Checked

Three minutes after ten. The Turkish authorities were late in their response. He glanced forward at Raschid, now stationed in the companionway with the portable transceiver. The half-Greek shook his head, indicating he had heard nothing.

Ismet barked an order to Hamzah. A hostage was dragged up to him, a terrified young man with stringy blond hair, a sleeveless sweatshirt, and a yellow plastic digital watch. Hamzah bound the hostage's arms behind him, as Ismet stripped off the sportwatch and fastened it on his own wrist, tossing overboard his own timepiece . . . The digital readout showed 9:56. The Turks weren't late, after all . . . Ismet stared defiantly ashore and placed his rifle against the young man's head.

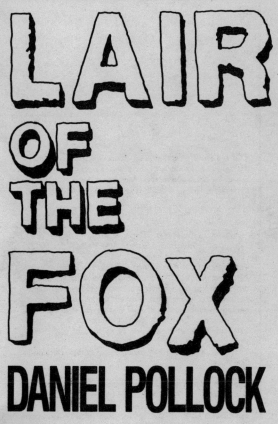

LAIR OF THE FOX

DANIEL POLLOCK

Harper Paperbacks

Harper & Row, Publishers, New York
Grand Rapids, Philadelphia, St. Louis, San Francisco
London, Singapore, Sydney, Tokyo, Toronto

Harper Paperbacks   a division of Harper & Row, Publishers, Inc.
10 East 53rd Street, New York, N.Y. 10022

This book is published by arrangement with Walker and
Company.

The lines of poetry by Hakim Sanai are quoted from *The
Walled Garden of Truth*, translated by David Pendlebury,
copyright in the U.S., its dependencies, the Philippine Islands,
and Canada by E. P. Dutton, Inc. Reprinted by kind permission
of The Octagon Press, Ltd., London.

Cover photography by Herman Estevez

First Harper Paperbacks printing: October, 1990

Printed in the United States of America

HARPER PAPERBACKS and colophon are trademarks of
Harper & Row, Publishers, Inc.

10 9 8 7 6 5 4 3 2 1

For my father and mother,
Louis and Cleta,
writers both
and lovers of books

The Fokiali sea caves are a feature of the island of Kastellorizo; the anchorite cave is not, but was transplanted from the peninsula of Athos by the author's imagination.

I want to thank my wife, Connie, and Don Michel, the Editor of the Los Angeles Times Syndicate, for their sacrifices and help in making it all possible; Dan Byrne, solocircumnavigator, for steering me in sailing matters; and my editor, Peter Rubie, for his advice and encouragement.

This world, O Brother, abides with no one . . .
It has cherished many like thee,
only to slay them.

—Sa'di, *The Gulistan*

LAIR
OF
THE
FOX

PROLOGUE

THE YOUNG ASSASSIN WITH THE BOOM BOX STOPPED TO watch the dancing bear. It towered over the summer afternoon crowd on the Bosphorus quayside, pirouetting on its hind legs to the drumbeat of the old Gypsy man who held its chain. But a sudden blast of sound from the boom box caused the beast to stagger, swivel its massive head, and gnash its teeth behind the thick leather muzzle.

"Very amusing," the middle-aged Russian said when the kid caught up, grinning at the havoc he had created. "Mind turning that damn thing down now?"

The kid reduced the heavy-metal fury a few decibels. The older man said nothing more. The GRU had sent him a *Spetsnaz* cowboy. As a KGB officer, there wasn't much Major Feliks Ilyinsky could do about that.

It was a generally fucked-up situation. Feliks needed this kid. The alternative—using Bessaraboff, his own KGB protegé, on a wet operation—was a sick joke.

They moved, without further incident, through the little street carnival beside the ferry landing stage of Emirgan on the Bosphorus's European shore. There were stilt-walkers, a fire-eater, fortune-tellers, and a huge, red-bearded martial artist, nearly as tall as the dancing bear, smashing stacks of roof tiles with his bare hands.

Farther on, a plane tree threw lacy shadows on the gray weather-beaten planking of an old boathouse. The two Russians entered. Behind the counter a swarthy young man lifted a single black brow over puzzled eyes and tried to shout above the cassette player: "A boat? For one hour, two—"

The young assassin pointed his *Spetsnaz*-issue P-6 silenced pistol at the single eyebrow and fired. The muffled shot was drowned out by the shrieking boom box. Ilyinsky made it around the counter in time to ease the dead weight to the floor, then continued through a swing door.

At the end of the open shed, silhouetted against a bright square of Bosphorus, were two men. One was crouched, shaking a can of spray paint; the other sat at a workbench tinkering with machinery. A half dozen geriatric wooden motorboats were tethered to the two-fingered dock. The kid joined Ilyinsky, after he shuttered the front.

The painter glanced up in annoyance at the blasting music. "Turn that thing off. You guys hire a boat?" Ilyinsky nodded. "So where's Torkom? Torkom, get your ass back here."

The kid fired successively at both men. Again the

explosive coughs of the P-6 were masked by the amplified din. Ilyinsky went forward to examine the objects being painted.

There were a dozen steel cylinders—three a flaky, bilious green; nine a wet chrome yellow. The necks had been fitted with standard SCUBA regulator J-valves. Ilyinsky unscrewed one. Underneath was a fuze pocket. Ilyinsky looked more closely at the metal object in his hand. The "J-valve," he suspected, was really an electronic timer. The unsprayed tanks bore coded markings indicating manufacture in Shikhany, the principal Soviet chemical weapons facility.

Ilyinsky rang his knuckles on the alloy-steel casing. They were all here—an even dozen unitary bombs, hijacked ten days before from a Bulgarian APC on Warsaw Pact maneuvers in the Dragoman Pass. They contained a new and specially thickened form of VX nerve gas, many times more lethal than anything in Western arsenals. The bombs had been designed as tactical weapons, to be air-dropped or fired as artillery shells. But, disguised and modified with the timers, they had been turned into fiendishly efficient terrorist weapons.

Ilyinsky had spent ten anxious days tracing the hijacking to Armenian separatists—a previously unknown faction which, unlike the Marxist ASALA, was working to overthrow the Soviet Armenian Republic. The last link—leading to this boat house run by three Armenian cousins—had been supplied by a pimply, fourteen-year-old terrorist in Yerevan, an orphan of the '88 earthquake. The boy had lost all his bravado and screamed everything he knew when Ilyinsky tapped the first finishing nail into his skull. The boy didn't know what mayhem the cousins intended with the canisters, but that question, thank God, was now academic.

"How many people could you kill with all this shit?" the young *Spetsnaz* asked.

"I don't know. Let's get busy."

Two minutes of concerted effort saw the dozen tanks loaded into a motorboat's back seat. The kid was complaining about yellow paint on his jeans.

"I'll buy you a new pair," Ilyinsky said. "Throw that tarp over the tanks."

As Ilyinsky squatted to free the dock line, a two-meter section of the boathouse wall buckled and splintered open, revealing the red-bearded giant hefting a wrought-iron bench as battering ram. Beside him a normal-size assistant began firing an AK assault rifle.

The young assassin crumpled and Ilyinsky dove into the water, kicking and clawing away from the boathouse.

Long seconds later, nearing blackout, he surfaced, and saw the motorboat—*his* motorboat, goddammit—snarling away into the Bosphorus traffic. A rifle barrel flashed in the sun. Ilyinsky gulped air and sank out of sight.

When he rose again, the boat was nowhere to be seen on the busy waterway. Ilyinsky trod the surprisingly cold water several minutes, hoping for a glimpse; but he saw only barges, fishing skiffs, motor yachts, ferries, and, to his left, a Soviet helicopter cruiser coming down from the Black Sea. The Emirgan quayside, meanwhile, had become a bedlam of shouts and sirens.

Finally Ilyinsky gave up the search and swam south with the current. Near the village of Balta Liman he drifted inshore. Somebody else had wanted the canisters, and very badly, he thought, hauling himself onto the dock of a shuttered seaside mansion, or *yali*. But who?

≡

Through the fading colors of evening, a uniformed motorcyclist roared down a street of slums in Usküdar on Istanbul's Asian shore. A pair of roosters in the middle of the unpaved road broke off their quarrel and scattered as he shot past. The mud-splattered fairing of the big German sports bike bore the insignia of the Turkish National Police.

A dismal block farther on the cyclist heeled sharply, skidding into a crossing, then snarled up through the gear-box, rear tires spewing dirt as they clawed for traction. He was now on a cart path, narrowed further by an open sewer trench and walled in with *geçekondus* or "night houses"—hovels thrown up overnight by the teeming Anatolian immigrant population. The shantytown, like many others fringing the city, was largely unmapped, but the cyclist never hesitated.

He downshifted and dived into an alleyway between two whitewashed shacks, plowing a furrow through a scrawny vegetable patch. Several meters ahead he veered again between flaps of hanging burlap into sudden enveloping darkness, braked to a stop and switched off the motor. He sat a moment, letting his vision adjust to lancets of dusky light that pierced a roof of scrap sheathing. Then he unhelmeted and pulled his goggles down.

"Ismet!" he called into the void. And again, "Ismet! It is Fahri."

Still there was no answer, only muted sounds from the street, and, somewhere in the distance, a *muezzin*'s

ululating call for sundown prayer. But the air was rife
with smells: the sewer stench outside; bacon fat, frying
fish and onions from a nearby cook fire; and, close by,
the burning-grass odor of hashish.

Then in the darkness came the slow sibilance of
someone snoring. The cyclist dismounted, whipped a
flashlight from his leather belt, and stabbed its beam into
a dark corner. On a filthy ticking mattress a man
sprawled on his side, a big red-bearded Westerner, bare
feet and thick forearms protruding from a dirty cotton
judo suit. Behind him a dozen large metal canisters were
stacked against the wall. Beside the man was a porcelain
narghile, the water pipe's mouthpiece still clutched in
grimy fingers. That, and the fact the man had not been
awakened by the motorcycle, indicated narcotic stupor.
The cyclist approached slowly, zeroing the flashlight on
the large head. Under the tangled red mane was a fighter's face—leathery, scarred, vein-mapped. The nose was
a flattened ruin, the mouth a swollen mass of flesh.

As the cyclist leaned closer, one malevolent eye
opened and thick lips curled back over yellow teeth. The
cyclist grabbed for his .45, but a huge leg scythed him
off his feet. He landed on his gun arm as the bearded
man exploded off the mattress. The cyclist swung the
heavy flashlight in self-defense, but it was knocked into
a corner as huge hands tore at his collar.

The two writhed in darkness. Without a weapon the
cyclist knew he was doomed. Then, as they rolled across
the earthen floor, the *narghile* shattered beneath them;
the bearded man, cut by porcelain shards, grunted in
pain and released his death grip. The cyclist wrenched
free and regained his feet, but the hulking figure loomed
up instantly between him and the burlap doorway.

This time the cyclist was able to unholster his side-arm and swing it toward the huge target. But the bearded man twisted and kicked sideways, his front foot knocking the cyclist's wrist aside as the gun went off.

While the darkness detonated, the cyclist was snatched up like a child and hurled through the air. He slammed into the motorcycle, rolling over with it and beyond into a pasteboard wall that collapsed under his weight. The cyclist kept tumbling, down a short muddy slope, the evening stars wheeling overhead. He came to rest with his face a scant half meter from crackling flames. On the far side of a cook fire hunkered a wizened old man in a cloth cap, masticating his supper and glancing about fearfully. Next to him a small sheepdog barked furiously.

The cyclist's entire left side, from cheek to hipbone, was one throbbing bruise, and his mouth tasted of his own blood. He looked back and saw the ragged hole in the pasteboard wall suddenly and violently enlarged. Through it, like some overgrown *djinni,* smashed the massive red-bearded man, bounding down the muddy slope and into the firelight. The cyclist tried to scuttle away, but his back was already against the hot stones of the cook fire. His holster was empty. His brain freewheeled in futile calculation. The dog continued to bark crazily. The red giant danced closer, grinning, playful, crouching into a martial arts stance. The cyclist called out in prayer to his dead mother. Then out of the night boomed a huge voice:

"John! No!"

The bearded man, on the verge of kicking his helpless victim in the face, halted and turned. Through the same hole a swarthy, mustached young man emerged.

He moved with a swaggering stride down the slope. But as he drew near, he seemed to diminish. The top of his head barely reached the bearded man's shoulder.

"Ismet, peace be upon you!" said the cyclist with heartfelt relief.

"And upon you, the peace and mercy of Allah, and his blessing."

Fahri's bearded assailant, meanwhile, spat and spoke in English. "Ismet, why did you stop me? I was about to kill this Turkish slime. He's with the fucking police."

"Yes," answered the small man in the same tongue. "But Fahri Bayram is also the husband of my cousin and a friend of Kurdistan. You must be more careful, John." Ismet knelt and helped the cyclist to his feet. "Forgive me, Fahri. This is John Courage, the big Angleesh. He arrived yesterday from Kastellorizo to do a little job for me. You must have startled him. Are you badly hurt?"

Fahri shook his head. He stood up, squared his slight shoulders, and made a show of dusting off his uniform. His beautiful leathers were mud-caked, his face scratched, and blood trickled from one nostril over his pencil-thin mustache and swollen lip. Tomorrow, he was sure, he would be rainbowed with bruises. But he was alive, Allah be praised, and nothing broken.

"No hard feelings," said John Courage, offering his hand. "But let me give you a piece of advice, Fairy, me lad. Never sneak up on an old soldier."

A moment later at Ismet's direction Fahri extracted an envelope from inside his leather jacket. Ismet opened it and unfolded a packet. On top were two glossy black-and-white photographs. One was of a dramatically lovely, dark-haired woman. The other showed a three-masted square-rigger under full sail. After a moment Ismet handed the packet to the Englishman.

John Courage bent close to the firelight and stared at the photo of the woman. "Holy Christ! You know who this is? Amanda bloody Morgan—only about the most delicious bitch in Christendom! She was right out of drama school when I first laid eyes on her ten, maybe fifteen years ago, as close to me as that mutt over there, half-naked in a West End farce. Of course that was before she started spouting off about nukes and Pakkies and all the rest of it. What's she gotta be now, near forty I guess, and look how good she looks, eh? What I wouldn't give to turn her upside down. Christ, Fairy, did you have to bend the frigging snap?"

Ismet pointed to the packet. "John, please read. It is in English."

"Of course I'll bloody read it." Reluctantly he turned from the glossy to the accompanying press release.

From the desk of B.J. Bracey: Media Relations
FOR IMMEDIATE RELEASE

AMANDA MORGAN LATEST TO JOIN CAST OF "BARBARY!"

British actress Amanda Morgan was announced today as the most recent addition to "Barbary!", Kronos Ltd.'s $35 million historical miniseries which begins filming soon in exotic Mediterranean locations, from Tunis to Istanbul. Ms. Morgan will be joining an all-star, international cast that already *boasts Jason Webb, Britta Milo, A. W. Kohout, Langley Peters and Ray Navidad.*

Executive producer Leopold Bouchard revealed the signing of Ms. Morgan Friday from Kronos's Paris offices, calling it "a master stroke." "Amanda is a wonderful actress with a worldwide following," said the producer. "But please don't ask me about her politics, or whether I'm paying her more than I paid for the ship." The reference was to the full-scale replica of an 18th-century twenty-four-gun frigate recently constructed in Italy from original U.S. Navy Department plans—at a hefty price tag of $5 million! The ship, christened the George Washington *after the original, is now en route to Istanbul, where principal photography for "Barbary!" will begin early next month.*

Ms. Morgan, a past Oscar nominee for "Little Girl Blue" and critically acclaimed for her title role in last year's PBS series "Rusudan," will be making her American network television debut in "Barbary!" She will portray the role of Lydia Markham, a celebrated American songstress in the year 1800, who is abducted while on a European tour from the stage of the Paris Opera by agents of the Dey of Algiers, Bobba Mustapha (A.W. Kohout). She is then smuggled, by Gypsy wagon, camel caravan and, in a bizarre plot twist, a U.S. naval vessel, to Constantinople, where she is presented to the Sultan as a gift for his harem. Like the legendary kidnapping of Helen of Troy, this incident launches a veritable whirlwind of events, including three naval battles and a heroic rescue attempt by an American privateer captain (Jason Webb).

"Barbary!" is romantic action-adventure in the grand tradition that stretches from "Captain Blood" to the latest Indiana Jones, compiled from historical and original sources. "Of course the emphasis is on entertainment value, and telling a good yarn," points out veteran British director Jack Woodhull, "but some of the parallels with present-day events are quite remarkable."

One such involves the voyage of the George Washington *from Algiers to Constantinople in the year 1800. It was this journey, in which a U.S. naval vessel was coerced into ferrying tribute (including, perhaps, an American songstress?) from one potentate to another, which caused the United States to escalate the war against the Barbary pirates. "Very few people know that Jefferson was the first American president to advocate the policing of the Mediterranean," adds Woodhull, "and so we try to point that out."*

The diminutive and dynamic Mr. Bouchard, who comes to the project fresh from the success of last fall's four-hour blockbuster version of Jules Verne's "Michael Strogoff, Courier to the Czar," envisions even greater logistical problems for "Barbary!" "Here we have secured cooperation from four separate governments, not just one as in 'Strogoff.'"

To underline this claim, Mr. Bouchard introduced Mr. Bekir Yagan of the Turkish Ministry of Trade, who read a special proclamation from his government, citing a 1982 maritime law in granting a one-time, five-hour suspension of all traffic on the Bosphorus waterway, to allow unimpeded filming of the ship not only on the Sea of Marmara, but within *the Golden Horn itself. Thanks to this dispensation, the millions of viewers of "Barbary!" will be treated to the sight of an historic American warship, once again under a cloud of sail, its bowsprit thrusting through the spray toward the graceful minarets of Constantinople . . .*

After several minutes of squinting in the flickering light, the Englishman folded up the pages.

"What do you think, John?" asked Ismet.

Courage scratched his hairy neck. "I like it. You take the ship, and I'll take Amanda."

1

MAJOR FELIKS ILYINSKY WAS A CONNOISSEUR OF WOMEN, not ships. But as tier upon tier of white billowing canvas swam into focus in his binoculars, he let out a grunt of visceral pleasure. Through clenched teeth he whispered, *"Krasavitsa!"*—"A beauty!"

The KGB officer pressed the zoom lever to bring the image closer. A topsail filled his circle of vision, bellied out and shining in the morning sun like a bedsheet on a washline. The square-rigger was coming straight at him. On the foredeck tiny figures moved; beneath its forefoot white bow waves creamed to each side. He recalled a nautical expression: She had a bone in her teeth.

Ilyinsky put down the binoculars and shouted for coffee. He was seated on the terrace of his summer house on the isle of Büyükada, scanning the Sea of Marmara between cypress trees and his own Adidas-shod feet on the wrought-iron railing. His morning exertions had smoothed the ironic lines of his broad face. His blue eyes sparkled, his cheeks were aflame, his monogrammed warm-up suit was sweat-soaked. He had just finished five up-and-down kilometers through the island's pine forests.

Noorsheen, his Azerbaijan serving girl, appeared a moment later bearing a tray of croissants, marmalade and coffee—not a demitasse of sweet Turkish coffee, but a French press full of his favorite Indonesian blend, poured black and steaming into a big breakfast cup. The girl was nineteen, slight and endearingly shy. Her nostrils were too large and a faint mustache shaded her upper lip. But her slim body was pleasing and her eyes were dark and fawnlike. She had excited Ilyinsky from the moment he'd first seen her, chopping onions and weeping in the scullery of the Soviet Consulate General. That very night he had contrived to possess the fragile creature, overpowering her shyness and ultimately awakening her eroticism. It had filled him with a sense of delicious violation. Moreover, as a poignant coda to their frequent couplings, the girl's whimpering, childlike cries of completion invariably awakened in the Soviet major feelings of paternal tenderness.

As she turned to go, he seized her small brown wrist. Her eyes went wide, but he smiled reassurance. "Not quite yet, Little Sweet," he said, translating the Persian meaning of her name. "Let me show you something first." He stood and looped the binocular strap over her black curls, pivoting her in front of him. He pointed and helped her focus. When she found the ship, she made a delighted sound. Ilyinsky laid his cheek against hers and began softly to recite a poem by Lermontov, one he had memorized as a boy in the Komsomol. It told about a solitary white sail lost in the fog of a dove-gray sea. By the time he had finished, he had grown hard against her and the rise and fall of her breathing matched his own. He lightly kissed the nape of her neck and watched with professional interest her shivering reaction. She was as excited as he.

He went on whispering in her ear: "Did you know, Little Sweet, a ship is just like a woman? Yes, yes, in many ways. Both are lovely, both changeable with the slightest breeze. And there are one or two other things. But in one way they are very different. Strip away her white plumage and the ship is no longer so beautiful. But undress a woman, and she becomes more exquisite." His palms cupped her small breasts. "As you are about to demonstrate for Feliks. Yes? Go inside then while I eat my breakfast, and lower all your sails. You understand? And wait for me like a good little girl."

He lifted the binoculars free and lightly swatted her rear. She moved away with an awkward and self-conscious gait, aware of his following eyes. At the door she gave a backward glance, her nostrils wider than usual. It was a look of such humid expectation that Ilyinsky felt the primitive urge to leap from his chair, throw her to the deck and mount her on the spot. He resisted it, though only just. To yield would give the girl exaggerated notions of her power. Besides, she would keep; his breakfast would not. He reached instead for a croissant.

On the Marmara, dove gray had deepened to shimmering blue as the sun lifted higher over the Asian hills. Ilyinsky forced himself to breathe deeply. Presently, even without binoculars, he was able to discern the approaching sails against the horizon.

Ilyinsky dispatched the second croissant, washing it down with coffee. He was rushing his breakfast. The deep lines bracketing his mouth reasserted themselves, mocking his feigned insouciance. Who was he trying to fool? Noorsheen? Himself? The glandular imperative was stronger than ever with him. When had he ever denied it?

The ship was swinging now onto a starboard tack, away from Büyükada and the other Princes Islands. Fore, main, and mizzen opened to view. She was carrying a full press of sail. "Welcome, Gollyvood." Ilyinsky saluted the vessel and the American movie capital with upraised coffee mug and sardonic smile. Not only had the film producers paid millions to build the replica in a Genoese shipyard, but, according to Ilyinsky's sources, they were continuing to pass money freely. He wondered, for instance, how much it had cost to persuade the Turkish government to invoke an obscure maritime law and suspend vital early morning traffic on the Bosphorus, turning one of the world's busiest waterways into nothing more than a movie backdrop.

Ilyinsky made a note to check on the filming schedule when he got to the consulate that afternoon. It would be amusing to watch the decadent goings-on at close range—especially any scenes involving the British actress, Amanda Morgan. For the moment, however, he had another female in mind. He gulped the rest of his coffee and headed inside toward the dark bedroom where his naked Azerbaijani waited.

≡

Forty minutes after Ilyinsky turned his attention indoors, Paul Cyrus, a thirty-six-year-old American, got his first glimpse of the *George Washington*. The frigate had left the Princes Islands in her wake and was on a long port tack, bringing her close to the Asian shore. Definitely within long-gun range, Paul decided. Not that he had any guns, long or short, at his command. The tall, sandy-haired man was perched on the flybridge of a fifty-foot motor yacht in the boat harbor of Fenerbahçe, focusing a pair of big Bushnells. But for the moment in his imagination he was Horatio Hornblower in a swaying foretop, spyglass to eye.

Paul had learned his sailing as a boy on Seattle's Lake Washington and had raced one-designs on the Chesapeake during college years at Georgetown. But he'd never sailed on a square-rigger, and the ache to do so now, to be one of those figures scurrying down the main deck to man the lee braces (if he recalled his nomenclature), was so intense it blotted out a throbbing hangover headache.

"Should be me," he said aloud, propping one long, denim-clad leg on a spoke of the stainless-steel wheel. Paul had the look of a blue-water sailor, and would be even more convincing in the part a few days hence when the Aegean sun buffed up his office pallor. The body was long and rangy, the face Huckleberry grown up, and the friendly gray-blue eyes had the requisite weather wrinkles at the corners. But he was not quite what he seemed.

In high school, inspired by the writings of explorers like Burton, Lawrence, Hedin, and Halliburton, Paul had started fooling around with Oriental alphabets. He amused his classmates and teachers by chalking cryptic blackboard graffiti in Tibetan, Sanskrit, and classical Mongolian. He then astounded his parents by not discarding the Asian fascination along with all his other youthful manias. At college he settled into serious Levantine studies, acquiring proficiency in Persian, Arabic, and Turkish, the principal languages of the Middle East. His romantic vision was to embark upon a life as a scholar-adventurer, like the masterful Burton, who used his linguistic skills to penetrate the bazaars of Islam in disguise, from Mecca to Harar.

That Paul failed to realize this vision was not remarkable given the academic pressures for specialization. What *was* remarkable was how close he came to attaining it. A master's thesis on "The Qur'anic Mandate for Pan-Arabic Terrorism" landed him a summer job in an interdisciplinary think tank on counter-terrorism. To his surprise, Paul found himself no more unqualified than his heavily credentialed colleagues to pontificate on this burning issue. Several such assignments led to detached consultation with the foreign service, which was in the process of hardening its embassies and consulates in the grisly aftermath of several car bombings.

Under these circumstances opportunities for adventure, and front-line danger, would seem to have been unavoidable. But Paul's day-to-day reality remained very much what it had been in graduate school. He labored long hours in airless cubicles, barricaded behind books and periodicals, his world reduced to the cold phosphor glow of a PC screen. He cooked up risk analyses, hostage scenarios, and foreign press extracts, all second- and third-hand stuff, warmed over with the requisite jargon. On holidays and weekends he took in local sights, worked on dialects, sent exotic post cards to friends. He was well thought of professionally and cut a handsome figure at embassy cocktail parties. But it did not add up, somehow, to the fulfillment of his childhood dreams. A fact which was poignantly symbolized by the approaching three-master.

His reverie and view of the ship were suddenly eclipsed. Forrest Watkins had come lurching up from the galley, a Bloody Mary in each fist. "Morning rations," he growled. Paul accepted the chilled glass as the big man collapsed in the swivel helm chair opposite. "The dockmaster's boy, Harut, says we can clear out of here in an hour. You watching the tall ship out there, or ogling my daughter like everyone else?"

Forrest's daughter, Darryl Ann, was sunbathing on the foredeck in a chartreuse bikini—and attracting considerable attention from neighboring boats in the crowded basin. Paul couldn't look at the lovely creature without experiencing a sense of strangeness about their relationship. They had spent so little time together since their first meeting at a weekend house party in Virginia during his last stateside leave. The physical attraction was mutual and undeniable, but in other areas he felt they were barely acquainted. "Hell yes, I'm ogling your daughter." Paul grinned. "But by my watch D.A. hasn't budged in twenty minutes, and that frigate's moving along pretty good. Have a look." He passed the binoculars over.

After a few seconds Forrest whistled appreciatively. "How many knots can she do?"

"Ten or twelve I bet, running free in a good wind. She's close-hauled now—as close as a square-rigger can get."

"Wide open, *Pegasus'* twin diesels will do over twenty."

"Yeah, good point. A windjammer doesn't hydroplane too well. But I'd like to be on her. In fact, I'd love to be on her."

"Once upon a time, so would I. Right now I'll settle for this tub. Air-conditioning, sauna, wet bar, VCR. You saw what we got in our stateroom. A goddamn bidet."

"Hey, not bad, skipper."

"Glad to see you're impressed, Paul. Drink up."

"Aye-aye, sir." Paul clinked glasses and willed his morning discontent to vanish, along with his hangover. Why the itch to escape into some unnamed adventure when he already had a one-way ticket home, via the Greek isles? What was his problem? He was on vacation as of yesterday afternoon, with paradise staring him in the face—a three-week cruise with Darryl Ann and her parents on this chartered luxury yacht. The fact that his two-year Turkish stint, split between Ankara and Istanbul, had concluded without incident was cause for rejoicing, not sour grapes. In his line of work, after all, theory was to be preferred infinitely to practice. It was one thing to devise intricate counter-terrorist scenarios, quite another to test them face to face with Uzi-toting True Believers.

"Allah be praised!" as a friend from the British Consulate had summed it up in a toast at last night's consular farewell party. "Our Yank colleague is not only escaping the Middle East. He's fallen right into the honey pot." The final reference, of course, was to Darryl Ann. When Paul had shown up at the Hilton with the dazzling ash blonde on his arm, the effect had been galvanic. Conversations evaporated, heads swiveled, loose males began eddying in their direction. Or *her* direction. Escorting D.A. anywhere was like being the Invisible Man—a situation Paul found oddly amusing at a party in his honor.

He took another bite out of the Bloody Mary. "Ought to feel damn fine," he said aloud.

"What's that, Paul?"

"Damn fine," he repeated, hoisting the chilled glass. Forrest grunted agreement.

The trouble was, Paul decided, when you got right down to it, he didn't belong on this idyllic little cruise. At least not with D.A.'s parents along. He couldn't escape the feeling of being taken for a test drive, couldn't help wondering how many other suitors had preceded him on family holidays, and failed the course, for one reason or other. Unable to hold their liquor, perhaps, or disagreeing with Daddy's opinions, or allowing D.A. to become bored. Now it was his turn. And it had been made clear to Paul that if everything worked out during the next three weeks, the engagement was definitely on and massive wedding plans would swing into effect. The funny thing was, he hadn't even proposed to the girl yet. His matrimonial willingness was apparently assumed.

He continued to sip his drink, glancing first at the sleek blonde on the foredeck, then at the balding, bearish individual who had sired her, his prospective father-in-law. And the real man in D.A.'s life, as Paul had discovered when he had tried to sell her on an alternate cruise—minus her parents.

"Daddy's already hired a boat," she had pointed out.

"We don't need a floating condo. We can charter a little sloop and sail her ourselves. And we can rendezvous with your mom and dad in the Aegean, wherever you like. It'll be great. Just pack your bikini and a couple cases of champagne."

"Daddy would *not* approve," she had answered flatly. "Besides, you know I don't *like* sailing. All that winching and hauling and fiddling with things. I *like* Daddy's boats."

Like most matters in their brief relationship, the debate had been settled in accordance with Darryl Ann's wishes. Ah, well, he thought, *amor fati*. Who'd said that? Old walrus-faced Nietzsche, wasn't it? Love thy fate. Or, to paraphrase the Limey toast, the honey pot may be sweet, but also damn sticky. Paul was not sure it was even possible to climb out, let alone advisable.

After all, the Watkinses were likable people, easy to be around. They could discuss a variety of issues at medium depth. Forrest was a political Neanderthal, of course, but Paul, who had overdosed on years of State Department double talk ("Always keep your options open"), found himself more than once agreeing with the man's hardheaded pronouncements.

And on at least one issue, both parents were more than liberal. Their willful daughter could do whatever she pleased. Had D.A. really wanted to go cruising with Paul, she damned well would have. The Watkinses certainly hadn't balked at letting her share her stateroom with him on a family cruise—a situation which Paul found a little hard to get used to. During their early morning lovemaking, D.A.'s orgasmic crescendo had resonated throughout the boat, if not the harbor.

"Good morning, boys." Bitsy Watkins emerged from below with a pot of coffee. She was a handsome, tanned woman, with close-cropped silver hair and a quick sense of humor.

"Morning," Paul said. "And bless you. I was beginning to think you folks subsisted on vodka and tomato juice."

"That's Forrie's wake-up tonic, not mine. Solid food in a jiffy—figs, yogurt, and some Turkish pastries. Did you children sleep well?" The last question was accompanied by a hint of smile and a tilt of the head toward Darryl Ann. Bitsy had obviously heard every decibel of her daughter's early-morning ecstasies.

Paul smiled blandly. "We were pretty late getting in. Hope we didn't wake you."

"Pooh! Don't give it a thought. This is a party boat, after all. So, how was your big farewell bash?"

"Great, I think. I don't remember much of anything after the fifth glass of *raki*. Anyway, hardly anyone noticed me after they met Miss Maryland."

"Really, Paul," Bitsy poked him in the chest, "you mustn't believe *all* Darryl's stories. She was first runner-up. And I'm sure your friends will miss you terribly."

"Oh, a few nice things were said, drunken toasts and all that. More in envy than affection, I suspect."

"We wanted to make an appearance. At least *I* did, but Forrie dragged me off to see the belly dancers at the Karavansaray." She struck a comical harem girl pose, palms clapping overhead.

Forrest glanced up from the back page of the *International Herald Tribune*. "I'm sure Paul doesn't give a damn where the old fogies went last night."

"My, we are gruff this morning. Have we had our injection?"

"Stow it, nurse. What I am is anxious to get out of this oil slick and head for the Dardanelles. Which I'll do, as soon as Hollywood is through filming out yonder. Here, take a look."

Bitsy accepted the binoculars and turned to Paul in mock earnest. "You heard Forrie. He wants action. You're with the government. Do something."

"Sorry, I'm on leave." Paul grinned, but he detected a hard edge to the husband-and-wife banter. Not a pleasant augury for a three-week cruise.

"Well," Forrest said, "do you see the damn thing or not? If it's gone, I'm revving up *Pegasus.*"

"It's there," Bitsy said. "But there's another boat—a little speedboat—"

"Christ Almighty!"

"Don't bite my head off. I only said—"

"Not you. It's the goddamned Orioles. They dropped a double-header. What the hell's going on back home?"

"Forrie, seriously, that speedboat is heading right for the ship. I thought you said they stopped traffic?"

"Probably a camera boat, my love. They've got to get the damned thing on film."

"Well, all right. But it's on a collision course. Paul, you look. Tell me I'm crazy."

Paul, squinting into the low morning sun, had already made out the lengthening white streak from the Asian shore. He cradled the binoculars, tracking and focusing in one motion.

It was an open-cockpit runabout, planing at full throttle and throwing up a rooster tail that feathered and sparkled in the light. It would have come from somewhere in Kadiköy, he figured, probably Haydarpasa, the next anchorage a mile up the coast. And it did seem on an intercept course with the *George Washington*. He counted four heads in the cockpit, but nothing that looked like camera equipment. Joyriders, he decided, disregarding the traffic suspension on the waterway and scooting in for a close look at the ship. The Turkish Harbor Police couldn't cordon off the entire approach to the Bosphorus for the benefit of a film company, no matter how much money had changed hands. The Hollywood folk would be furious at having their expensive shot ruined, but that wasn't Paul's problem. Mike Mitchell, consular first secretary, could soothe the savage moguls.

Paul was about to lower the binoculars when he caught a metallic flash from the speedboat, not from the brightwork, but the cockpit itself. He steadied the image and saw an automatic rifle with a curved magazine like the Soviet Kalashnikov—the worldwide weapon of choice for revolutionaries and terrorists. The next instant his view of the cockpit was lost behind a curtain of spray as the boat veered.

Joyriders—with automatic weapons?

Or a fanciful scene from the movie—twentieth-century pirates attacking a Colonial man-o'-war?

But this was supposed to be a swashbuckler, he knew, not a time-travel flick. On Paul's last day in the office the movie press kit had come across his desk. He had given it short shrift, after admiring the glossies of the leading lady, the oval-faced, sloe-eyed Amanda Morgan, and of course the ship itself. The synopsis was the standard historical pastiche, replete with bodice-ripping corsairs, harem kidnappings, and Yankee bravado, against the backdrop of America's war with the Barbary states. There was even a sketch of the original *George Washington* under attack by an oared xebec. Bearded and burnoosed pirates were hurling grapnels and swarming aboard. But they were brandishing cutlasses, not Kalashnikovs. So the runabout was definitely not ferrying props out to the ship.

He spun the helm chair around. "Gotta make a phone call," he said, moving toward the aft ladder. In a feet-first vault he reached the deck, jumped onto the transom and across the stern gangplank.

"Wiat," Forrest called after him, "the marine operator can patch you through on VHF."

"No time," Paul yelled over his shoulder, dodging a playful dog as he raced barefoot along the dock. He took the harbor office stairs in a stride and burst inside, shooing little Harut out of his father's chair. He dialed the desk phone, tucking the receiver under his chin to free his hands for the binoculars.

A familiar, perky voice answered on the first ring. "United States Consulate General."

"Louise, it's Paul. This is an emergency. Give me Mike Mitchell quick."

"Hold on, Paul." His heart and head were both pounding now, from exertion and hangover. Elevator music percolated in the earpiece. "Moonlight in Vermont." Where was the damn speedboat? Had it veered off again? Then he saw it, coming up on the quarter, the classic point of attack. Where were the Harbor Police? Dockside probably, obeying their own fiat.

"Paul, where the hell are you? Don't tell me the party's still going?"

"I'm in Fenerbahçe. Mike, we got an emergency here."

"Out of vermouth?"

"No, I'm watching a powerboat attack a frigate."

"Run that by me again."

"The *George Washington*. Someone just took a boat out to it, and—holy shit!—they're throwing a grapnel—"

"A what?"

"A grappling hook. There's a guy scrambling up the side of the ship." Paul's angle of vision prevented him seeing what happened when the figure reached the frigate's entry port.

"Where are you?"

"I told you—Fenerbahçe, about a mile away, watching through binoculars. Mike, for Chrissake, they've got assault rifles."

"Paul, has it occured to you that you are watching them make a movie?"

"It's no movie. It's a fucking terrorist operation, and we gotta move fast. I know what I'm talking about. Call Colonel Ozsahin. Don't hang up—use another line and get back to me quick. I'll stay right here so I can tell you what's happening."

There was a decisive change of tone. "All right, Paul. Hold on."

The elevator music resumed, bizarre accompaniment for the distant drama he was watching. The powerboat was tethered alongside. He had counted four men, each slung with a weapon, up and over the frigate's side. Four ruthless men, armed to the teeth, and a helpless crew—and he could see nothing. The ship was now hove to, canvas slatting helplessly against the yards.

Paul tightened his grip on the binoculars. Then his name was shouted. He glanced up to see Darryl Ann prancing toward him in her awkward, coltish stride, palomino mane whipping side to side. She was still clad only in bikini, her body sheened with perspiration. It made for quite a spectacle. Even in the midst of crisis Paul felt the stab of desire, but it was tainted with irritation. She must have been alarmed at his bolting the ship, and had come on the run to fetch him back.

He couldn't remember ever saying no to her, but he was about to. Terrorists had just tipped over his honey pot. At the very least his Aegean cruise was on hold, along with his escape from the Middle East. If only they'd left an hour ago, they'd be halfway to the Dardanelles by now and out of reach. Instead Paul felt himself drawn into a vortex created by whatever was happening out there on the motionless three-master.

2

THE STOLEN ITALIAN SPEEDBOAT WENT SNARLING ACROSS the blue Marmara, as if carrying the millionaires whose plaything it normally was—and not four desperate and destitute *pesh merga,* Kurdish freedom fighters. Again and again the gleaming white projectile bucked and reared, smashing its fiberglass belly against the water, while the Kurds held fast to the stainless-steel grab rails.

Ismet had demanded speed. It was essential to reach the sailing ship and overwhelm the crew before the Turkish Harbor Police could intervene. But that fool at the wheel, Raschid, was overdoing it. Had they carried trembler-fused explosives among the arsenals on their persons and in the nylon bags at their feet, they would have blown themselves out of the water by now. Ismet stood to shout in the taller Raschid's ear, but his words were drowned out by the shrieking wind, high-revving outboard, and hull-hammering water. Raschid, knowing only that an order had been given, grinned and nudged the throttle-clutch control farther forward. The bow surged higher, and Ismet was punched back into his white vinyl seat.

Raschid, a half-Greek raised in the port of Salonika, was the only one of the four at home on water. But the two *pesh merga* in the plush stern couch took the bucketing stoically enough. Hamzah, Ismet's baby-faced cousin, had let go his Czech Skorpion machine pistol to hold onto the upholstered wing panel, but his soft features bore no trace of anxiety. Beside him, Taufiq, bearded and saturnine, was buried in a Sufi trance state, eyes shut behind spray-coated spectacles. Like the others he was garbed in a black nylon athletic suit and had a webbed belt hung with fragmentation grenades. But he alone retained an item of traditional Kurdish clothing, a headpiece of blue-checked cotton, now beginning to unwind in the wind blast.

For Hamzah and Taufiq, following Ismet into danger was nothing new. As children they had roamed together over the dun hills of the Kurdish homeland, near Ruwandiz along the Great Zab. When they were old enough for their first rifles, they had hunted together— partridges at first, and then, at Ismet's urging, ever larger game, from wild sheep and ibex to jackals and wolves.

One of Ismet's childhood exploits, smoking a silver fox out of its hole, had earned him the title "the Little Fox." The name stuck, thanks to the boy's large ears, keen face and darting eyes. But he was never an object of derision. By sheer force of personality, he became the dominant figure in their young lives, maturing early and developing a commanding voice which compensated for his lack of stature.

In Ismet's fifteenth year an incident occurred which was to assume the proportions of local legend. While hunting in a mountain pass, the young marksman came upon three brigands attacking an old traveler. The youth shot and killed one brigand and chased off the other two. The old man turned out to be the Murshid of a famous dervish order, who began proclaiming that Ismet had not only delivered him, but would one day do the same for the entire Kurdish nation. According to the Murshid's revelation, he himself represented long-suffering Kurdistan, the three brigands were Turkey, Iraq, and Persia, and young Ismet the leader destiend to drive them off.

The Little Fox pretended to dismiss this grandiose prophecy, but secretly it took hold of him. His life thereafter became a crusade to fulfill the Murshid's word. At fifteen he joined a nomadic band of *pesh merga,* skirmishing against the local Iraqi garrison, then retreating to limestone caves in the mountains of Qara Dagh. At eighteen Ismet had assumed command of this unit, increasing both its numbers and scale of operations. The fame of the Little Fox and the rallying cry, *Biju Kurdu Kurdistan*—"Long live the Kurds and Kurdistan"—soon spread from Sulaimani in the south to Siirt in eastern Turkey and northeast to Persian Mahabad. The sharp-featured youth grew into a fierce-visaged warrior, with dark mustaches drooping beside an implacable jaw. He favored Cossack dress—pantaloons thrust into Russian top boots, blouse festooned with cartridges, and, protruding from his silk sash, a dagger in a hammered-silver scabbard.

His followers boasted that their leader was not merely fearless, but careless of danger. As his reputation grew, village headmen—Aghas and Mukhtars—trekked to his camps, bringing gifts and seeking patronage. Turkish and Iraqi militia units also sought out the Little Fox, but failed to smoke him from his hole. As a chieftain of the Barzani clan, Ismet began to be mentioned in the same breath with the great Mullah Mustafa, the most famous Kurd since Saladin, and the man who had come closest to uniting the Kurdish tribes against their oppressors.

Then the inexplicable happened. The Little Fox struck a bargain with the enemy. He ended his rebellion, leading his men out of the mountains and into the service of Iraq. Only to his closest comrades could he confide his reasons; only they knew that patriotism, not treason, lay behind his bizarre actions. He had been made certain promises by emissaries from Baghdad, which was then in the fifth desperate year of war with Tehran. In exchange for helping to harass Iran's northern borders, Ismet was to receive automatic rifles, grenade launchers, mortars, wireless equipment—in other words, enough weaponry to prosecute large-scale guerrilla operations against Turkey, and thereby exert political pressure on Ankara to proclaim an autonomous Kurdish state. The Little Fox was still pursuing the Murshid's vision.

He kept his word, leading his *pesh merga* north to the salt plains of Lake Urmia and raiding across the Persian frontier as far as Maragegh. But the promised weaponry never materialized. Instead, after a year's combined insurgent operations with Iraq's First Army Corps, Ismet and a hundred of his men were dispatched south by railway to Basra and thrown into the trenches for defense of the city.

During the ensuing campaign, the bloodiest of the Gulf War up to that point, the *pesh merga* were cut to a score, then a dozen. Finally, when the bloodbath in the Hawizah Marshes was over and the human waves of the Ayatollah's Dawn Eight offensive receded, only a handful of Kurds had survived. This pitiful remnant, which included his childhood friends Hamzah and Taufiq, Ismet was determined to save. With the help of a British mercenary known as John Courage, they deserted, escaping overland to Kuwait.

The years since, in some ways, had been the worst yet. The outcast warrior-patriots had found themselves reduced to Levantine criminals, drifting from Bahrain to Cyprus, turning their hands to smuggling, drug trafficking, even piracy. And yet they never abandoned their dream of Kurdistan, or their faith in the Little Fox. And he had led them, on this fateful summer morning, to a stolen speedboat on the Sea of Marmara and an enterprise more desperate than anything they had undertaken yet.

Suddenly they were hurled to the side, as Raschid spun the wheel. The boat slewed, sending up a fountain of spray. Ismet, peering through the misted Perspex windscreen, saw a storybook image rising and falling before him. It was the *George Washington,* magnificent and cloudlike, the Stars and Stripes rippling from its jackstaff. Ismet did not allow himself to be awed by the sight. It was simply a target, and a small one at that, less than fifty meters from bow to stern. Compared to the ship John Courage had originally proposed—one of the supertankers calling on Iran's Sirri Island oil facility—

this was a toy. The Little Fox smoothed his large mustache, in the manner of a Mullah, and waited for Raschid to slow.

But Raschid did not slow. They continued to leap over the water with the full muscle of the hundred-thirty-horsepower Evinrude, closing rapidly on the frigate. At fifty meters the half-Greek was still grinning. Had he lost his senses? Was he bent on smashing them to death against the ship's side?

Ismet made a lunge for the throttle, just as Raschid slotted it back to neutral. The outboard wailed in protest and the nose slapped down, lifting the Kurds out of their seats. Still, they had considerable headway, pushed along by a swell of their own making under the lee of the frigate's gallery. In a display of insouciance Raschid spun the wheel while reversing the engine. The speedboat slipped sideways, gathered sternway and missed the frigate's counter by an arm's length. While the three passengers remained braced for a collision, the boat glided out along the starboard quarter and sidled up neatly against the wooden wall.

Ismet didn't bother to congratulate his pilot. He was already on his feet, grabbing his Kalashnikov and coiled grappling line. He moved quickly back through the cockpit between Hamzah and Taufiq and onto the transom above the swimstep. Bracing his legs against the rocking of the boat, he began whirling the grappling iron at his side.

"Wait!" Raschid pointed forward where steps projected from the frigate's waterline to the entry port at the mainchains. But the Little Fox had waited long enough. He heaved the three-pronged hook aloft, heard it lodge behind the rail, and pulled it taut. In an instant he was moving quickly and skillfully up the side, hand over hand, rifle slung behind. From above came shouts, answered by a firecracker burst from below—Hamzah's machine pistol. The shouts were replaced by an agonized cry that cut off abruptly. Scrambling between two gun ports, Ismet grabbed a thick shroud attached to the chainplate and vaulted the rail. He nearly landed on Hamzah's victim lying face down in a bloody pool in the scuppers. All around on the quarterdeck people were screaming and running for cover.

Ismet fired his Kalashnikov in the air. "Everyone stop!" his voice boomed. Those on deck, thirty or so, froze in a tableau of terror. Ismet swooped and pried a revolver loose from the body's lifeless fingers. The man had caught Hamzah's burst full in the face. "One hero is dead. Who is next?"

The black-clad terrorist swaggered forward, staring scornfully at the costumed actors and extras. Several were uniformed as naval officers in blue coats with brass buttons, white waistcoats, and breeches. A few, including the actual sailing master and his crew, wore the outfits of sailors before the mast, tarpaulin hats with checkered shirts and red kerchiefs. About a dozen, for whom Ismet reserved the most contemptuous glances, were darkskinned extras of various Mediterranean races, sandaled and burnoosed as Arabs.

The rest, members of the film crew, were in casual clothes, blue jeans and T-shirts, shorts and tank tops. These included the cameraman, camera operator, sound man, mike boom operator, still photographer, grips, propmen, gaffers, and several Turkish counterparts. In charge of the company was the second unit director, a sixty-year-old Englishman with a grizzled ponytail and granny glasses, which lent him the mournful look of an aging hippie. Lyle Johns's bony frame was buttoned into a cowboy shirt and Levis, and in his hand dangled the bullhorn through which, a moment before, he had been blocking out the next scene for the Arab extras. They were to swarm up on deck en masse to perform their prayers facing Mecca. Whenever the helmsman tacked, they were all supposed to spin their prayer carpets accordingly. Lyle had already decided that the more confused the extras became, the funnier the scene would play.

Now, swiftly and irrevocably, all their elaborate make-believe had been punctured—with real bullets and real blood. A likable French rent-a-cop lay lifeless, cut down in the line of duty, and in their midst moved a pint-sized intruder, wielding the power of life and death. Lyle had directed mock battle scenes all over the world, but he hadn't experienced live fire since being an eighteen-year-old infantryman with the British Expeditionary Force in Flanders before Dunkirk. His reaction now surprised and shamed him—his knees had begun to tremble and nausea curdled his bowels.

For a moment the only sounds came from the ship itself. Overhead canvas flapped and volleyed in disarray, while a welter of cordage creaked against the stresses. Forward of the mizzenmast the big wheel, abandoned by the helmsman, revolved its spokes of its own accord. Underfoot the deck tilted in slow, undulant motion.

Then Ismet shouted: "Everybody down!" There was fearful hesitation, as people looked to one another. The command was repeated with violent gestures, and bodies dropped, squatted, or fell prostrate all over the deck. Lyle Johns lowered himself gingerly, favoring an old hip injury. He had the ghastly premonition that the little madman intended to shoot them all in the back. He visualized his ignominious death under the sunshine on a splendid morning in Istanbul Harbor. Anger boiled up amid his sick fears. He wished for some means to destroy the terrorist-assassin, to blow him away like the vermin he was, off his set and into the sea.

Again the menacing voice bellowed above them: "Guns, knives, all of them, give to me!"

Next to Lyle several costumed actors began writhing about, trying to unbuckle their sword belts while remaining prone. A dozen paces away a pistol slid across the planking to Ismet's feet. The eventual heap of prop weaponry, Lyle saw, included cutlasses, antique pistols, and a scimitar encrusted with fake jewels.

"Okay, listen to me now. I am Ismet. I am *pesh merga.* This means a soldier in Peoples Army of Kurdistan. You know my country, where it is?" Who bloody cares, thought Lyle Johns. A bunch of filthy, nomadic beggars with rifles, holed up in some barren rockpile of a country. All he knew was that the British had tried several times to make something of the Kurds, and each time had written them off as an impossible lot, and that the Iraqis had finally resorted to poison gas to crush their rebellion. "We *pesh merga* are the same like George Washington, the name of this ship. We fight for freedom. Turkey, Iraq, Persia, Syria, to us all are enemies. We are not afraid—"

Breaking off, Ismet whirled, aiming the Kalashnikov from the hip. Across the deck a young man had leaped to his feet and was sprinting toward the rail as if to dive overboard. Lyle recognized him as one of the Turkish trainees they had taken on in Izmir. The boy had been tireless in running shoreside supply errands. The Kurdish terrorist tracked his dash for safety, seeming to take his time before firing a stuttering burst. As the rifle swung, splinters flew in a short swath from the mizzen fife rail to the break of the quarterdeck. The running figure gave one throttled cry and went sprawling in a lifeless heap.

Lyle Johns's reaction was violent nausea. As he lay doubled over, retching up his breakfast, revulsion echoed around him in horrified chorus. Ismet, meanwhile, had resumed his speech: "Now two heroes are dead. And I have many bullets. Do you understand? If you do not do what we tell you, all of you will die."

As if to confirm the reference to "we," three more armed *pesh merga* suddenly boarded amidships, storming over the railing with blood-curdling cries and fanning out fore and aft. A shipful of hostages might have overpowered a single fanatic, but against four men, Lyle knew, their chances were nil.

The black quarter of *pesh merga* began to shout orders. People hiding below decks were herded topside. They included the sound crew, hairstylist, makeup man, three caterers, costumer, seamstress, and finally, the matronly Irish nurse and her lone patient, a seasick propman. More weapons were confiscated. The old Italian sailing master was summoned and ordered to sort out the chaos of canvas and rigging aloft. Under his direction the ship was hove to, the main topsail backed, and the weather braces secured. The terrorists strode back and forth over decks covered with bodies. The boarding operation had taken less than ten minutes.

"Who is the boss?" Lyle turned to see Ismet prodding the terrified wardrobe mistress with his rifle.

"Leave her alone!" Lyle cried out. "I'm the boss!" The terrified woman looked up, profound gratitude in her eyes. Ismet rushed up the companionway. The next moment Lyle found himself staring up the Kalashnikov's wicked snout.

"Up, Mr. Boss!" Lyle stood, his knees again turning to jelly. He was terrified, but no longer shamed by his reaction. He had spoken out. "What is your job, Mr. Boss?"

"I'm the second unit director."

"What means?"

"I work for the director." In the terrorist's dark eyes Lyle found no flicker of humanity, only the hair-trigger rage of a caged predator. O Lord, he thought, have mercy on us all.

"Where is the director?"

"He's in Istanbul. Listen. I don't know what you want, but we have no money on board. And we are not your enemies. We are from everywhere here, all countries. I'm British. We have people from Italy, England, Canada, the Middle East. That man was a Frenchman"—he pointed first to one corpse, then the other—"and that boy was Turkish. In the name of humanity—"

"Okay, okay, Mr. Boss." The Little Fox's eyes had been tracking the power cables snaking alongside flemished coils of rope and racks of belaying pins. "I tell you what I want. Do what I say, nobody dies. You make video of me."

"I don't understand."

"Video! Everybody knows video. I want all world to see me, hear about my country. On video."

"But we don't—we simply don't have that kind of equipment. This is film, not video. There is a difference."

Ismet shifted the Kalashnikov forward on its web sling to jab Lyle's belly. "You lie, Mr. Boss. Look up there." Ismet pointed aloft where a small microwave mast protruded from the maintop. "That is for video. See?" How did the little bastard know? Lyle wondered. The company did have a through-the-lens video system mounted on the film camera. It was used mainly for dailies, which were transmitted to a station ashore.

Then, like a child distracted by a new toy, Ismet reached and snatched a walkie-talkie from Lyle's belt. He turned it in his hand a moment, extracted the flex antenna, thumbed a button and began speaking loudly into the microphone: "Hello, I am Ismet. Who is there?"

He paused, cocking his head to listen. There was a faint pulsing sound—but from the sky, not the radio. Soon everyone on ship could hear it, growing louder. A moment later it became recognizable as the thrashing of an approaching helicopter.

≡

Five hundred feet below the chopper the surface of the inland sea sparkled in the morning sun like a sheet of hammered Byzantine gold. Beyond Üsküdar the forecourt of the Asian continent stretched to the horizon in shimmering haze. To the north were the familiar spires and mammary domes of Istanbul, sprawled like Rome over seven hills. The Turkish pilot, who had seen these things countless times, still marveled at their beauty. He recalled lines from Fitzgerald's *Khayyam:* "And Lo! the Hunter of the East has caught / The Sultan's Turret in a Noose of Light." As they continued westward at sixty knots, there came a sight of equal loveliness. A lone white speck far below on the gilded sea gradually re-solved itself into the majestic outlines of a three-master, on course for the Golden Horn.

Seated beside the pilot and tracking ahead with bin-oculars, Jack Woodhull was oblivious of the magnificent panorama. As the director of "Barbary!" and the man charged with bringing it in on schedule and under bud-get, he was more concerned with the lack of radio re-sponse from the *George Washington*.

"Their bloody transceiver must have packed up," he muttered into his headset. He glanced to his right, where the cameraman was sitting half out of the wide-open starboard door, guiding the 35-millimeter Arriflex on its over-the-shoulder mount. "How's she look, Mike?"

"Like a million bucks," the voice came back, chuck-ling against the background din of wind and rotor. It was a standing joke between them. At Jack's insistence, the company had laid out *five* million for the frigate.

Jack nudged the pilot. "Hagop, to hell with the radio. They can damn well hear us coming. Take her way down and come in along the wake, right on the wave tops. Mike, see if you can get Saint Sophia and all the rest of 'em through the rigging, okay? Then, if they've got their act together on deck, we'll do some hover shots and three-sixties."

The pilot nodded and forwarded the collective pitch of the little Turkish-made Augusta-Bell. They dropped quickly, watching the surface trade its sungloss for dark aquamarine. As they approached the frigate Hagop was the first to notice something wrong. "Jack, there's no wake. She's dead in the water."

"Get close," Jack snapped.

They altered course and swept in over the maintop,

so low the downdrift from their rotors began to luff the slackened canvas. As they passed, the cameraman swung the Arri down and around on its pan-and-tilt head.

Close up a full-rigged sailing ship can inspire awe, but the sudden, stunned silence in the cockpit was due to another emotion: horror. What they had just seen had chilled them to the bone. The *George Washington*'s entire deck surface was covered with bodies. Bodies face down. Motionless.

Jack Woodhull was the first to find his voice. "Christ, no." He felt the rush of nausea, and not because the pilot had stomped on the right rotor pedal to swing round for a second pass. Jack didn't want to look down again but knew he had to.

As they came out of a sharp banked turn, they saw, tethered alongside the frigate, a speedboat, a grappling line dangling into it from the quarterdeck. Jack had to will himself forward against the windscreen to look as they dived in over the stern.

The nightmare rushed at them. Corpses strewn everywhere. Then something they'd missed on the first pass. Among the flattened bodies four figures stood upright. And all four were swinging rifles up at the chopper's belly.

"Get the fuck out of here!" Jack screamed. Hagop hadn't waited to be told. He was already fighting collective and cyclic levers to lift and slip sideways. The cameraman, the most exposed of the three, continued to roll film.

When they were a thousand yards off the frigate's port quarter, a strange voice growled briefly in their headsets.

"What the hell language is that?" Jack asked the pilot. "You get any of it?"

"English, I think, with a Kurdish accent. He definitely mentioned Kurdistan. He asks for the big boss. I think he means you. If you wish, I can hover right here, okay?"

"Yeah, sure. Just keep us way the hell out of rifle range." Still fighting sickening fear, Jack forced himself to come to grips with the crisis. What did he or any of his company have to do with Kurdistan, for Christ's sake? It wasn't even a country, just another back garden gobbled up by history, like Macedonia or Ruthenia. More luckless bastards with machine guns. He replaced the headset and spoke slowly, emphatically: "Hello, repeat please. This is Jack Woodhull calling the *George Washington.* Is there somebody who speaks English?"

He repeated the call several times before a familiar voice came on. "Jack, this is Lyle Johns."

"Lyle, Christ Almighty! Thank God you're alive—"

"Jack, listen! Don't fly over the ship—not again. They'll shoot."

"Don't worry, we won't. Lyle, are you okay? What the bloody hell's happened? It looks like Jonestown down there."

"Yeah, yeah, it's bad, but . . . but we're alive. They made everyone lie flat."

"Who's 'they'?"

"You heard the man—the Peoples Democratic Army of Kurdistan. Jack—"

"You're telling me everyone's okay? Lyle, you're damn sure about that?" There was a pause. *Too long,* Jack thought. *The bastards have a gun to his head.*

"Yeah, everyone's okay," Lyle's voice came back.

"So far. But please, don't do anything crazy. These guys are very, very serious. Jack, you got to get us out of here."

"Damn well right we'll get you out of there, Lyle. Count on it." The bravado promise was in stark contrast to the way Jack actually felt. He saw his helplessness reflected in the face of the Turkish pilot. Lyle was going on, his voice beginning to crack under the strain as he read a prepared statement. Hagop was getting it all on the flight recorder. It was an unintelligible manifesto, full of the usual political claptrap and non-negotiable demands, including a live TV hookup. Jack had the awful conviction he was listening to a dead man. *Like the coal miners,* he thought. There had been an incident during his boyhood. A cave-in somewhere in Wales. The whole family had watched it on the telly. There had even been a phone line to the trapped victims. The miners had sounded exactly like Lyle, and the authorities had made the same brave promises. *Don't worry, mates, we'll get you out.* They'd come out, all right—days later, on stretchers, into the back of the undertaker's van.

It's my own goddamn fault, Jack told himself. I had to have authenticity. Build a full-scale ship, pay three million pounds, sail 'er right into the Eastern Med, fly the Yankee flag. Smart move, Woodhull. Next time why not just send a telex, attention all terrorists? Leo was right. We could have shot the whole damn thing with balsa models in a studio tank.

Finally Lyle signed off, conveying the terrorists' ultimatum for a response on the same frequency on the hour. The pilot pulled out of hover and began beating westward toward Istanbul's Yesilköy Airport. Crouched in the starboard doorway, obeying the instincts of his profession, the cinematographer continued to roll footage till the sailing ship vanished in his tele lens.

3

AMANDA MORGAN HAD BEEN UP HALF THE NIGHT DOING business on the phone from her suite at Istanbul's Pera Palas. Her California calls began at 4 A.M. and she continued, working her way eastward over the globe. As first light leaked through the window curtains, she was propped up in bed, prophesying against nuclear power to a late-night radio talk show audience in Boston. After eight, wrapped in an emerald silk sari from Islamabad, she had moved onto the terrace, which had a view of the Bosphorus and the Golden Horn. In between bites of brie and crackers, she was making wake-up calls to London.

Tony, her agent, was enthusiastic about an offer for her to do Shaw with the Royal Shakespeare Company at the Barbican the following spring. *"Caesar and Cleopatra,* Mandy. You'd be perfect."

"Tony, don't hate me, but I can't possibly, and you know why. The time is already committed."

"Then uncommit. It's only for a few weeks. World peace can wait, the RSC won't."

"Don't push, luv. I've made promises, and I intend to keep them. Now if it were *Saint Joan,* I might reconsider . . ."

Her accountant, too, was being a bit of a nag, fussing over the number of causes and committees she was funding.

"I know, Reg. I should cut them all off at the ankles and move to Monte Carlo. But I like being parasitized. Not to fret." The fee from "Barbary!" would go a long way toward calming Reginald's fiduciary anxieties, while enriching the coffers of the Inland Revenue.

Her ex-husband Roy, thank heaven, wanted nothing. He was looking after her house in Hampstead and her cats. He told her some amusing stories about their neighbors and said he was still in love with her, which was sweet and quite possibly true.

Sybella, her secretary, read her the headlines from *The Times,* traded gossip, and asked for her verdict on a half-dozen pending invitations.

"The only one that sounds amusing," Amanda responded, "is the Jordanian Embassy reception. But we'll be filming in Tunisia that week."

"What about Lake Como?"

"What was it again?"

"A symposium on Oriental eschatology, it says here. End-of-the-world scenarios, whatever that means."

"Caca, dear, it means pure, unadulterated *caca.* But

find out who will be there. I'm curious. Let's see, there is something else. Tell Morty he's not to publish that interview till I go over his changes. Be firm, Syb. You know how sneaky he is. Listen, why don't you have him fax the pages to me? Ring up the Kronos offices there and find out if they have one of those machines, would you, dear? Good. And Syb, just keep telling everybody that I'm booked clear through till next fall."

Which was nearly true. Amanda had several TV guest shots lined up after "Barbary!" wrapped in November. But basically, from the end of the year until the following September, she was keeping off the greasepaint to become a full-time activist. It was essential. She could ignore the nasty little epithets the tabloids used to describe her political involvements—Marxist Tart, Red Starlet, Bolshe Vixen. And she was flattered by comparisons, favorable or unfavorable, to Fonda or Redgrave. But when a smarmy right-wing MP had recently stood in Parliament and labeled her a "politically misguided, albeit delicious dilettante," Amanda had been incensed. Dilettante she damn well was not! As he, and others of his ilk, would soon find out.

There was to be a combined European "peace offensive" in the spring. Amanda had volunteered to spearhead the UK drive. Aside from attending endless coordinating sessions from Amsterdam to Athens, she would need time for intensive study. It was not enough to put on the mantle of righteousness and orate passionately on behalf of the cause. She had to know her stuff: facts, figures, and dates, as well as throw weights, megatonnage, radiation levels, and casualty estimates. Fortunately her ability to memorize pages of dialogue helped her spit back statistics on demand.

When Amanda finished her last call, to a radical Milanese journalist, it was nearly nine—and she was due to meet her producer, Leopold Bouchard, at ten-thirty for a tour of the Topkapi Palace. A tour unfortunately listed in the press kits of media junketeers flown in from all over Europe and America. Which meant it would turn inevitably into a Fellini parade, with a horde of publicists and Turkish officialdom and the usual *paparazzi* swarm. Jack Woodhull would join them later for a harborside lunch, and between mouthfuls of lamb *kebab* they might actually have a few minutes to discuss character and motivation.

Amanda's first scenes were scheduled the following day at the palace. These were all exteriors, travelogue stuff really, posing in front of minarets. The Harem interiors would be shot in Shepperton in the fall. The script was open on a brass tea table, where she had abandoned it after memorizing a few pages of rancid dialogue. She'd done worse things, though not in recent memory. And never for such an obscenely large sum of money. Her salary would allow her to take most of next year off and damn near bankroll the peace movement.

"Of course the script is tawdry," Tony had said. "It's designed to be interrupted every nine minutes to sell hairspray and frozen yuk. You might as well cash in. British actresses are hot this year." And of course Tony's percentage would fund his own avocation—frequent trips to Cannes in quest of sun and Mediterranean men.

Amanda stood and stretched—and experienced near blackout. The room swirled and an electric *frisson* swept her. Her sense of identity was vacuumed out and for an instant she was a hovering presence, an otherness looking out through strange eyes.

Then identity returned, the odd moment leaving a piquant and mystical residue. She turned to an ornate cheval glass set into a seven-foot armoire. There was the image that had been splashed onto glossy magazine covers, magnified across cinema sheets in darkened movie halls, etched in phosphor across television screens. Long black hair spilled onto the sari's emerald silk shoulders. In the olive oval face, dark gypsy eyes, one ever so slightly lower than the other, stared back. Black brows, unplucked, like twin caterpillars. Button nose—adorable en face but, in profile, the bane of cinematographers. Exaggerated bottom lip. Near the corner of the frank mouth, the beauty spot copied by English schoolgirls—and boys.

"Whoever I am," she thought, "I'm bloody well trapped, aren't I, locked inside a film star." Then the contrary mouth smiled, and she turned, knowing she had no more time to indulge in introspection. She entered the enormous bathroom and stepped into the large mosaic shower stall, fighting sudden urges for a cigarette and a man, in no particular order. The former she was quitting—had done without for nearly two months. And the latter—well, it had been nearly as long since she'd given the boot to Alf, a red-headed carpenter who'd come to fix the floors in Hampstead and had stayed the month. Still, men weren't the same kind of vice as smoking. And if they were, Amanda didn't care. Since Alf, the right type just hadn't come along—and she wouldn't have had time for him if he had.

She steamed and lathered, singing "Eleanor Rigby," and felt better than she had any right to. Lately she had been getting along on three and four hours of sleep, eating carelessly, drinking far too much coffee. The small, compactly muscled body—the physique of a tumbler or circus girl—stood her in good stead. It was nearing forty, and she made more demands on it now than in her teens.

She turned off the shower and heard the phone shrilling. An instant later she stood naked and dripping on the Oriental carpet, listening to Leopold Bouchard, in agitated *franglais,* tell her about an attack on the sailing ship. She attempted to piece the disaster together, but Leo was nearly incoherent. Terrorists of some stripe had apparently taken over the *George Washington,* causing the cancellation of their day's outing, perhaps the entire miniseries, and a resultant financial disaster of unutterable proportions involving his studio and an international consortium of investors and insurance underwriters.

"What about the hostages?" she finally broke in. "Has anyone been hurt?"

"I don't know it. Perhaps, yes!" He was sending for more security and ordering her not to leave her hotel room.

"Leo, I realize you're in the midst of a crisis. But please, just give me information. Don't tell me what to do. Who are these terrorists? What have they done exactly? And what are their demands?"

"They are Kurds, didn't I say it? From Kurdistan, where is it, I don't know. But they are criminals!"

"There *isn't* any Kurdistan. That's why they've turned to terrorism. That doesn't make them criminals, Leo."

"Merde! Always *la politique!* I should have expect this from you."

"Of course you should. I hope you'd be a terrorist too if someone occupied your homeland."

"Someone 'as. And I do not misbehave of it."

"Really, Leo, are you talking about your house in Beverly Hills? Paris hasn't been occupied since the Nazis, and you were too young to be in the *Maquis.*"

"I am talking of the Pyrénées, eh? *Ma mère,* she was Basque, you didn't know it? And Mandy, there is in your contract a thing that forbid political activity. *Absolument.* So I am telling you, speak to no one all this crazy stuff you are thinking."

"Leo, people have been trying to shut me up since first form, and I assure you it can't be done. Besides, your little clause is unenforceable, as our solicitors have discussed. Actors aren't chattel. You cannot restrict their fredom of expression, as unfair as that must seem to you. If I want to speak out"—she found herself fumbling for cigarettes, stopped herself—"or, heaven forfend, even leave my room, I'll bloody well do it."

"No, no, no! You will not! I pay million dollar for you, Mandy! Do what I say! *Ne bouge pas!*"

"Leo, I intend to find out what's going on, and if you won't tell me—" She broke off. He had hung up on her.

She swore. She was furious. Why couldn't the impossible little man simply tell her what was happening? After a moment of indecision, she went to the door, opened it a crack, and smiled at the young Turkish security officer stationed outside. He smiled back. He would be no problem when she decided to leave.

She clicked on the television and saw bare-chested men in leather britches, bodies slathered in oil, grappling in intimate, almost erotic positions on a soccer field.

Crowds cheered. The other channel had talking heads at a desk beneath a clock. Morning news, in a language that could have been Martian for all Amanda could comprehend. She'd been told there were occasional bulletins in English, but when?

Still naked, she went onto the terrace overlooking Mesrutiyet Caddesi. To her right across the intersection a half-dozen cars were drawn up in front of the four-building compound of the U.S. Consulate General. She could see people bustling in and out of both the main office building and the four-story annex. Something was indeed afoot. But directly below, in front of the historic hotel, the media scavengers were loitering, apparently unaware of any hostage crisis under their noses. They were fiddling with lenses, drinking coffee, littering the sidewalk—waiting for her. If one of those oily characters with zoom lens and motor drive *had* chanced to glance up now, she thought, he could shoot enough celebrity skin to qualify for *paparazzi* heaven.

Down the street she spotted a van from Turkish TV, TRT, with microwave mast. That meant the video crews could feed live remotes back to the studio and on the air. A chancy thing to do under the current Turkish constitution, she would have thought. But it could be useful if she chose to make a statement. Leopold Bouchard was not going to keep her under house arrest. One way or another, she was going to find out what was going on, and stir things up in the process.

She hurried inside to get dressed.

BLUE AND YELLOW LIGHT FILTERED INTO THE LONG ROOM
through a tall stained-glass window depicting a Mussul-
man saint slaying a sea serpent. The bright hues tinted
the marble-tiled floor and patterned the long refectory
table, which was strewn with ash trays and coffee cups.
High along the walls overhead, visible through a cumu-
lus of tobacco smoke, dusty crossed oars and faded banners commemorated regattas of yesteryear.

Emergencies always bring out committees, thought
Paul Cyrus, as he glanced around the crowded conference room of the Harbor Police headquarters in Galata.
This crisis had summoned to the same gleaming expanse of mahogany an extraordinary assembly. Movie
moguls sat side by side with Foreign Service types. A
phalanx of dark-suited Turkish Cabinet ministers stared

across at the oddly garbed Hollywood contingent, or rather movie contingent, since none of them were actually from California. Leopold Bouchard, the diminutive executive producer, was unmistakably Gallic, dressed in Gucci leather and chain-smoking Gauloises in his curled paws. The director, Jack Woodhull, a red-faced, sad-eyed Yorkshireman, had come straight from a helicopter flight and was still bundled in a parka vest, as was his cameraman, a young Canadian introduced as Mike Babka. The unit publicist, by the name of Billy James Bracey, was a pudgy American Southerner who spoke in a tenor twang and looked like a child evangelist with his blond pompadour and white-on-white suit. Paul was seated near one end of the table. To his left, busily scribbling notes, was a Turkish press spokesman sporting a Stanford University tie, and a double-chinned representative from Turkish Radio-Television's board of directors. On Paul's right were the impeccable Townsend White, U.S. Consul General, and his preppy Vice Consul, Mike Mitchell.

As Paul had predicted, Colonel Celal Ozsahin was running the show. The chief of Turkey's counter-terrorist apparatus had the look of a plump banker or civil servant. He was overgroomed, with pomaded hair and mustache, gray silk suit, and heavy gold jewelry, and he spoke with disconcertingly effeminate, limp-wristed gestures. All this was camouflage, Paul knew. For Ozsahin was a war hero, had won a chestful of combat medals with the famed Turkish Brigade in Korea, and had made his political mark during the martial law years of General Evren by ruthless and effective suppression of gang warfare. When he spoke, Paul noticed, the heavyweights from the Turkish National Security Council and National Military Council paid close attention.

Ozsahin, obviously operating against the clock, had been briefing them rapidly, in both Turkish and English, which he spoke in clipped, Oxonian tones. Four terrorists, as Paul had observed through binoculars, had boarded the *George Washington.* So far they had identified themselves only as Kurdish separatists, but Ozsahin possessed an extensive dossier on their leader, a terrorist known as Ismet al-Azzawi, the Little Fox.

While still in his teens Ismet had been charged with the assassination of Turkish administrative officials. More recently, after an unlikely stint in the Iraqi army, the Little Fox and several of his men had resurfaced in the Eastern Mediterranean, where they had apparently become involved in the Lebanese drug trade. It was claimed they had been supplying heroin refineries in the Bekaa Valley with opium smuggled from Afghanistan and Iran—"Two of many countries," Ozsahin pointed out to Townsend White, "which make no attempt to cooperate as do we with your DEA's strictures against poppy cultivation."

Ismet and his *pesh merga* had also been linked to a series of bank robberies in eastern Anatolia—in Diyarbakir, Siverek and Hakkari—"undertaken obviously to finance further terrorist operations. So you see, the hijacking of a large target like the *George Washington* is a logical escalation."

According to the movie company's call sheets, there were forty-three people aboard, actors and crew, all now held hostage. At this point in the recital Ozsahin shook his head. "I am sorry to inform you that the number has been reduced by at least two."

A VCR and a large monitor were wheeled in, and they were shown a video transfer of helicopter footage shot that morning. As the camera pivoted down over a deck covered with bodies, Ozsahin halted the tape and turned to the horrified audience.

"What you see are hostages lying flat in obedience to orders issued by their Kurdish captors. At least that is what Mr. Woodhull here was told, during radio contact with a colleague aboard the ship. Unfortunately it is not entirely true." Ozsahin pressed the remote control, zooming in on the image, then tracing with one plump finger the unmistakable outline of a dark stain around one of the bodies on the deck. "Everyone can see this? Yes? And there is more." He fast-forwarded the tape, then froze and enlarged a second figure, partially eclipsed by an edge of sail. But clearly visible, in addition to bloodstains on the deck, were bloody patches on a white shirt. "You are looking at a corpse, shot many times in the back."

Deathly silence fell over the room. Paul found himself gripping the arms of his chair, his teeth clenched. Jack Woodhull began slowly pounding the table. "I knew it!" the Englishman said. "The sodding bastards!"

"Quite so, Mr. Woodhull. The Little Fox has something of a reputation as an assassin. The bodies have since been removed, by the way, so we must thank your cameraman for this proof that we are dealing with murderers." Ozsahin switched off the playback.

In the stunned aftermath Leopold Bouchard continued to stare at the now dark monitor, a cigarette hanging slack on his lower lip. Paul watched the little producer stub it out and cross himself as he fumbled to

light another. Meanwhile Townsend White had leaned
forward: "Colonel, exactly what is happening now?"

"If you are asking, Mr. Consul General, are we simply sitting on our backsides, waiting for these criminals
to shoot more innocent people, the answer is no." Ozsahin strode to the wall, yanked down a large map of
the city and surrounding waterways. "The *George Washington* is anchored here," he said. He jabbed a spot in
the Sea of Marmara, off Istanbul's southern shore, due
south of the Blue Mosque. With his curiously fey gestures, the colonel began sketching the deployment of his
counter-terrorist forces.

$$\equiv$$

Along the Marmara sea walls a dozen long-range
marksmen had been in position for more than an hour.
These men were all competition sharpshooters from the
main Turkish hostage rescue unit, the Jandara Suicide
Commandos, known in Turkish as the *Ozel Intihar Kom-
mando Bolugu* or OIKB. They were equipped with
H&K NATO sniper rifles and Zeiss Diavari telescopic
sights, which afforded startling close-ups of the deck of
the square-rigger a kilometer offshore.

The marksmen were spaced at intervals along the
seafront: overlooking the rail line and the coastal road;
atop the old defense towers that marched eastward
along the sea toward Seraglio Point; amid the crumbling
ruins of the Great Palace of Byzantium; among pigeons
on the tile rooftops of hotels and houses. They waited,
alert to commands from their headset transceivers, eyes
glued to scopes, fingers caressing triggers.

A soccer field, just north of the rail line and west
of the Sergius and Bacchus Church, had been selected
as a staging ground. A CH-47 Chinook transport heli-

copter settled its skids on the muddy turf and disgorged a squad of what looked like futuristic shock troops. They wore black polycarb ballistic helmets and Kevlar vests, and were armed with H&K machine guns, Colt .45 autos, and stun grenades. These were the elite Jandara commandos, from a hundred-and-fifty-man company stationed near Yesilköy Airport. Already on the field were SEALs from the nearby Naval Training Command on Heybeli Island in the Marmara, choppered in moments before and now forming up by the single dilapidated goalpost.

The combined forces were making final equipment checks before heading several blocks west to the tiny fishing harbor of Kumkapi. Here, behind the little sea wall, Special Boat Units (SBUs) and submersible Swimmer Delivery Vehicles (SDVs) were being readied for an assault on the terrorist held ship.

While detailed plans were being worked up, a standby assault group of several SEAL teams was already in the water. These men were disguised as fishermen in a scattered flotilla of wooden skiffs, loitering in the frigate's general vicinity. Weapons concealed beneath nets, they were ready to attack instantly should the terrorists begin shooting hostages.

Also targeting the *George Washington,* from a balcony on the top floor of a rundown seaside hotel, was an array of electronic surveillance gadgetry—thermal imagers and parabolic microphones. To gather more data on the terrorists, Ozsahin had ordered listening devices placed on the frigate's hull. SEALs in SCUBA gear were in the process of carrying out this mission.

Feliks Ilyinsky watched the counter-terrorist deployment with avid interest from the top of Istanbul's First

Hill. In response to an urgent call from his consulate, the KGB major had cut short his morning's dalliance and, in his twenty-foot ski boat, commuted at full throttle back to Beyoglu. Instead of monitoring the unfolding crisis from the Soviet Consulate on Istiklal Caddesi, he had summoned a car and driver, collared his deputy, and headed across the Galata Bridge to kibitz firsthand.

He had selected a favorite overlook atop the Sphendone, the great curving south wall of the ancient Hippodrome. At a garden railing, Ilyinsky slowly swept his binoculars from Seraglio Point all the way west to the Marble Tower, where the ancient Byzantine land walls met the sea. On the sparkling horizon the Princes Islands were etched sharply against the Asian shore. Over there in his villa Noorsheen no doubt would be neglecting her chores, probably sunning herself on the terrace, or perhaps curled up inside on his elephant-gray velour sofa, flipping the pages of the latest European fashion magazines. Whatever she was doing, she would be humming one of her little tunes, Feliks thought, for he had managed to extricate himself from her clutches with full erotic honors.

He tilted the binoculars down, past a rooftop on which he was able to pick out another sniper. That made half a dozen so far. He reckoned them no more than a thousand meters from their targets, well within effective range. The trick, of course, was to take out all the terrorists simultaneously.

"Feliks, can we go now? I'm freezing my ass out here." The plea came from a cadaverous young Russian beside Ilyinsky. While Feliks was enjoying the light easterly breeze in his shirtsleeves, the young man, Anton Bessaraboff, was shivering inside a heavy corduroy coat with a wool scarf wound round his scrawny neck. Feliks gave him a sympathetic glance. For Bessaraboff it had been a long influenzal summer, despite regular dosages of *pyenitsilin.*

"Poor Toshka, freezing in splendid weather. Suppose we were assigned to a missile base on Kamchatka? How would you survive?"

"How about Brazil?"

"Neither of us speaks Portuguese."

"I could learn it in three weeks."

What would have been a joke or an idle boast from anyone else was from Bessaraboff a simple statement of fact. The repulsive-looking prodigy had solved the intricacies of Turkish grammar and pronunciation in the course of the summer, while Ilyinsky, who spoke a half-dozen Slavic and European tongues, was still stumbling about like a schoolboy after nearly a year.

Feliks draped an arm about the young man's shivering shoulders. "Of course you could, Toshka. But my assignment is here, and what would I do without you?" Feliks had met Bessaraboff two years earlier in Bucharest in the qualifying round of a chess tournament. At first he had been fascinated by his opponent's obvious grotesquerie—gangly, ectomorphic body, elongated, insectile head. Twenty-five moves later, when the youth suddenly turned a King's Indian Defense into a blitzkrieg counterattack that swept Ilyinsky from the board, it was the power and elegance of his opponent's brain that intrigued him. The strange young man had gone on to win the tournament without a loss. A week later Ilyinsky had recruited him into the Committee for State Security.

On the Istanbul diplomatic list Bessaraboff was simply one of several second secretaries of the Soviet Consulate, specializing in science and technology. In reality, however, the young Russian was Ilyinsky's deputy in the Eighth Department of the First KGB Directorate, a division responsible for foreign operations from the Balkans to Afghanistan.

"Feliks, would you mind if I went back to the car now?" A half-block away their dark Mercedes was nosed against a mesh-wire fence at the end of a cobbled cul-de-sac. The driver was lounging outside, reading a newspaper spread on the fender.

"Endure a few minutes more for my sake, Toshka. There's a great deal going on down there, and I may wish to benefit from your analysis." Ilyinsky was observing National Police SWAT units spilling out of vans and cordoning off Kennedy Caddesi and the approaches to the sea walls. Word of the crisis must have spread rapidly; crowds were already gathering behind the barricades.

Bessaraboff turned his back to the scene, coughing quietly. Feliks pivoted him around and offered the binoculars. Bessaraboff declined.

"Really, Toshka, you're being such a dismal fellow. I know you have *la grippe,* but where's your sense of drama? Here we are, privileged to look down through a heavenly proscenium, like old Jove spying on the plains of Troy. Not a bad allusion, really, considering where we're standing." Feliks flung his arm back toward the site of the Hippodrome. "You realize charioteers took this corner at breakneck speed while a hundred thousand people cheered. And on this same ground the great Belisarius put down a rebellion against the Byzantine empire, trapping thirty thousand rebels in the stadium and slaughtering every last one of them. Makes you wonder how *he'd* deal with a handful of ragged terrorists, eh?"

"You know I'm not interested in antiquity, Feliks. And if you want to find out what's really happening down there, you can learn more in five minutes from Yefim back in the comm center than standing up here all day with a telescope."

"True, Toshka, but also very sad. Modern generals no longer seek the high ground to observe the battle. They must remain at HQ, plugged into their headsets. Where is the sense of human drama?" Ilyinsky sighed. "We'll go back to your beloved computers in a minute. First, tell me what you think of the Jandara Commandos."

"No one ever said Turks couldn't fight."

"You don't think they'll ask for help?"

"The British already offered."

"How do you know that?"

"Yefim monitored the call an hour ago. I meant to tell you. Guess I'm too doped up on antibiotics. Turns out they've got a crack SAS unit training practically next door on Malta. They could be here in two hours."

"And?"

"Colonel Ozsahin turned them down."

"What about the Americans? Did Yefim intercept a call from them as well, about which you also forgot to inform me?"

"Delta Force? No, at least nothing Yefim has heard. I assume they're back home in North Carolina, still savoring the glory that was Grenada." Bessaraboff shut his eyes and exposed his gums, a facial contortion Feliks had learned to interpret as a smile, and a sign that Toshka had just made a joke.

The Marmara breeze freshened, stirring the wispy hair on Ilyinsky's broad skull. "So tell me, Toshka, what do you think will happen here today?"

"Too many variables. Besides, it doesn't really matter. Neither side is ours."

"Surely there is some gain to be made from even a small bloodbath."

"This is nothing. A big show for TV, that's all. What we need is for the Persian Gulf to blow up again, or for the Shias to cut the oil pipeline from Iraq. Feliks, please, let's go. I have to piss."

"So, water the geraniums over there," Ilyinsky raised his binoculars again.

"I can't piss out here. People could be watching."

"Who? Spies, lurking behind the cypress trees over there? Going to send incriminating snaps to your little Babushka in Odessa?" Ilyinsky was tracking a helicopter as it lifted off the soccer field below, and then another vectoring in low from the west. Bessaraboff made perfect sense based on the facts at his command, yet there were one or two things Ilyinsky had kept from him. The major swept the panorama below one last time then lowered the binoculars, his face creased by a wide, saurian smile. "All right, my brave Toshka, let us see to your needs."

Ismet leaned on the teak quarter railing, staring up at the clustered domes of the Blue Mosque. Somewhere out there, probably lower down along the sea wall, snipers would be staring back at him. His head would make a fat target centered in a sniperscope's cross hairs. But he was betting his life the Turks wouldn't shoot unless they were sure of bagging all four terrorists at once.

At the moment Ismet, standing on the quarterdeck, was the only one exposed. Hamzah and Taufiq were sheltered between two of the foredeck carronades and Raschid was below, sorting the confiscated passports and valuables. The hostages were also hidden, huddled together amidships under the shade of an inverted longboat and an awning-rigged staysail. Ismet had ordered the caterers to supply food and drink all around. Many like Ismet were drinking coffee, while several, despite the crisis, partook of pastries that had been passed out.

Unfortunately for Ismet's comrade-in-arms, John Courage, the famous actress was not among the captives. Since the Big Angleesh had taken so obvious a fancy to his dark-eyed countrywoman, Ismet had made a final search for her below decks, descending the wooden steps into the bowels of the eighteenth-century replica. Instead of the low-ceilinged gun decks and wooden bulkheads he had expected, the companionway had opened into a spacious commissary with tile floors and formica tables gleaming under fluorescent lighting. The adjoining galley sparkled with stainless steel fixtures; a technical bay was crammed with video monitors, mixing consoles, and playback units. In a carpeted alleyway he opened the doors of one plush dressing room after another, peered into the porcelain glare of a half-dozen bathrooms. A deck lower he wandered past electric generators, fresh water tanks and then, under the floorboards, discovered the ship's true power source, a pair of big German diesels. Dizzied and disoriented, the little Kurd made his way back topside, emerging into the sunshine of the square-rigger's spar deck and the glory of the ancient Stamboul skyline.

Off to starboard, at the Bosphorus mouth, white-

and gold-smokestacked steamers could be seen plying between Haydarpasa and the Princes Islands. The city was resuming its commerce, but giving the hostage ship a wide berth. Only a few fishing skiffs ventured near, none closer than a kilometer; a helicopter hammered the air high overhead. Ismet assumed all this attention to be hostile reconnaissance.

But he was used to being stalked. He could hardly recall living *without* a price on his head. In the mountains of his homeland he had waited many times as enemies closed in. The Little Fox had always managed to outmaneuver his foes. He had even escaped the Iraqi Army and the endless siege around Basra, those marshlands of the Tigris-Euphrates delta into which so many Iraqis and Iranians had drained their life's blood. Yet never had the odds been stacked so fearfully against him. Here death was his only certain escape.

Ismet was not afraid to die. "When Allah's time arrives," the Prophet had written, "none shall put it back." That time might arrive for many this very day. Ismet had threatened to execute all on board, and, if put to the test, he would do so. What his will had resolved, his hand would carry out, no matter what the cost. Ismet counted his life already forfeit. His pilgrimage, foretold by the Murshid, was to a Meccah that did not yet exist, and one he would probably never see—a sovereign Kurdistan.

Yet often Ismet longed to follow a different path, to live for a wife and family rather than for a country and cause. His visions of this other existence always conjured up a girl he had known in Ruwandiz. Adila was a strong-willed beauty, quiet and stubborn. Contrary to the wishes of her father, the Mukhtar, she had been devoted to Ismet, her childhood playmate.

His memory projected her into the morning air, looking as she had on a fine spring day, gleaming black coils of hair adorned with scarlet and blue wildflowers. He could feel her small, warm hand slip into his own, feel her breath, thrill to her whisper, lose himself in the depths of her eyes. The vision faded, but the memory lingered.

In a peaceful world Ismet might have looked for no richer prize than Adila. Instead he had been swept early into his people's struggle, taking up his rifle and fleeing with his young comrades into the mountains. Two years later he had returned to Ruwandiz, a *pesh merga* chieftain and a fugitive from the Turkish militia. For three nights Adila sheltered him and his small band in her family's stable, fed them, listened to their stories, and favored Ismet with swift, stirring glances. Before dawn of the fourth day the Turks had attacked. Ismet and two of his men escaped, but Adila and all her family were butchered in their beds. Whatever secret dreams she had harbored had died with her.

How could he fear death now, when Adila, stubborn and tender spirit, had gone to that final lonely place before him? Where she had led, surely he could follow.

Ismet addressed the shining city on the hill, where a moment before he had beheld the vision: "Adila, it may be that I will come to thee today." There was comfort in that thought. Also a kind of intoxication, a flirtation with the inevitable.

The Little Fox checked his watch. Three minutes after ten. The Turkish authorities were late in their response. He glanced forward at Raschid, now stationed in the companionway with the portable transceiver. The half-Greek shook his head, indicating he had heard nothing.

Ismet barked an order to Hamzah. A hostage was dragged up to him, a terrified young man with stringy blond hair, a sleeveless sweatshirt, and a yellow plastic digital watch. Hamzah bound the hostage's arms behind him, as Ismet stripped off the sportswatch and fastened it on his own wrist, tossing overboard his own timepiece, a bright piece of junk he had bought off a Portuguese sailor in Bahrain. The digital readout showed 9:56. The Turks weren't late, after all. Still it was time to stir them up. The captive was forced to kneel on the planking. He was sobbing now, actually slobbering as he pleaded for his life. Ismet stared defiantly ashore and placed his rifle against the young man's head.

5

DARRYL ANN'S LEGGY, BIKINI-CLAD IMAGE KEPT DARTING like a phantom flasher through the life-and-death proceedings. In the middle of one of Colonel Ozsahin's tactical explanations, Paul pictured her bending over, awkwardly and provocatively, to free a dock line, while Big Daddy Watkins fired up *Pegasus'* twin diesels. Soon Bitsy would be breaking out the sandwiches as they put Istanbul astern, along with the captured frigate, forty-one hostages, two dead bodies, four terrorists, and one expendable ex-fiancé. Tomorrow the whole happy clan would be in the Aegean, cleaving the sunshine on the way to Lesbos. D.A. would be splayed on the foredeck half nude, guzzling diet cola and listening to Springsteen on her boom box. Before the cruise was over, Paul decided, she'd pick up some oily Adonis to share her state-room and her strenuous ecstasies.

To hell with her, he thought. Staying behind in Istanbul had not been simply a question of duty. He was where he *wanted* to be. The crisis atmosphere—the stomach-churning tension in the room—heightened his sense of reality, his energy, and his perception. Moreover, he enjoyed studying Ozsahin's methods and the man's air of command in a situation that offered such limited options. Paul only wished some of the Turks would loosen their collars, so he could do likewise. As the morning wore on, the room had grown hot and stuffy. Eventually an aide was sent round with a long pole to open the clerestory windows, but the effect was negligible.

The real stumbling block to Paul's concentration, of course, was that he had no part to play. It was like attending a class in which he was well prepared but never to be called upon. The Turks were totally in charge. The question of jurisdiction had been resolved as far back as the Vienna Convention of 1924, and reaffirmed under Nixon, Carter, and Reagan. The host country was responsible for all people within its boundaries. Townsend White and Mike Mitchell may have been glad to have Paul on hand, but he was clearly superfluous.

About thirty minutes into the briefing the colonel was called suddenly out of the room and an aide took over. Quickly Paul found his thoughts wandering back to Darryl Ann and their final, painful moments together. After his call to the Consulate from the *Pegasus*, he had thrown on a suit and grabbed the first transport available on the Fenerbahçe waterfront—a battered and piebald vintage DeSoto *taksi*. Darryl had insisted on coming along. They had fought all the way up the Asian coast, over the Bosphorus Bridge, and into Beyoglu. D.A. simply could not accept that Paul was defying her wishes.

Finally, as they were nearing the Consulate, she had grown desperate and turned sexual terrorist herself. Snuggling close, she had presented her ultimatums in a flurry of seductive whispers. He could meet briefly with his boss to soothe his sense of duty or wounded pride or whatever was making him behave so childishly. She understood, she really did; it obviously had something to do with Daddy's money. But then he must return promptly, like a good little Pauly-Wolly, to his real boss. She would be sipping a daiquiri across the street at the Pera Palas. She consulted her Patek-Philippe; she would give him an hour, no more. Then the two of them would sail off into the sunset on Daddy's boat, get bombed on Dom Perignon, lock themselves in her cabin, and screw their brains out.

Had Paul agreed—and he'd come shamefully close, with D.A.'s hands all over him and the young Turkish driver staring goggle-eyed in the DeSoto's rear-view mirror—his life would have been forever altered. He'd be cruising now, not only into the Aegean, but into a life of leisure. Also, of course, a life of doing whatever D.A. desired, as an obedient husband—well-heeled and well-leashed. Lighting her cigarettes, mixing her drinks, and working for Daddy's wallboard company or maybe just fetching and carrying for D.A. like the rest of the hired help.

There had been a moment when he'd almost bought the whole cozy package. But self-respect had gotten in the way. His willingness to pursue compromise, a quality that made him a good negotiator, finally gave way to intransigence. It was damn well time for a showdown, a showdown he must win if there were to be any future for them. He disengaged from her tentacles and uttered the forbidden word. She had seemed genuinely puzzled. "What do you mean 'no'?"

"I mean I can't promise anything, Darryl. It may take an hour, it may take six days. Can't you understand? Back off. Don't wait for me."

For an instant, as they had pulled to a stop in front of the Consulate, she'd been speechless. As he opened the door to get out, he'd nearly blown it and told her he would try and fly out later to meet them on Lesbos. But her full fury had ignited, rescuing him from last-second equivocation. She had goddamned him all to hell, screamed at the driver to return to Fenerbahçe, and vanished from his life in a carbonous belch of DeSoto exhaust.

What Paul felt now was not so much emotional loss as erotic withdrawal. He couldn't dispel the clinging vision of all those vanished goodies. There was even a touch of self-pity, like a child locked out of a favorite candy store. And he'd done it to himself. Had he only paid her price, he might have been locked inside—for life.

"How is your Kurdish?"

"Pardon?" Paul focused, realizing Ozsahin had come suddenly back into the room and was addressing him. Indeed, everyone in the room seemed to be looking in his direction.

"I asked you, Mr. Cyrus, how good is your Kurdish?"

"Serviceable," Paul answered.

"You are better in Farsi, I trust? Your surname is, after all, that of a Persian conqueror."

"My Farsi is quite good," Paul admitted. In fact his Farsi, or Persian, was probably better than his Turkish. "Why?"

"Because most Kurds like to speak Persian."

"Excuse me, are you asking *me* to negotiate?"

"I suspect the Little Fox would prefer to deal directly with—well, someone other than myself or my staff. You, Mr. Cyrus, might be considered somewhat more sympathetic. You are available?"

"Of course he's available," Townsend White said.

"Absolutely," Paul agreed.

"Please come with me then. You also, Mr. Consul-General, and Mr. Woodhull. Quickly, gentlemen, if you will. We haven't a minute to lose."

≡

Paul followed the colonel's broad back out of the long conference room, along a corridor and down and around a tight spiral staircase. The idea of being pressed into use as negotiator made sense, Paul thought, as their footfalls on the iron-shod treads echoed in the stairwell. The anti-Americanism Paul associated with Kurdish separatists was mostly rhetorical. Their hatred of Turks, on the other hand, was intense and visceral. In fact, Turkey had never officially acknowledged the existence of the millions of Kurds within its borders. They still persisted in referring to them as "Mountain Turks."

The procession reached the floor below and strung out single file in the colonel's wake down a narrow hallway that reeked of disinfectant. A right turn fetched them into the air-conditioned chill of a square, windowless room bristling with electronic equipment. Against a far wall were magnetic tape units and line printers coughing out fan-folded paper into catch trays. Another wall was given over to tape storage and rack-mounted hardware with blinking LEDs. In the center of the room two men were seated at a long console in front of four video monitors. Paul could hear one of the men speaking Turkish into his headset.

Paul moved closer to the monitors. Two of the screens showed wide-angle shots of the *George Washington,* yards braced, sails furled. The others had identical long-lens closeups of two figures on deck—a mustached terrorist holding a walkie-talkie in one hand and in the other a rifle to the head of a kneeling long-haired hostage.

It was a sickening sight, though one that had become horribly familiar in terrorist drama. Instinctively Paul's mind struggled against accepting the reality of the nightmare image, as it had the first time back in 1972 in his dorm at Georgetown, when the TV screen had flashed from Olympic Stadium to a telescopic glimpse of a hooded figure on a Munich balcony holding a gun to the head of an Israeli athlete. At first the tableau had seemed stagy and unconvincing, the Black Septemberist a comic book figure of evil. But the evil had been all too real, as the world had soon discovered.

"There, gentlemen, is Ismet al-Azzawi, alias the Little Fox." Ozsahin pointed at the monitor, then introduced the negotiating team. Dr. Orhan Ziyal, a psychiatric consultant with the National Police, was a middle-aged man with a strabismic stare and a ballooning midsection. The actual negotiation was being handled by a Major Hamid Yoruk, Ozsahin's colleague, who was at that very moment locked in fruitless dialogue with the terrorist.

"The major is an experienced negotiator, mostly in dealings with trade unions." The colonel smiled, a humorless tightening of thin lips. "But dealing with animals, especially the Kurdish variety, is a different matter. Major Yoruk speaks only rudimentary Persian. I have the tongue, but not the temperament. There is someone en route, then I thought of you, our American linguist." Ozsahin turned a knob on the console, and the room speakers amplified Yoruk's voice in Turkish, an insistent monotone:

". . . European and American networks are already here. If you shoot this innocent boy, the world will see it and condemn you for it. Is this what you wish? Or is it not precisely the opposite of what you wish? People inclined to sympathize with your cause will repudiate you, don't you see?"

Paul could not fault the persuasive tack, but there was a double edge of didacticism and desperation in Yoruk's voice that bothered him. Even with the air-conditioning the major was perspiring heavily and mopping his face with a soggy handkerchief. Paul turned to Ozsahin:

"What does Ismet want to let the boy go?"

"Who knows? We cannot give in to his demands, only promise to consider them."

"Give him something. A gesture. What about the TV hookup?"

"I cannot authorize a broadcast. That is up to TRT's Supreme Broadcasting Council. The matter has been referred to them."

"But you can set up the equipment while you wait. That might buy some time."

"We are investigating it."

"Stop investigating. Let's do it now. Let's get that boy out of there."

Ozsahin considered a moment. "Perhaps you are right. Personally I recommend against an actual broadcast. It would set a foolish and dangerous precedent. But the equipment could be quite useful . . . as a means of diversion, perhaps even distracting the terrorists while we mount our attack. Yes, I like this."

"Then let's do it." Paul turned to Jack Woodhull. "What do you need?"

"There's really nothing to install," the Yorkshireman answered, obviously eager to contribute. "The video hardware's essentially in place, as I told the colonel. We have minicams aboard and a microwave transmitter. My camera guy has already been on the roof here. They've got a dish up there he can adjust. If you give us the go-ahead, we ought to be in business pretty fast."

Paul turned back to Ozsahin. "Okay, you asked me to negotiate. Let's start now."

Ozsahin nodded, and Paul slipped on a headset. A moment later, like a pilot handing the controls to a copilot, a grateful Major Yoruk introduced him to the Little Fox and the job was his.

6

"YOU WANT TO MAKE SOME BUSINESS, MR. AMERICAN?" asked the Little Fox.

"Yes, I do." Paul's mind honed in like a laser on the small black-garbed figure on the monitor before him. The terrorist held the transceiver to his ear; in his other hand the rifle never wavered from the head of the kneeling hostage. Paul had answered in English, but now allowed his thoughts to coalesce in Farsi. "First we are willing to provide the video connection you wanted."

"Mr. American, you speak Persian?"

"I assumed you would prefer it."

"Say your name again?"

"Paul Cyrus."

"So, you are ready for me to speak on television?"

"Yes, as soon as we are able to transmit a picture

from the ship to this building. We're in Galata, about two kilometers away, but there are hills between. They tell me the signal must be relayed—"

"Enough! Two hours ago I told the men in the helicopter to arrange all this. Why has it not been done? Do you think I am a fool? Perhaps if I shoot this prisoner, you will believe me?"

"Ismet, listen to me. We *are* ready here. But we need to test the video equipment on the ship. It's quite simple."

"Of course. You wish to bring many Turkish soldiers aboard, dressed as technicians. I promise you, Mr. Paul Cyrus, whoever tries to come on this ship will die."

"No one is coming aboard. All I'm asking is for our technicians to speak for a few minutes with those on the ship."

"To plan your attack, yes?"

"You can listen to every word they say. They will arrange what you want swiftly. Let's not waste any more time. If you could locate for me a man named Lyle Johns—"

"I know him," said Ismet. "He is second unit director."

Paul was surprised by the response. He checked with Jack Woodhull before answering: "Yes, that is exactly right. Could you find him for me?"

"How much time will all this require?"

"Thirty minutes I'm told, perhaps less. All depends on how quickly they can begin. They will set up a video camera for you somewhere on the ship, probably on a deck below, and send the picture to us with the microwave transmitter on the mast."

"Yes, I have seen this."

"But first we need you to give your radio to Mr. Johns so we can speak to him. The sooner you do this, the sooner we can put you on television."

Paul was now sweating as much as Major Yoruk had been. He had run out of words and found himself waiting desperately for the terrorist to react. Several seconds passed, as the frightening figure remained poised like an executioner over his victim. Paul heard Yoruk's voice behind him: "You're going too fast, Mr. Cyrus. You cannot push him like this."

"Leave him alone," Colonel Ozsahin said.

But Yoruk might be right, Paul thought. He *was* pushing hard. He had purposely severed all continuity with Yoruk's negotiation, giving Ismet no opening to control the conversation. It was a risky gambit, adopted more on intuition than analysis. No matter what, he had decided, he must keep his energy level higher than the terrorist's. Now he prayed it would not backfire. He willed the angel of death to pass over, the Little Fox to lift the Kalashnikov from the bowed blond head.

And it happened just that way. Suddenly the black-suited terrorist backed away, leaving the kneeling hostage alone in the video frame. In the room behind Paul there was an explosive gasp of relief. Then Ismet's voice rumbled in his headset:

"Okay, Paul Cyrus, I do what you ask. I will find Mr. Johns. It is ten forty-two. If you speak truth, five minutes beyond the hour I will be on television. If I am not, for each minute beyond that, I shall shoot one hostage. Do you hear what I say? One hostage each minute. It is a fair bargain, you agree?" Ismet made a sound like a cackle and the voicelink went dead.

"Don't worry." Ozsahin's big hand rested briefly on Paul's shoulder. "I think it is good, what you have done."

"Good?" protested Yoruk. "Mr. Cyrus has stuck us with an impossible deadline. What happens in thirty minutes if we can't acquire their video signal?"

"Then we lie," said Ozsahin.

Meanwhile on the monitor the blond man remained on his knees, head slumped forward. "For Christ sake, somebody help him!" cried Jack Woodhull. But nearly a minute passed before two hostages appeared on the screen and helped the exhausted, terrified victim to his feet. The camera's long lens tracked the three figures as they crossed the deck into the deep shade of a sail awning.

"How long was he under the gun?" Paul asked.

"Fifteen minutes," answered Dr. Ziyal.

"Christ, that's an eternity."

Townsend White nodded. "It's barbaric. That poor young man will have nightmares forever."

"If he lives," said Jack Woodhull. "If any of them live."

Fifteen minutes later Paul stood in the hallway outside the computer room, tasting a scalding mug of black coffee. Inside Jack Woodhull and Mike Babka were huddled before the monitors, conferring with their colleagues aboard the *George Washington.*

Beside him Colonel Ozsahin lit a stubby oval cigarette with a gold Dunhill. The colonel had just informed Paul that the Supreme Broadcasting Council had vetoed any live broadcast from the ship; all footage of the terrorists would be restricted to edited news programs. By Paul's reckoning the Turkish authorities had not yielded a millimeter on any demand. Their strategy was cast in stone: try and talk the Kurds into surrendering, or into releasing more hostages. Failing that, just keep talking and stalling. If an assault on the ship had to be made, the Jandaras wanted to wait for darkness. The longer the wait the better, for it would increase the likelihood the terrorists would become fatigued.

"If we could just open up a negotiable factor," Paul said to Ozsahin. "Say fifteen or twenty percent. Even the Japanese Red Army conceded that much."

"Spoken like a think-tank commando," Ozsahin replied. "You may be prepared to give these bastards eighty percent of what they are asking; we are not. Not even five percent. If we do, we will end up paying for it in blood, again and again."

"There has to be some room for maneuver. What about the prisoners?" Ismet had demanded liberation of all Kurdish prisoners, including those in custody awaiting trial.

The colonel shook his head. "You're talking about hundreds of criminals. This would open, how you would say, *une boîte de Pandore.*" The Kurdish separatists were an active group, Ozsahin emphasized, convicted of crimes ranging from murder and armed robbery to political offenses, such as anti-state propaganda and defaming Turkey abroad. Although Major Yoruk had tried to convince Ismet that arrangements were under way, with lists of detainees being drawn up and places of incarceration verified, in actuality nothing had or would be done.

The government was equally adamant there be no ransom payment and Townsend White had confirmed the U.S.'s total accordance with that stand. The Kurds had initially requested two million U.S. dollars for freeing the hostages. During this last contact Ismet had upped it to five million Swiss francs. "It is like the carpet merchant in the bazaar," Ozsahin said. "Next time who knows what he asks? It is not the prime issue here."

"But perhaps it could be," Paul protested. "What about Bouchard's offer?" During the general briefing, the little Frenchman had vowed to raise any amount of money to save the lives of his employees, no matter what the governments said. "Why not let him do it?" Paul asked. "It could be kept strictly back-channel, like Ross Perot in Iran."

Ozsahin made a little flourish with his cigarette. "You have my permission to tell the Little Fox that all of Hollywood plus Mickey Mouse is procuring money for him, if you wish. Perhaps he will believe you."

The final terrorist demand was for safe conduct. Ismet had outlined a bizarre sequence of transfers—via speedboat, helicopter, airplane, and finally, parachute drop somewhere over the Iranian border. Several hostages were to be taken along as insurance. "It would be much easier," Ozsahin had commented at the briefing, "to remove these criminals from the ship as corpses in body bags." The colonel's grim smile indicated that he not only welcomed that eventuality, but the confrontation that might lead to it.

Paul's preferred scenario was one in which the Kurds surrendered peacefully and the hostages climbed safely down into waiting boats. He wanted to defuse the ticking bomb before it went off in their faces. But, according to Paul's watch, they had only fifteen minutes left to get the Little Fox on television.

Inside, the technicians were still conferring. What,

Paul wondered for the twentieth time, was taking so damn long? He turned to the colonel: "You really think he'll start shooting?"

"He already has."

"We know that. But he doesn't know we know."

"You're being wishful, Paul. We're talking about a psychopathic killer. You agree, Dr. Ziyal?"

"Yes and no," said the portly psychiatrist who had just joined them, blocking the narrow hall. "That the man is a psychopath is perhaps debatable. But that he enjoys killing is not. You can see it in his eyes, I think, even if you had not read it in his dossier. Yes, on balance I agree, Colonel. He is less likely to surrender than to kill again."

"I intend to attack *before* that happens," said, "not after."

$$\equiv$$

"We're ready to go in here," Jack Woodhull motioned the group in the hall. "The Little Fox has a lapel mike and a small earphone, so he can hear the negotiators, and we can all hear him from the headsets and room speakers. Stand by."

Ismet appeared a moment later on two of their console screens. They'd squeezed under the thirty-minute deadline with three minutes to spare. The scene was below decks, one of the movie mixing rooms with a bank of monitors in the background.

"Picture's too bloody contrasty," Woodhull complained.

"Leave it," Paul said. "We can see him fine."

The Kurdish chief was in a large, baroque chair with carved lion heads on the armrests. Though dwarfed by the ornate prop, he struck a commanding pose with the Kalashnikov in his lap.

"The little shit thinks he's Napoleon," commented Mike Babka, Woodhull's cameraman.

"Silence," said Ozsahin.

The Little Fox had slicked his hair back and even combed his mustache, Paul noticed, studying his adversary. Ismet al-Azzawi had what sculptors would call a fine head, with a strong brow and jawline, and high, flat cheekbones. He also seemed to have an actor's or model's abnormal self-awareness. Could vanity be the key that wound this little criminal? If so, unwinding that key might be one way to save the forty lives now held hostage.

One of the monitors behind Ismet repeated the closeup which they were receiving, the second showed a soccer game, and the third a black-and-white movie in which fighter planes flashed low over a carrier flight deck.

"Why does Ismet keep turning around?" Jack Woodhull asked.

"That's TV-1 and 2 back there," Paul answered. "He's expecting to see himself on it."

Ismet's deep voice broke in, speaking English and confirming Paul's supposition: "Why am I not in there also?"

Paul opened his mike and improvised: "You will be, Ismet, as soon as we can arrange it. We see you and hear you perfectly, by the way. Engineers from TRT are here now. They are trying to relay the signal to their studios in Beyoglu for national broadcast, but there are a few problems to work out."

"You are lying, Mr. Paul Cyrus, just like the Turk.

Do you remember what I told you would happen in such case?"

"Ismet, I am also anxious to proceed more quickly. But we *are* making progress. The problems will be solved in a few minutes." Paul heard in his own voice the same desperate tone he had criticized in Yoruk. He sensed himself losing control.

"I warned you!" Ismet flew into a sudden rage. He leaped out of the big chair, then lurched forward out of focus. An instant later the audio cut off as he presumably lost his microphone. The camera flash-panned in time to catch him leaving the room.

"You promised too much!" Yoruk shouted in Paul's ear. "The madman is going to start shooting now."

Ozsahin, meanwhile, was yelling into a phone, putting the hostage rescue team on full alert, then ordering a technician in the room to get a close-up of the hostages on the frigate's deck.

Sick with dread, Paul hung on. With the earphones and lapel mike gone, Ismet was beyond recalling. They could only wait and pray, or attack the ship with guns blazing. Ozsahin, riveted to the monitor, was weighing that decision now. The bomb was about to blow up in their faces, and Paul had triggered it with his bungling eagerness. Ozsahin was staring now at a video monitor which swept the main deck. The hostages were as before, huddled in the shade. There was no sign of the *pesh merga* chieftain.

Then a new voice filtered into Paul's headset and through the room speakers: "This is Lyle Johns. Can anyone hear me?"

Paul identified himself. "What in hell's going on, Lyle? Are you okay? Should we attack?"

"Oh Christ, I dunno. The little bastard's gone berserk again. Smashing things outside. Wally's gone to check."

"Is he shooting people? The commandos are ready—"

"No, hold off. He's just down the passageway, by the dressing rooms. He yelled at Wally to grab a minicam. He's fucking nuts. You should have a picture of the whole damn thing in a moment."

A few seconds later they indeed regained the picture. It was a bizarre scene of a small man in a black athletic suit and rifle laying waste to a dressing room. He swept jars, vials, and bottles off a makeup table with the Kalashnikov barrel, then used the butt to smash the bright mirrors. Next he whirled and began karate-kicking the folding chairs.

"It's all a goddamned show," said Woodhull.

"Perhaps," said Ziyal. "But the man is still dangerous. He could start shooting at any moment. We must be ready."

"We can do better than that," Paul said. "I've got an idea."

"And so have I." Yoruk grabbed him. "I will take over now. Your ideas have already endangered too many lives."

Paul pulled away. "Listen to me, damn you. You can't stall him forever. He's proved that. Let's give him what he wants!"

7

"You're as crazy as he is!"

"No, I'm not. I'm going to trick the little bastard into *thinking* he's on TV." Paul spoke into his headset. "Lyle, are you still there?"

"Go ahead."

"If we get the terrorist back in his high chair, can you feed a picture of him into the other monitors?"

"I don't follow you."

"So it'll look to him like he's on Turkish TV."

"Sure, I can do it. Matter of fact, we can rig a switch on the console so it happens right before his eyes."

Paul turned to Ozsahin, still on the phone to the Jandara field commander. "What do you say? It's worth a try."

Ozsahin hesitated only a moment. "I agree. But tell them to be quick."

"I heard that," Lyle Johns cut in. "You guys just hang on. I'm working on it already."

"Okay, but slap it together fast. He's running out of steam out there. He may come back any second."

Ismet's rampage, as tracked and relayed by mini-cam, had indeed lost much of its fury. The little terrorist now stood in the commissary, surrounded by unyielding surfaces—formica, vinyl, stainless steel. The floor was strewn with plastic cups and cutlery, paper napkins, packaged hamburger buns, garments ripped from wardrobe closets. Against one wall was a sliding green splotch, where he'd hurled a gallon of pickle relish. Paul found himself hoping the terrorist would regain his destructive momentum and give Lyle more time to rig the video switch. Ozsahin, meanwhile, was ordering his commandos to hold fast.

Finally the word came from Lyle Johns: "Paul? We're ready."

"Okay, go tell Ismet TRT is standing by."

Moments later the studio setup flashed back on their monitors—Ismet in his chair, mike pinned in place, hair combed. The terrorist swiveled to check the monitors, reminding Paul of a boy in a barber chair. But Lyle hadn't thrown the switch yet. Both channels were broadcasting what Paul recognized as "telenovelas," one a family drama, the other what looked like a Mongol Western. High-rated foreign imports, like "Dallas" and "Dynasty," usually aired in prime time.

"Ismet, can you hear me?"

"Where am I? It is not working!"

"Hold on. The TRT engineers are going to interrupt

both channels and put you on. You did ask for TV-1 and 2, didn't you?"

"Yes, yes, of course. How long will I have?"

"As long as you like."

Behind Ismet both monitors blinked and came back with a closeup of the seated terrorist, his head turned away. Seeing himself, Ismet twitched in his chair, as though quickened by an electric current, and whirled to face the camera. He's bought it, Paul thought. In the Kurdish leader's dark eyes there was a rekindled dementia.

He introduced himself to the imaginary audience in stilted Turkish. Ozsahin provided a running translation for the benefit of Townsend White and Jack Woodhull. Paul caught himself listening as though the terrorist speech were an actual broadcast, and not a closed-circuit sucker job. Ismet began to pour his fanatic soul into the void, playing it like an Arafat, a beleaguered statesman without a nation. *Just pray he doesn't catch on to the trick.*

Fifteen minutes went by, and the Little Fox scarcely paused for breath. He had changed to Persian, and the cadences flowed rapidly, phrases concatenating into sentences that ran on into paragraphs and seemed never to end. Zoroastrian mythology metamorphosed into Kurdish history, and thence into Ismet's childhood memories, with no clear demarcations.

Ozsahin was smoking. He had stopped translating, and provided only minimal commentary.

Townsend White shook his head. "Does he really think TRT would broadcast this drivel?"

"Or anybody would watch it?" added Jack Woodhull. "How long do you think he can keep it up?"

"The longer the better," Paul said.

"I agree," said Dr. Ziyal. "This farce could save many lives."

≡

Ismet had given little thought to what he would say. He fixed his gaze on the camera's hooded eye and the blinking red light above it. Beyond it, he saw a great cloud of faces watching and waiting for him to speak. And behind him, invisible and voiceless, he felt the presence of the scattered millions of his own people, the Kurds of eastern Turkey, of Iraq, Iran, Syria, and Russia, plus all their numberless ancestors who had struggled and perished before them.

He drew vast strength from the knowledge that he had this one brief chance to be their voice. The video camera was like a great magnifying mirror, collecting his image, multiplying him a millionfold.

As the words were drawn out of him, he felt his spirit dilate and rise out of the chair, hovering about his head. His voice also seemed to be coming from somewhere beyond him. Its pitch was higher than usual, the tone more measured and modulated, with an effortless eloquence. At times he spoke in Turkish, or Arabic, or Persian, or Kurdish, shifting tongues without conscious thought.

He felt as if he had finally fulfilled the Murshid's vision and become the spokesman for his people. Time meant nothing now; he was aware only of the power flowing through him. The Western technicians in the room, the cameraman and second unit director, were merely instruments.

Inevitably Ismet came to speak of the heroes of Kurdistan, the ancient Medes who warred against Cyrus the

Great, and the mighty Saladin, greatest of Islamic warriors and conqueror of the Infidel Crusaders. Ismet told of the marvelous trek of Mullah Mustafa Barzani, who led his tribesmen to freedom through Iraq, Turkey, and Persia. And of the *pesh merga* who had fought and perished in the recent Iraqi genocide—the five thousand martyrs gassed at Halabja, including women and children, and tens of thousands more in Butia, Dahok, Zakhu, Al Amadiyah, and in hundreds of other villages in Iraqi-occupied Kurdistan.

The blood of these heroes, the Little Fox said, would never permit his people to abandon their centuries-old quest for a sovereign homeland, or to bend their knee to usurpers. They would fight for their freedom, if need be, until the very last drop of Kurdish blood had been spilled.

Finally Ismet subsided against the thronelike chair, made one gesture of farewell to the camera, and motioned to the technicians that he was finished.

But he could not resist turning to catch a final glimpse of himself in the monitors—a vanishing microcosm of even tinier figures also turning round to look at themselves. Then both channels flashed back to their regular programming, and Ismet was returned abruptly to himself. If he expected some comment on his oration, he was disappointed. On one channel a Japanese tourist was being interviewed in Taksim Square; on the other screen barnyard cartoon animals sang a nursery rhyme, their animated mouth movements out of sync with the Turkish words.

It did not matter. Ismet knew what he had said. It was up to the arrow to fly true.

≡

By Paul's watch, the Little Fox had talked for forty-seven minutes—and had managed to vilify every country within a radius of several thousand miles. Yet some of it, particularly the Persian, had been quite lyrical—though, of course, he could have been paraphrasing Sa'di, or Khayyam, or some other Farsi poet. And the peroration, with its impassioned condemnation of Iraqi gas attacks, made Paul wish this part of the speech *was* being heard by the world.

Of course the critical thing was that the Little Fox seemed totally taken in by the electronic sleight-of-hand. And, judging by the glazed look in his eye, he had given it his all.

Paul felt a touch on his shoulder. He turned, expecting Ozsahin. Instead it was Major Yoruk. "Well done, Mr. Cyrus."

The consensus in the room seemed to be that there had been a breakthrough. Their cautious optimism was confirmed moments later when Paul spoke with Ismet, who was now apparently willing to negotiate. He yielded none of his demands, but when Paul tossed out the idea of Ismet's releasing all female hostages as *quid pro quo* for a subsequent freeing of Kurdish prisoners, the Little Fox nodded thoughtfully. "Yes, perhaps. This I will consider." First, however, he wished to confer with his comrades.

"All right. Can we resume in fifteen or twenty minutes?"

"Yes. Twenty minutes."

As the little Kurd rose, he turned and glanced back one last time at the Turkish TV monitors.

And then it happened.

The left-hand screen behind Ismet, tuned to TV-2, flashed from a studio anchorman to an on-the-street interview. The subject was an attractive Western woman. Extremely attractive, Paul thought. Then, as the camera closed in, he saw that it was Amanda Morgan.

Apparently the Little Fox also recognized the famous face, for he halted, staring at the screen. The British actress was standing in front of the Pera Palas hotel, glossy black mane aswirl in the breeze, as traffic passed behind her on Mesrutiyet Caddesi. She was tucked into a tight and trendy buckskin outfit, like some high-fashion Pocahontas, and she accompanied her speech with a flurry of vivid gestures. Despite what seemed like a lot of affectation, the cumulative effect, Paul decided, was one hell of a vital woman.

"Hey, that's Mandy!" Jack Woodhull exclaimed. "Turn up the sound, I want to hear this."

"What's she got to say?" Townsend White wondered.

"Something trivial, I hope," Paul said. "We've got an explosive situation here."

"Knowing Mandy it'll be political," Woodhull said, "but not to worry. She probably doesn't know about the crisis." The director raised his voice: "Hey, can we get that channel in here?"

Colonel Ozsahin, irritated by the interruption, switched on a monitor. The actress burst into the room in mid-sentence:

"—my point is, it's a national liberation movement, like any other, and I espouse them without distinction. In fact, I've heard the Kurds compared to the Poles in the nineteenth century, or, for that matter, to the Poles of today—"

"Who allowed her on television?" Ozsahin said, reaching for the telephone. "This woman is a lunatic!"

She paused, as the interviewer translated her words briefly for the camera. And, Paul realized with a certain amusement, the interviewer went beyond mere translation; he totally sanitized her remarks, deleting all reference to either Kurds or Kurdistan. What emerged were humanitarian banalities. Ms. Morgan, meanwhile, flashed her high-voltage smile, obviously unaware that the Turkish people were being denied her eloquence. One person who *had* heard, though, was the little Kurdish terrorist staring at the monitor. And his English, Paul knew, was quite good enough for him to get her meaning.

She launched forth again, sweeping aside a trivial question to return to politics: ". . . I'm not in the slightest concerned with delays in filming. Good God, this crisis makes all that irrelevant. There are human lives at stake here, brave men and women of the film crew, many of whom I know very well.

"I agonize for the fate of the men and women on that ship, and yes, forgive me, but I also cannot help but be sensible to the plight of those who hold them, whose suffering has driven them to commit this desperate act. I don't condone what they have done, but I wish to say one thing directly to the Kurdish leaders on board.

"Please, if you can hear me, or if these words can be conveyed to you, I beg you, in the name of your God, Allah, the Compassionate, the Merciful, do not harm these innocent hostages. Let them go, please, and let me offer myself in their place. In fact, I will come now in faith that you will carry out this exchange, and so that

I may speak with you and listen to what you have to say. I am absolutely sincere in this. I beseech you, let us—"

There was an abrupt cut back to the studio where a deadpan newsman began to read statistics about cropping patterns and grain yields on the millions of hectares of Turkey's arable land. There followed footage of a tractor cultivating a field.

Too late, Paul thought, the damage was done. The poor dumb bastard at TV-2 who had been asleep at the switch would probably be out of a job tomorrow, or worse. An instant later Paul's worst fears were confirmed when Ismet whirled, grabbed his lapel mike, and began speaking excitedly in English: "I accept! Tell her I accept this offer!" He pointed at the monitor from which Amanda had just vanished. "Bring her to me, this lady, and hostages are free! Do you hear me, Paul Cyrus? Bring this lady to me!"

Paul could only stare at the monitor—and a terrorist once again rampant with energy. *Goddamn that gorgeous bitch, the meddlesome, arrogant little bitch! Who did she think she was? And why couldn't she stay the hell out of it?* With one bleeding-heart, grandstand gesture, she had blown away everything they had so painfully achieved. And she must have known she was quite safe in doing so, that she would never be permitted to give herself up to terrorists.

But she should be, Paul thought bitterly.

AMANDA MORGAN WAS IN A CONTROLLED FURY. IT WAS A
state of emotion she used often to subdue antagonists,
from officious hotel clerks to temperamental film directors. But against a carload of Turkish police her smoldering wrath had little effect.

Moments after she'd finished her television interview a half-dozen swarthy, dark-suited types had surrounded her on the sidewalk in front of the Pera Palas.
The two local security men Leo Bouchard had assigned
her quickly vanished, along with the three-man video
crew from TRT. Only the intrepid *paparazzi* remained,
pressing in from all sides with their camcorders and mo-
torized SLRs. For once, Amanda was thankful for their
presence, as she was forcibly steered by the police toward a dark Mercedes sedan parked by the curb. For the

paparazzi's benefit she increased her struggles and pitched her protests at full stage volume.

The next moment the actress found herself wedged between plainclothesmen in the rear seat as they accelerated through the narrow streets of Pera. A revving chorus of motorcycles and motor scooters behind indicated a posse of *paparazzi* in pursuit. In the front passenger seat a sinister-looking man with hooded eyes and pitted cheeks spoke rapid Turkish into a radio, then turned with an undertaker's smile.

"Miss Morgan, I am admirer of your films. But this was not necessary what you did, to make drama on street. Why you did not come when I ask you?"

"Excuse me, who are you?"

"You have seen my papers this minute ago. I am Captain Adnan Erol, National Police."

"Captain Erol, I do not recall being shown credentials or asked anything on the street. What I do recall quite clearly is that you and your men put your hands on me and forced me into this car. I now consider myself your prisoner. If I am not, please stop and I will get out at once."

"If you please, is best not to do."

"I thought not. Can you at least tell me where I'm being taken and why? And what is happening with the hostages on the ship?"

"Please to calm yourself, Miss Morgan. We are going only five minutes to Galata where your friends are waiting."

"Friends? I don't know what you're talking about."

"Mr. Giddings of British Consulate, and your employer, *un petit français,* I do not recall name."

"Leo Bouchard," she said. "Of course. The little bastard."

"Also my commandant, Colonel Celal Ozsahin. Most urgent, you see, Miss Morgan. They are making negotiations with terrorists. There your questions will be answered. Now it is clear?"

"Perfectly clear, Captain. And perfectly unacceptable. I protest the orders you were given and the way you carried them out. Both you and your colonel will regret this."

She settled into the seat, her fury unabated, but directed now at Leo Bouchard as well as the Turkish police. This time, instead of a limo, the little despot had sent the local storm troopers for her.

Her anger was tainted, however, with a perverse satisfaction. For, in her defiance of Leo and her need to find out what was happening aboard the ship, she had damn well intended to stir things up. She had waded into the media camp in front of the Pera Palas and begun firing questions. The ensuing melee had attracted the crew from TRT. When the minicam began blinking its red light, she had no notion what she would say. But the questions translated to her were so inane ("Who has been your most sexy leading man? Clint? Jason?") that she plunged immediately into politics and was carried away by the momentum of her own soliloquy. Having made her impassioned offer to exchange herself for the hostages, she was fully committed to follow it through. Her waiting "friends" would find that out soon enough.

The driver aimed the Mercedes through the seven-pointed confluence of Sishane Square without letting off the gas and headed downhill to Karaköy. Amanda was thankful for the speed. Not only was she eager to confront Leo and anybody else awaiting her, she urgently wanted out of this crowded sedan with its reek of sour perspiration and high-octane cologne. Did Turkish cops always scent themselves? Was it some ingenious new form of police brutality? Or had they simply taken a bath in the stuff for her benefit? Despite their seeming stolidity, all four were obviously aware of her. The beefy pair on either side had been straining their ocular muscles with peripheral glances. Captain Erol was doing the same, on the pretext of tracking the pursuing press. And the bull-necked driver, who needed every ounce of attention ahead to avoid motorists, cyclists, porters, pedestrians, and other solid obstacles in his path, had his mirrored sunglasses locked instead on the glamorous face in his rearview mirror.

From the heights of Pera they were descending now into the harbor district. Between monotonous files of stone buildings and over red pantile roofs, Amanda caught glimpses of the Galata Bridge and, at the far end across the Golden Horn, a shimmering cluster of domes.

"Yeni Cami, it is called," Captain Erol explained, "the Mosque of Valide Sultan. Is beauty-ful, yes?"

"Am I in police custody, Captain, or on a sightseeing tour?"

"Pardons, Miss Morgan?"

"Never mind. The mosque is lovely."

The following thunder of cycles grew suddenly louder. Amanda glanced behind. In place of the ragged corps of *paparazzi* they had acquired a derrière-garde of Turkish motorcycle cops. Farther back a few *paparazzi* were barely visible. Doubtless he had radioed for the official escort to keep the press corps at bay.

More sedately now the noisy entourage entered a

street of warehouses behind the Karaköy Maritime docks east of Galata Bridge. They passed an Armenian church, then turned into a private alleyway palisaded with spear-tipped wrought iron. Beside a gatehouse, a white-clad Harbor Police sentry with auto rifle waved them through a lifting barrier arm. A few meters beyond they halted under a porte cochere. The motorcycle escort roared in behind them, dismounted, and threw open the Mercedes' doors.

"Miss Morgan, your long journey is finish," Captain Erol announced. "Inside many people are happy to see you."

Amanda exited without acknowledgment, but Captain Erol caught up to her outside: "May I request a last favor from such beauty-ful lady?" The police captain produced a fountain pen and pocket notebook. His brows were lifted in coquettish appeal.

"Really, Captain, you can't be asking for my autograph. It's too bizarre."

"If you please. Is not for me."

"Oh, don't beg. It's not manly." She snatched the pen, made her flourish, and handed it back. Her withering look was wasted on the policeman, however, as he peered closely at his keepsake, evidently trying to decipher her scrawl.

Finally he glanced up with his unctuous smile. "Many thank-yous. Now, please to follow me." He led her inside across a barrel-vaulted, tiled foyer where their footsteps echoed and into a narrow corridor. A short way down a young policeman stepped out of a cross passage and collided with Amanda. The officer, dressed in motorcycle leathers and barely taller than she, leaped back, apologizing in Turkish.

"Clumsy fellow," Captain Erol said in English for the actress's benefit. "What is your name?"

"Officer Fahri Bayram."

"Have more caution, Patrolman. You are okay, Miss Morgan?"

She nodded. In the instant of contact the young officer had pressed a folded square of paper into her palm. As they continued, she slipped it into a pocket.

At corridor's end double oak doors opened before them. Captain Erol beckoned her into a Victorian reception room with damask walls of faded rose and large potted palms. Of the eight men in the room, Amanda recognized four. Her producer was first on his feet, but she turned instead to Jack Woodhull.

"How bad is it, Jack?"

"Mandy, thank God you're here! You had us a bit worried. It's very bad. I better let them tell it."

The other familiar faces belonged to Leo's American unit publicist, B.J. Bracey, and the British Consul General. The Honorable Bertrand Giddings was a kind of Foreign Office caricature, complete with toothbrush mustache, overbite, and stammer. Thumbs in vest pockets, he performed the brief introductions.

Three of the four strangers turned out to be American diplomats. Giddings' opposite number, Townsend White, was white-haired and patrician, with a tennis tan. His youthful deputy, Mike Mitchell, was blandly good-looking. More attractive in a boyish way was the man who, Giddings said, had been handling the negotiations with the Kurds. To Amanda, Paul Cyrus was a bit young to fit the profile of counter-terrorist consultant. In fact, his lazy posture, appraising blue eyes, and faint smile reminded her of Alf, her erstwhile Hampstead house pet.

The fourth man, a well-fed Turk with an Italian suit, flashy gold jewelry, and penetrating eyes, was introduced as Colonel Celal Ozsahin, commander of the National Police and Captain Erol's boss.

The captain, thus officially relieved, made his exit, and Amanda took an armchair facing the masculine array. Despite the circumstances, she could not resist the obvious sally: "I suppose you're all wondering why I've brought you here today?"

"Really, Am-amanda," chided Bertrand Giddings, "this is hardly a m—m—moment for levity."

Her reply was icy: "Do forgive me, Bertie. I've just been kidnaped off the street in broad daylight by the local Gestapo. I'm in a jolly mood."

A moment before, she had caught the British diplomat staring at her crossed, bare legs, or perhaps at her sandaled feet with their opalescent toenails. Was it a stare of disapprobation or longing? Had he expected her to arrive dressed for consular high tea with floral print, white gloves, and picture hat? She wore minimal makeup. The little suede dress was sleeveless and cut above the knee, exposing a slice of thigh along with her tanned calves. Her black mane was in its typical windblown, Medusan frenzy, what her Parisian hairdresser termed her *"tohu-bohu* look." But Amanda made no attempt to pat her hair into place or to tug southward on her hemline. She was quite comfortable being the cynosure of male attention. Alone in a roomful of men she usually felt supreme; this was no exception.

"Miss Morgan." Colonel Ozsahin rose and began to pace slowly, a barrister addressing the court. "Let me offer again apologies for any inconvenience you have experienced." He made a florid gesture which, as an actress, she considered excessive. She interrupted:

"So, Colonel, at last I meet my kidnaper?"

He came to a surprised halt. "Hardly that, Miss Morgan."

"How would you characterize it? Being seized against one's will, dragged into a car, one's protests ignored?"

"Force majeure, if you wish, dear lady. Captain Erol assured me your cooperation was requested, but that you chose to dramatize the moment as an abduction for certain elements—" he made a look of eminent distaste, "—of the European popular press."

"Dramatize!" Amanda was livid. With a jangle of silver bracelets she thrust a finger at the Turkish officer. "You're wrong, Colonel. I haven't begun to dramatize. Wait till I get back to London and talk to my friends at Amnesty International. That will be a performance, one I hope you will hear about."-

"Mandy, please." Jack Woodhull was quickly beside her, coaxing his leading lady back to the scene at hand. "The colonel has apologized, perhaps clumsily, but he has apologized. We're all running scared this morning. They had to get you here fast."

"Thank you, Mr. Woodhull," the colonel said, "for explaining my clumsiness. May I retract any remarks that have offended?" He cocked his head at the British actress, as if reassessing how to approach such a volatile creature.

"Please proceed, Colonel. I realize there is a crisis. God knows, I've been trying to discover its dimensions all morning."

"The dimensions are grave, Miss Morgan. Lives have been lost."

This was a blow for which she was quite unprepared. "God help us, I had no idea. Who? How many?"

"Two men at least are dead. Executed in cold blood. Mr. Woodhull can identify them."

"I don't think you would know either one of them, Mandy."

"That hardly matters, Jack."

"No, of course it doesn't. One was a French security officer, whom Leo hired in Marseille—"

"A real tough guy," Leo cut in. "They call 'im Dufy, like the painter. He—he—'ad two little girl. Is 'orrible."

"I think the other was one of the Turkish boys we picked up in Izmir."

"You know they're dead? There's no hope?"

"We 'ave picture, Mandy!" Leo cried out. "Is bloody mess!"

"Don't shout at me, Leo. Do you think I did it, for Christ's sake, to sabotage your stupid film?"

She cradled her head. She felt, for the first time, the crushing weight of events that had been occupying the men in this room for some hours. In a moment she glanced up. "What do you want me to do, Jack? I'll do anything. I assume you know I've already made an offer to the terrorists?"

"That's just it, Mandy. The colonel wants to put you back on television and have you withdraw that offer."

"We can't 'ave you meddling, Mandy," Leo began, but was cut off by Woodhull.

"Leo, for God's sake, keep out of it."

"I didn't mean to meddle," Amanda said. "They pointed the camera and—and I simply said what I felt.

What harm could I have done? The Kurds can't know what I said."

"They know precisely, Miss Morgan," said Ozsahin. "Their leader was watching at that moment."

"And?"

"He accepted your offer. He is waiting for us to produce you."

Amanda stared in astonishment. "He is willing to release the hostages? For God's sake, then let him do it. I'll carry out my side of the bargain. Why are you standing in my way?"

"Mandy, you can't be serious," said Woodhull.

"I certainly can be, Jack. I'm bloody serious."

Ozsahin shook his large head. "But we cannot permit this."

"The risk is not yours, Colonel, it's mine. And I choose to take it."

"You choose nothing!" Leo was on his feet. "You are in Turkey under exclusive contract to Kronos. And I am Kronos and I forbid it!"

"Oh, rubbish, Leo. Sit down. You're making a fool of yourself."

"Excuse me, Colonel. May I say something?" Paul Cyrus spoke for the first time.

"Proceed, Mr. Cyrus." The colonel smiled. "Perhaps your negotiating skills can aid in a swift resolution here. We have little time."

"I understand." He turned to Amanda. "More than anything else, Miss Morgan, these terrorists—"

"They're Kurds, aren't they? Why don't you call them that?"

"Yes, they are Kurdish terrorists, and they've made the usual sorts of demands—release of political prisoners quote unquote, ransom, safe passage. But the crucial demand seems to be publicity. And they're getting plenty of that. The TV cameras are everywhere already, and of course the world is watching, or soon will be. The colonel would like to prevent that, and frankly so would I. But we can't. We can only try to control the atmosphere of spectacle, to limit it. But we certainly can't do that if Amanda Morgan injects herself into the middle—"

"But already she has!"

"Yes, Monsieur Boucher, I realize that." Paul paused till the French producer resumed his seat, then continued: "But Colonel Ozsahin has instructed TRT not to furnish the tape of that interview to any other networks. We're trying to quarantine the damage. But, Miss Morgan, were you actually to carry out your offer to give yourself into the hands of these terrorists, the publicity would be stupefying, a kind of media inferno. Offhand, I can't think of anything comparable. The Lindbergh kidnaping maybe. Patty Hearst. In PR terms, one international film star is worth more than a shipload of ordinary people."

"This is all very obvious," Amanda shot back. "But so what? If the Kurds hadn't been denied attention all these years, they might not have been driven to this terrible act. The Iraqis gassed thousands of them before the world even noticed their existence—and then promptly forgot it again. Isn't a little publicity, or one hell of a lot of publicity, worth forty lives? Wouldn't you trade ink for blood, Mr. Cyrus?"

"That may not be the bargain, Miss Morgan. You would certainly be forfeiting your liberty, if not your life. The Kurds would reap the world's attention only so long as you were captive. That would seal your fate. They'd have everything to gain by keeping you, nothing by your release. I call that an unacceptable risk."

"What's an 'acceptable risk,' then? Negotiating long-range, while others face the guns? That's not the way I live my life. I'm a risk-taker. Unlike you, I'm willing to talk to this terrorist face to face. Perhaps we should swap jobs, Mr. Cyrus. I don't think you've got the balls for yours."

9

"REALLY, AMANDA!" BERTIE GIDDINGS PROTESTED.

"I say what I feel, Bertie, always have done." She smiled sweetly.

She had stung the American. He had the bewildered look, even the suffused cheeks, of a man who has just been well slapped by a woman—a look she'd observed at close quarters more than a few times. *Dear boy, if you're no match for me, how do you expect to deal with a real killer?*

Jack Woodhull spoke up: "Mandy, that really was uncalled for. Nobody's questioning your motives, or your bravery."

"He is." She pointed at Paul. "And why shouldn't he be jealous? I achieved a breakthrough, and he didn't."

Woodhull went on: "For argument's sake, Mandy,

let's say your involvement would help the situation. The point is, we still can't allow it."

"Who's we? You, Jack? The male establishment? Her Majesty's Government? The colonel's secret police?"

"There is no question of secret police," said Ozsahin. *"I* do not permit it."

"How do you propose to stop me? Am I in official custody?"

"Amanda," Bertie Giddings said, "you m—must not persist. This is a Turkish domestic c—crisis, with many lives at issue—"

"Don't tell me what's at issue, Bertie. I'm not some brainless starlet. Because of my involvement—and for no other reason that I can see—this Kurdish revolutionary is willing to release our colleagues, all of them. Why do you want to stop that from happening? What do you have to offer, any of you? What concessions have you been able to extract from him? Will attacking the ship protect those innocent lives? No, I have the clout, gentlemen. You may not like it, or admit it, but you damn well know it. And I'm not going to let jealousy or paternalism or anything else stop me."

"Our concern for your safety, Miss Morgan," said Townsend White, "can hardly be dismissed as paternalism."

"Call it what you like. If it's intended to stop me, it won't work."

"I wish to say something now, Miss Morgan," Colonel Ozsahin began in a peremptory tone. "And then we will conclude this discussion. I applaud your speech. You are a person of eloquence and passion."

"I'll second that," added Bertrand Giddings. "One

disagrees wholeheartedly, Amanda, yet at times one must admit you make him p—p—proud to be English."

"I can't think why I should, Bertie," Amanda countered, "since I happen to be Welsh."

"Let me conclude, Miss Morgan," said Ozsahin. "First, you are not in custody. Neither will you be permitted anywhere near the *George Washington*. I am in command here, and I will permit no such exchange. But I do ask you, Miss Morgan, to use your passion and your eloquence, not on us, but on this criminal. Plead with him to carry out his promise to free his captives. Blame us, if you wish, for refusing to support your original offer, but tell him that he can best serve his cause by releasing these people unharmed. This you may do on behalf of your colleagues on the ship. Nothing further."

"Why don't you write it all down for me, Colonel?"

"Use your own words, of course."

"Jack, give me a cigarette."

"I thought you quit."

"I did. Dammit, give me a smoke." She took one of his unfiltered Players, bent to his light, and inhaled deeply. After months of non-smoking, the nicotine rushed to her brain and made her giddy. She contorted sideways in the armchair, grimaced, surveyed the room. I'm surrounded by bloody cowards, she thought. What do I do now? Then she saw, posted in the corridor, the young policeman who had passed her the scrap of paper. She had forgotten all about it; it was still in her pocket, unread. She turned to the colonel.

"Is it permitted, Colonel, to visit the powder room?"

"Powder? You are referring to explosives?"

"Not exactly. The loo. The WC. I don't know the Turkish word."

Ozsahin saw his error and, slightly chagrined, gestured acquiescence. As he spoke quickly to the young policeman at the door, Amanda got up and walked past into the corridor.

≡

Notwithstanding her startling crude remark at his expense, Paul Cyrus found himself fascinated by Amanda Morgan. After several compulsory forays into the D.C. cocktail party circuit, he considered himself immune to celebrity bedazzlement. But the actress's magnetism was of another order, a palpable force. She tended to blot out everyone else in the room.

And every man there had felt that energy, Paul was sure, even Ozsahin. In the wrong, outranked and overmatched, she had charged into them like an angry lioness, spitting and clawing, keeping them all off balance. She hadn't won, but she'd damned well made a fight out of it.

Paul, of course, bore the fresh scars to prove it. Her well-aimed, elegantly voiced vulgarity had found its target. Darryl Ann at her bitchiest hadn't been able to penetrate his defenses so neatly. In fact, he hadn't felt so flattened by a female since his first year of high school, when a senior cheerleader had greeted his do-or-die request for a date with hysterical giggles. His despair had lasted weeks. These days, fortunately, injured pride healed more quickly. As she sailed out of the room followed by one of the guards, Paul set about piecing himself together.

What the hell did it matter what a film star thought or said about anything? Negotiators who offered themselves as potential hostages were not courageous, they were damn fools—like Amanda Morgan. She could be expected to make irresponsible statements. That's what celebrities usually did when mouthing words not scripted for them by their intellectual superiors. Left to their own devices they were liable to espouse any damn thing from UFOs to Trotskyism.

The really infuriating thing was that, knowing all this, Paul was still vulnerable. He did care what she thought, this abundant little creature with the purring feline voice and the flashing feline claws. He had regressed into the spurned schoolboy of years ago, yearning for heroic deeds to convert her disdain to admiration.

Leo Bouchard, meanwhile, was apologizing for his employee's bad behavior: "Of course she is difficult. With *artiste,* sometimes you must treat them *comme les enfants.* I think she calm down, but, if not, leave me alone with 'er a few minute—"

Jack Woodhull broke in: "Leo, I suggest you let the colonel handle it. You're paying her upwards of two million pounds, for Christ's sake, and she still treats you *comme merde.*"

≡

In the bathroom stall, Amanda unfolded the yellow flimsy sheet and read the crudely inked note: "DESTROY PAPER AFTER READ. IF YOU DESIRE SEE ISMET AL-AZZAWI, HERO KOORDISTAN, MAKE YES SIGN WITH HEAD, EYES, SPEAK NOTHING. I WILL TAKE YOU ISMET. HAVE GREAT CAUTION OF PERIL. DESTROY PAPER."

After reading it through several times she wadded it up, pulled the chain, and with a great roar, the note was flushed into the Stamboul cisterns. As she emerged from the bathroom, the eyes of the young policeman standing guard sought hers almost shyly. They were alone in the corridor.

Amanda had made up her mind. She might be saving forty lives, she might be throwing away her own. But the game was definitely worth the candle. She nodded fractionally. The policeman looked alarmed, then nodded back. With a tilt of his head and quick turn of his shoulders, he conveyed that she was to follow.

≡

If those instants were vertiginous for Amanda Morgan, they were truly terrifying for Fahri Bayram. The young policeman with the pencil mustache seemed outwardly at ease, but his uniform was soaked through with nervous perspiration and his heartbeat had accelerated to full gallop. Because of his intrepid stupidity in purposely colliding with the actress and passing her the note, his fate was now in her hands. No matter how she responded, Fahri stood to lose—and the stakes included his life.

Suppose she were foolhardy enough to accept his offer to take her to Ismet. Then Fahri would have the impossible job of spiriting one of the world's most recognizable women out of a crowded police compound in broad daylight.

If instead she revealed the note to Ozsahin, Fahri's doom would come more swiftly. Imprisonment was a certainty, torture and execution strong possibilities. Despite the government's avowed efforts to outlaw the *bastinado* and other hallowed methods of police persuasion, Fahri suspected an exception would be made in his case. The authorities would be extremely desirous of learning the identities of his Kurdish accomplices and could hardly be expected to abandon overnight a tradition that stretched from the post-Atatürk juntas back through the Ottoman Empire to Byzantium and the infamous dungeons of Theodora. All this did not bear much thinking about, of course, but Fahri, who had an extremely low pain threshold, had been thinking of it constantly. Had already decided, in fact, to confess all.

His only real hope lay in the actress's ignoring the traitorous note while sealing her lips to its contents. Fahri besought this outcome with his whole soul, as he waited in the corridor for Amanda's reappearance. *May it be so,* he prayed, *that my life may continue and that I may say to my wife and all my accursed in-laws that I have tried my best.*

A chain of idiocies had placed him in this precarious position. It had been idiocy to boast of his assignment to guard the film star; compound idiocy to promise to deliver the note into her hands; rampant idiocy actually to make good the deed. But father to all his many idiocies had been falling under the spell of a Kurdish beauty and marrying into her fanatic clan. The Al-Azzawis—cousins, uncles, brothers—were seditionists all, devoted to carving a Kurdish homeland out of contiguous chunks of Turkey, Iran, Iraq, and Syria.

To her credit, Guldasa—slim, graceful, and usually softspoken—had revealed her commitment to the hopeless family cause before the marriage was sealed. But it was already too late. For her power over Fahri had been established early in their courtship, when he discovered the sudden and savage temper which surfaced when he opposed her on even the smallest matter. It was like walking through paradise and stepping on a land mine. Ever after he trod more carefully and was prepared to undertake the most arduous detours to avoid suspicious terrain. Soon he found himself routinely risking his police career—cycling out to that hovel in Üsküdar while on duty, carrying messages, money, supplies, and finally state secrets. His domestic tranquility was purchased at the daily price of on-the-job terror.

Though Fahri still had not the strength to oppose his wife, it was becoming increasingly difficult for him to forgive her for the demands she made upon him. His devotion had been tested to its limit; the only sane course left was to take back all the powers he had so foolishly granted the Kurdish woman over his heart. But knowing this was one thing; doing it another.

In the midst of his anguish, the door opened before him and Amanda Morgan emerged. Fahri's frail hopes plummeted at once. For the eyes of the beautiful actress were alight with conspiratorial mischief. She'd obviously read the note. Now, seeing Fahri, she threw back her head and lifted her eyebrows. In Turkish this upward nod signals no, but in the West, Fahri knew, it meant yes.

It also meant Fahri's cherished civil service career was finished; he was now a criminal. He unbuttoned the holster flap on his .45. From this instant forward he could be shot on sight. He beckoned the actress to follow.

Several steps along a side corridor he led her into a small alcove, told her his name, then pulled from beneath his tunic a folded black fabric and shook it out. The actress understood at once. With a skill born of theatrical quick changes, she wrapped herself in the dark gauzy material, then took a smaller square of white cotton from the policeman and tied it neatly around her tumbling black curls. With a last playful tug of the head scarf, the lower half of her face was concealed.

Fahri watched with relief as the actress was transformed by the flowing garment. Only her dark, mischievous eyes remained in an orbit of olive skin. Her flagrant beauty had been reduced to coquettish promise. She could pass now for an Anatolian peasant woman, some of whom still went veiled in public; though most Turkish women, especially in the cities, favored the Western attire so long encouraged by the reforms of Atatürk.

The policeman took her left wrist. Before she realized what was happening, he had snapped a handcuff on it. His other hand stifled her attempted cry for help.

"No scream," he hissed. "They stop us, they no kill me if you my prisoner, understand okay, lady?"

When she nodded, he lifted his hand from her mouth and locked the other cuff to his own right wrist. It was a feeble ruse, but he needed a plausible story if they were apprehended.

The policeman and the black-robed figure moved in locked tandem down the corridor. Five nerve-wracking minutes later, they snuck past the open doorway of a basement pistol range, reached the temporary sanctuary of an underground workshop, and closed the door behind them.

The actress was out of breath, and barefoot after abandoning her designer sandals on a spiral staircase. Fahri was wet to the knees after tripping over a bucket left on the same stairs by a charwoman. Amanda felt as if she'd just been filming a slapstick movie chase—the frenzied flight of the disguised film star and the Keystone Kop shackled together. Though, she decided, with his pencil mustache, precise movements, and soulful eyes,

Fahri was more of a Chaplinesque figure. All they lacked, thank God, was a small army of Turkish police in hot pursuit.

Fahri unsnapped their cuffs and began crawling about the floor. After a moment he located a recessed ringbolt and heaved open a hinged trapdoor.

"Here is!" he said, dropping into the hole. "Come!"

Amanda did not share his enthusiasm at the prospect of further descent. They were already in the basement. Where in God's name was he proposing to take her? Did the Kurdish terrorists hide out in the sewers of Istanbul? But, since there was no alternative, she gathered the voluminous garment around her waist and lowered herself down the ladder on which Fahri had already disappeared.

"Shut door!" the call came from below.

She swung the trapdoor down over her head.

"O Christ!" Her voice echoed in sudden and utter darkness.

Well, Mandy old girl, she thought, *this certainly ranks right up there with some of your madder escapades.* Like her Lady Godiva Gallop for Peace. Or the Aboriginal Music Festival. Or the time in Alaska she'd let that big, bearded stuntguy take her storm-kayaking. Maybe Leo was right, and the American, Paul Cyrus. Maybe she'd gone beyond mere risk-taking once again into the realm of sheer lunacy.

Though she could see nothing, her other senses were fully occupied. Below them, water was dripping steadily, slapping rhythmically against something. A tidal current, then, probably an affluent of the Golden Horn. And there was a pervading rankness—salt water and sewage, perhaps industrial waste in the mix. She'd read that the waterway was terribly polluted; the point was no longer moot.

Then she heard Fahri's boots scraping about below. A light flared from a low-wattage bulb suspended from a projecting girder. The feeble glow revealed a cavernous void.

Just beneath the rung on which she stood was the top of Fahri's head. Below him stone steps disappeared into black water. Beyond, stone columns marched off into obscurity, their vaulted arches and capitals lost in gloom. The guidebooks boasted of the ancient Roman cisterns; this one, she suspected, would not be on the tour bus circuit.

Fahri, meanwhile, was again searching for something. A boat seemed like a good idea. Surely he wasn't expecting her to wade into the muck? Even the Phantom of the Opera provided his victims some kind of transport.

But the moment she lowered herself to the ground beside him, he began tugging her off into the darkness.

"Wait!" she cried. "Where are we going?"

"Going Ismet. Must to hurry, lady!"

"I *can't* hurry. I'm barefoot, Fahri—no shoes, see? So don't go so bloody fast!"

Mercifully, he did slow, and she followed him onto a narrow stone shelf, barely wide enough for their passage. On her right was a wall of slime-covered, moldering brick; to her left an oleaginous sheen on the foul black water. Then the light bulb faded and died behind them, stranding them in pitch blackness.

Merde! Just like those damn stairwell lights in all the Left Bank fleabags she'd lived in during her student years in Paris. She was developing the symptoms of full-fledged panic when Fahri guided her hand to the bottom of another ladder. Thank God! How her Welsh forefathers could have spent their lives mucking about several miles down in mineshafts had always been beyond her comprehension. She climbed rapidly in the darkness, without a thought for her precarious position on the ladder.

The policeman stopped suddenly above her. She heard him grunting, wrestling with something, then muttering—cursing in Turkish, no doubt. The hatchway must be sealed or stuck fast up there. Which meant, obviously, they were trapped down here. Her panicky thoughts returned with a vengeance. How the hell were they going to get out?

They would have to retrace their passage back through the catacomb, step by blind step, that's how—all the way to the police building, up the spiral stairs and down the corridor to surrender to a whole roomful of gloating male faces. Well, it wasn't going to happen. She'd be damned if she'd go back.

"Come on, Fahri, you little bastard, push!"

There was a sudden, hollow, grinding sound like the opening of a sepulcher. An arrow of light pierced the shaft. Fahri yelped in surprise, then braced his shoulder and heaved again. Light showered in, giving Amanda a view of the policeman's legs wriggling and vanishing upward.

A moment later, as she shielded her eyes against blinding brightness, she was pulled out. They had obviously surfaced beyond the Harbor Police compound. They were in a big shipping yard, surrounded by aisles of stacked pallets and aluminum cargo containers. She smelled manure. Still, it was preferable to the stench below. Fahri was wrestling a manhole cover back into place, jumping back as it settled with a heavy clang.

Then they were running again, and she was hit with dizziness. Worse, her bare soles stung with every pounding step on the macadam, but she kept the pace. Like Fahri, she was now a fugitive, fueled more by determination not to be caught than by her original urgency to intercede in the hostage crisis.

The little policeman halted at the corner of a warehouse to peek ahead, and Amanda sagged back, catching her breath. It had already been a long day, starting with her predawn phone chats to California. Her Gucci leather Day-Planner had not indicated that noon would find her fleeing barefoot from Turkish police—a scene hokey enough to be included in the "Barbary!" script. And the day was young. Where might she get to by sundown?

She adjusted her veil and glanced at Fahri. His whole body was tense, like a hound catching a scent. And there were plenty in the air. The manure was fainter, replaced by the smell of quayside fishmonger stalls and the fuel oil belch of the Bosphorus ferryboats. They must be near the Galata Bridge.

She peeked around the corner. The Harbor Police compound was just down the block. Under its porte cochere was the dark Mercedes that had brought her. There was no sign of pursuit, but she could imagine the frantic search inside the building when they realized she was not coming back from the loo. Leo would be balling his tiny fists and turning puce like an apoplectic two-year-old.

"Okay, we go." Fahri set off at a deliberately casual pace away from the police building. Amanda followed at a little distance, as directed. Like a Moslem wife, she supposed. Just ahead there loomed the small horde of *paparazzi,* armed with telephotos, massed behind a police barricade. They were being held at bay by a couple of Turkish cops. Fahri gestured to these as he came up. A quick exchange brought guttural laughs from the cops and appraising glances in her direction.

That's all right, have your little sexist chuckle. Wait till that bastard of a colonel found out whom they let slip through their net. The cops opened a gap between the barricades to let her pass and shoved aside the nearest *paparazzi.* They gave way reluctantly, wary like all scavengers of forfeiting their place in the feeding frenzy to come. The woman in black they simply ignored. Their eyes were locked on the police building, zoom lenses focused on infinity. Amanda walked through with a sense of utter triumph. If these jackals didn't spot her, she thought, she could fool anybody.

They continued to the end of the block, turned the corner, and fetched up in front of Fahri's big German motorcycle. The policeman seemed extremely pleased to find it untouched. He mounted quickly, helmeted, and fired it up, gunning the engine impressively. Then he patted the seat behind him.

"Okay, lady, you ready go?"

Amanda nodded—the nod that meant no in Turkish. The sober-faced policeman grinned in spite of himself as the Western woman hitched up the black robe and suede dress underneath to free her legs. He got a quick vista of tanned thighs as she hopped up behind him and straddled the pillion. Then she rapped her knuckles on his helmet and shouted in his ear: "Okay, Fahri, let's get the hell out of here!"

The moment he felt her arms snake around his leather jacket, he released the clutch and they snarled away into the maze of waterfront alleys.

Amanda Morgan had vanished into the East.

10

IMMEDIATELY AFTER THE BOMBSHELL OF AMANDA'S DISAPpearance, Billy James Bracey, the unit publicist for "Barbary!", had slipped his considerable bulk out of the Harbor Police briefing room in quest of a private telephone. This was a very ill wind indeed, and he intended to be the somebody it blew some good. The time to make a move was obviously before all the fallout hit the ground. B.J. commandeered the first empty desk in the first open door down the hall, dialed an outside line, and started making calls.

In the wake of the morning's catastrophic events, some heavy media hitters based in Europe and the Middle East would be booking flights to Istanbul—the op-ed pundits, the trenchcoat brigade, the network glamour boys. But B.J. didn't have to wait for them. As it happened, some major players were already here, and at his beck and call, on the "Barbary!" junket. Of course they were not hard-news types, but the traditional hard-soft boundaries were rapidly disappearing. These days it was all show biz, and B.J. was in perfect position to take advantage of it.

On the second call he hit pay dirt. Mary Alice McVicker was still in her suite at the Khedive Palace—sleeping off a late night, no doubt. When B.J. had first met Mary Alice, at the SMU chapter of Sigma Delta Chi in the early seventies, she was noteworthy only as a relentless party girl. B.J.'s own career climb since had been worth a few letters home, but Mary Alice's had been spectacular.

She had started on a society desk in Biloxi. A couple years of hard work and unremitting self-promotion had landed her the dubious editorship of a small Gulf Coast tabloid. Within a year she had turned it into a national supermarket weekly. In another six months it was acquired by the Bruce Media Group of London, and Mary Alice crossed the Atlantic to become feature editor of Gaylord Bruce's worldwide publishing empire. Within a few eventful months, she had become Bruce's chief consort as well.

Incredibly, Billy James found this world-class gossip-monger totally unaware of the hijacking. "Lord God, B.J.," she complained in her whisky twang, "I just this minute started taking calls. Okay, give it to me quick and dirty. I'm gonna have to call Gay on this one. He's down on his island, gaffing marlin and banging slave girls, or versa vice, whatever the hell he does down there."

B.J. synopsized rapidly—the attack on the ship, the

two verified deaths, Ismet's demand to be put on TV, the ruse that had satisfied it, Amanda's televised offer to exchange herself for hostages, her disappearance from police headquarters.

"Listen, Beej, you're real positive about all this shit? You're not freebasing or anythang? Mandy's been snatched by terr'ists?"

"Or she's run off with them. It amounts to the same thing. Either way she's a hostage, only she doesn't know it yet. The cops have turned the building upside down, and all they found was a pair of her sandals."

"Give me the designer."

"What?"

"The sandals, silly. Which designer? Gucci, Amalfi, Garolini? What we do is get us a pair and shoot 'em close up, so you can see the logo. Readers love these li'l details and we make companies pay through the schnozzola."

"Mary Alice, I believe you're even more mercenary than I remember."

"I've grown in so many ways, darlin'."

"Well, I didn't actually see the shoes. Make up the brand."

"We will. Listen, B.J., who knows about all this so far?"

"I think you're the last to find out."

"Not the hijacking—Mandy's disappearance."

"Only a half-dozen or so, outside the police." B.J. recited the short list. "I give it an hour, maybe three or four at the outside, before word spreads. You gotta move fast, Mary Alice. And I mean really fast."

"I'm afraid this is just too dang perishable for us,

B.J. Even with satellite printing, it takes us forever and a half to hit the newsstands."

"So peddle it to the networks. Cut your own deal. I've got to hang up."

"How much, B.J.? You wouldn't be doin' this for old time's sake?"

"Let's just say you owe me a big one, Mary Alice. I'll think of something."

"Sure you will. But if you're screwin' me on this deal someway, honeybunch, so he'p me, I'll get my Uncle Bodie's boys down in Amarillo to cut on you here and there with their gelding knives."

"Don't get graphic, Mary Alice. *Ciao.*"

B.J. hung up. Jack Woodhull was standing in the doorway. The publicist raised one plump palm. "Right with you, Jack. I'm rescheduling the whole goddamned afternoon for fifty journalists."

Woodhull kept coming, leaned across the desk, grabbing a fistful of white silk shirt, yanking B.J. out of the chair. "Bracey, what the hell you think you're doing? If you've leaked this—"

"Hey, hey, whoa boy. Who said anything about leaking? I got a job to do, just like you. Do I tell you how to direct, Jack? Uh-uh. Now I got me a busload of flaks out there, potential terrorists themselves if they don't get all their freebies and perks and gourmet eats and hot copy, and I got a whole fucking agenda that just got blown out of the water. So you take care of the big stuff, and you let ol' Billy James do his—hey, what the—?"

Woodhull seized the publicist's upper arm. "Leo may trust you, Bracey," the director said, propelling the larger man out of the office and down the hall. "But I sure as hell don't. And I don't think Colonel Ozsahin will either. He made it absolutely clear nobody says anything unless it's okayed with him. And you're definitely nobody, in my book. If you've got a statement to issue, then you hammer it out and you damn well show it to us, word for bloody word. Got that?"

"Okay," B.J. said. "No problem. I can work with that." He wrenched away from Woodhull's grasp, straightened his collar and necktie. "But let me tell you something, Jack. If you think you're gonna keep the lid on this, you are real mistaken. This story is gonna blow sky high, my friend. That little lady is big news. And if you're worried about saving the miniseries, forget it. 'Barbary!' is dead."

Woodhull stuck his face close to B.J.'s. "It's not the damn picture we want to save, Bracey, it's Mandy's life. Got that?"

Woodhull stared into the publicist's brown-cow eyes. Too late, he decided. Bracey wasn't threatening him about the story leaking; he was boasting after the fact. *The slimeball already made his phone call. He knows it, and I know it, and there's not a fucking thing we can do about it. Like he said, it would have happened sooner or later, only Bracey made sure it was sooner.*

≡

Amanda's impromptu tour of Istanbul continued. She had already been treated to a view of the Galata district from the back seat of a police sedan, followed by a barefoot crawl through a Byzantine sewer. Now, still barefoot, she was seeing the Bosphorus from the buddy seat of a full-dress BMW motorcycle, weaving in and out of car, van, and lorry traffic on the crowded coastal road at fifty miles per hour.

The experience was exhilarating. It had been twenty

years since Amanda had last ridden tandem on a cycle. She had forgotten the kinetic high—the explosive accelerations, the screaming wind, leaning hard on the curves to counter the G-forces. For sheer physical intoxication it belonged right up there on her thrill list—beside roller-coaster rides, downhill runs on untracked powder, and long, galloping, sexual climaxes.

Immediately after the Paris riots in '68, the teenage Amanda had gone off on the back of a "moto" with a blond French boy named Max. As a close friend of Danny Le Rouge, Max had decided the better part of valor required him to get out of town. They'd headed south, for the Dordogne. In time's long gallery Max's face was less than distinct, but Amanda remembered vividly his machine-gun laugh, freckled forearms, and lean, pungent body. On the bike she had pressed herself against him exactly like this, her legs spread, smelling leather as she lay her cheek against his old aviator jacket, holding on for dear life as picturebook countryside streamed past.

A long blasting diapason jerked her head around. A Soviet cruise ship flashed sleek white sides in the sun, gliding down the Bosphorus from the Black Sea. Red pennants fluttered from the rigging, decks were packed with waving tourists, and seabirds circled the fantail. It sounded its horn again, as if to scatter lesser watercraft from its path. Ahead on Amanda's right, needling above shoreline pines, were the minarets of a small mosque. Farther on was the long Moorish marble wedding cake she knew to be Dolmabahçe Palace.

What she ought to be doing—instead of reliving her wild youth—was questioning where she was being taken. She knew damn well the hostage ship lay diametrically opposite the direction in which they were so rapidly proceeding. But her worries were flung away by the wind, which a moment before had plucked off her headscarf and now whipped her hair into frenzy. Amanda could think of nothing but holding on, shielding her face in Fahri's lee and watching the Bosphorus spread its loveliness beside her, like an exquisite blue carpet unrolled in the Grand Bazaar.

≡

"Policeman Bayram was married to a damned Kurd. One of the Al-Azzawis." Colonel Ozsahin lounged against the corridor wall, puffing on a flat cigarette in an amber holder and brushing ashes from his gray silk lapels. "But the chief idiocy is that my own internal security did not even suspect the man was married."

"Well, now we know why Ismet's been stalling us," Paul Cyrus said. Inside the command room Major Yoruk and Dr. Ziyal were still seated before the monitors, which showed only long shots of the frigate. "He's just waiting for a signal from his people that they've got her. But where will they take her? I assume Bayram's apartment has been abandoned?" Ozsahin nodded. "That figures. And they know they won't get anywhere near the *George Washington*. In any case she'd be more valuable as a hostage away from the ship, to assure safe conduct for him and his men."

"But I do not intend to wait for any of this to happen, Mr. Cyrus. If we do not find her very soon, we will attack the ship." Ozsahin paused and arched his brows. "You disagree?"

It was a surprising question from the colonel. Paul could not imagine the head of the national police soliciting a second opinion once he had formed his own. Paul had heard of his exploits as a field commander in Korea. During the November nightmare of 1950, when a million Chinese poured over the Yalu in sub-zero weather and routed the entire Eighth Army, Ozsahin's Turks had actually continued to advance north, attacking in the teeth of the Chicom onslaught.

But forty years later the man was in a different kind of war. In counter-terrorist confrontation the rules of engagement were not so clear-cut. Ozsahin's granite countenance was marked by signs of self-doubt: a tic at the corner of an eye, a fine sheen of sweat on the bullet forehead, as one cigarette followed another into the amber holder.

Paul spoke: "I would hold to your original plan. Stall, talk, wait for darkness, *then* attack."

"And Miss Morgan? If they threaten to kill her?"

"They have threatened to kill everyone on board. And she has chosen to place herself in jeopardy."

"Quite so," Ozsahin said, with an air of summing up. "Our first concern must be for the forty innocents, not the one celebrity who has complicated matters for us all. She was warned. She is perhaps brave, certainly foolish, but innocent—no, that she is not."

Paul thought that one over and silently disagreed. The actress's very idealism argued a kind of stubborn innocence. And he had a hunch that her sophisticated, tough-talking veneer was at least in part a defense against unusual vulnerability. But whatever her virtues and vices, she was now in way over her head.

≡

Two hundred feet above the Bosphorus on the great suspension bridge between the continents, wind streamed around the big motorcycle, causing Amanda to clutch even tighter to the leather-clad policeman. Through the flashing suspension cables and the noon haze she was able to savor the spectacular vista. On both sides of the meandering waterway the great city sprawled in all its contradictory, millennial splendor: industrial blight and modernist high-rise, shantytowns and Arabian Nights fantasy. And beyond, just over the horizon and beckoning to her imagination, lay the great plains of Europe and Asia.

In a moment they were off the bridge and flowing with the quick-eddying traffic south through the urban canyons of Usküdar. In narrow streets beneath crisscrossed washlines their backfire echoed off stone and stucco.

As they idled explosively beside a busy street market Amanda shouted into Fahri's helmeted ear, "Where are we going?" Her question was drowned out by the cycle, which the policeman kept at high revs. *The little bastard's ignoring me,* thought Amanda. *How dare he?* She could get off right here. Just slide backward off the bike and disappear into the crowd. One phone call and in a few minutes she'd be in the sybaritic saloon of a Kronos limo, a chilled bottle of Dom Perignon at her elbow, solarized glass between her and the swarms of Asia, tooling back to her suite at the Pera Palas.

She didn't do it, of course. Instead, she hung on as Fahri accelerated away. It was her old Capricorn stubbornness. Once she'd made up her mind, almost nothing could turn Amanda Morgan aside. Accumulating evidence as to the wrongheadedness of her course was ruled out or flatly ignored. Once, in the late seventies, for instance, she'd worked nearly a year on a doomed film without a penny of compensation rather than quit and simply admit she'd made a mistake.

This time she'd been warned by three governments, been handcuffed and dragged through sewers, and now was having her shouted questions ignored—and still she hung on, determined to see it through.

Well, too bloody bad. That's the way I am. She'd paid the price for it before, and she'd pay it again.

Moments later they entered a street of torn up cobblestones and rundown apartment buildings of weathered wood. The policeman braked, took off his helmet and handed it to Amanda.

"What for?"

"Is for hide, okay? Nobody see your face."

She strapped it on.

A few minutes more brought them into a district of out-and-out slums. Cobbles and macadam gave way to gravel, packed earth, and rutted mud. They motored past dismal blocks of jerry-built structures pieced together out of old brick, stones, broken tiles, scrap wood, and signboards. In the interstices, goats and chickens wandered, children played, old men smoked and loitered, women beat clothes on flat stones beside a trickling faucet. That was probably the extent of the local plumbing, Amanda thought. She doubted they had sewers out here, not to mention other basic municipal services.

Amanda had read of these vast slum tracts on the outskirts of the larger Turkish cities. They were squalid encampments for the large immigrant peasant population, made possible by an ancient law dating back to Ottoman times, which forbade the pulling down of any two-walled, roofed structures that could be built during a single night. The result were these *geçekondus,* or night houses. They reminded Amanda of the *favelas* of Rio, the *bidonvilles* of North Africa, or the shantytowns of South Africa, all of which she had visited. She wondered if anything was being done to improve the primitive conditions. When this present crisis was over, she decided, she would make it her business to find out, and to lend her voice to something more worthwhile than the brainless drivel of "Barbary!"

Fahri accelerated away from a band of raggedy children, then swerved twice in quick succession, guiding the big bike toward a ramshackle wooden structure. They plunged through a burlaped opening into enveloping darkness and Fahri cut the motor. Faint light filtered through a scrapwood roof; the cooling engine ticked in the interior silence. Amanda smelled rancid cooking oil and a pervading rankness that recalled the Stamboul sewers. She unsnapped the straps under her chin and Fahri helped her lift off the helmet.

"Come," he said, dismounting.

A little shakily, she slid off, put her bare feet down on cold earth—and then on something sharp. She swore.

"Is problem?"

"Christ, Fahri, this place is full of broken glass. I've got to have something on my feet."

"Shoes, yes?"

"That's the general idea."

Fahri took a step in the darkness, heard the crystalline crunch beneath his boots. *Ah,* he thought, *the broken narghile of the bearded Angleesh.* The sound brought back all the rushing horror of that encounter.

"Yes, yes," he instructed the actress, "please, not to move."

"Don't worry, I shan't."

He stooped, positioning his arms under her.

"What are you doing?" she demanded.

"I—I take you up." He sucked air, heaved, staggered.

"Oh, for heaven's sake," Amanda said as he finally straightened, grunting with the effort. "I'm not *that* heavy, Fahri. You mustn't groan like a piano mover."

≡

Beside an unglazed window in the next room of the *geçekondu,* a slim young Kurdish woman bent over a small gas stove, brewing tea. Guldasa Bayram had heard everything—the big cycle roaring in a moment before, the woman crying out, and then the two voices. She turned now at the heavy footsteps to see her husband come staggering through the doorway, the Western woman in his arms.

So, her timid little policeman had actually done the intrepid deed. Guldasa recognized Amanda at once. Though swathed in cheap black muslin, without makeup, her hair a windblown tangle, the lady was not quite the glamorous creature of her photographs. And yet, Guldasa decided, as her inquiring gaze was returned in full measure, none of those things could disguise Amanda's sheer vitality. Guldasa was impressed. It was the first time she had ever seen a film star in person.

She spoke sharply to her husband in Turkish: "Put her down this instant!"

11

"SHE HAS NO SHOES," FAHRI BEGAN TO EXPLAIN, "SO I—"

"I'm not blind. Fetch her the black Reeboks from my bag. They should fit. But first change your clothes. Wait! Before you do anything, you must send the radio message to Ismet. You have the book?"

"Yes."

When the officer had departed on these errands, the Kurdish woman smiled at Amanda, revealing a crooked eyetooth. "I am Guldasa Bayram. Fahri is my husband. My cousin is Ismet al-Azzawi, the leader of the Peoples Army of Kurdistan. I am pleased to welcome you, Miss Morgan, as my guest"—Amanda accepted the slender, proffered hand—"as Fahri tells me you have come here out of sympathy with our cause. This is correct?"

When Amanda said it was, Guldasa added, "Of course it is a pleasure, too, as I have enjoyed your appearances on *Dynasty.*"

"Dear God!" Amanda said. If Guldasa were not simply confusing her with Joan Collins (horrifying thought!), she could only be referring to some tawdry cameos done years before, and best forgotten. Amanda forced a gracious smile. "Thank you. I've come to do anything I can, really. If you know anything about my career, beyond *Dynasty,* you know I've supported revolutionary movements all over the world."

"We Kurds consider ourselves patriots, Miss Morgan. If we are revolutionaries, it is only by tragical imperative."

"Well, that's usually the case, isn't it? Please call me Mandy."

"Very well—Mandy."

"Your name is quite lovely, by the way. Is it Kurdish?"

"Yes, Guldasa is a type of flower, or perhaps what you would call 'bouquet.' "

"It suits you." The young Kurdish woman had the look of a ballerina—ethereal features, no chin, arched back, undeveloped breasts, even the swan neck. Her skin was paler than Amanda's, the color of old ivory. She wore tight French jeans and a green velour pullover, and a Liz Claiborne scarf was knotted in her dark plaited hair. Yet this sylph-like creature had a subtle *hauteur,* Amanda observed, and talked to her husband like a sergeant dressing down a new recruit.

Guldasa responded to a compliment on her English: "I worked for THY, that is Turkish Airlines, for two years, and before this I attended the American College in Bebek. Please, sit down. I am preparing tea." She indicated an unraveling wickerwork chair.

"Thank you, but have we time for tea? All I need, really, is something for my feet, and I'm ready to go."

"Go?"

"To the ship. The sooner you take me to this Ismet al-Azzawi, the better for all concerned, I should think?"

"I have instructed my husband to notify Ismet of your safe arrival. We are to remain here until he contacts us."

Amanda shook her head. "You may do, but I shan't, at least not for very long, I'm afraid."

"Of course you are offended by such a filthy place. Obviously we do not live here. It is merely, how do you say, a clandestination?"

"That's not it at all. I've lived in places—well, nearly this bad. But I've come here expressly on Ismet's promise to exchange myself for the prisoners on the ship. You're aware of this? I simply must insist that this promise be carried out as quickly as possible, or I shall leave. Is that clear?"

"Perfectly."

"Then please instruct your husband to tell Ismet what I have just said."

"I'm sorry, Mandy, but it is Ismet's orders that I follow, not yours. So there is nothing more to do but wait. How do you take your tea?"

Amanda was becoming angry with this serene and officious *aparatchik,* who was being just as thick-headed as the striped-pants brigade Amanda had just left. With forty lives held at gunpoint on the Marmara, she was not going to sit politely in some hovel in Scutari, sipping tea and making phrase-book chitchat. She had taken lunatic risks to get here, and was in fact prepared to take more—to be smuggled right through the ranks of Colonel Ozsahin's commandos, if necessary, as she had walked through the *paparazzi*—in order to reach the *George Washington* and *do* something, for Christ's bloody sake.

She weighted her words with theatrical emphasis: "Guldasa, you realize that your leader—Ismet—wants to see me?"

"Yes, of course."

"But he happens to be a prisoner on a ship, you realize that as well? I don't care what his last instructions to you were. Right now the whole bloody Turkish army have their guns on him. I *know* this. I was just at police headquarters, from which, thanks to your brave little husband, I escaped. Ismet can't just walk away, is that clear? That is *why* I need to be taken to him, and that is precisely why he wants to see me. Now please, take me to him, or I'll go myself."

Guldasa gave her a small, infuriating smile. "You do not know my cousin. If Ismet says he will come to us, then he will do so. If he makes a promise, he will keep it. And if we are not here when he comes, he will be very angry."

Fahri came back dressed in jeans and windbreaker, a pair of black high-top aerobic shoes in hand. At a nod from Guldasa he handed the shoes to Amanda, then spoke in Turkish: "I'm starving. Is there any food?"

"And what about the woman? Do you think of her?"

"Yes, of course. Her, too. Do you have any yogurt?"

"There is only tea. I have had no time to prepare food for any of us. If you must eat, go ask my great uncle next door. He was cooking fish. No, don't go now! We must watch her closely."

Amanda was lacing on the shoes. They were a size large, but she was grateful for them. They were exactly what she needed to call their bluff—march right out the door and through the shantytown to the nearest phone. She rose.

"They are fitting good?" Fahri inquired.

"Yes, thank you. I'm leaving now."

At his wife's barked command Fahri leaped and seized the actress from behind, pinning her arms in the voluminous black robe and dodging her back-kicks.

"Please, do not fight us, Mandy," Guldasa said as the actress was wrestled back into the kitchen chair. "We intend you no harm. But you must wait for Ismet, as we must wait. He will come to you."

"They'll kill him, you realize that? They bloody will. I can save his life."

"They won't. The Little Fox can escape anything."

"Ah, well, how fortunate for him. What does he need me for, then?"

"I, too, am curious about that. We shall find out soon enough. Now, will you take some tea?"

Amanda took a deep breath, confronting her captors. Finally she nodded. "Please."

≡

"There is your signal, Mr. Cyrus," Ozsahin said.

The members of the hostage negotiating team were clustered around a mixing console in the basement of the Harbor Police building, listening to a playback. The brief Persian exchange had been intercepted on the ship-to-shore band several minutes before. A quick voiceprint confirmed the likelihood that one speaker was Ismet al-

Azzawi; they speculated that the other could be ex-Officer Bayram.

"Do you by any chance recognize the aphorisms, Mr. Cyrus?"

"Rumi?" Paul ventured.

Ozsahin arched his brows. "Good guess. But I am informed they are lines from Hakim Sanai, one of the great trio of Sufi teachers along with Rumi. Obviously the lines constitute a childish code." He shook his head pityingly. "Why do they play these stupid games? Why doesn't Bayram simply come right out and say, 'We've got her'? and Ismet answer, 'Damn good'—or just 'Roger' like you Americans?"

"Too prosaic," Paul said. "Kurds love poetry."

"Yes, well, in any case now we know they've got her, and it's time to take action."

≡

In the Soviet Consulate on Istiklal Caddesi in Beyoglu, not only the intercepted playback but the comments of Ozsahin, Paul Cyrus, and others were being monitored. The voices were being picked up and amplified from a small tube embedded in the plaster of the Harbor Police communications room, and technician Yefim Arbatinsky was justifiably proud of the signal strength.

"So," Major Feliks Ilyinsky said, "it interests me more and more, *l'affaire Morgan.* I tell you, Toshka, Moscow will also take an active interest in the capture of such a key personage in the European peace movement."

"Perhaps," Anton Bessaraboff said. He was still snuffling, standing as far as possible from the open window on Istiklal Caddesi. "But perhaps not. This woman is a very active and volatile personality. But her effect is indiscriminate. For instance, she has denounced Warsaw Pact weaponry as well as NATO's, and Chernobyl as vociferously as Three Mile Island."

"But this is in her favor, Toshka, and exactly in the spirit of *Perestroika*. Have we not denounced Chernobyl ourselves, and punished those incompetents responsible for it? Evenhandedness only enhances her prestige. And pressures for mutual withdrawal, mutual force reduction in Europe—are these not exactly what we seek? To use the language of chess, with numerical advantage, can we not afford to make even exchanges as long as NATO is foolish enough to accept them? I tell you, Toshka, if this woman is not a queen, she is certainly worthy of saving from capture."

Bessaraboff attempted a smile. "Dear Feliks. What exactly are you proposing, that we attempt to rescue a film actress?"

"I propose nothing. I am simply studying options."

But Toshka knew the signs all too well. One way or another his patron was determined to get deeply involved in this Kurdish terrorist affair. And Toshka would have to go along with him, at least for the time being, though he would certainly document his misgivings in appropriate memos.

≡

By one PM the anachronistic image of the three-master, hove to and motionless against the Stamboul skyline, had been satellite-dished into homes around the globe. Video reporters waited for just the right breeze off the Marmara to ruffle their hairdos as they filmed identical stand-ups, chroma-keyed against the dramatic backdrop.

Along the sea wall, swarming behind the police barricades, the phalanx of camera crews and video trucks grew by the hour, competing for unobstructed views. The focus of all this worldwide attention, the *George Washington,* swung lazily to its bow anchor in the three-knot current down the Bosphorus. On its spar deck the only movements were occasional stirrings under the canvas sun dodger rigged amidships, and, at forepeak and taffrail, a riffling of the Stars and Stripes in the fifteen-star configuration of Jeffersonian America.

By order of the Turkish National Council, all ship and air traffic was being routed around the sector. Except for the frigate, the Marmara roadstead, usually a busy commercial anchorage, was deserted. Fortunately, several cargo ships had reberthed the night before, to comply with the request for the filming. News helicopters had been grounded, although on the soccer field near Kumkapi, Ozsahin's helicopters remained in readiness. Networks had to make do with endlessly replaying the footage taken by Jack Woodhull's cameraman—made available for a tidy sum by Leopold Bouchard—during the first flyover of the ship.

The next break in the story came shortly before two in the afternoon when an American cable network, citing unofficial Turkish government sources, released the shocking news that Amanda Morgan had disappeared shortly after offering to exchange herself for the hostages, and was now presumed to be in the hands of the terrorists.

This bombshell turned a regional media circus into a worldwide media frenzy. On most European and american video coverage this sensational sidebar overwhelmed the main hostage story. File footage was instantly exhumed in order to compile a video assem-

blage of the actress-activist in all her manifestations—
shouting down hecklers at Hyde Park rallies; fleeing
swarms of *paparazzi* along Boulevard de la Croisette in
Cannes; in jeans and leather jacket leading an anti-nuke
march through the rain in Düsseldorf; swathed in blue
fox, emerging from a limo in a starburst of strobe units;
in Slavic finery as the Empress Rusudan from the BBC-
PBS series; and, in some embarrassing early cheesecake
glossies, as a hopeful starlet, camping it up on London's
Carnaby Street clad only in bikini and body paint.

As the first media shock waves hit the Harbor Police command post Ozsahin grabbed a phone and began
speaking quietly in Turkish, but Paul Cyrus could see
a vein throbbing at his temple. A desk away, Jack Woodhull punched the air: a short, violent uppercut into an
imaginary gut. "That fat-ass Bracey," he said, "that slimy
bastard!" The publicist, predictably, was no longer to be
found.

Ozsahin slapped down the phone and stared at a
video monitor, saying nothing. Paul looked over the colonel's shoulder at a full-screen image of Amanda Morgan in a diaphanous harem outfit. There was, Paul
thought, a surprising amount of cleavage for TV, especially Turkish TV. Somehow he'd missed that particular
shot in his quick perusal of the "Barbary!" press kit. And
when he'd been sitting across the room from her upstairs—had it been only a couple hours ago?—he'd not
realized she was quite so well endowed.

He smiled in spite of himself. He had a wild impulse
to turn to Ozsahin and say, "Okay, so she demolished
all our plans and sabotaged our negotiations, but how
about those tits?" A glance at the colonel convinced him
such a joke would not be well received.

≡

Thirty miles away on the Sea of Marmara, in the well-appointed galley of the *Pegasus,* Bitsy Watkins was microwaving frozen *tortes provençales* for a late lunch when Amanda Morgan's face flashed on her little Sony TV, superimposed on a long shot of the frigate. Bitsy turned up the sound—it was the English-language broadcast. A moment later she interrupted her daughter's marathon sunbath to inform her of the sensational sequel to the hostage crisis.

Darryl Ann became agitated. She demanded details and, when her mother was unable to supply them, switched on the larger television in the lounge, pacing to and fro like a caged lioness till Forrest came down from the flybridge and told her to, for God's sakes, sit down.

She complied, popping the top on a Tab and sucking the contents without taking her eyes from the set. She was not sure herself why the sudden injection of the glamorous British actress into the middle of the crisis should alter her opinion about Paul's involvement, but it did. Finally, reaching consensus with her conflicting emotions, she blurted out:

"Daddy, turn around, we're going back now!"

"What in hell for, punkin?"

"I have to apologize to Paul . . . because . . . because I've been a royal bitch, that's what for."

Forrest Watkins shook with laughter.

"Well, I have been!" D.A. protested, looking hurt.

"I'm not arguing with you, honey," Forrest said. "If you say you were a bitch, well, maybe you were—just a wee bit." He chuckled again. "You *can* be sometimes, guess we know that. And your mother and I like Paul, and kind of hoped you wouldn't be giving him all these ultimatums."

"Well?"

"Well, what?"

"Aren't you going to turn around?"

"Hell, no, I'm not going all the way back to Istanbul just so you can tell the man you're sorry. If you want to apologize, you just write it all down in a cable and we can send it on the radio. And don't go into a pout. I'm the captain and what I say by God goes." He winked at his wife, who had just emerged from the galley with the heated French puff pastry shells and olives.

"Lunch, me hearties," Bitsy said.

"I'm not hungry," Darryl announced, and stalked out of the salon.

Forrest smiled. He had witnessed these stormy exits from the time she was two, whenever she had encountered parental intransigence. Too damn often, he thought, they had worked.

But not this time. He kept the *Pegasus* on its heading while he and Bits devoured the lunch. As he maintained his lookout forward through the big amber-tinted windows, he could not help but see his spoiled, thwarted, voluptuous girlchild once again splayed out in the afternoon sun. Now she was mad at him instead of Paul. She'd get over it.

But in the midst of sunning and sulking, Darryl Ann was actually taking her father's advice and trying to frame an apology she could fit into a ship-to-shore cable. It was a tricky assignment. The wording had to be just right, apologetic without seriously damaging her pride. She had to admit her . . . well, bitchiness, and yet make it seem like he might have overreacted just a tiny bit. Something like that. Fuck! She felt like Scarlett composing a cable to Rhett!

Finally, unable to work it all out in her head, she stalked inside for pen and notepad, past her mother, who was napping through *Lawrence of Arabia* on the VCR, and then back topside to belly flop on her towel. She ignored the little wave from her father up on the shaded flybridge, turned to her paper, squinted out the glare of the westering sun, chewed on her tongue, and was soon in the throes of serious composition.

"Pauly Wolly . . ." No, that wouldn't do. She couldn't babytalk her way out. The opening had to be serious.

"Paul darling, forgive me . . ."

≡

As late afternoon shadows deepened on the domes of Saint Sophia and the Blue Mosque, below them, in Kumkapi Harbor, the Jandara Suicide commandos remained at attack readiness. Officers studied plans and timetables, pored over the blueprints of the ship's modern interior provided by Kronos Limited. Out on the water emergency teams continued to patrol in fishing skiffs as close as possible to the frigate.

What they needed was darkness, and it looked like they were going to get it. At least that was Colonel Ozsahin's feeling two kilometers away at the Harbor Police command post. It was now apparent that Ismet was stalling for time. But why? With Amanda Morgan in his grasp, why didn't he simply announce the fact and use her to gain his demands and his own release?

≡

As the sun dipped below the Istanbul land walls, and the recorded and amplified call of the muezzins drifted out from the minarets over the sea, Ismet spread his prayer carpet on the quarterdeck of the *George Washington* and bowed toward Mecca.

Amidships and forward, Taufiq and Hamzah did likewise, while the half-Greek Raschid continued to watch the huddled hostages, AK-47 cradled on his knees. But his ferret eyes continuously darted this way and that, betraying his thoughts. For Raschid was a reluctant terrorist, who now wanted desperately out of this position—to recapture his prized anonymity, to be able to wander freely once again the streets of his native Salonika, lost among ten thousand mustached men in white shirts and dark pants, able to slip into any doorway, shop, club, cinema, foodstall, to explore and savor unobserved the endless tributaries of life. He was *not* ready to die, as the others seemed to be. And Ismet's revised escape plan, which he had elected upon the capture of Amanda Morgan, seemed now a sure way of death.

Taufiq, making his prayers amidships, felt similarly the presence of death, but counseled himself not to fear it. He bid his spirit be ready to free itself from his body, like a kite catching the first wind and straining at the string. At the conclusion of his devotions he recalled the words of Sanai: *"Arrange things so that when death calls, he finds your soul waiting in the street."*

There must be many more martyrs, he knew, before Kurdistan could finally claim its rightful place in the family of nations. Death would be the price. And he would pay it, again and again, if need be, as many lifetimes as he was allotted. In the end they would win.

Hamzah, forward, finished his prayers quickly and

reached for his binoculars. His were more practical concerns. How many elite forces were marshaled against them, and where were they emplaced? Behind the sea wall, and in the harbors, and in the boats around them, surely. They would miss nothing. And helicopters would be seconds away.

Like Raschid, and unlike Taufiq, Hamzah was not eager to die, but inaction ate at him, frayed his nerves, dried his mouth, made his skin itch. More and more, he found his thoughts turning to sex—violent sex. He thought vividly about taking one of the captive women, dragging her below, and violating her. There were several who would do nicely, and who would probably enjoy it. But Ismet would never permit it. And, of course, he was right. Allah had set his law unequivocally against such things. Still, it would be deeply satisfying, and what else could a man think about for hours on end?

But the breakout would come soon.

Amidships, with the onset of dusk, the captives no longer needed the shade provided by the sailcloth. But they continued to huddle together under it, taking comfort in their closeness and the illusion of shelter it provided. They suffered now the adrenal exhaustion of prolonged crisis, glandular reserves drained dry from too many emergency responses to the terrors of the moment . . . moments that had stretched into hours of unremitting fear.

What could one do against automatic weapons that could colander a man or woman into lifeless gore in an instant, a transformation they had witnessed twice at close quarters? Yet more terrifying than the weapons were the unholy eyes of the young men who wielded them, eyes seemingly without pity, eyes that did not acknowledge the humanity of their captives. What had driven them to turn their savagery on innocents, like the blond Scandinavian boy who now lay sleeping fitfully in their midst, fleeing his nightmares down the dark corridors of unconsciousness?

And they had other fears. They prayed for rescue, yet dreaded a Turkish assault that would loose a hailstorm of bullets over the ship, and instant retribution, sworn by the Kurds—the lobbing of grenades into the midst of captives. "You will die first," Ismet had promised, and they believed.

Beyond this night no certain future beckoned. It simply was not there for them anymore. The God who had given them birth and carried them thus far through all the dangers of the world had now abandoned them to an unthinkable fate . . . or, at best, a blind chance at survival.

And the odds were not very good, thought Lyle Johns. At first glance the Kurds appeared boys—underfed, untempered. But this was illusion. For the assistant director had observed them carefully, and found their movements precise and coordinated. They handled their weapons like seasoned fighters. If their postures occasionally displayed fatigue, their overall vigilance was unwavering. The little bastards were very good indeed.

And despite their boyish appearance, Lyle could find no forgiveness in his heart for them. He could not put himself in their place and justify what they had done—not for any cause in the world. He'd heard about the Stockholm Syndrome, the tendency of some hostages to identify with their captors. But he detected no trace of this in himself. He despised these animals and longed to destroy them. He would gladly bring it about with any weapon known to man, or his bare hands if necessary. He imagined it in various ways in vivid detail, over and over, till he was glutted and shaken with hatred.

Several feet away, the plump nurse, whom Lyle Johns had protected earlier from Ismet's wrath, now sat exhausted with her back against a wooden gun carriage. Even so, her terrified heart continued to race. Only by ceaseless prayer (which Saint Paul had commanded all Christians to do) could she subdue it and find the moment-by-moment strength to endure her fears.

Earlier she had glanced up from her prayers to see one of the black-clad terrorists, a lank man with beard and headscarf, also saying his prayers, prostrating himself on a small carpet while a brother terrorist stood by, machine gun in hand. The sight filled her with such rage that she had to redouble her devotions to bring peace back to her soul—and still, the anger lingered. What could those murderers be praying for? How dare they seek divine sanction for this hideous reign of terror!

≡

Back at the command post Paul sat idly, watching a slight tremor in his right hand that was holding a coffee cup. He willed the tremor to cease; it did not. So much for mind over matter. What did he expect? He had drunk far too much of the damn stuff. His kidneys felt drained. Not to mention his brain, which had run out of ideas hours ago. He felt hopeless. It was strictly a military operation now.

Across the room Ozsahin was endlessly on the phone, totally involved in the tactical questions of the coming assault. Since Amanda's disappearance Ismet had responded to nothing, only reiterating his demands and sneering at their threadbare excuses for failing to meet them. During the last brief conversation he had given them a new ultimatum—until sunrise, or executions would begin—but Paul did not believe he meant it.

Neither did Dr. Ziyal or Colonel Ozsahin. It was apparent to all that the Little Fox was only playing a game, obviously waiting for something. Whatever happened would happen this night.

And Ozsahin was determined to strike first. The assault had now been advanced to midnight. Three or four in the morning would be better if they wanted to catch the Kurds at low ebb, but the colonel was afraid to wait that long.

"We came damn close," Paul thought to himself. *If only Amanda bloody Morgan hadn't fucked it up. Or mucked it up, wasn't that the appropriate Briticism?*

On the monitors, masts, spars, and crosstrees showed now as a lovely dark etching against evening purple. How peaceful it all looked, he thought. And, as he watched, the first flames leapt up the masts.

12

"FIRE!" PAUL SHOUTED.

Others, too, had seen. Tumult erupted in the small room, crescendoing into ear-splitting static when someone switched the video monitors to full volume. Mercifully the thunderous crackling abated an instant later, becoming recognizable as the roar of flames amplified by parabolic mikes.

"Oh Christ!" Jack Woodhull cried out. "Christ bloody hell!" Anguished oaths continued to spew out of him as he watched like a father helpless to aid a child in peril. The anguish, Paul knew, was not for the magnificent ship burning before their eyes but for the hostages in the midst of the inferno.

Fanned by a steady breeze, the fire climbed the masts and spread through the rigging and across the decks. Paul and the others crowded around the screens in horrified fascination as flames and smoke hemorrhaged upward into the night sky, coiling into thick, swirling columns that blotted out the horizon.

Above the confusion, Ozsahin could be heard shouting into the phone, ordering an immediate rescue-assault.

"Into fire?" Major Ergun Akalin yelled back on the command net from Kumkapi Harbor. "I'm sending all boats—"

"Everything! Choppers, Jandaras, SEALs!"

"Celal, you want Jandaras to rappel onto a burning deck?"

"Idiot! Not rappel! Drop SEALs and IBSs—now!" The colonel slammed down the handset, punched another number.

Now is already too late, Paul thought. He remembered a September evening in 1985 in his Georgetown apartment watching CNN's satellite pickup of a hostage crisis forty-five hundred miles away in Malta. EgyptAir Flight 648 had been parked on the tarmac against a night sky like this, after the shooting of five passengers and an all-day standoff in negotiations. The ending, televised live, was swift and terrible. In an operation now considered a textbook fuck-up, Egypt's Force 777 hostage rescue unit blew the escape hatches and went in, guns blazing. On Paul's fifteen-inch screen the denouement lacked dramatic realism. Just a static long shot of a plane with interior lights flashing and a distant sound like corn popping. The awful statistics came later. During the assault fifty-seven hostages lost their lives—from the firefight, grenades, and smoke inhalation. Paul suspected he was now witnessing another such tragedy.

Had the terrorists accidentally detonated their explosives, igniting the ship? But there had been no flash or bang. Had the hostages set the fire, or had the Kurds themselves? Did they intend to perish, along with their captives, in a fanatic immolation? Paul could not believe that of Ismet. The Little Fox would have contrived a speech first.

In the close-ups Ozsahin demanded, there were no life-boats, no heads in the water, no bodies leaping overboard. Nothing but flames and smoke, as the ship became one combustible mass.

Jack Woodhull, beside Paul and searching the screen like everyone else for some sign of life, slammed the table and shouted: "Where are the fucking boats?"

"Haven't they all burned?"

"The ones on deck are just fucking props. The real boats are below—Zodiacs that release through big watertight doors on the other side of the ship. They've still got a chance."

A damn slim one, Jack thought. The poor bastards had better be out of that bonfire in the next minute. It was going up too damn fast, fueled by Jack's own fanatic insistence on authenticity. From the planks that skinned the steel ribs to the holystoned decking, the *George Washington* was built of solid oak, all hand-rubbed with linseed oil, which made her photograph like a dream—and, as was now bloody evident, burn like a torch. Further enhancing her combustibility, every inch of the miles of rigging was natural hemp, and the thousands of square feet of sail, though sprayed with fire-were all canvas cotton. Jack had commissioned a floating tinderbox.

Ozsahin was in a fury. He had been desperate for

action—to end the standoff, rescue the hostages, destroy the Kurdish vermin. Instead he had gotten chaos, sending all his careful planning up in smoke just like the damned ship. His commandos were converging on disaster. The colonel was reduced to staring at flickering images on a video screen like every other damn idiot in the room. By the time he got his reports, the crisis would be over, hostages saved or lost, terrorists captured or dead.

And, like Jack Woodhull, Ozsahin found cause to blame himself. He should have attacked an hour ago.

≡

At his command post in Kumkapi Harbor, Major Ergun Akalin was no less frustrated. He and Ozsahin had spent the day drafting the assault plan, anticipating every contingency—including a fire eventuating from the assault. They had even considered starting one, using incendiary devices instead of stun grenades to create a diversion. But this inferno changed everything. Now they could only rush in, circle the fireship, and try to rescue survivors—hostages and terrorists alike—making themselves targets in the process. Akalin had radioed for fireboats, but they wouldn't arrive in time to save anyone or anything.

Ozsahin's order to "send in everything," Akalin feared, would only increase the chaos—hostages mistaken for terrorists, SEALs shooting Jandaras and so forth. Confusion was already rampant in Akalin's headset, as the various assault-rescue elements reported in on the tactical net, seeking coordination—which, in too many cases, the major could not provide.

As he had countless times that day, Akalin polled his counter-sniper teams along the sea wall. Now that they finally had clearance to shoot, it was too late. Even with low-light optics, there were no terrorist targets on or around the burning ship. And their long-range thermal imagers, which could penetrate the shrouds of smoke, were rendered useless by the fire's intense heat. The marksmen, too, were reduced to spectators, as impotent to effect the outcome as all those who now massed behind the sea wall barricades and crowded the First Hill's steep streets to gaze down upon the conflagration.

Thirty seconds after relaying Ozsahin's launch order, Akalin watched two Agusta-Bell 212 choppers lift off the adjacent soccer field in Kumkapi. Each carried seven Turkish SEALs. In seconds they were above the flaming frigate. The original heliborne assault plan required commandos to rappel onto the ship. With flames shooting skyward, the hovering AB-212s instead dropped a half-dozen seven-person CO_2 inflatable boats, followed instantly by the SEALs, who swarmed out on the drop bars, one after another, letting go to fall the six or seven meters into the water, as near the ship as possible.

Meanwhile, in a variety of small surface craft disguised as fishing skiffs, Jandaras closed in on the inferno from all quarters. And on the muddy bottom a dozen meters below the *George Washington*'s keel, a Turkish-type 209 Atilay-class submarine flooded its escape trunks and released four more SEALs in SCUBA gear, each propelled by a swimmer delivery vehicle. The main body of Jandaras embarked from Kumkapi in two Jaguar III-class patrol boats armed with .50-caliber deck guns, searchlights stabbing the smoke-roiled surface.

The magnesium flares called for in the operational

order had been rendered unnecessary by the *George Washington*'s own pyrotechnical display. The entire Marmara seafront was lit up in a lurid *son et lumière,* the soaring flames rouging even the floodlit facades of the Blue Mosque and Saint Sophia.

=

The fire was no accident. It was Ismet's diversion, an option he had considered the moment they had discussed an attack on the square-rigger. But it had originally been a last-ditch option, to cover an escape only when all else had failed. But with the stunning news that Amanda Morgan was in Fahri's hands, Ismet had decided to use the fiery diversion as soon as possible. The ship and the other hostages had served their purpose— providing him a worldwide television audience, then attracting the film star into his net. With this one famous hostage, the forty were expendable. It was now time for the Little Fox to stage his most spectacular escape—before the eyes of the world.

As darkness fell Hamzah and Taufiq herded the hostages below while he and Raschid poured petrol around the three masts and into the cordage coiled on the belaying pins. He struck a match from a fancy box whose lid bore the film company's gold-embossed logo; it seemed an appropriate way to touch off the blaze.

Then they stood back as the flames sprang to life like a basketful of serpents unleashed from hell—slithering up the masts and shrouds, racing from yard to yard, writhing along the well-tarred rigging of the tops. Finally Ismet had to force himself to flee below, yelling at Raschid to follow.

In the bedlam below decks, meanwhile, Hamzah and Taufiq were waving their guns and shouting ineffectually at the terrified hostages, who pushed forward en masse toward the side loading-doors where four large Zodiac inflatables were stacked. The smell of smoke, the explosive crackling overhead, the intense heat in the confined space all added to the cumulative terrors of the day, had driven the hostages into collective madness, which prevented the evacuation they sought.

Ismet, taking in the chaos at a glance, fired his Kalashnikov in the air and summoned the full force of his voice: "Stop now! You, Mr. Boss, you, Mr. Captain, give orders! Everyone do what they say! Quick, quick!"

Lyle Johns and the Genoese sailing master—the two men Ismet had pointed to—seized the opportunity. Emulating Ismet's stentorian tones, they bullied their fellow hostages into four groups and cleared the first Zodiac for launching. While Lyle directed the first group into the inflatable, ordering them to keep down, the sailing master threw a switch. Two large steel doors slid apart on their tracks, letting in a blast of superheated air and windowing a smoke-streaked square of night. Above the roar of flames Ismet heard the thrashing of rotor blades, glimpsed through veils of smoke the sea's molten surface whipped into a froth from a chopper's downdraft.

So the Turkish attack was on, and time running out for the *pesh merga* to make their escape. Hamzah rushed to Ismet's side, while Taufiq stood guard against any last-second reprisals from hostages.

But where was Raschid? The quiet, dependable half-Greek should have been right behind him, but the main companionway was now sealed with smoke and, beyond that, a wall of fire. Was Raschid trapped up there? Ismet shouted his comrade's name.

Meanwhile the first Zodiac, with a dozen hostages huddled on the floorboards, was run out and launched on the waves, while a dozen more people scrambled into the second. But instead of pulling away, the first boat drifted in a circle, while hostages rowed at frenzied cross-purposes and a costumed crewman fumbled with the outboard. Suddenly the motor growled and the inflatable leaped forward, just in time to evade a flaming mass of rigging that fell hissing into its wake.

Ismet tried to force his way up the smoke-filled companionway, but staggered back, coughing, till he was seized from behind and dragged the rest of the way down.

"Ismet!" Hamzah was screaming at him, his face contorted with urgency. "Forget Raschid! We must go *now!*"

The Little Fox glanced around. The fourth Zodiac was launching. Raschid's fate was in his own hands—or Allah's. But now where was Taufiq? The Sufi was no longer standing guard. Had he too fled? As the last boat vanished into the smoky sea, they were suddenly alone in the doomed ship.

Hamzah was ripping open their dive bags, breaking out the SCUBA gear they had brought for underwater escape. Ismet buckled on the weight belt Hamzah tossed him and shrugged into his buoyancy compensator while Hamzah attached regulators to the air tanks. Both men strapped on their backpack harnesses. Ismet's Kalashnikov, with butt folded and spare magazines, and Hamzah's Skorpion machine pistol were sealed into two large waterproof 20-gauge PVC diving pouches, along with confiscated currency and several passports.

The two cousins now strapped on their fins and

waddled through the smoke. They paused an instant on the threshold, hearing even above the roar of flames the droning thunder of helicopters and the angry Doppler whine of boats churning the water. Hamzah produced a grenade, pulled the pin, and hurled it far out into the smoky night as a parting gesture. Then they spat into their masks, bit down on their mouthpieces, and stepped into the sea, sliding below the fiery surface into liquid darkness.

13

TAUFIQ HAD GONE IN THE THIRD ZODIAC, HUDDLED IN THE sternsheets and disguised in Arab burnoose. He was counting on the confusion ashore to give him a chance to slip away.

One lucky chance had already come his way. Below decks a costumed "Arab" fled the crush at the Zodiacs. Taufiq pursued, yelling for the man to stop. Brought up short by flames, the "Arab" whirled, a kitchen knife in his hands. Taufiq squeezed off a burst from his AK-47 and watched the man topple to the deck.

The bearded Sufi looked down at the man he'd just killed and saw a way to go on living. He stripped the bloodstained burnoose off the corpse and pulled it over himself, discarding his headscarf. Then he flung his rifle away and hurried toward the loading doors, where Lyle

Johns and the Genoese were herding people into the big rubber boats. En route Taufiq walked past Ismet and Hamzah frantically getting into their SCUBA gear, while looking round for him.

It was a turning point in his life, a moment of clear betrayal. He was abandoning not only the sacred cause of Kurdistan, but two boyhood friends. And he was betraying the Sufi code that schooled him to embrace death. Yet once in the Zodiac, his headpiece pulled down to mask his features, Taufiq felt only elation—tempered by the fear of being discovered.

As they raced over the waves and the night erupted around them in flashes and explosions, he glanced back at the ship. Even in destruction it was a magnificent spectacle, hypnotically beautiful. It was aglow from within and blazing at every port. The masts were fiery columns whose capitals flowed upward into vast, billowing whorls that filled the sky.

≡

Raschid's escape was not spontaneous like Taufiq's, but wholly premeditated. The moment Ismet resurrected his fire-and-water plan, Raschid had privately counted himself out. Despite his years on boats in the port of Salonika, he was a poor swimmer, and the cursory SCUBA training the *pesh merga* had undergone with the Trucal-Oman UDTs had done little to alter that. In fact, it only reinforced his preference for staying on *top* of the water, not *under* it.

After emptying a jerrican around the foremast, Raschid had watched with revulsion as the masterpiece of shipbuilding begin to yield its beauty to the consuming flames. The burnished teak fife rail blistered and blackened; its nexus of rigging burned through and parted before his eyes, so that lines and tackle gave way aloft and came tumbling down, forcing Raschid to leap back. More than anything else Ismet had done, including murder, this wanton act of destruction repelled Raschid.

Instead of hurrying below after Ismet to put on diving gear, Raschid headed aft, dodging as a welter of flaming cordage from the maintop hit the deck ahead. Sparks and greasy smoke swirled about him in an oven draft. Tar, boiling in black rivulets along the deck, burned his feet through his rubber soles. Raschid ran faster, feeling like a bug on a skillet.

Behind him a thirty-two pound carronade, left shotted and loaded, exploded as flames struck the primer, its slide recoiling, carriage trucks rumbling over the deck. Praise Allah, it had not been pointed in his direction! It would have been the perfect death for an arsonist—struck down by a cannonball discharged by a fire he himself had set.

Raschid gained the quarterdeck, slung a leg over the railing, and then stopped in dismay. The speedboat was gone! But of course—he was at the port rail, and he'd left the boat by the starboard mizzen chains. As he whirled, a square meter section of deck crumbled before him into charcoal and flames. Raschid leaped over the smoking hole and across the quarterdeck.

Grappling hook and rope were gone, but the boat was where he'd left it that morning. He scrambled down to the chain plate between tongues of flame that lashed out from the gunports, licking the ship's sides. Holding the mizzen shrouds and searing his palms, Raschid steadied, then let go, falling three meters into the stern couch of the little speedboat.

He was stunned, but took no time to assess his injuries. With his knife he sliced the painter. The key was still in the ignition. The throaty engine coughed and burbled to life, as if grateful for a chance to flee.

Raschid throttled forward and was slammed back into the cushions as the four-cylinder Evinrude bit into the sea. The wheel spun and the V-hull began carving an escape trench through the water. He doubled the frigate's counter, then knifed off to the west toward the darkness of Yesilköy.

The outboard's banshee song filled his head, the spray stung his face as the boat began to buck and lift and slap its strakes on the waves. Raschid was suddenly happy. He looked straight ahead, heedless of pursuit or the pain of his burned palms on the wheel. He thought simply: "I'm going to make it!" Soon he would head inshore, tie up, and steal away into the night. Become again the Greek citizen his papers proclaimed him— Raschid Georgiades. His Kurdish misadventures were nearly over.

Then a hundred meters out on the starboard quarter a flaming rooster tail was thrown up by a patrol boat, a wall of spray spectacularly refracting the firelight behind it. A magnesium star flare exploded a hundred meters overhead, ten thousand candlepower flooding the speedboat and the sea around it in blinding white luminescence. Simultaneously came the cry from a loudhailer, ordering him to cut his engines and put his hands in the air. Or be blown out of the water.

Raschid wrenched the wheel to port instead, slewing around, punching the throttle all the way forward. The boat careened, smashed into its new course. What a little Italian hellcat he had in his hands!

Another craft was converging on the port bow. Another star flare blossomed, blinding him, followed by more amplified orders. Raschid ignored them all. Only when a fusillade shattered the Perspex windscreen, ripping into the fiberglass snout, did he know his glorious ride was over. He throttled back, stood up, raised his arms.

It was too late. He was snatched into the air by salvos from fifty-caliber deck guns firing five hundred rounds a minute. As his lifeless body vanished into the wake, the little sportboat went snarling off into the night as if intent on its own escape.

$$\equiv$$

Considering the chaotic conditions and the potential for disaster, the rescue-assault on the *George Washington* came off with admirable efficiency. The illumination from the burning vessel allowed the converging surface craft to quickly surround the Zodiacs. The order went out on the tactical net to fire only if fired upon, and then only with rifles on semi-automatic to prevent spraying hostages. The Jandaras were to escort the boats into Kumkapi and quarantine everyone there to separate any terrorists from the hostage group.

Meanwhile four SEALs were surfacing and a dozen more splashed down from the choppers. They joined forces in the CO_2 inflatables to search for survivors in the water, ready for a rescue operation or a firefight. They were also to look for anyone who might still be aboard the burning ship.

In fact, as the first two SEALs paddled their raft toward the loading doorway, one person *was* still aboard—a Turkish boy named Okyay. He was the half-brother of the youth shot by Ismet in the first moments of the attack. Okyay had hidden during the loading of the Zodiacs, praying for a last chance at revenge and willing to give his life for it. When smoke drove him from refuge, he stumbled upon the body of the "Arab" shot by Taufiq. A little farther on, he saw the AK-47, exactly like the one with which Ismet had cut down his brother.

Its stock was hot to the touch and Okyay felt its unholy power flow into him as he cradled it in his arms. Once before he had handled one of these satanic instruments, shown off to him by a cousin in the gendarmerie. He flicked the fire selector to full-auto and leaped out to the loading area—just in time to see Ismet and Hamzah in SCUBA gear disappear over the side.

Okyay stood there, his vengeance swamped by futility and grief. Why had Allah provided the weapon, and then taken away the target? The youth began to sob, his convulsions lost in the hellish chorus of flames. The bulkheads around him, the deck overhead, all were now engulfed.

Then, through his tears, he saw his prayers answered. Ismet and Hamzah were clambering back aboard in their dripping black dive suits! Allah had delivered his enemies back into his hands! The AK-47 leaped in Okyay's arms, the spent shells ejecting and the steel-core slugs ripping into the black-clad bodies and pinging off their metal air tanks. Okyay savored the agonized screams as one terrorist crumpled to the deck and the other tumbled back into the sea.

He had killed two Turkish SEALs come to rescue him. Before Okyay got close enough to discover his horrible mistake, a third diver, who had witnessed the killing of his comrades, fired a three-shot burst from his H&K submachine gun. All three nine-millimeter rounds struck Okyay in the chest with a terrible force. He died with a final rejoicing thought: He was not only revenged, but martyred. He would awake in Paradise.

Another Turkish casualty resulted when a SEAL, holding too long to the drop bar of a hovering AB-212, landed in the *George Washington*'s flaming mizzen shrouds and suffered second-degree burns before he was able to cut himself free with his commando knife and fall into the water.

The only other hostage death—the fourth of the day—was discovered as the last Zodiac arrived in Kumkapi. The British nurse was found unconscious on the floorboards, her plump face darkly cyanotic in the flashlight beams directed on her by Jandaras. She was lifted onto the dock, given CPR, then evacuated by helicopter to the American Hospital in Nisantasi. All to no avail: she never regained consciousness.

The largest number of fatalities at one blow occurred when a raft of four SEALs was hit by a fragmentation grenade. Three men died in the blast. A fourth survived; his maimed body was found floating in the Marmara and was choppered to the hospital in Nisantasi. The grenade was the one thrown blindly by Hamzah as he and Ismet abandoned the ship.

The final assault toll came to nine dead: six rescuers, two hostages, and one terrorist shot fleeing in a speedboat. Two more commandos were grievously injured.

And Taufiq?

As his Zodiac was convoyed into Kumkapi, the bearded Sufi fingered the cyanide pill in a pouch of his tracksuit. Like all the *pesh merga* he had sworn to swallow the capsule rather than fall into enemy hands and undergo torture and its inevitable consequence, betrayal of his comrades. But Taufiq was already far beyond betrayal this night. And, at least to his fevered mind, the possibility of escape still flickered.

That faint hope was extinguished moments from landing. Beside him a crew-cut French girl saw his scarab ring flash in the firelight. As the company's continuity person, trained to record the most minute details of filming, she remembered seeing it that afternoon, gleaming on a finger wrapped around the trigger guard of an assault rifle. She cried out in horror.

Several men shouted, and a long arm flung back the burnoose. Taufiq scrambled over the side, but was dragged back. Hands tore at his clothes, then his flesh. When a patrol boat came alongside he was screaming like a butchered pig, and the Turkish commandos had to move quickly to save his life.

Moments later he was spread-eagled face-down on the dock while hostages screamed obscenities at him. He was body-searched, his wrists shackled behind him, a gun barrel thrust against his neck. They were shouting questions at him in Turkish, then Arabic. Taufiq, already bruised and bloodied by the hostages, pleaded ignorance and was kicked in the ass and legs.

He was yanked to his feet and rushed through a gauntlet of bright lights and shouting men and into the back of a police van. The cold steel floor smelled of vomit and disinfectant. Then he was dragged onto a bench and propped between two guards with guns digging at his ribs. The door slammed and the van jerked into motion, siren keening. Taufiq lurched sideways into a guard, who shoved him back and promised to shoot him in the balls if it happened again.

Taufiq's mystic abilities had abandoned him. He

tried and failed to extricate his consciousness from his doomed body. Fear and panic gave way to genuine terror. Even had his hands been free, the pants leg and pouch that held his cyanide capsule were gone, torn off in the raft. If only he had followed Ismet, even into a watery grave! Not been a traitor, and a coward.

What methods would the Turks use to torture him, he wondered? As his mind conjured vivid horrors, he felt his bowels loosen with fear.

≡

Five meters below the fiery surface Ismet followed his flashlight beam through the murk, keeping it trained on the slow, undulant scissoring of Hamzah's fins. For long minutes he had seen nothing else, and was thankful for it.

The worst moments had come right at the start when they had glimpsed several divers around them. Had they been challenged, Ismet had no illusions that he and Hamzah could have held their own against combat-trained Turkish SEALs. But the size and confusion of the operation had worked in their favor. The divers must have assumed them to be part of the waterborne assault.

He checked his compass bearing. They were still headed eastward, cutting across the three-knot Bosphorus current. They moved leisurely, tethered by a three-meter buddy line. Ismet's idea was to surface near the ferry landing in Kadiköy or, depending on the drift, upstream in Haydarpasa. It was a considerable distance—a night SCUBA swim on compass course of more than fifteen hundred meters; one of the qualifications, Ismet recalled, for the Trucal-Oman UDTs.

After the nerve-wracking tension of the past twenty-four hours, Ismet welcomed the enveloping quiet, the uterine sense of safety. But he was also sensible of his deep exhaustion and the labor for every breath as he fought the constriction of the heavy backpack harness, air tanks, and leadweighted belt.

He checked his watch, then his pressure gauge. They'd been in the water for thirty minutes and still had half their air. That was just about right, Ismet figured. At five meters depth, a full tank should easily last an hour, more than enough time for them to reach the Asian shore. It wouldn't hurt to have a look.

He gave three pulls on the buddy line—"going up"—and Hamzah echoed the signal. Ismet ascended carefully, scanning the aqueous ceiling for the darker shape of a passing ship. It wouldn't do to get carved up in prop-wash. As his mask barely broke the surface, he filled his buoyancy vest and switched from regulator to snorkel.

The air was thick with the smell of ashes. Perhaps two kilometers away the frigate was etched in red-orange against the Stamboul skyline, its fiery calligraphy snaking across the dark water. The next instant a tongue of flame shot high into the sky, followed by a muffled thunderclap. One of the ship's big diesel fuel tanks exploding, Ismet realized. As he trod water, braced for another *ka-boom,* an ear-splitting whistle caused him to spin round. Fifty meters off a searchlight stabbed the night. A Turkish patrol boat? Ismet made ready to dive, and then saw the gold-and-white-striped funnel. It was one of the Bosphorus ferryboats, or *vapurs,* packed to the rails with passengers ogling the spectacular pyre across the waterway. Hamzah surfaced silently beside him.

The current had washed them farther south than he'd figured, well past Kadiköy. In fact, they had drifted all the way down to the mouth of Calamis Bay by the Moda Yacht Club. The *vapur* must have just pulled out from its dock.

There was no need to dive again. A few minutes of dog paddling with the current brought them to an old wooden dock midway between Moda and Fenerbahçe. They slid in under the pilings and hauled themselves out of the oily water onto some crosspieces. Quickly they divested themselves of diving gear, stripped off their sodden tracksuits, wedging everything under the pilings. Then they opened their dive pouches and pulled on dry jeans, T-shirts, and sneakers and climbed up onto the timbered dock.

Across the Marmara the night sky was still livid from the smoldering ship, the air still tinged with smoke and ash.

Five minutes later, they had flagged down a *dolmus,* a big, chrome-laden Pontiac Star-Chief from the fifties. They squeezed into the crowded back seat, their still sweating dive pouches at their feet. An adenoidal dash speaker was blasting Albanian folk songs from Radio Tirana. Ismet leaned forward and, with a few thousand Turkish *liras,* persuaded the driver to take them out of his route into the neighborhood of their *geçekondu* in Usküdar.

"You are in a hurry?" the driver shouted over the radio.

"Plenty," Ismet yelled back. "A most beautiful lady is waiting for me."

14

DAWN CAME AS A DISTANT GOLDEN FIRE OVER SCUTARI, THE ancient Chrysopolis. The light shot fanlike from beneath a layer of altocumulus, paling the gray cloud ceiling into a soft white, then gilding its edges and piercing it with shafts of seraphic blue.

Paul Cyrus stood by the coastal road east of Kumkapi, hands jammed in his windbreaker, ignoring the technicolor effects overhead. His attention was fixed nearer to hand.

Fifty meters away the burnt-out hulk of the *George Washington* had washed up against the sea wall. The police had cordoned it off, but a crowd of curiosity seekers and reporters pressed against the barricades. Video crews worked the fringes, their trucks strung out along the road. Shoreline traffic along Kennedy Caddesi was at a crawl as motorists ogled the wreckage and the surrounding mob.

Under the lightening sky, the ghastly details of the thing on the rocks stood out starkly. Yesterday Paul had thought the ship one of the most beautiful objects he had ever seen; she was now a charred skeleton. Above the hull only the jagged, blackened stump of the mizzenmast remained, pointing at the sky. Most of the oaken planking was gone, revealing a carbonized metal carcass of curving steel ribs and deck beams which framed a yawning pit washed by Marmara wavelets.

Down among these entrails an autopsy was in progress. Salvage experts and investigators from both Turkish intelligence and a British firm of marine insurance underwriters sloshed through the muck with flashlights and cameras, sifting through heaps of sodden, blackened debris and ash. What in God's name did they hope to find, Paul wondered?

The death toll for the "rescue" now stood at seven—two hostages and six commandos. Two more of Ozsahin's men were in critical condition.

One terrorist had been killed fleeing in a speedboat and another was in custody, but the other two Kurds had escaped.

Not as grim as it might have been, perhaps. But for Paul Cyrus, looking at the charred wreckage this morning—a morning without breakfast after a night without sleep—the sense of futility was pretty near complete.

Darryl Ann was right, he thought. He should have kept the hell out of it. The Turks could hardly have done worse without him. He didn't figure to be much in demand as a negotiator in any future terrorist-hostage crises on the basis of this first outing. Even before yesterday he'd been pretty well burnt out as a "think-tank commando." The crisis had reinforced what he'd already decided: what was needed were hands-on people, not post-graduate theorists like himself.

Paul's career had petered out. Or Peter-Principled out, he thought with a sour smile. He had been propelled by bizarre circumstance, for a few critical hours, into a chair he had no damned business occupying. Maybe nobody was qualified to negotiate with madmen for human lives, but certainly some more than he. Anyway, the end was ashes.

Late last night at the Consulate he had approached Josh Nevins, the top CIA man at the U.S. Embassy who had just flown in from Ankara. Paul had volunteered his further services for the duration, mentioning his Kurdish language skills. Josh had been in his shirtsleeves, tie loosened, trying unsuccessfully to look as battle-fatigued as everybody else. He'd been talking to Bertie Giddings, who had his little flock of bright-eyed, youthful Foreign Office types hovering about.

Josh had patted Paul on the back, told him to go home and forget all about the Kurds and the crazy actress. Paul noticed both men had carefully waited until he was out of earshot before continuing their discussion on Amanda Morgan.

Ozsahin had sent the same signal with his effete handshake, hearty thank-you-we'll-take-it-from-here, and a hollow promise to keep Paul briefed through the Consulate.

Most of Paul's belongings had already been crated and shipped stateside. As he stood now on the sea wall, he was down to a bulky seabag at his feet. He sat down on it, his attention drawn to a pretty sloop tacking in for a closer look at the wreckage. All packed, nowhere to go. *What do I do now, Coach?*

He fished in his windbreaker, took out the cablegram that had arrived for him this morning at the consulate, and read it for perhaps the dozenth time:

PAUL DARLING, FORGIVE ME. I'VE BEEN IN HELL SINCE I LET YOU GET AWAY. I WAS WRONG WRONG WRONG TO STOP YOU FROM YOUR DUTY. AND I'M PAYING FOR IT. MY COZY CABIN IS SO EMPTY WITHOUT YOU. WHEN YOUR CRISIS IS OVER, IF YOU STILL WANT ME, COME TO ME PAUL. IN LESBOS, OR CHIOS, OR SAMOS . . . OR WHEREVER. I'LL BE WAITING. YOUR BIG BAD SAD BLONDE, D.A.

All about *her, her* pain, *her* desperate need. Nothing had changed. Except that, at this particular moment, Paul's resistance to her was minimal. Maybe he should fly to Lesbos, patch things up between them. Darryl had obviously already written and rehearsed the script. She'd probably even supply his side of the dialogue. He'd just nod once in a while and mumble something sincere; she'd be all tears and conciliation and unbridled eroticism. But the truth would be—and they'd both know it— she'd have won.

He folded the message carefully and put it away, feeling like an alcoholic soberly contemplating his next bender. But why the hell not? He had no better plans for the rest of his life, did he?

Only one thing, perhaps, something way out of his league: find Amanda Morgan. But the polite dismissals had been pretty damned demoralizing.

Still, he couldn't help thinking about the British actress. Where was she this morning? In danger or duress, trussed up or being treated like royalty? The Little Fox might be in for a surprise, Paul conjectured, and allowed himself a brief smile.

Amanda's disappearance had led off the morning BBC radio report, taking precedence over the burning of the ship and the rescue of hostages—not to mention an earthquake in Indonesia and an oil platform fire in the North Sea. The news reader even lent his cultivated tones to some highly gratuitous speculation, making reference to the eighteen-month detention of Patty Hearst by the Symbionese Liberation Army in the early seventies. It was Beauty and the Beast all over again, Paul thought, Fay Wray in the clutches of King Kong.

Yet despite his professional cynicism, Paul was not immune. He found himself worrying about Amanda's safety, recalling with unvarnished admiration the stormy interview in which she had defied them all, insulted his manhood, and then vanished. Every bit as stubborn as Darryl Ann, he thought, except the two women's motives were light years apart—will as opposed to whim. Amanda was totally wrong-headed—Paul was still convinced of that—but it was now clear the actress believed in the things she so passionately espoused, and had the uncommon courage to act on them. Of course, the same might be said of Ismet or any other true believer with a righteous cause. But Amanda Morgan had endangered no one but herself.

It was all pretty admirable, Paul decided. What did *he* believe in? Shallow pragmatism, elastic ethics? Helping old ladies across streets, if it didn't take him too far out of his way? Did he really believe in anything enough to follow through to the limit, run the risks *she* had?

No. He only dreamed improbable deeds.

Crashing into the terrorist hideout like James Bond, hosing down the bad guys with an Uzi, carrying Amanda off over his shoulder. "Hi, remember me?" Comic-book stuff.

He heard footsteps and glanced up. A man was walking toward him, away from the crowd at the wreck. A blocky man in a burgundy-and-white warm-up suit, long-armed, long-waisted, legs slightly bowed. There was something familiar about the broad flat skull.

A few paces nearer the man called out: "Good morning. Paul Cyrus, is it not?" The broad face creased into a smile. There was a thickening of Slavic accent.

Paul hesitated. "Ilyinsky? I can't remember the rest."

"Feliks Demianovich."

"Good morning." Paul shook the proffered hand and recalled what he knew of the man, pieced together from cocktail party gossip and consular briefings. Ilyinsky, nominally a military attaché at the Soviet consulate, was actually a major in the KGB. Josh Nevins had called him a man with a future.

"Damn awful sight." Ilyinsky waved an arm toward the wreckage. His eyes were ice-blue. "Especially for you, I would think. You are a sailor, isn't it true?"

"Sailing's a hobby of mine."

"I remember things, you see!" Ilyinsky shook his head sadly. "Damn awful. I saw her yesterday morning for first time, sailing out there by my summer house on Büyükada. She made me think of a beautiful lady. I speak a metaphor, you understand?"

"I'm familiar with it."

"Also she made me think of a little poem by Lermontov. Then I made love—*fortissimo!* But in my mind

I am seeing only this ship. Now, I cannot look. It is a piece of obscenity."

Paul agreed. What the hell did the man want? Surely he hadn't walked over to share this little anecdote. Did the Russian know of Paul's role in the hostage negotiations? Might he have even followed him here? If so, why? Then Paul realized he didn't care why. It was over. "I guess there's no point hanging around. Feliks, if you'll excuse me—"

"Paul, wait please. I wish to speak a little more."

"Well, the truth is, Feliks, I'm just starting my vacation, and I've got a plane to catch."

"A moment only."

"Sure." Paul let his bag drop. "But why me? My name was last on the diplomatic list, last time I looked."

"You are being modest. Your work has been known to us from the day you arrived at the Consulate. And you did very well yesterday, my friend. Do not blame yourself for what happened."

Paul waited for the gambit to develop, but the Russian only smiled. Paul broke the silence: "Look, thanks, but I'm not looking for sympathy. I did my best, and things got out of control, as they usually do. Now I'm off the case, on holiday. That's that."

"On holiday? Perhaps *hors de combat* is a better phrase. Services no longer required. Not appreciated."

"What the hell are you talking about?"

"You do not know? I am under the distinct impression that you made several offers last evening to help find a certain famous lady. It is not so?"

"For Christ's sake!"

"It is a small place, Istanbul, and secrets, like the day's catch from the Marmara, do not last very long here.

It is hardly surprising that I should hear of it. To me it is only surprising that you were rejected."

"Wait a minute, Feliks. Let's stop playing games here. Just tell me where the hell you're going with all of this."

"I am saying that the authorities were unwise to refuse your aid. I don't think they will find her, you know."

"I suppose *you* know where she is?"

"Unfortunately about *this* group of Kurds—this Little Fox and his cohort—no one seems to know very much. But we know perhaps a little more than everyone else."

"I wouldn't underrate Colonel Ozsahin."

"A strong man, but in this case, believe me, the colonel is helpless. He will make a big show, arrest Kurdish street porters, close down pamphlet-makers. But he will find nothing."

The sun was well over the horizon now, and directly behind Feliks, so that Paul had to squint against the light. "Suppose you're right. What's your idea?"

"We have certain contacts with Kurdish elements in our own country, and throughout the Near East. This Little Fox is almost a legend with them, it seems, and also a mystery. And we have uncovered a few facts here in Istanbul. It is at this point that your knowledge of Kurdish could be useful, you see, in pursuing inquiries. Excuse me, did you come by taxi?"

"Yes, why?"

"I have a car and driver just over there. Rifat is an excellent man, a very devil in traffic. Perhaps if you would accompany me to a certain café—you like Greek food?—we could discuss our business further."

"You're forgetting about my plane, Feliks. Anyway,

it's not really your problem, is it—a British film star, I mean?"

"Ah, but a most remarkable lady."

"Agreed. So?"

"Let us just say that my superiors are desirous of seeing her returned unharmed."

"On humanitarian grounds, or because she's a Marxist?"

"Or perhaps because the General Secretary admires her films? No, it is none of these. Miss Morgan is a person whom others follow, a person of great influence. Nothing more."

"A nice speech."

"But you do not believe it?"

"Not the part about your needing my linguistic abilities. That fellow Bessaraboff must speak about ten languages."

"Kurdish is not one of them."

"Then find somebody else. There are plenty of interpreters around."

"All right, now I will explain it, so even you will finally understand. We want this lady, this famous lady, returned very fast, with every hair on her head. But we wish to keep a big distance from all the publicity that will come from her rescue, publicity which could injure Miss Morgan's officially nonaligned persona." Ilyinsky paused, his smile impish. "Now, you see how you would be useful in our endeavor?"

"I'm not sure. You want me to help you track her down, then you disappear and let *me* take all the credit?"

"Precisely."

"It's lunatic, Feliks. Besides, it wouldn't work. Say we succeeded, which I absolutely doubt. Amanda would damn well know who rescued her, and you can bet she'd tell the world about it. She's not shy, and I can tell you she can't be controlled."

"But we could arrange matters so even *she* thinks you are her rescuer. Ha! You begin to like my plan a little, I can see."

Paul shook his head. But it was hard not to be tempted by something so totally in line with his recent fantasies, especially coming on the heels of rejection by three governments. And it was halfway plausible. That was not to say Paul believed one damned word of it. The motives of a guy like Ilyinsky and his Kremlin spymasters were beyond fathoming. In any case, it was out of the question. Paul had only heard the Russian out to satisfy his curiosity. No matter the pretext, knowingly working with the KGB was not a recommended career move for a U.S. diplomat.

Besides, Paul wasn't in the market for any job at the moment. If he was going to succumb to temptation, it would be D.A.'s, not the KGB's.

He hefted his seabag. "Thanks for the offer, Feliks. It's one of the most imaginative sales pitches I've ever heard. And it's nice to feel wanted for a change. But like I said, I've got a plane to catch." Two steps beyond the Russian major, Paul turned and added, "Good hunting."

15

THE OLD VOLVO PANEL TRUCK WENT RATTLING THROUGH the night, across the Turkish peninsula toward the Mediterranean. But in the back, wrapped in a blanket with her legs curled beneath her in wet straw, Amanda Morgan had no idea where she was being taken—and was almost too weary to care. The most stressful day of her life was drawing into its twentieth hour, with no end in sight.

What energy she had left was spent bracing herself against the incessant jolting, for the postwar vehicle had long outlived its suspension. Worse, its interior reeked of fish, even after the iced smelt they had started out with had been unloaded an hour outside of Istanbul.

There were other smells: sour perspiration from five bodies in the confined space; gun oil and cleaning solvent, as Ismet, beside Amanda in the darkness, was stripping, cleaning, and lubricating his assault rifle. Between the fetid air and constant jostling, it was to Amanda's credit she kept her stomach. What pushed her on was the thought that as long as the others could take it, so could she.

Across the narrow truck bed a dark lump emitted a snore—Fahri Bayram, lying on his side in the straw, his face tucked inside his leather coat. She envied him his sleep, for, despite exhaustion, it would not come to her. Next to him, revealed as oncoming headlamps caught the wet sheen of her eyes, was his wife, Guldasa, cross-legged and, like Amanda, wide awake.

Forward in the cab Amanda could see Hamzah's round head silhouetted behind the wheel, hear the tinny pulse of his transistor radio hung from the rear-view mirror. It was tuned to the AM Arabic broadcast of Radio Monte Carlo—a constant barrage of pop rock and news flashes covering the Eastern Med from powerful transmitters in Cyprus.

From time to time Hamzah would turn and cheerfully update his cousin in Kurdish: "We have disappeared." Or: "All of Istanbul has been sealed off! No one can get out!"

"What will the Little Fox do now?" Ismet would chuckle, translating the news for Amanda's benefit. "Those clever Turks have caught him in their nets at last!"

Once Hamzah reported: "The whole world is looking for her, and for us. People have seen her everywhere—still in Istanbul, on a Russian ship in Odessa, even in Beirut!"

"Find what the BBC says," Ismet ordered.

"Up the bloody Brits!" Hamzah replied in English.

"My cousin only knows a few phrases in your language," Ismet explained to Amanda, "and this is one of his favorites."

"I've said it myself, more than once." In actuality, Amanda was scarcely registering the ambient sounds—the Volvo's drone, the static crackle of Hamzah's radio, the snickety-click of Ismet's AK-47 being reassembled. Her mind was adrift, spinning back over the bizarre circumstances that had placed her in the back of this truck, among these unlikeliest of traveling companions.

When she had met Ismet earlier that night in the hovel in Usküdar, she'd been surprised both by his smallness—he was at least an inch shorter than she—and his intensity. Amanda, accustomed to being the focus of attention wherever she was, sensed the instant shift in polarity as the Little Fox, in gray pullover and faded jeans, swept into the room with a swagger that should have been comical, yet somehow was not. He carried it off with his remarkable, well-sculpted head, aristocratic bearing and judicial manner. But behind long lashes his dark, feral eyes conveyed other messages—lurking danger and repressed sensuality. His cheeks and strong jaw were darkly shadowed and scratched in several places after a hasty shaving to remove his mustache.

Not Amanda's type at all, thank God! But many women would disagree, she thought, and gladly overlook his diminutive size. Under other circumstances, she could even visualize this charismatic fellow up on the cinema screen. Of course he would need to be surrounded by other small actors, as was commonly done for shorter leading men—Alan Ladd, say, or Sly Stallone.

And the Kurdish chieftain's voice was quite masterful, as he had announced the crisis was over, all hostages freed. She, too, would be free, he promised, and very soon if she chose. But first Ismet wanted to take her with him, to show her something.

Amanda drew herself up and replied: "I'll go with you when I am satisfied you've kept your side of the bargain. But I must have proof."

The little Kurd was obviously stunned at being challenged by a woman, and then became angry. "I have told you. That is your proof. I am a man of honor. In any case, you must do as I say."

"That is a different thing, is it not? I am a captive, then. And you are no man of honor, but a kidnapper. Also a killer, if I am to believe what I was told by the chief of Turkish security."

"You were told lies. I am a warrior—this is what means *pesh merga:* 'those who face death.' We have faced death many times, and yes, we have killed. But," and he spat on the floor, "we are not murderers!"

"Then prove it. Prove to me that the hostages are safe—and I'll go with you willingly. Otherwise I refuse."

She glared back at him. When the fire came over her, she could face down all comers—street bullies, neo-Nazi hecklers, belligerent drunks, batteries of attorneys, film producers, even a band of Hell's Angels once on a location shoot in Nevada. Never before, however, had she confronted a terrorist.

Without turning, Ismet called out in English: "Hamzah. Your radio. Give it her."

She was handed a transistor by a round-faced

cherub in a Popeye T-shirt with a pistol sticking out of his waistband. The radio's plastic case resonated noisily in her hand, evidently trying to convey some sound beyond its feeble capacity.

"What is this?" she asked.

"Stones," Hamzah grinned. "Rock and roll."

Ismet snatched it from her and turned down the volume. "I will find a Turkish station for you. There will be news very soon in English. Perhaps you will believe filthy Turks."

He turned the dial till he found a shrill, singsong voice stringing out a plaintive Middle Eastern melody. He handed the radio back, but the wailing went on. Ismet gestured for her to wait.

Finally a man's voice came on, speaking what Amanda first took for Turkish, then realized was oddly inflected English. He was reading a bulletin about the hostage crisis and the night rescue operation. Four members of the film crew had perished, two "executed ruthlessly" by terrorists claiming to represent the Peoples Democratic Army of Kurdistan. The other hostage deaths were still under investigation.

But the broadcaster confirmed that the remainder of the film crew was safe, as Ismet had said. Amanda breathed a silent prayer of thanks. Whatever else happened now, she felt she'd made a difference, achieved something worthwhile.

The announcer went on. One terrorist had been killed and another captured, while two were missing, although their capture was imminent.

At this Ismet snorted, almost causing Amanda to miss her own name. The "film star," according to the announcer, had "foolishly sought to involve herself in the crisis" and been "lured into capture by these insidious criminals." A ransom demand was expected at any moment—

Ismet snatched the radio back, switched it off, tossed it to Hamzah. "Now you see? Even Turks say hostages are free, okay?"

"Yes, I'm very grateful for that. Thank you for letting them go. But why did four innocent people have to die?"

"People die because it is war! As people are dying every day in my villages, from poison gas from Iraqis or from Turkish bombs. These are innocent people too. And we are soldiers, fighting for our country, only our country is taken from us, so we fight here, in enemy country, and we cannot always know who are innocent and who are not."

"I know about the Iraqi genocide. I've condemned it. And I'm familiar with all the justifications for terrorism."

"So you understand?"

"No, I don't." The truth was, now that the hostages were free, she wanted to go back to her hotel and take a nice hot bath, mission accomplished. She didn't want to be standing in this hovel among wild-eyed Kurds, being bombarded by revolutionary rhetoric she could quote herself chapter and verse. And she damn sure didn't look forward to going off with them, dodging bullets and hiding out in squalor, no matter what she'd said on Turkish television.

But she'd given her word. Besides, she knew her stubborn streak would force her to finish whatever she'd started.

=

Amanda found sleep at last, but was awakened a few hours later for what Guldasa explained was a "comfort stop." Amanda stumbled out into the night after the others, locating a suitable shrub to squat behind. Wouldn't this make a nifty news item, she thought, as a chill wind whipped the black muslin robe above her hips. Amanda Morgan, freezing her ass off somewhere in the Anatolian hinterland, doing her business while trying to count all the stars in the Milky Way. She really should be thinking something more profound, but she was too bloody tired. And cold. Which wasn't surprising; under the muslin robe, she had on only the buckskin minidress—hardly an all-purpose travel garment.

She was grateful to crawl back into the Volvo and cocoon herself in her blanket. Her next awareness was of shivering in pre-dawn chill, sore and stiff from the unyielding floor.

Within the hour a faint gray light seeped into the squalid interior, revealing her companions. Ismet slept on, but Fahri was stirring in the soggy straw. Guldasa still sat cross-legged, her gaze unreadable.

And with the light came something else—an unmistakable salt tang. Amanda dared to lift her head and saw a faint silver-blue streak on the horizon off to their right.

She did not know what ocean it was, but her heart lifted at the sight, as it had during her childhood in Wales whenever she spied Carmarthen Bay. For an instant she was in pigtails again, with Small Tom beside her in the back of her parents' old Morris, off to the seaside. Odd, she thought. Now, as then, she was heading into adventures over which she had no control.

Out of the corner of her eye she saw Guldasa shaking Ismet's shoulder, whispering to him urgently. The

Little Fox sat up, fastened a fierce look upon Amanda. "You must *not* be seen, Amanda!" his voice rumbled. "You make big crazy danger for us!" He spoke in Kurdish to Guldasa, and she produced a black scarf from her bag, looking pointedly at the actress.

Amanda glared back. "I'm warning you, Guldasa. You bloody better not try it."

"It is for your well-beingness," Ismet said, as though placating a child. "So no one can ask you where you go with *pesh merga*. Please. It is only for a short time."

"How long is 'a short time'?"

"A few hours, perhaps less."

"Give it to me then. I'll tie it myself." She secured the scarf around her head, pulling it down over her eyes. Her last sight was of Guldasa's tight smile of satisfaction. *Happy, are we, you cow?*

At least she'd had one good glimpse of the sea.

The morning was full upon them before they finally halted at the end of an unpaved road beside the water. Amanda knew it was the seaside, because she could hear it now as well—the slosh of surf, the cry of gulls. She was helped out and felt the sun, glorious on her back and shoulders, and rejoiced to stretch her limbs. The thought had occurred more than once during the long night that she was a little old for this sort of thing. She drank in the fresh sea breeze, with its traces of honeysuckle and pines.

Ismet guided her quickly along a rocky path. "We must go very fast. We get into a little boat now, and you must stay down." Behind her she heard the old Volvo grind away in low gear.

Moments later she was handed down from a stone jetty into a wooden boat, only slightly more stable than a dinghy, and seated on the floorboards where sea water sloshed to and fro, soaking her clothes, while the others scrambled for places around her. She imagined a map of Turkey, surrounding it with bodies of water. They could be most anywhere. On a bay of the Marmara or the Black Sea, even the Mediterranean.

They cast off and moved out through light swells that slapped the wooden hull, pushed along by a noisy little motor. She was handed goat cheese, black olives, and bread—remnants of the food they'd passed around during the night.

Was she being taken to an island or a ship? She did not inquire. She would know soon enough, Ismet had promised. In the several hours of being blindfolded, she had lapsed into a decidedly uncharacteristic docility. *Watch yourself, Mandy, old girl,* she thought. *Remember—you're a voluntary observer here.*

=====

In the sternsheets of the weatherbeaten *caique,* Ismet took the tiller, while the boat's owner, a fisherman called Ugur, was vanishing in the Volvo behind a bend in the Lycian coastal road on his way to Antalya. Before them the Mediterranean danced in the sunlight. Quickly they opened up the little bay of Kas, off the starboard beam, its breakwater marina asparkle with a flotilla of pleasure craft moored stern-to—Club Med charters, private yachts, sleek runabouts. Amanda's world, Ismet thought. But not this morning.

Less than three kilometers ahead through the morning haze lay their destination, the tiny island the Turks called Meis, and the Greeks Megisti or Kastellorizo. But their journey would be longer, for they were steering for the far end of the island, away from the harbor town and Greek immigration.

Ismet had hoped to make the unauthorized crossing before dawn, but they'd started too late from Istanbul. Still, they had made decent time, using secondary roads whenever possible and covering nearly nine hundred kilometers in twelve hours of darkness. By now the Turks would be tearing apart Istanbul's Kurdish community, seeking the fox's lair. But they would not find it, and nothing could lead them hither—except, perhaps, old Salah, the great uncle of Hamzah and Guldasa, who had let them use the *geçekondu* in Usküdar. And this Salah had recently suffered a stroke that rendered his left side useless, his memory inaccessible, his speech slurred. Otherwise they would not have left the old man behind, to die as he wished among his dog and pigs and chickens.

While Ismet meditated thus, something brushed his bare arm—the soft hair of the Western woman seated below him, fluttering in the breeze under the black blindfold. Ismet looked down upon the crown of Amanda's head, black hair touched with burnished highlights in the sun, scalp exuding an earthy pungency. He was reminded sharply of Adila, his soul's other half, and experienced a sudden pang that left him weak with longing.

Gently he touched Amanda's shoulder.

Her head did not turn. "Yes?"

"We are going to an island, Amanda. We will be safe there. But I must tell you about a man on this island. We call him Angleesh. He is what you call 'merc.' You know this word?"

"A mercenary?"

"Yes. Only this big Angleesh is one of us now. He

has saved our lives in Iraq, years ago, during the siege of Basra. He has sworn the *pesh merga* blood oath and joined the brotherhood of Al-Islam."

Guldasa made a contemptuous sound.

"Why are you telling me this?" Amanda asked. "Is the man dangerous or something?"

"Is no question about your safety. I'm saying only sometimes this man is acting crazy."

"An Englishman? What's his name?"

"John Courage."

The odd name brought a touch of fear, yet Amanda could not remember where or how she knew it.

16

JOHN COURAGE WAS A BIG MAN, A GIANT BY MOST ORIENtal standards—six-foot-four and nearly sixteen stone—with huge, ursine forearms and wrists. His matted hair and beard were Viking red, framing the scarified face of a pugilist, which he had in fact been while serving in the British Army. One way or another he'd been fighting and soldiering for as long as he could remember, clear back to his rough-and-tumble boyhood on the Deptford waterfront in east London.

But to really feel good, John Courage needed a war, much as Sherlock Holmes needed an "interesting" case. Without the trip-hammer stimulus of battle, the brute nervous system of the "Big Angleesh" raged within him like a caged predator, driving him to the nearest, strongest anodyne, as Holmes had sought the needle.

Although Courage would ingest or inject whatever was at hand, he preferred hashish, Middle Eastern or North African, crumbled and smoked in the traditional Oriental *narghile*. A sufficiency would send him reeling, and conjure up the most sanguine battle scenes. In these narcotic reveries, he might go charging through carnage on a huge warhorse, bellowing at the top of his lungs, swinging a scimitar or claymore, cleaving casks and breastplates to left and right—till he toppled into unconsciousness.

But the blasted supply of Turkish cakes had run out two days ago. He had not allowed for a fivefold increase in usage caused by enforced idleness. Bloody hell! On an island, without!

For the past two days he'd had only a dwindling case of Greek brandy. Courage had been swilling the sweet, gooey stuff most of the night, and here he was, well into the morning, still on his feet, lumbering to and fro in the tiny camp, cursing the black fate that had hounded him all his forty-some years. He had achieved a kind of lingering stupor, but fallen well short of oblivion. If only the Little Fox would show up with some high-quality *cannabis* among his booty.

At first light, Courage had stumbled along the rocky mule path that traced Kastellorizo's southern spine, squinting through field glasses across the island and the narrow channel beyond to the Turkish mainland. He'd seen a few boats, all right—a motor launch, probably a day-tripper out of Kas, and Greek fishermen from Kastellorizo harbor. But nowhere on the shimmering azure field of vision could he pick out the little apple-green *caique* loaned them by old Ugur. Where the hell was Ismet?

Brandy-soaked or not, Courage had remembered to tune in the short-wave radio during the night. He knew Ismet and at least one other had gotten clear of the burning ship, so there was nothing for it now but to wait. Courage stumbled back to his tent, traded the field glasses for another bottle of resinous brandy and began belching out choruses of "I can't get no . . . sa-tis-faction" between long swallows, seeking unconsciousness at its bottom.

"Better up here anyway," Courage decided. If he was down on the jetty when they came in, Ismet would be pissed. Keep a low profile, that's what the little Kurd had said. Stay in camp. Don't go anywhere—except bloody bonkers.

"Izzy don't have to trust me," Courage addressed the dark amber bottle. "What did I ever do for him anyway, but save his hide now and then?" Not to mention the fact that he, not Ismet, had masterminded the attack on the ship, a good bit of it anyway. And who had told Ismet all about Amanda-bloody-Morgan and her bleeding-heart sympathies, and how if they really wanted a lorryload of publicity for Kurdistan, she'd be just the ticket? Plus her straight market value, celebrity flesh on the hoof. Ransom Amanda and you could buy yourself a year's supply of SMGs and SA-7s and RPGs and other little necessities for carrying on your armed struggle. From the radio reports, it wasn't clear if they'd snatched the actress. But at the moment, Courage was more concerned about Ismet bringing him a resupply of hash.

≡

At the first glimpse of the pastel-colored houses tiered around Kastellorizo's horseshoe harbor, Ismet steered the *caique* to starboard, rounding the craggy headland of Agios Stefanos. For the next hour, the ancient two-cylinder engine pushed them slowly along the base of the island's steep, western wall toward the deserted southwestern tip.

Guldasa, seeing her first Greek isle of any size, was fascinated by the vibrant, barren beauty. Scattered about the island, according to her guidebook, were the ruins of Minoan and Mycenean graves, Dorian inscriptions, prehistoric stone axes. But mostly it was nine square kilometers of sunblasted rock, all but depopulated due to its remoteness and lack of commerce, and sparsely vegetated due to infertile earth. Only the primal elements reigned supreme here—earth, air, fire, and water.

In the steep walls that slowly slid by, Guldasa saw red-veined traces of the ferrous rock used by the Knights of Saint John to build the fortress that had long ago given the island its variously translated name—Kastellorizo, Castelrosso, or Red Castle. The rust-colored rock rose out of a sea that shone sapphire in the sunlight but in the deep cliff shadows turned a dark indigo.

Fahri seemed equally affected by the scenery, gripping his wife's hand, perhaps in mingled anticipation and apprehension of this new chapter in their lives. Hamzah and Ismet, meanwhile, who had both been here many times, scanned the cliffs and surrounding water, alert to danger, careless of beauty.

About a half-kilometer from Pouliou Folia, the island's southwestern tip, Ismet pointed the *caique*'s blunt bows into a tiny cove—a mere scallop out of a rock bulge. At the base of a winding path in the cliff face were the rotting remnants of a wooden pier. Ismet nudged against this, Hamzah made them fast, and the boat was unloaded for the slow trek to the clifftop. Ismet, Ham-

zah, and Fahri went ahead up the rocky switchbacks with
the bulk of the weapons and supplies, while Guldasa
guided the blindfolded actress.

Amanda trod carefully on the steep, stone-flagged
path, grateful as much for Guldasa's borrowed Reeboks
as the Kurdish woman's arm. As they climbed, the tem-
perature grew hotter and the sound of surf faded. Now
Amanda heard the buzzing of insects and once, high
overhead, a jet ripping the stratosphere.

Several times she paused to catch her breath, but
finally, to her considerable relief, felt herself descending,
first through dappled shade, then into the coolness of
what felt like a tunnel. A moment later Guldasa helped
her onto a camp stool and removed the blindfold.

They were in a tent camp, pitched in an oblong excavation, perhaps twenty paces long and ten across. This
pit was further gouged by two trenches, one of them
man-deep with a rusted traveling crane above it. Mounds
of debris lay scattered about, and along one wall of rub-
ble were three blue sleeping tents. Above the excavation
she could see the tops of some wind-twisted trees, probably olives. Outside one tent Ismet was stacking gear,
while Fahri and Guldasa inspected a second tent. On a
deal table nearby Hamzah was fiddling with a short-
wave radio.

"Is this Kurdistan, then?" Amanda asked blithely.

It took Ismet a moment to look up and catch the
joke. "Ah, perhaps yes, Amanda! Many times we live like
this in my country—in caves, in mountains, hiding from
Turks, Persians, always fighting. So yes, let us say, here
is Kurdistan."

What it was, obviously, was an old archeologist's
dig. Whoever had worked it had run out of either signifi-

cant finds or funds, or both, Amanda theorized, and somehow these *pesh merga* had inherited it, like a hermit crab in an abandoned shell.

Abruptly the flap on the third tent was pushed open and a red-bearded giant of a man emerged. His thermal undershirt was soiled, his khaki pants filthy. He scuffed through the dust toward them in thick leather sandals. To her surprise, Amanda knew who he was, and now connected the name—John Courage.

She had seen him only once, ten years before in Tunisia on the set of "Zenobia." He had pushed past the local security people and come right up to her, chatting away in Cockney like an old school chum. Said they had a lot in common, even asked her to come back to his hotel for a drink later on. Amanda, though adept in dealing with the occasional obnoxious admirer, became quickly alarmed. For this huge man out of nowhere had the look of wreckage, of violence and derangement. It was stamped in his face. She'd excused herself and taken refuge in her trailer, locking herself in till assured the giant had left.

The following day one of the co-producers had brought a tweedy little pipe-smoking man to see her, a British embassy "official" who wanted to chat about her strange visitor. John Courage was, apparently, something of a legend among soldiers of fortune, having surfaced in PLO training camps in Lebanon and among the rebel forces in Mozambique. More recently he had been seen in Angola, working with the SWAPO insurgents.

The embassy official had advised Amanda to steer well clear of Courage, and report any further contact. Thank God, there hadn't been any—until this moment. As he lumbered toward her, larger and scarier than she remembered, she felt naked and vulnerable. There wasn't even a trailer to flee to. She wished desperately for a gun, and a damn big one, as she recalled what the official had told her about the man.

The story had begun in Belfast in the early seventies, shortly after England assumed direct control of the Ulster government. One night while patrolling the Falls Road an SAS paratrooper named Oliver Fitzgibbon had turned his Sterling submachine gun on his fellow paras and taken out a half-dozen of them, before defecting to the Provos. The astonishing thing—at least to Amanda's pipe-smoker—was that the man had done it for a lark and a bit of money, or so he later claimed. His adopted *nom du guerre,* John Courage, was based not on any martial virtue but his favorite brand of English ale.

Now the Big Angleesh halted, bear-hugging Ismet and swinging him off the ground. "Izzy, me old son, you did it, didn't you? How much money did you get? And I bet you didn't forget to get old John some good shit to smoke, eh?" The giant's small, ursine eyes quested around the camp till they lighted upon Amanda. At this he broke into a huge, snaggle-toothed grin. "Why you foxy little bastard! You actually did it! Brought me Amanda Morgan!"

Courage set down Ismet and took several lurching steps toward the actress.

"John!" Ismet yelled after him. Amanda tensed, ready to flee. But the giant only dropped to one knee in the dust at her feet, then bent his shaggy head and put his bearded mouth to the hem of her black robe. The mingled reek of booze and body odor was overpowering, but it was a sense of danger, more than revulsion, that swept Amanda.

"We've met, you know, you and me," Courage said, grinning up at her grotesquely. His eyes glittered with admiration.

"I don't recall," Amanda heard herself say. "Please, get up."

"Well, the Beast recalls, if Beauty don't." He cackled and stood up, swaying a bit before catching his balance and making a sweeping ringmaster's gesture with one huge arm. "Welcome to Kastellorizo!"

Ismet shouted again: "John, you damn bastard! We are bringing her here all the way with eyes blind!"

"Don't worry, Izzy, old boy. She probably don't know where fucking Kastellorizo is, anyway. Do you, luv?"

"No. And if I did, I certainly wouldn't tell anybody, including the Turks. The blindfold was unnecessary." In fact, Amanda not only recognized the name Kastellorizo, but had actually set foot on the place years before on a private cruise. She could now visualize herself, vaguely, on a map of the Eastern Med—on a tiny teardrop island only a mile or so off the Turkish coast between Cyprus and Rhodes.

"You see, Izzy, not to worry—" Courage trailed off in mid-sentence. His roving eyes had found something else, something evidently more compelling than a film star. Amanda followed his gaze over to Ismet, who was lifting a foil-wrapped parcel out a field pack. Courage snatched at it like a striking shark. Then, as quickly as he had burst upon them, the huge man turned and, without further word, disappeared back into his tent.

Drugs, Amanda thought. *So he's an addict now.* Which made him more dangerous, if that were possible. As the tent flap closed behind him, she sank back on her stool, releasing some of the terrific tension from her body. For long seconds every nerve, every muscle, had been on full alert. In the aftermath she was exhausted, and made no response when Ismet knelt before her, very much as Courage had done.

He touched her arm: "Hey! You are okay?"

"Yes, I suppose so. I mean of course I'm not okay. Definitely not okay. Christ Almighty!"

"This is true what he said, you have met him before?"

"No," she lied, without knowing why precisely.

"Then I tell you about him. Big Angleesh is a great soldier, but maybe a little crazy now, also bad manners. It is from having no shit. Hashish, you understand it? Now he have big supply and when he is getting shit-faced he will be okay. But you must not to worry, Amanda. Hamzah and I watch John very good. Okay?"

Amanda shook her head. "Look, I already said it's *not* okay. I've got to talk to you, Ismet."

"Ah, you think is a bad situation for you?"

" 'Bad' doesn't come close. I can't stay here any more." She pointed at Courage's tent. *"That* wasn't part of the bargain. I must leave right away, do you understand?"

"Your bargain is with me, Mandy, not Big Angleesh. I keep him away."

"No, you can't, Ismet. I saw you. You just sat there and did nothing. I want off the island. Now."

"You have promised to help Kurdistan."

"And perhaps I shall, when I can think. Look, I said I didn't know the man. That was a lie. I do. He's a psychopath—a crazy man, a murderer. Now, obviously he's a dope addict. I don't care what he's done for you. I won't support him. And I won't support anybody or any-thing associated with him."

"You must calm yourself, Amanda. I can do noth-ing at this moment."

"Oh Christ, well that's clear enough. Let's stop the stupid pretense then, shall we? I'm your prisoner. And you're not patriots, or freedom fighters, or anything of the kind. Just criminals, the lot of you—like him." She whirled and stalked away, confronting a solid rock wall, trembling with rage and absolutely determined not to cry.

"I promise I send you back soonest I can do it," Ismet spoke behind her. "But is not easy thing to do. Make danger for everyone. But I do it, if you make for us video to show the world. Then also we must leave, so Turks not find us. Do this, Amanda. And I keep this man from you, I swear it."

She glared at him. "How soon can I leave?"

"Two days, soonest I can do."

"You have video equipment here?"

"Sure, all best Japanese kind."

"What do you want me to say precisely?"

"Say about yourself, that you are safe here, which you are, but whatever you wish. So no one worry for you."

"Let me go, Ismet, and the world will *know* I'm safe."

But what choice had she? An hour later she was sitting on a camp stool in one of the tents, her hair brushed and tied straight back, wearing one of Guldasa's blouses, unbuttoned somewhat to accommodate her larger dimensions. She talked for a few minutes into a home video camera held on Hamzah's shoulder.

Afterward she could not remember what she'd said. She wolfed down some barley soup and cheese and fresh fruit prepared by Guldasa. Then, overcome with exhaustion, she fell fast asleep on a filthy cot inside the tent Ismet and Hamzah had pitched for her.

She dreamed, not of being confined by terrorists on a remote Levantine island, but of a breezy summer day at the Welsh seaside thirty years before. There were saltwater taffy and strawberry ices and a stroll with Mum and Dad and Small Tom in front in the pram. And as they walked, the pale sun slipped away and the sound of their laughter lingered in the evening air.

$$\equiv$$

An hour later she sat up groggily on her cot, awakened by the sounds of argument. It took her a moment to place herself, and for the incredible events of the previous day to coalesce in her memory. Then she heard the quarrelsome sounds again and lifted the tent flap.

John Courage and Ismet sat across from each other at the deal table. The Englishman was pointing a huge fist, with a pipe stem sticking out of it, at the smaller man. She caught the sweet, burning-grass odor of hashish, but could not hear what they were saying.

$$\equiv$$

"Look, we can't stay here, Izzy. If Taufiq ain't dead, they've got his fucking nuts in a wringer by now and he's squealing like a stuck pig."

"Taufiq will tell them nothing. He is true *pesh merga,* also Sufi. A Sufi can fly away from his body, whenever he wishes."

"Right. And I can blow reveille through me bleedin' arse."

Ismet folded his arms. "John, I ask you, who is boss here?"

"Okay, Izzy, if you're gonna pull rank, we stay. But how long, just tell me that?"

"This is Greek island. No Turks are coming here."

"Somebody's fucking coming. Believe me, Izzy."

"When I say we go, we go."

"Fuck it! Let 'em come, then—Greeks, Turks, the American Sixth Fleet—who bloody cares? At least we got us a hostage, eh?"

"You are talking about Amanda?"

"Who else? We can ransom her for millions."

"For this we have poison gas. She is not for ransom."

"Glad to hear it, Izzy! I was afraid you wanted to keep them tanks hidden here on the island forever. Or maybe you agree with Hamzah, who don't care if we get a penny out of 'em so long as he can squirt 'em on Baghdad and give the Iraqis a taste of their own medicine. Now if you ask me, we should take 'em to some big posh city—Paris, Rome, London, maybe. Not enough to do a big town up proper, mind you, but enough for a little demonstration, make some headlines, scare the authorities into paying up."

"Perhaps. We will decide soon."

"Yeah, well, they'll keep awhile where I've stashed 'em. But *she* won't." He turned toward Amanda's tent, caught sight of her just pulling her head back.

"Look who's up, then," he bellowed. "Come on out and join us, darlin'. We was just talking about how you could do some good for fucking Kurdistan. Fundraising's right up your street, ain't it?"

Amanda pushed through the tent flap and headed

straight for Ismet. "What the hell is going on out here? You gave me your word to keep him away from me. Can't you do it!"

"John, please go back to your tent. Take this with you." He pointed to the hash pipe smoldering away in an ancient pottery shard. "You are acting very shit-faced."

"Christ, Izzy. I'm sorry."

"Be sorry later, John. Go."

"But I didn't mean nothing." Courage sprang from the table, and Amanda stepped back warily.

"Don't come any closer. I mean it." She was waiting for Ismet to stand up and take charge.

The Englishman was very far gone, his eyes not focusing. "It's really in your interest, as well as ours, Mandy. All of us—" Again he flung his arm in a sweeping motion, and suddenly, as if conjured out of their tents, Guldasa, Fahri and Hamzah were all standing there, watching.

"I mean, we gotta get some money out of this deal, right? So let's get the word out fast, do up a proper ransom note. You could write it yourself, luv. Nobody'll know you're in on the deal. Hey, you'll come out of it smelling like fucking roses. What do you say, Mandy? The sooner we do it, the sooner we can all get off this bloody awful rock and back to fighting Turks and Iraqis. And you can get back to your silk sheets and bathtubs full of French fucking champagne, am I right? The only bleedin' question the way I see it is how much? What's your price these days, Mandy? A few million quid, I bet?"

Finally Ismet stepped in and grabbed the Englishman's arm. "Enough. I told you she is not here for that, John."

"What the hell is she here for then?"

"Amanda is our guest. She has come here as student."

"Oh, has she now? Are we playing bloody schoolteacher, then? She going to be a *pesh merga* too? Gonna issue her a rifle, are we? Oh, do it, darlin'! Be one of us!" He pulled away from Ismet and began raving and stumbling about the camp like a ham actor doing Lear. The trio of *pesh merga* stayed alert but well clear, avoiding the huge arms that scythed the air as if wielding a sword. Evidently, they'd decided to let the fit run its course.

"That what you want?" he roared. "Queen of the *pesh*-bloody-*merga*. Don't sound half bad, does it? What'll they pay to get you back? A queen's ransom, I'd say. Enough to make us all bloody rich. Richer than robbing a thousand fucking Turkish banks. You wouldn't begrudge us that, now would you, luv? Come on, what do you say?"

For a frightening second his wild eyes found her, and he lurched forward. At a shout from Ismet, Fahri and Hamzah jumped in from either side, pinning his huge arms. But the giant simply shrugged them off and came straight on. Amanda froze in terror. Out of the corner of her eye, she saw Ismet swinging his rifle. *Yes!* she thought wildly, *Shoot the bastard. And keep shooting!*

Courage stopped suddenly, finally reaching the brink of that blissful oblivion he had been seeking for so many hours with the help of *metaxa* and hashish. Almost on top of Amanda he threw back his head and vented a blood-chilling war cry. The same instant Ismet's rifle butt slammed into his hamstrings, and the giant buckled, his knees giving way. With his last flicker of consciousness he smiled benignly and pitched forward into the dust.

Amanda watched Hamzah and Fahri roll the big Englishman over and drag him, snoring lustily, feet-first back to his tent. Her legs were trembling, but she made herself stand firm.

"Very bad thing," Ismet summed up. "Tomorrow he will say he is sorry to you. And he will do everything only what I say, stay far away from you."

Amanda spoke quietly: "Ismet, if you don't let me go right now, you may as well kill me. Because if I ever get free, I'll denounce you and your *pesh merga.*" As always, she had said what she felt, and damn the consequences. *Let him answer me,* she thought, *if he can.*

Ismet glared back at her. Then he shook his head. "I tell you, Amanda, I can't send you back now. Is too dangerous."

"What's dangerous? I don't have the faintest idea where I am. Blindfold me, throw me in the back of your damn bloody truck, and drive me back to Istanbul. I can't hurt you."

"Why am I bring you here? To learn nothing?"

"This isn't Kurdistan. What will I learn here? How to avoid rape? How to camp out, rough it? Play solitaire? For Christ's sake, I've spent endless months on locations like this. Besides, I'm out of the bloody mood to learn anything. Can't you tell?"

"I am not finish with you, Amanda. I swear by Allah, you will be safe, and you will be free. Soon. But you must stay."

"Then get rid of him."

"No. I can't send John away."

"So what *are* you going to do? Ransom me, like

he says? Let me tell you, my brave Little Fox, if you do that, you will have betrayed everything you stand for." She stared down at him, her eloquence spent, and still he sat. She walked away.

≡

That night, with only Fahri on watch, Ismet made a last tour of the camp. Hamzah had curled up with his cassette player wired to his ear, Courage was still snoring like a bear, and Guldasa and Amanda were likewise asleep. But when Ismet crawled back into his own bedroll in the tent he shared with Hamzah, sleep would not come.

He had too much on his mind. For both John Courage and Amanda Morgan had been right in what they said.

It was a great dilemma. He had brought the actress to the island to share the *pesh merga* struggle, so when she returned to the world she could speak with true knowledge. But this could no longer be. The Big Angleesh had frightened her so much that only against her will could they keep her now. The thing to do was set her free, as she demanded. Unless they were going to ransom her for a great sum of money, as Courage suggested.

It was very clear, was it not? And yet, Ismet could not embrace either choice. To ransom her would be a betrayal, exactly as she had said. And simply to let her go would be a futility. Besides, he did not wish her to go.

When he asked himself why this was so, the answer had little to do with Kurdistan, much to do with himself. Even now her heart-shaped face hovered in his mind, and in his memory played the proud music of her voice.

It was a very fine thing to look into the eyes of Amanda Morgan. They made him think of the "Dark Eyes" celebrated by the Kurdish poet Guran. In their womanly depths one could lose oneself. In this, she was like no other creature for him since Adila—the other half of his own soul. Whatever this elusive thing was, he did not wish to lose it.

So he must keep her awhile. But he could not tell her why.

17

PAUL CYRUS SAT IN THE BACK OF THE CROWDED AIRPORT bus, returning to Istanbul from Yesilköy Airport. He was surrounded by a boisterous West German soccer team—an explosive pack of apple-cheeked, towheaded Boris Beckers, mauling one another like lion cubs and filling the air with Teutonic shouts and a deafening crossfire from several boom boxes.

Paul tuned out the youthful mayhem as best he could, as the bus passed through the Topkapi Gate in the Theodosian land walls and headed along Millet Caddesi into the Old City. He was preoccupied with his own thoughts.

In his pocket was a nonrefundable Olympic Airways ticket to Lesbos via Athens—back to Darryl Ann. After buying it he had sat for a half-hour in the departure lounge, stood for the boarding, turned aside at the gate, walked to the Pan Am counter, stood in line to buy a ticket home to Washington. Then, when it was finally his turn, he walked away and out of the airport.

He had opted for the bus back to the City instead of a taxi because he had no particular destination. All he had, really, was the faintest shadow of a plan—a plan which, under scrutiny, bore a striking resemblance to adolescent fantasy.

He would find Amanda Morgan.

Nice work—for a Lancelot or a Lone Ranger. Paul didn't qualify as either. But, at the moment, there was nothing else he wished to do.

He got off the bus in Aksaray, glad to escape the noisy footballers, and began working his way up the Third Hill through side streets to avoid the clamor of Aksaray Square. He came out on Ordu Caddesi east of the Laleli Mosque, in the center of the hotel district. He was looking for something quiet and preferably off the Frommer list. On a narrow street west of the university his eye was caught by a small third-class hotel sandwiched between more prepossessing neighbors. The Vartan—the name, he recalled, of an Armenian warrior-saint.

In a corner of the lobby four Orientals bent over a large board game Paul didn't recognize. Behind the desk a thin, bespectacled Armenian barely glanced up from a medical textbook as he handed Paul a key to a fourth-floor single in exchange for six thousand *liras.*

Upstairs Paul tossed his canvas bag on the swaybacked bed and pushed open the tall wooden shutters. Off to his left, over the orange pantile rooftops and through the television antennas, he could see the twin minarets and golden ocher dome of Laleli, the baroque "Lily Mosque."

He turned around to regard the dingy room, and was surprised by his own reflection in a flaking mirror. This was the first Istanbul hotel Paul had ever stayed in. Not exactly the Pera Palas or the Divan, but for what he had to do, it felt about right. It was as though he had just taken the first step outside his own life.

Which was basically the plan. Feliks Ilyinsky had planted the seed when he solicited Paul's linguistic aid in tracking Amanda. Later, Paul had thought about the KGB offer. Maybe he *could* help. Trouble was, given the present circumstances, the Kurdish community would be extremely wary of any Westerner, especially a Kurdish-speaking one. There was one obvious way around that. The idea had occurred at the airport and, with a rush of adrenaline, had pulled Paul right out of the Pan Am ticket line and put him on the bus back home.

He would become a Kurd.

Go native. He had daydreamed about it for many years. The first time had been as a precocious fourteen-year-old back in Seattle, when, on a long, rainy weekend, he had curled up on the sofa with Sir Richard Burton's *Pilgrimage to Al-Madinah and Meccah* and lost himself in the mysterious East.

How delicious it had all seemed—the masterful Burton, Europe's greatest adventurer, linguist, and swordsman, squatting on the deck of a Nile steamer in dervish robes and turban, telling his beads, invisible to the upper-deck world of Occidentals. Delicious, yet dangerous. For, in undertaking his masquerade and penetrating Islam's holiest shrines, Burton had run the constant risk of detection and death.

Though Paul's risk in impersonating a Kurd might be less, there would be danger nonetheless. Yet in contemplating it, Paul felt mostly stage fright; the prospect of danger actually attracted him. He *wanted* to run a risk.

The reason was not hard to figure out, he thought, confronting himself again in the mirror. It was because *she* had run risks.

Paul had been doing a good bit of thinking about Amanda Morgan this morning. At the airport, waiting in the lounge, even queuing for the flight to Lesbos—it was not D.A. who had occupied his thoughts. It was the Englishwoman, or rather the Welshwoman. He marveled again at her star turn among the roomful of powerful men at the Harbor Police building. Amanda had simply blown them all away, including Ozsahin. It had been a magnificent performance, part calculated effect—the theatrical gestures, the tossing of her tangled ebony mane, the twining of elegant legs in that flagrant minidress—and part moral passion. Joan Collins as Joan of Arc. She had defied them all with her smoky, cultivated voice—then vanished into thin air, leaving them befuddled.

Where might she be now? Would those talismanic eyes ever look into his again? Paul's chances of tracking her down were impossibly slim, he knew. But maybe he could find out *something*, some useful piece of intelligence, and take it to Ozahin.

Even if he achieved no part of this unlikely quest, just going through the motions offered a temporary release from feelings of frustration about his own life, and exercise for his growing preoccupation with the actress.

Anything was better than doing nothing—than being captured back into D.A.'s orbit or going home with the taste of ashes.

Which gave him an impulse. He dropped D.A.'s comehither cablegram and the ticket to Lesbos into the bathroom sink, set both aflame, and watched the paper blacken and curl into smoke and cinders. Was he burning a bridge, or making a pretense of it? The path back to Darryl Ann would remain open awhile longer, he knew. If his resolve weakened, she would be waiting.

He chuckled, amused by his own harbored weakness. He washed the ashes down the drain.

Now, for the transformation.

He opened up the seabag, sorting the stuff out on the bedcover. He needn't duplicate Burton's elaborate preparations—shaving his head, assembling a complete Oriental wardrobe, assuming his disguise in England before taking ship for Alexandria. Burton had even gone to the painful extreme of submitting to circumcision at the age of thirty-two.

Paul would get off considerably easier. His sandy hair would need to be dyed, his skin darkened, though not indelibly as with the walnut juice and henna Burton had used. Paul thought he could get by with one of the liquid-tanning products favored by bodybuilders before contests. Kurds were not Arabs, and many were fairly light-skinned. More critical would be the shape of face and features. Paul's well-defined profile, though less than aquiline, should serve him well.

And for the finishing touches . . . he rummaged through his toiletries and pulled out a little zipper pouch. Inside were a fake mustache in a plastic envelope, a bottle of spirit gum, and brown contact lenses in saline solution. Darryl had given him the costume makeup kit for an elaborate Valentine's party thrown by some of her Virginia friends. Paul had suffered the silliness—and ended up thoroughly enjoying the masquerade, to the point of affecting a British accent. He'd kept the kit and taken it overseas on impulse, thinking he might use it at some consular bash. A suitable occasion had not arrived—till now.

He still lacked a few items, mostly wardrobe. Though a few Stamboullu Kurds could be seen in traditional peasant garb, and some were identifiable by flat gray caps, most wore Western clothes. Paul drew up a shopping list.

The expedition took three hours, including a lunch of street food—a *döner kebab,* dark Turkish beer, and *baklava.* In the flea markets around the Covered Bazaar he bought shirts, sweaters, and trousers. He had no trouble finding black hair dye and mustache wax from an *eczane,* or pharmacy. But he spent nearly two hours searching for the quick-tanning gunk, even crossing the Golden Horn to comb the pricey hotel shops of Beyoglu, before locating a few bottles at a basement weightlifting club in Tophane.

He also picked up a transistor radio, an old leather satchel, and cigarettes. Paul hadn't smoked since college, but he knew that most Kurds, like most Turkish men, were heavy smokers.

Back in his room at the Vartan, he dropped his parcels, tuned in some Arab music on the transistor, stripped off his clothes, and stepped into the shower. Two hours, a hair-dye and body-paint job later, he stood naked before the mirror admiring a black-haired, sepia-skinned stranger. A slightly jaundiced-looking stranger, he thought. His "tan" would look better after a second coat tomorrow, but it would do.

"You're better-looking as a wog," he told himself. His smile had more wattage, the teeth were whiter.

He stuck the mustache on with spirit gum, darkened it with mustache wax, trimmed it with scissors. The contact lenses irritated a little, but were bearable. Burton had suffered far worse, Paul reminded himself.

He parted the sleek black hair down the center, then combed it to each side with a little gel. Put on a white shirt, maroon sleeveless pullover, black polyester slacks, jogging shoes, wire-rim glasses with no discernible correction. Practiced gestures in the mirror.

How do you do? I am Jiraz Shikak. I am born in Cairo, attended London University. Also McGill in Montreal. Typical of the background of a homeless race after a diaspora, Paul thought. Jiraz would have worked as editor and writer on several Kurdish-language publications. Other details and embellishments fell quickly into place, as if he were an actor fleshing out a character.

Paul was startled out of his reverie by the amplified ululation to evening prayer from the nearby Laleli Mosque. Dusk had settled over the rooftops. It was time for Jiraz Shikak to leave his cocoon.

≡

The following morning "Jiraz" began his investigations in earnest, walking east on Ordu Caddesi, crossing the vast gray expanse of Beyazit Square with its hordes of pigeons and stately mosque, and through the monumental gateway into Istanbul University. He carried the battered satchel, mingling with the student throng. He was more shabbily dressed than most, but Jiraz was, after all, an underemployed journalist.

On campus bulletin boards he found, as expected, no postings for Kurdish groups. On abrupt hiatus, he thought. In any case Paul had not really expected to be conveniently directed to the nearest hotbed of Kurdish student radicalism. Ozsahin's boys would have been snooping around here yesterday.

The next stop on Paul's list was close by. Reentering Beyazit Square he headed left behind the Mosque and through an open-air teahouse crowded with students and professors. Just beyond was the Gate of the Spoon-makers, one of many entrances into Istanbul's Covered Bazaar.

But the Bazaar proper, a teeming tourist maze of nearly a hundred streets and thousands of tiny shops and stalls, began its assault on the senses a little farther on. Here, just inside the stone portal, was a more tranquil precinct, a vine-shaded courtyard around a softly plashing fountain. This was the picturesque *Sahaflar Carsisi,* or Old Book Market, lined with secondhand bookshops whose wares spilled out through narrow doorways onto crowded tables and barrows.

Many of the booksellers, Paul had been told, were dervishes of the Halveti Order. The man he sought was also reputed to be a Sufi—and a Kurd. Just off the courtyard Paul found the faded letters on a filthy awning: *Cherif Antiquariat.*

He stepped into musty gloom. The only illumination, aside from the doorway, leaked through a skylight nearly opaque with dirt and filtered through dust motes from a desk lamp in back. Only Braille readers could browse under these conditions, Paul thought. He shouldered by teetering, head-high stacks of paperbacks, feeling like a spelunker in a labyrinth of stalagmites. Then he heard a querulous female voice ahead and saw, on the floorboards, ghostly footprints.

Around a high shelf he came upon an odd tableau. Behind a desk in a pool of lamplight sat a little old man in a skullcap, being railed at by a big, broad-hipped woman in headscarf and floral print dress. In fact, the woman was nearly screaming as she stood before the desk, clutching a purse in one hand and high-heeled shoes in the other. At the woman's white-powdered, stockinged feet the trail of ghostly footprints ended.

She spoke in a rough Greek dialect, which Paul suspected was Cretan, but could not fathom. Whether or not the bookseller understood the torrent of words rained upon him, he kept nodding and smiling politely. This proved effective, for the woman, without ceasing her tirade, tossed a wad of bills from her handbag onto the desk, picked up a book, and stalked out.

Paul stepped forward, noticing that the bookseller's quilted smoking jacket was dusted with cigarette ash.

"Allah keep you," Paul began in Persian.

"And thee." The wizened face continued to smile.

"Was she a madwoman?"

"She was very angry."

"With you?"

"With all men, I think, and with the world, such as it is. She wished me to recommend a book on love. I named several. Then she demanded to know what love was, real love. 'Not the cruel kind,' she said. She knew all about that kind."

"What did you say?"

"I told her I understood very well what she meant. Love can be extremely cruel, and predatory. I tried to tell her about a different sort of love, the kind our glorious sun has for its planetary children. But *c'est un peu difficile*. In any case, she had not come to listen."

"At least you sold her a book. What was it, if I may ask?"

"A translation of an American work. *The Love Machine* by Susann. Do you know it?"

"No," Paul answered with a straight face.

"Neither I, but it was the only thing I had on the topic in Greek. Now, how may I help you, sir?"

"Mine is not a metaphysical question, Dr. Cherif."

"Ah, you know me?"

"Only by reputation. I am trying to locate some friends." Before Paul could proceed, Cherif held up his hand.

"A moment. I have just brewed some tea. Won't you join me?"

Paul agreed, introducing himself as he took the proffered chair. After a discreet interval, sipping the sweet tea out of a glass in the Russian fashion, he began his story—of a Kurd, who, like so many of his brothers, had lived his life abroad, but who had returned only the day before, from Frankfurt, wishing at last to play some part in his country's struggle.

"But you know, of course, what has happened?" Dr. Cherif said, smiling benignly—and switching to Kurdish.

"How could I not?" Paul replied in the same language. "When I went to inquire at the one address I had—in Usküdar—I was detained by the police. It seems, since this incident yesterday, every one of us is being watched."

"*C'est ça.*" Dr. Cherif inclined his head. "Just along the courtyard there is a little tea garden. On your way out, if you look at the first table under the red-and-white umbrella, you will see a man with a white mustache feeding the cats and reading the *Cum Hurriyet.* " The bookseller's little eyes crinkled. "He is either a secret policeman or a very slow reader."

"They are everywhere today, I think," Paul said.

"And who was this friend of yours in Usküdar, Mr. Shikak? Perhaps I would recognize the name?"

"His name is Davud. He is here himself only a few weeks from Geneva. But I am informed by the police that he is a cousin to one of the Kurds who has been captured—Taufiq Hamed al-Mahmeed."

"Ah! And was this Davud also detained?"

"No, he had wisely left that very morning, to avoid the kind of harassment to which I have been subjected."

"You were not tortured?"

"Oh, no. But the questioning was far from pleasant."

"And when the police released you, you came straight here? Dear me! Have you a letter to me as well?"

"No. But your name was mentioned to me by certain people."

"Such as?"

"Journalists, academicians."

"Tell me some of their names, could you, please?"

Paul named several, people whom he in fact knew, and Dr. Cherif nodded. "Look here, I would like very much to help you, Mr. Shikak. But your timing is very poor. I have in the past allowed my shop to be used for certain meetings, and my old letter press over there, you see, for the printing of certain materials. All this the police know. However, I am a very old man. What can they do to me? If they set their hands upon me, I will simply instruct my feeble heart to stop its beating.

"But several weeks ago my daughter comes to me and tells me that my activities have made certain problems for her son-in-law, who is a teacher at the Bosphorus University in Bebek. A fine boy. My daughter, Mr. Shikak, she speaks to me in a manner very much like this woman you just saw here. Most persuasively. So we have come to an understanding, my daughter and I. All such activities on my part have ceased as of that discussion. This also the police know. So, of the circle of friends whom you seek, I know nothing, and wish to know less. *Dommage.*" Dr. Cherif took a sip of tea, smiling over the rim of his glass. "Now, if you only wished to fathom the mysteries of love, perhaps I could help."

"I'm sorry," Paul said. "Of course I appreciate your position. One does not wish to make trouble for one's children."

"*C'est ça.* However, a thought occurs. In Usküdar there are also the offices of the KPU. Surely someone there—"

"I have been there. They are closed until further notice."

"Ah, I see."

Paul watched the wizened face become extremely bland. Yet behind the forehead and glittering eyes Paul sensed intense mental activity. A decision was being weighed. Finally Cherif spoke, refilling Paul's glass from a brass teapot:

"Do you like belly-dancing, Mr. Shikak?"

"Excuse me?"

"I don't mean the sort you will see at the Hilton or the Divan, for which they bring the big buses full of holidaymakers. This is a kind of *betise*. And neither do I mean that which is found in the *striptiz* clubs, for sailors off the boats. Those girls are *consommatrices,* nothing more. No, I refer to something equally erotic, yet considerably more authentic, do you see?"

"Authentic belly-dancing?"

"Exactly."

Paul sipped and nodded. Was the bookseller toying with him, or leading somewhere? "Where is it to be found?" he asked.

"Do you know the City at all?"

"I have a map."

"It is very near the Edirne Gate—along the Theodosian Walls. You passed through them if you landed at Yesilköy."

"Yes, I remember."

"Not the gate you came through—that was Topkapi—but Edirne. There is a mosque, Mirimah. Lovely. Around this mosque there are some districts, very poor, populated by Gypsies. And there are some *boites,* you see? The music, alas, is too loud for me, but the dancing is quite *énergétique.*"

"Any club in particular you recommend?"

"N'importe. Where thou wilt." The bookseller smiled.

"I see. And the dancing, it is there tonight?"

"Oh yes. Most do not open until nine, but do not wait too long. By midnight sometimes they are all shut up, and you will see only a dark street and think I have sent you on a fool's errand."

Paul thanked him.

"If you are at a loss till then, I suggest a cruise on the Bosphorus, or a waterside table, perhaps a bottle of *buzbug.* An excellent red wine. And, of course, you must have a book." He produced a slim volume. "Five thousand *liras.*"

Paul paid. It was by Pierre Loti.

"You read English, Mr. Shikak?"

"Yes."

"I thought you might." Cherif twitched his smile. "Please try not to step in the talcum on your way out. And if you see a small boy with a broom in the courtyard, send him to me. *Salaam aleikum.*"

Outside Paul could not find the boy, but noticed the old man behind the *Cum Hurriyet* as he exited into Beyazit Square. When he was sure he was not being followed, he stopped and leafed through the book. A folded handbill fell out. It was hand-printed on goldenrod, advertising a nightclub called "Zenobia" on some street in the Edirnekapi district. There was a crude drawing of a belly-dancer, improbably proportioned.

Paul smiled. Apparently the bookseller's daughter had not persuaded the old man to abandon all his "activities."

≡

Paul spent the next several hours vainly pursuing other leads, then phoned Mike Mitchell at the consulate.

"Absolutely nothing so far, Paul. Nobody's seen Amanda or the damned Kurds. Anyway, I thought you were going home."

"Any moment now, Mike, don't worry."

He thought of calling somebody else, but who? Ozsahin, Josh Nevins, the little French film producer? The only one likely not to give him short shrift was Ilyinsky, and Paul still wasn't ready to do business with the KGB.

He walked away from the phone and took out his

list. Everything was crossed off, including his only "inside" information, an address in Sishane he'd overheard from Ozsahin. It was supposedly the apartment of the Turkish policeman, Bayram, the man suspected of spiriting Amanda out of the Harbor Police building. While searching for the skin dye, Paul had gone by and found the place cordoned off by police. Another dead end.

In fact, Paul realized, he had no other lead than the ridiculous one given him by the old bookseller. Nine o'clock, Cherif had said. It was now a little short of three, and Paul was suddenly very tired.

He flagged a *dolmus* back to his hotel, walked past the same four Orientals intent on the same mysterious board game, and pocketed his key from the same oblivious desk clerk. Paul had been prepared to switch lodgings after his radical change in appearance, but so far the little Armenian had not glanced up long enough to notice. As far as Paul could tell, no one had noticed, or cared, and thus far his elaborate masquerade was a complete waste of time. Would anything ever come of it? Something had to happen. While the old cage elevator was jerking its way up the shaft, he imagined himself opening the door to his room, like the reluctant hero Latimer in Ambler's *Coffin for Demetrios,* finding the contents "tossed" and some Peter Lorre-type waiting, with a sad face and a loaded automatic.

But the dingy place was exactly as he'd left it. The call to afternoon prayer was just dying away from the minaret loudspeakers of Laleli Cami. Too tired to undress, Paul took off his fake spectacles, fell onto the bed and slept.

≡

A little after ten, Paul stepped off a bus near the Edirne Gate. Inquiries led him to a little alleyway off Sulukule Caddesi. He saw at once several "nightclubs," what in Turkish are called *payvon*—exactly the sort of *striptiz* joints with B-girls that Cherif had spoken of with contempt. Paul couldn't imagine why the bookseller had sent him hither. There was certainly nothing Gypsy about the first two Paul walked by. Inside he could hear the inevitable Turkish drum and clarinet accompaniment to the belly-dance. Touts worked both doorways.

Zenobia was the last one in the alley. It had the usual red-plush portieres hung with framed glossies of provocatively posed, bejeweled dancers. As Paul paused, a thin, faintly mustached young man stepped between him and the photographs. Entrance was for members only, he was told nervously.

Paul took out the handbill he had found in the book. "Look," he protested, "it says nothing here about private club."

The young man peered at the handbill, then at "Jiraz" through watery eyes, taking in the shabby sweater and shiny slacks. He smiled furtively. Of course, if he were prepared to purchase a "guest ticket," an exception might be made. Paul paid the exorbitant price, wondering if, as himself, he would have been allowed to walk right in, or required to pay more.

The entryway led down several steps into a corridor draped tent-like with more worn velvet. Saint-Saens's "Bacchanale" filtered through this, the volume swelling as Paul pushed through the curtain into a smoky interior that smelled of stale beer.

A bass guitarist and Turkish flute player slouched on folding chairs at the back of a foot-high stage. Around two walls was a crude, faded mural depicting the captive Zenobia, dressed mostly in chains, being led into Rome. The artist had made her look both haughty and pneumatic—and very like Sophia Loren, Paul thought. The seated, leering Aurelian seemed copied from a picture of the young Brando.

In front of the stage male patrons were spaced out over a dozen bottle-littered tables, being worked by the bar girls. Paul stepped inside, crunching pistachio shells underfoot, and slipped into the first empty table as the next dancer took the stage.

She was not quite what he expected. She was barefoot, with the usual jeweled halter and girdle, bracelets, bangles, and finger cymbals. But rather than brazen and rubbery, this dark-haired girl was tiny, apparently shy, and quite young. Paul was not alone in noticing. Several men stirred from lethargy, sitting up and scraping chairs closer to the stage apron.

As the music resumed, the slim girl began her dance. It was obvious that she was untrained and not especially talented. Rhythmic contractions of the stomach muscles, rapid, hypnotic pelvic movements—these techniques of the belly-dance were quite beyond her. Even if she could have attempted them, she was much too petite to bring them off properly. She only undulated, slowly and repetitively, before their jaded eyes, sidestepping self-consciously from patron to patron. Yet Paul found himself responding to her awkwardness and the nymphet sensuality she exuded, something to which he had not thought himself especially susceptible.

A B-girl drifted his way, a hefty, smiling redhead who trailed her fingers over the back of his shoulders. She offered *viski, konak, bira, sampanya.* Paul ordered a bottle of locally brewed Tuborg, automatically fending her off, until it occurred that she might be his contact— if there was such, and Cherif had not sent him on a fool's errand.

"You like her better, huh?" the girl grinned, revealing an expanse of gums and lipstick-smeared teeth.

"Like who better?" Paul asked.

"Her. I saw you looking."

"She's awfully young, isn't she?"

"I think so, too, honey. Me, I'm better for you. My name is Sally." She was Greek and Albanian, she said, and had lived for five years in Australia. When he told her he was Kurdish, he discerned no particular reaction. But she was quick to notice his attention wandering back to the stage as the dancer moved closer.

"Hey, you be a good boy now while Sally gets your beer, okay? Don't go touching her." She slapped his hand and pranced away with her tray. Paul turned quickly back to the stage. The girl was directly in front of him.

This is silly, Paul thought, as his pulse accelerated. The girl wasn't that attractive. She did have a nice figure—tiny waist and narrow back setting off blossoming hips and small, hemispherical breasts. But her nostrils were unusually large, and her mustache almost as pronounced as the doorman's. It was her eyes that drew him in.

They were wide and unblinking as they searched his for a response. When they found what they were looking for, a faint smile of triumph played at the corners of her mouth. It was all a game, Paul thought, a naughty little trick she had picked up somewhere, this Eastern Lolita. And, because she was such a tiny thing, the response she evoked carried with it a residue of shame, as a father would feel catching himself momentarily lusting after a nubile daughter.

Quickly enough she flashed him a last humid glance, clashed her cymbals softly, and sidled to the next eager patron.

The little devil! What she needed was a good spanking.

"What do you think of her?"

Paul looked up. The nervous young doorman was standing next to the table.

Paul mumbled an agreement and turned back to the stage. The doorman sat down beside him. "I'm Ishmael," he said.

And I'm Moby Dick, Paul thought, ignoring the man as pointedly as he could. It didn't work.

"You want a smoke?"

"No, thanks."

"You're Shikak Bey, correct? First name, Jiraz?"

Paul nodded. Sally, the bar-girl, must have told him.

"You're looking for somebody, also correct?" The unexpected question came in Kurdish.

Paul turned back in surprise. So, this little nerd was his contact. Paul responded: "Yes, this is so. I am hoping—"

"Hey, keep it quiet, and talk Turkish. I was just showing you how it is, Jiraz. See that guy over there?" Ishmael pointed two tables away at a plump, well-dressed man leaning precariously toward the stage with a wad of *liras.* His intention clearly was to stuff them into the dancer's skimpy costume. But she kept her distance, shaking her head stubbornly, till he shrugged and tossed the money at her feet. "Secret police," said the doorman.

To Paul, the man looked more like a professor, or banker perhaps. If he were indeed a policeman—and the Kurds were in a position to know such things—he was certainly making free with government money.

"These people you're looking for, no one knows where they are. But I'll do what I can to help you. Jiraz, you know your way around Usküdar?"

"If you give me an address, I'll find it."

"There's no address. It's in the *geçekondu,* one of the big shantytowns, understand? I have to take you there, or as close as I feel like. You should know, it's going to be dangerous."

Paul nodded.

"Which is why it's also going to cost you."

"How much?"

The doorman hesitated. "Fifty thousand *liras.*"

"I can't pay that much. I have no work." Paul unfolded three ten-thousand *lira* notes from his wallet.

"Not enough."

"It's all I have." Paul shrugged and folded the notes. Before he could put them away, they were plucked out of the air by Ishmael's fingers.

"Okay. I can't do anything until tomorrow night. I'll meet you at the railroad station in Haydarpasa at eight. Right out front, the main entrance."

"I'll be there."

The young man stood up, but didn't move away. "Hey, Jiraz, I bet you'd like to meet Noorsheen, am I correct?"

"I don't know. Who is she?"

"That little Azerbaijani you've been staring at. She's brand-new here. It's her first night. Pretty good, eh? I can't promise anything, understand. But for a certain consideration, maybe I can do something."

Paul felt the swift ignition of lust. Sure, why not? Just what he needed tonight, a quick tumble with an underage Azerbaijan hooker. Followed, perhaps, by a knife fight in the alley with her pimp. Tomorrow they would fish his perforated body out of the Bosphorus, and, if they ever figured out who the hell he was, Mike Mitchell would get the pleasure of filling out the triplicate paperwork to ship him home.

"She's a lovely girl, but no thanks. I'd better go." Indeed, he better had. He put some smaller bills on the table. "Please see that Sally gets this. Tell her I couldn't stay."

Paul exited through the smoke and faded plush into the air, filling his lungs. By the streetlamp his watch read only ten-thirty. He had until seven tomorrow. The thing was, after ogling that damned succubus in there, he really *did* need to get laid.

Instead, he decided to walk the four miles back to his hotel.

18

SHORTLY AFTER SUNSET THE FOLLOWING EVENING, AS A wet, smoky mist settled over Istanbul, a ferry swung out from the Karaköy landing stage into the Bosphorus. Sipping tea on the upper deck, Paul Cyrus was amazed how quickly the magical city folded its tents and disappeared into obscurity. Halfway across the waterway even the floodlit domes of Saint Sophia and Sultan Ahmet had vanished astern into pewter-gray fog. Paul, feeling clammy wetness on the back of his neck, went into the saloon for another glass of tea.

After the twenty-minute crossing they debarked at the Haydarpasa pier, and Paul flowed with the crowd toward the large German baroque station, the terminus for all of Turkey's Asian rail routes. It was quite cold now, and Paul, still disguised as Jiraz, wished for something more substantial than his sleeveless pullover.

He also had the queasy sensation of being played for a fool. He had given thirty thousand *liras* to a tout in a dive who happened to speak Kurdish, a furtive-looking guy eager to sell the favors of a belly-dancer he hardly knew. Really, the likelihood of Ishmael showing up at the rendezvous was not very good. How long was Paul prepared to stand shivering outside the station before admitting he'd been had?

But fifty yards from the entrance, through the eddying currents of travelers, Paul spotted his man. He was leaning against a pillar under a light, flagrantly conspiratorial in aviator glasses and leather jacket.

As Paul came up, Ishmael took his elbow and, without a word, steered him into the huge station, dodging through the middle of a peasant family queued up for the evening train to Ankara, and out a side exit where a Turkish-made Fiat coupe was parked with the motor running.

Ishmael directed Paul to squeeze into the back then took the front passenger seat. Behind the wheel was a girl in a red trench coat and jaunty beret. She turned around and showed Paul her gums. It was Sally from the club.

"Hi!" she said. "Remember me?"

Ishmael also turned around and took off the dark glasses, revealing a face rigid with tension. "Jiraz, I got to have another ten thousand."

"What for?"

"I had to hire this car."

"That's your problem. I gave you thirty thousand *liras.*"

"Sally, turn off the motor. We're not going anywhere." She did as she was told. "Get out," Ishmael ordered Paul.

"What do I get for what I paid, then?"

"You got here."

"You're quite a guy, Ishmael. If I agree, are you going to stop the car every block and ask for more?"

"He's got a point," Sally said.

"Be quiet. Here's the deal, Jiraz. You give me ten thousand more, I take you where you want to go. Plus, I loan you this." He produced a plastic flashlight. "Go ahead, try it. It works."

Paul thumbed the feeble light on. "What for?"

"You'll need it where you're going. I'd like it back when you're done. You can leave it for me at Zenobia."

"I tell you what, Ishmael. Take me wherever you're going to take me, and I'll give you five thousand. And another five when you bring me back."

"That's basically the same deal as mine. Why don't you just pay it all up front?"

"No. Half when we get there, half later, and nothing till you start driving."

"Sally, start the car," Ishmael barked, and the tiny Fiat leapt away from the station. They took an erratic course, with Ishmael calling out last-minute turns Sally had difficulty making. Paul peered through the back window, wondering if they were trying to elude pursuers. Whatever the intention, Paul was soon lost, especially with only the Fiat's fog lights to probe some of Üsküdar's darker neighborhoods.

At one point the land rose into dark, rolling hills. Paul caught the distinctive calligraphy of tall cypresses and jumbled Moslem headstones. This could only be the vast cemetery of Karaça Ahmet, an odd detour. Paul was relieved when they exited back into a residential area of old mosques and weathered wooden houses, which gradually gave way to grim blocks of concrete apartment buildings.

After a quarter-hour of meandering, the Fiat began to bounce around on deteriorating roads. This was Paul's first indication they had entered one of the many *geçekondu* encampments that were continually springing up on the city's outskirts, beyond the outreach of municipal services. In the absence of electricity, the jerrybuilt structures they passed were illuminated only by the occasional flickering of oil lamps and candles.

Here Ishmael was clearly unsure of his way, and several times made Sally turn around and retrace their bumpy course. Finally, he had her pull over and cut the engine. In the sudden silence Paul could hear raindrops pinging on the car roof.

"Are we lost?" he asked.

Ishmael turned quickly, his thin head a silhouette against the night. "The place you're looking for, it's at the end of the street up there, on the right."

"How can you tell? This looks like every other street we've been on in the last ten minutes."

"I've been here. The *geçekondu* is built around a courtyard. If any of your friends are left, they'll be there. If not, ask for an old guy named Salah. He's got a dog. He may know where they've gone." He stretched forth his palm. "Five thousand *liras,* Jiraz. That's the deal."

Paul peered out into darkness. This was the moment, then. Amanda Morgan had plunged into such a void, maybe at this very spot. Could he do the same? If not, this was also the moment, maybe the last one, to turn back. He pocketed the flashlight, handed over the money, and stepped outside—into squishy mud.

"Good luck!" Ishmael called, sticking his head out the window as the Fiat fired up.

"Wait!" Paul yelled. "Where are you going?"

"Sorry, Jiraz, we can't stay. This is Sally's father's car. It has to be back by nine-thirty."

"You told me you hired it!"

"I did. From her father."

"Ishmael, we had a deal! How the hell am I supposed to get out of here?"

Paul began to run after the Fiat, but it gunned away, rear wheels flinging mud on his trousers. Ishmael called back, "If you walk, maybe you can find a *dolmus.*" Then the coupe turned the first corner and disappeared from sight.

"Asshole!" Paul yelled, abandoning Kurdish for Mother English. "Fucking little shit-faced asshole!" Paul had counted on the extra five thousand *liras* being enough to keep the mercenary little creep hanging around. Slight miscalculation.

For a few moments he just stood, listening to the flatulent, dying echoes of the fleeing Fiat. Then he turned and walked through mud and drizzle and shredding fog, toward the end of the deserted street.

He was cold and frightened. He wished for a gun. He wished he'd come here in daylight. He wanted to turn and head back toward the faint neon haze over the horizon that marked the beginning of the City, and civilization. He even hoped Ishmael *had* deposited him here at the end of a wild-goose chase, and there was nobody in the dark structure he was approaching. But, for the sake of self-respect, he had to take a cursory look.

The "night house," he saw, was really a series of ramshackle shelters, joined with hoardings of pasteboard and rotten sheathing, built around some kind of courtyard. Roughly what Ishmael had described. Maybe the little asshole *had* been here, and this *was* the place. Paul heard the sudden rooting of a pig within and, a moment later, winced as the wind shifted and he caught the sinus-searing odor of pig manure.

He walked quickly around the *geçekondu,* seeing no opening. With a running start, he could probably smash through one of the flimsy walls. But he didn't fancy landing in some Anatolian family's communal bedroom.

He switched on the flashlight and swept the outer wall again. This time he spotted an opening, draped in sacking. *Okay. You've got to go in there. Don't think about it. Just do it. They're probably long gone.* He slipped behind burlap into total darkness and froze, senses alert. He saw and heard nothing. Smelled a great deal—most of it pretty rank. He waited a few seconds, then switched on the flashlight.

He moved the beam along walls of rotten sheathing, past old water-stained pinups torn from magazines—big-breasted women and soccer stars. In one corner, on the dirt floor beside some wooden crates, was a filthy ticking mattress. Scattered around it were pieces of broken glass and pottery, beer bottles, refuse.

The next wall was pasteboard, with a ragged, man-sized hole punched out of the middle of it—about what Paul figured he'd make with a running start. Something had happened here.

The last wall wasn't any more reassuring. Someone had spray-painted a human target on it, then blasted away, and pretty damn accurately. Head, heart, and groin were pocked with bullet holes, nicely grouped. Littering the base of the wall were empty, rusted food tins, also bullet-riddled. Paul's shoes crunched shell casings from all the rounds that had been fired.

Get the hell out of here, came the inner command. When Paul was ten, he and a friend had gone hiking and discovered a hobo hangout. It had looked and smelled just like this. One room—latrine, bedroom, kitchen. Empty cans. Girlie magazines. They'd made brave jokes. Then they'd seen the strange tall man standing there, and run like hell.

Okay, he thought, *I'm going. Wherever the hell they've taken Amanda, it isn't here.* He turned, reaching for the burlap, when a sudden groan from the next room lifted the hairs on his arms. Paul froze, and heard it again—fainter.

Against all his instincts, ignoring his hammering heart, Paul inched forward, turned a corner, poked ahead with a flashlight beam that wavered in his hand. A narrow passageway led off into obscurity. He took a step, listened, took another, yearning for a weapon.

Then, from the side came a gurgling, strangulated sound. Paul whirled, pointing the flashlight down several earthen steps into an alcove. At the bottom the feeble beam found a body on a pallet. It was an old man, his frail torso bared, bottom half draped with a sheet. Was he still alive, or had Paul heard his death rattle?

He moved down, stared at the grizzled face. The eyes were shut, the skin deeply cyanosed. He set the flashlight down and went to work on the emaciated body. The parchment flesh was still warm to the touch.

Paul's brain raced, trying to recall the CPR checklist. He found the carotid under the whiskered jaw, but no pulse.

He cradled the head, shouting in Turkish: "Breathe, damn you! Come on, breathe!" There was a faint gurgling deep in the throat. Paul lay his ear to the man's chest, heard nothing. He tilted the head back, probed in the toothless mouth to make sure the tongue was free, then sealed his mouth to the whiskery lips, ignoring the foulness and his own revulsion, blowing with all his force. After the second exhalation he was rewarded with a deep, gravelly rumbling, perhaps a fluid trying to come up. Frantically, Paul shifted position, squatting, fitting his hands below the breastbone. How many times? Fifteen, wasn't it? He began, counting and pressing.

He had done ten rapid compressions when, directly behind him, someone coughed.

Paul grabbed the flashlight, stabbing the darkness. A few feet away was a man in a black windbreaker, leaning against the earthen wall. It was Feliks Ilyinsky. He was smiling—and pointing a revolver at Paul's face.

"Do svidanya, glupi Turok," Ilyinsky said.

"Good-bye" was one Russian word Paul knew; "stupid Turk" he did not. Waiting in outraged, helpless disbelief for the explosion that would end his whole world, the American could not comprehend why Feliks was going to kill him. Then he realized the Russian wasn't aiming at him at all, but at "Jiraz Shikak." The ultimate absurdity—he was going to die by mistake, thanks to some costume-party makeup.

He screamed in English: "Feliks, don't shoot! I'm Paul Cyrus!"

The world did not explode. It went on existing another heartbeat, and another. But the gun remained fixed between Paul's eyes. "For Christ sake, Feliks, it's me! Put the gun down!"

Finally, in excruciating slow-motion, the hammer was lowered, then the revolver. The Soviet's face creased into a wry smile.

"So! I congratulate you on your clever disguise, Paul. It nearly caused your death. And I commend your attempt at resuscitation. And on reaching the wretched headquarters of our Kurdish bandits in advance of the security services of Turkey and Great Britain, as well as your own government. I myself was only a little ahead of you. How did you manage it?"

"I don't know. Luck, I guess. Look, Feliks, I think this man is still alive. You heard him just now."

"Organic sounds. In any case, with the help of my translator here, I have found out everything I need to know from this relic. There is no further use for him."

"Translator?"

"You may switch off your torch. There is a candle beside me, which I blew out when I heard your blundering arrival."

A match flared, transferred to a candle flame, which bloomed into wavering light that revealed the tiny alcove. Crouched grasshopperlike in a far corner was a cadaverous figure, also smiling, also with a gun.

"I believe you have met my colleague, Anton Bessaraboff? Look here, Toshka, it's the American linguist and hostage negotiator, Paul Cyrus. And we thought he had gone home."

Bessaraboff grinned. "What's happening, dude?"

"Forgive Toshka, Paul. He cannot resist American slang."

Paul, though still under the spell of near death,

prodded his petrified brain back into activity. He sensed his own life precariously in the balance. He found himself calculating the angles up the stairs, how he might flee into the night if he had the chance.

"You see, Paul, I was right to try and recruit you."

"Except you didn't need me. How did you find this place?"

"Alas, since even Toshka doesn't speak Kurdish, I was forced to employ another language."

"Which one?"

"Pain."

"You—you tortured him?"

"Well, we tried gentle questioning, but the old fool was stubborn. Alas, his last few minutes in this world, before *Allah* claimed him, were not pleasant ones. But they went swiftly. Fortunately he had a bad heart."

Paul clamped his jaw, fighting nausea at this smug revelation of casual murder. But Feliks was not finished:

"As a student of terrorism, Paul, surely you are familiar with how we won the release of our hostages in Beirut in '82?"

"I know the story." It was popular in counterterrorist circles. Other nations might be paralyzed by the fanatic Shia bands who kidnapped their countrymen, but not the Union of Soviet Socialist Republics. When four of their own were captured, and one killed, the KGB retaliated quickly by seizing four Shia terrorists at random, castrating one, and sending the evidence as a calling card to Shia headquarters. The remaining Soviet hostages were freed within twenty-four hours.

"The moral of the story is inescapable, you agree? Your Western pundits are fond of saying there is no answer to terrorism. In fact, as we proved in Beirut, that is not so. The answer to terrorism is greater terrorism."

Ilyinsky studied the effect of his words on the man he had nearly killed. The disguised American had obviously been badly frightened. Still, Cyrus had done remarkably well in getting this far, a feat which Ilyinsky had only accomplished through a bit of luck, and certain tidbits picked up by Noorsheen at the Kurdish club in Edirnekapi. As Feliks had suspected, after her initial reluctance, the little Azerbaijani had rather enjoyed disrobing before strange men.

But the American would have gotten no farther, Feliks judged. Even had he been able to persuade the old man to talk, as Feliks had done, a civilized fellow like Paul Cyrus wouldn't have a chance against the ruthless Kurds. From here on the chess game became serious, with deadly exchanges—which Feliks was prepared for. This relic on its grimy pallet, and the sheepdog outside in the mud with a bullet in its stupid, loyal brain, were in all likelihood only the beginning of a bloody business.

"This is a little out of your depth, Paul, is it not? But compose yourself. If I intended to kill you, I would have done, in or out of disguise. But it is not necessary. You cannot stop me. You may, if you wish, even call Colonel Ozsahin and tell him everything you have learned. He cannot stop me either."

"Stop you from what?"

"Rescuing Amanda, of course. I told you that yesterday."

"You really know where she is?"

"Of course I know."

"Where?"

"Torture me and perhaps I shall tell you. Otherwise,

I fear you will learn nothing for your ingenious masquerade."

Ilyinsky got to his feet, stuffed his revolver into his windbreaker. Then he beckoned to Bessaraboff.

"Feliks. Wait." Paul stood up, blocking the exit. His knees were shaky, his stomach awash. But he felt possessed by a strange resolve. Even his voice sounded different to his own ears: "I'm not going to talk to Ozsahin. I'm not going to talk to anybody. There's only one thing I want to do—help you rescue Amanda."

"You are serious?"

Paul nodded.

"I believe you are. I'm sorry. I no longer need a linguist. To rescue Amanda I have real fighters. *Spetsnaz,* you know?" Feliks stared at the young American. In the flickering candlelight, with his stained skin, black mustache, and intense, darkened eyes, Paul Cyrus seemed now a terrorist himself. Had something snapped in the American's mind, Feliks wondered?

"Excuse me a moment." The KGB major turned to his companion and spoke in Russian. "Toshka, what do you think of this?"

The gangly young man screwed up his face in thought. "Like you said, we already have two *Spetsnaz* guys. *Afgantsy.*"

"Exactly. But this place the old man told us of, this little island . . . don't say its name."

"Yes?"

"How shall we approach it?"

"From the air?"

"It has to be quick and surgical. But I can't mount a full-scale counter-terrorist strike. It is best if the Greeks on this island suspect nothing till we have departed. So we will not arrive by chopper, or by parachutes or hang gliders, or courtesy of a nuclear submarine from the Black Sea Fleet. We must decide and begin quickly. Tonight. Or forget the whole thing. Think, Grandmaster."

Bessaraboff blinked his goggle eyes, a sign, Feliks knew, that he was indeed flexing his considerable brain. "First, we must know exactly where the Kurds are hiding on the island."

"Yes, I'll arrange for intelligence. But then?"

"Well, perhaps we could come by sailboat . . . at night, silently?"

"Good, Toshka. And for this we must charter a boat, in Rhodes, I should think. A motor-sailer, so we need only sail the last bit. And for this we will need a captain. Our *Spetsnaz* do not qualify, nor I, nor you. But Paul Cyrus can do these things for us. I happen to know he is an experienced sailor. Of course, in the actual rescue he will be of no use. But then, I don't know about you either, do I?"

"I can shoot, you saw me!"

"Really! You killed a stupid dog, Toshka. Anyway, we'll see about that when the time comes. Afterward, we can do with the American as we choose. And, of course, taking him along is better than killing him or letting him talk to Ozsahin."

Bessaraboff pondered. "It computes."

"From you, Toshka, a rare compliment." Ilyinsky turned to Paul and spoke in English: "All right, my American friend. Welcome to the KGB."

19

THE VIDEOTAPE WAS DISCOVERED AT A NEWSPAPER OFFICE in Bodrum on Turkey's southern Aegean coast. It was poorly lighted, unedited, the sound scratchy. More distracting, the camera was unsteady, so the distinctive head and shoulders floated about in the frame. Amanda Morgan was seen in front of a blue cloth backdrop, without makeup, khaki shirt open at the throat. Her dark hair was pulled back and tied with a scarf into a ponytail that spilled forward over one shoulder. Her forehead and upper lip showed perspiration, but there was no apparent sign of duress.

She began by giving the correct score of a Turkish football match played the day before the tape was found—and two days before it aired on Turkish television, and then worldwide.

"I want to make clear straightaway that I am not a prisoner," she said, looking earnestly into the lens, speaking without theatrical emphasis. "I am here of my own choice, to keep a pledge I made to a Kurdish leader to exchange myself for hostages he had taken, hostages whom he then released.

"My being here, of course, does not mean I approve of terrorism. Absolutely the contrary. I came forward to try and stop a terrible situation from getting any worse than it already was. To save lives, if I possibly could. And I am on record many, many times as condemning violence of every sort, whether terrorist or government-sanctioned.

"I am of course distressed that my sudden disappearance may have caused suffering among many friends and loved ones. In part to alleviate their anxiety, the Kurds have offered to make this video and deliver it to the world.

"I am perfectly fine, dear ones—Mum and Auntie Del, Syb and Tony and Reg and Roy and so many others—not to worry. Knowing me, you will understand that I did what I did because I felt I had to. Because the authorities—both British and Turkish—would not permit me to keep my word. While I'm sure they had their reasons, I cannot and do not operate that way. I try to be a person who does what she says she will do. So, here I am.

"I have also come here to learn something, I hope, about the Kurdish people, and what they're fighting for, and will go on fighting for, which is a homeland. Something most of us take for granted, but which many, many people around the world can only dream of, and struggle for, and, in too many cases, die for. It is a dream that can also drive some people to the kinds of desperate acts which brand them as terrorists in the eyes of people whose own nationalist struggles are safely behind them.

"One thinks of so many places and peoples, really . . ." And, closing her eyes as if to visualize global suffering, Amanda began ticking them off—Kampuchea, Poland, the West Bank, and southern Africa; Native Americans, the Islamic tribes of Soviet Central Asia, and the starving refugees of the sub-Sahara, whose land, she said, had simply dried up and blown away.

"Sometimes, I know, it seems there are just too many voices crying out for our help and concern. But one does what one can, and so again, that's why I'm here, to share for a short while, in a tiny, symbolic way, the day-to-day struggle of the Kurdish people, and to help bring it to the world's attention . . ."

The tape ended abruptly after five minutes, with no specific appeal or clue as to when, or under what circumstances, she expected to be coming home.

Yet there *was* more. The cassette had been left at the newspaper office with a note signed by the Peoples Democratic Army of Kurdistan. The note reiterated one of the Kurds' original "non-negotiable demands"—for a sum of money equivalent to five million Swiss francs, in various currencies.

The threat for nonpayment was unveiled, in amateur legalese, toward the end: "To bring about the immediate and safe return of this heroic woman, it is imperative that the demand herein stated be met completely. All monies collected shall be used to further those causes espoused by Amanda Morgan." The note concluded by saying that detailed instructions for delivery of the "charitable donation" would be communicated to the authorities with another videotape in the next few days.

≡

Ismet watched the video on a small black-and-white television in an open-air restaurant on the long beach at Olü Deniz, near the Turkish Mediterranean resort of Fethiye. In fact, to see the screen he had to leave his table, only a few steps from the sand, and worm his way through a noisy, three-deep crowd of bathing-suited Europeans around the shaded bar.

Several glanced his way as he pushed through, seeing only a small, strong-featured Levantine in dark glasses, sport shirt, and French jeans—one who wore no jewelry besides a yellow plastic sportwatch and had no facial hair.

The Europeans glanced back at the screen and chattered annoyingly throughout the broadcast—in a Babel of Anglo-Saxon tongues. Since Olü Deniz, with its golden, two-kilometer beach and crystalline lagoon, had gotten itself plastered on European tourist posters, the heliotropic Northerners had been arriving in increasing numbers. Ismet wanted very much to silence them to better hear Amanda, but decided not to call attention to himself. His altered appearance and false Turkish identity papers might be good, but as the target of a nation-wide manhunt, it would be better to avoid any possibility of police scrutiny.

So he stood there, overshadowed by the Nordic types around him, tuning out their chatter and concentrating on the image and voice of Amanda Morgan. When the video ended and Turkish commentators came on to analyze it, the Little Fox returned to his beachside table.

It is very wrong, what I have done, he thought. The woman had kept her word, and he had betrayed her. Refused to let her leave the island. And now was in the process of trading her very life for money.

The previous night in Bodrum he and Hamzah had delivered the videotape, along with the ransom demand drafted by Guldasa. The two cousins were due to return in the van to Kos later this evening and slip across to Kastellorizo after nightfall.

They would have no trouble collecting the money, that's what everyone said—not just Courage now, but all of them. The only real disagreement had concerned the size of the ransom to demand.

When Ismet had flatly rejected their plan, he had been shocked by their reaction. For the first time in his memory, they had protested his decision. Ismet was listening too much to the Englishwoman, they had argued, and not enough to them. They *had* to get some money out of this operation, Hamzah said, to pay for all the risks they'd taken and the loss of their two comrades. Courage, the obvious instigator of the rebellion, pointed out that if Amanda Morgan truly wanted to help them in their struggle, let her make them rich. Besides, it would be no worse for her. The millionaire film producers would gladly pay.

In the end, despite his promise to Amanda, Ismet had given in, for there was much truth in what they said. Perhaps the actress *had* bewitched him for a time. And what if she did discover she'd been tricked and ransomed? By the time she was safely back in Turkish custody, the Little Fox and his band would be far away.

As the Big Angleesh had said, why should Ismet care what a film actress thought?

Something whacked Ismet in the back of the neck. He leaped out of his chair, knocking over his Orangina and landing in a karate stance—till his foot skidded on a plastic Frisbee that sent him sprawling in the sand. As he scrambled back to his feet, he heard Hamzah's shouted laugh. His grinning cousin, wearing only his Popeye T-shirt and hacked-off jeans, was sprinting up the beach toward him, followed by two shrieking blondes in skimpy bikinis.

Allah be praised, Ismet thought. Hamzah had once again found his quarry. Hunting was, after all, the only reason his cousin had insisted on this scenic little detour from the coastal road back to Kas. And he had flushed not just one little pigeon out of the beach flock, but a matched pair.

The three of them, in an apparent footrace, came skidding into the sand by Ismet's table. When they stopped laughing and got their breath back, the two blondes plopped their sandy selves down around the table, and Hamzah ordered a round of beers. He introduced them as Britt and Susannah, Aussie schoolteachers on holiday, and himself and Ismet as Hayri and Salim, "businessmen" from Bodrum.

Britt, closer to Ismet, had a tousled, pixie hairdo, a snub nose, and a mask of freckles around pale gray eyes. She poked a stubby forefinger into his chest and apologized for hitting him in the back of the head with the Frisbee. "Honest," she said, "I wasn't aiming!" Susannah, leggier and more darkly tanned with long, straight hair, said Salim should just be glad it wasn't a bloody boomerang. The Kurdish men joined in the laughter, without understanding the joke.

"What do you think of them?" Hamzah asked his cousin in a rapid Kurdish aside.

"I don't know how you do it. I like this one better, with short hair, it is okay?"

"Of course. She is your type, cousin. I knew it."

"Now, now," Susannah broke in with schoolmistress tones. "We'll have none of that filthy talk around here." The shrill laughing started all over again.

The Aussies were as uncomplicated and playful as two puppies, Ismet thought. Here they were, practically naked in front of two strange men, and they acted not the least self-conscious. They licked beer foam from their lips, jabbered away in their strange nasal English, threw each other all kinds of eye signals. Every now and then they'd give him and Hamzah outrageously flirtatious glances, then explode into giggles as if shocked at their own boldness.

Hamzah, in obvious command of the operation, signaled the waiter for another round of beer and a large pizza. "Okay, drink, girls," he said beaming, "fun, fun, fun."

"There's a song called that," said Susannah. "The Beach Boys, innit?"

Hamzah pointed to himself. "Me and Salim, we are the only beach boys for you girls."

The Aussies eyed each other and giggled hysterically.

Hamzah smiled. "Hey, you girls like to dance? There is a really groovy disco in Fethiye."

Britt and Susannah exchanged quick glances. "Could be. How long you blokes staying on here?"

"We must leave tonight," Ismet said sternly.

"Hey, Salim," Hamzah objected, "why you want to go so soon? Britt, talk some sense to my friend, okay?"

"Well, I might do. He is kind of cute, you know?" She swung around in her chair, her tawny haunch brushing against Ismet's leg. Her round impish face was suddenly so close he could count the freckles on her nose, see the tiny chip out of one front tooth. And he couldn't help noticing the plump, freckled breasts spilling over the bikini top, and savoring the tangy, sun-cooked girl-scent.

Over her pretty shoulder Hamzah was grinning like an idiot. Ismet nodded back. Okay. They would stay over, get back to the island the following night. What was another stupid promise broken? He'd gone far too long without a woman. And this sandy little imp beside him would remedy that quite nicely. And maybe help banish the thoughts of the lady he had betrayed.

Britt snapped her stubby fingers in his face. "Hey, there, wake up. So tell me, Salim, what kind of business are you in?"

The Little Fox thought it over. "I am an international terrorist," he said with a straight face.

For a second he saw her register fear. Then her eyes crinkled up and the automatic giggle switched on.

Nine hundred kilometers to the north, in Istanbul's aluminum-and-glass city hall on Atatürk Boulevard, another roomful of people had just finished watching Amanda Morgan's videotape.

Assembled in Colonel Celal Ozsahin's ornate, seventh-floor office, overlooking the clustering domes of the Sehzade Camii complex, were many of the same high-powered functionaries who had been summoned after the ship hijacking—two Turkish cabinet ministers; Ozsahin's staff assistants, Majors Akalin and Yoruk, plus Captain Erol; the British Consul General, Bertram Giddings, with two secretaries and three military attachés; less directly involved, Townsend White and Mike Mitchell of the U.S. Consulate, along with Josh Nevins of the CIA; and Leopold Bouchard and Jack Woodhull representing Kronos films.

Bertie Giddings was in mid point: "Obviously, Colonel; Mandy's been d—d—duped and doesn't realize the k—k—kind of danger she's in. But c—c—can't you learn anything from the tape, and where it was delivered, to p—p—pinpoint where they might be?"

Ozsahin drew on one of his unfiltered oval cigarettes and walked to a wall map. "That blue cloth behind her looks like a tent. Using the delivery point as a center," he scribed a sweeping oval with his forefinger over his country's entire southern Aegean and Mediterranean coastlines, "they could be camped out anywhere in here." He smiled. "Or perhaps not."

"Quite a large area, Colonel," Townsend White said.

"Several hundred thousand square kilometers. Nevertheless, all the *jandarmas* within the area have been alerted, supplied with photographs and descriptions of Miss Morgan and the terrorists, and so forth."

"Your circle takes in nearly half the Dodecanese," Josh Nevins pointed out. "Greek territory."

"So it does. Which brings me to the next videotape I have to show you. Captain Erol?"

The captain went to the VCR, switched tapes. The video showed a harbor in bright sunlight, the viewing angle down, as from an upper-story window, onto a line of yachts stern-to on a stone quayside beside a crowded outdoor cafe.

"Is she there? I don't see 'er!"

"Please, be seated, Monsieur Bouchard," Ozsahin said, freezing the frame. "I have no idea where Miss Morgan is at this moment, but I can assure you she is not on that screen. You are looking at a picture of Mandraki Harbor on the island of Rhodes. It was taken yesterday afternoon."

The lens zoomed in on a single table, framing three men under a Cinzano umbrella behind an array of bottles and glasses, occasionally eclipsed by people passing in the foreground.

Josh Nevins reacted first. "What the hell is Feliks Ilyinsky doing in Rhodes? And what are you following him for?"

"Excellent questions. Perhaps you also recognize the man beside him?"

"*I* do," Mike Mitchell jumped in. "What's-his-name, the chess player."

"Bessaraboff," Nevins said. "Ilyinsky's protegé."

"Very good again," Ozsahin said. "And the third man?" The camera panned slightly to a striking dark-skinned young man with center-parted black hair and neatly clipped black mustache.

"Al Pacino," quipped Mike Mitchell.

Ozsahin whipped out a notebook. "Say again, please."

"Sorry, just a dumb joke. He looks kind of familiar, but I can't place him. I gather you can't either?"

"We are working on this. From his appearance, he could be a Semite, or Aryan, any of the Mediterranean or Levantine nationalities. A mystery man." He clicked off the video.

"Well, Colonel," prompted Bertie Giddings, "why don't you just torture that K—k—kurdish bastard you've got in jail and have d—d—done with it? He'll tell you what you want to know."

"Please, Mr. Giddings."

"Another poor joke, I apologize. But surely you have something m—m—more to tell us. Or do you just enjoy spying on KGB blokes on holiday?"

"Yes, there is more. Immediately after Miss Morgan's disappearance, both Ilyinsky and Bessaraboff were observed in certain locations in the City, places known to be frequented by Kurds. I ordered them followed. They disappeared, but were observed again at the airport boarding a plane to Athens. At Hellinikon they transferred to a flight to Rhodes. Since arriving there they have been under constant surveillance.

"The possibility exists, then, that these Soviet operatives have discovered something we have not, and are planning to act on this information."

"Why should they care?" Townsend White asked.

"Precisely my p—p—point," Giddings said. "Mandy's politics may be off kilter now and then, but she's by God not one of theirs. She's ours, and we'll fetch her b—b—back, thank you very much. And I'm going to ring up Nikulin and tell him so."

"Mr. Giddings, I already brought this information to the attention of the Soviet Consul General, and was told that Ilyinsky and Bessaraboff are pursuing no investigation, and are in fact enjoying a brief holiday in the Dodecanese."

"Well? How d—d—d'you know they're not?"

"Perhaps if I may continue? This third man, who we originally suspected to be a Kurdish informer, this morning paid a large sum of money to a Mandraki yacht broker for a one-week charter of a forty-foot sailboat."

"What's wrong with that?"

"Nothing, Mr. Giddings. Except for the crew. We have just received these facsimiles of photographs taken today of this boat with a telephoto lens. Please pass them around."

The faxes were fairly good halftones, a dozen views of a sailboat cockpit. Ilyinsky, Bessaraboff and the "mystery man" appeared in most of the faxes; along with them were two new faces: young-looking muscled men in T-shirts, loading gear aboard from dockside. One was nearly bald, the other crew-cut.

"Who are these guys?" Leo was the first to ask.

"We think—indeed, we are quite sure—that they are Soviet special forces. *Spetsnaz.*"

"But *Spetsnaz* work for the GRU, military intelligence, not the KGB," Nevins pointed out.

"Well, here they are 'all in the same boat,' as you say." Ozsahin smiled, obviously pleased at his little joke. "Whoever they are, Mr. Nevins, they seem to be bringing on board a good deal of equipment, and I daresay it isn't all Coca-Cola."

"Why don't you just stop them?" Jack Woodhull asked.

"Hell, no," said Josh Nevins. "Let 'em go."

"Exactly. We are extremely interested in their destination. If it is just a holiday cruise, they are welcome to enjoy themselves as much as they like." The colonel moved back to the map. "As I mentioned, we have alerted our police all along the Turkish littoral. But, as

Mr. Nevins observed, half the Dodecanese are within a hundred kilometers of Rhodes—" his finger hopped from one island to another, "Karpathos, Kasos, Simi, Halki, Tilos, Nisiros, Kos."

"Couldn't they charter a boat out of any of those larger islands, say, Kos? Why Rhodes?"

"Yes, Mr. White, they could. Which indicates perhaps their target is a much smaller island, closer to Rhodes. Halki, for instance, is surrounded by islets. And along the Lycian coast are several small Turkish islands, in the Gulf of Fethiye and the Gulf of Antalya, here and here. Also, just off our shores we have the last of the Dodecanese, tiny Meis, which the Greeks call Kastellorizo. But this is traveling perhaps too far, almost a hundred-twenty kilometers from Rhodes, and a rough sail."

"Have you rung up Athens about all this?"

"Naturally, Mr. Giddings. We do cooperate, you know. Elite units of the Greek Army's special forces and paracommando brigades are standing by, waiting for this little sailboat to leave Mandraki."

"Excuse me, please, but may I offer another suggestion?"

"Of course, Monsieur Bouchard."

"You must understand, my concern is not killing terrorists. It is the saving of the life of my dear wonderful friend Mandy Morgan. And this, gentlemen, we can do without guns, Greeks, sailboat. It takes only money, Colonel, nothing else."

"M. Bouchard, everyone in this room shares your concern for the life of Miss Morgan."

"Bullshit!"

"Please, Monsieur Bouchard. I have told you—with the full support of Mr. Giddings and Her Majesty's government—that there will be no ransom paid to these criminals. As long as the demand is received on Turkish soil, it will not be done."

The little Frenchman stood up, jerked away from Jack Woodhull's restraining hand and stalked to the door, where he paused a moment. "You don't care about 'er, none of you. But I do care. And you cannot stop me from 'elping 'er!"

20

THE KNIFE WAS A TINY THING, BONE-HANDLED, WITH A three-inch, drop-point blade. Amanda turned it slowly in her palm, watching the stainless-steel blade glisten in the moonlight streaming through the tent flap.

"If it makes you feel better," Guldasa had told the distraught Englishwoman, "please take it. But I know Ismet and Hamzah will return at any moment. It will be all right."

"It will *not* be all right!" Amanda had protested, pocketing the weapon gratefully all the same. She could not believe Ismet would leave the island without telling her, accompanying his cousin to the mainland to deliver the videotape. The idea of being alone on the island with John Courage—except for Guldasa and her henpecked little husband—was utterly terrifying.

But why was she waiting? What she should be doing was escaping—anywhere, in any direction. The Turkish mainland was only a couple of miles off. She ought to be able to swim that—or die trying. And Kastellorizo's harbor town couldn't be more than five or six miles. There was no way to miss it, if she followed the shore. With Guldasa's Reeboks and a full moon to guide her over the island's rocky terrain, she could reach it.

But first she had to slip out of camp undetected.

Fahri was on sentry duty, somewhere at the top of the excavation. Amanda remembered how soundly the little Turk had slept in the back of the van. Perhaps he had already nodded off.

In the patch of sky visible through the tent opening the moon was briefly shadowed by scudding clouds. If some larger, darker clouds would only sail by, she thought, she could steal away from the camp.

She stared up at the luminous silver disk, her decision made, as one dark veil trailed another across the bright surface, none lingering sufficiently. Then a smoky wisp ushered in a dark, drifting cloud bank. Within a few hammering heartbeats the moon had vanished. *Now,* she thought. She gripped the knife, drew back the tent flap—and walked right into John Courage.

"Going for a stroll, luv?"

She gasped and tried to wrench free. He chuckled and ripped her shirt half away, knocking her against the tent pole. She caught her balance, then remembered the weapon in her hand. She lunged upward, felt the blade slice into flesh.

The giant bellowed in pain. "You fucking whore!"

Again Amanda stabbed, but Courage stepped aside and slapped her, sending her tumbling to the ground like a rag doll. For moments she could not remember where she was, or who she was. There was only a faraway sound, an eerie buzzing, and in her skull a sick numbness. She tried to locate her body, make it move, could not. Was she paralyzed?

Then she felt her fingers clawing gravel, her legs thrashing on the ground, trying to crawl away like a wounded animal. Before she could reach the tent opening, she was snatched into the air, swung around, and dropped onto her cot.

She lifted her head to see him looming huge against the moonlight, whipping off his belt, fumbling at his pants. Where were Fahri, Guldasa, with their guns? Couldn't they hear her screaming? But she *wasn't* screaming! She was making only a faint, growling vibrato. She began instead to pray.

The Englishman was naked now, twisted oddly around. She realized he was inspecting himself. "Bitch!" he cursed, pressing his wadded shirt against his left buttock. "Fucking bitch!" She must have stabbed him in the ass then. She wished she'd castrated him!

He whirled around. Too stunned to protect herself, she watched in horror as he came toward her. She tried to quell the waves of panic that swept her. It wasn't her any longer. It was somebody else the Englishman was yanking upright, whose shirt was being ripped off her back, whose jeans were being peeled off her legs. Amanda was totally naked now, a helpless, splayed-out doll. But her real self had taken refuge deep in the cave of her mind, huddling there, waiting till the nightmare was over.

As the unspeakable, corpselike thing lowered itself onto her, she spoke the Lord's name over and over like a *mantra.* She felt the cot groan beneath the weight, then canvas tear loose from the frame, and they crashed together to the ground. Amanda was nearly crushed, but the grunting, slobbering beast on top of her didn't seem to notice.

As she fought for breath, his foul, bearded mouth came down on hers, making her gag. Why was no one helping her? Had Courage killed them first, both Fahri and Guldasa? Was she all alone on the island with this monster?

Then, abruptly, his weight shifted, and he rolled off her and stood up. She expanded her aching ribs, filled her lungs, dared to open her eyes

The trouserless Englishman towered astride her, his hand flogging away at his huge flaccid penis, cursing himself the while: "Get hard, damn you! Fuck the bitch!" But the tone was despairing, and his furious efforts unavailing.

Amanda watched in horrified fascination. The giant would-be rapist couldn't get it up; drugs had apparently rendered him impotent. Despite herself, she began to laugh hysterically.

She knew at once it was a mistake. Courage reacted instantly, ceasing his futile labors and glaring down with pure malevolence. "I'll give you something to laugh at, you little slut!" He drew back his leg to kick her in the face.

"Angleesh! Get away from the lady!" cried a voice outside. Fahri! Thank God!

Courage stopped.

"Come out of there, Angleesh, or I come in and shoot you! Guldasa! Guldasa!"

"Go ahead, you little wog! Come on and kill me. Then explain it to Ismet, if you bloody can!"

"Angleesh!" This time it was Guldasa. "I order you! Come out of there at once!" But Guldasa didn't wait. Amanda looked up as the Kurdish woman slid into the moonlit opening, rifle leveled at Courage. The giant backed away, grabbing for his trousers.

"The bitch stabbed me!" he said.

"You deserve much worse than this! Get out!" Courage, trousers in hand and still muttering, edged carefully past her and exited.

"I have him, Guldasa!" Fahri called from outside.

"Good. Watch him closely. I will see to Amanda."

Guldasa came forward then, slinging her rifle and kneeling beside Amanda. "You poor child," she whispered, her hand touching the Englishwoman's forehead. "You are all right?"

The kind words brought on Amanda's tears.

≡

The same night, at the wheel of the forty-foot chartered sloop *Alcyone,* Paul Cyrus watched the full moon play hide-and-seek through a ragged stratus cloud cover. They were heading east southeast, paralleling the bulge of the southern Turkish coast several miles off the port beam. For the past several hours they had been running before the *meltemi,* the prevailing westerlies, which were blowing at about force four.

It was the happiest Paul had felt in weeks. He was finally getting to sail the Greek Isles, as he'd wanted to do with Darryl Ann. Of course, instead of a beautiful blonde his crew consisted of a quartet of Soviet agents. *Oh well, can't have everything.*

They'd taken *Alcyone* out of Mandraki harbor at

sunset, past the old windmills and through the entrance once straddled by the ancient Colossus, into Rhodes channel, where he'd switched off the auxiliary engine and raised sail. The *meltemi* had obliged at once, wrapping them in a stiff, twelve-knot embrace and sending them scooting along on a broad reach.

Gradually in the past few hours Paul's problems had lost their death grip and been carried away by the wind, along with the fake mustache of Jiraz Shikak, which had come loose and been cast into *Alcyone's* wake. Paul still thought of Amanda, of course, visualized her out there somewhere in the night. But his mind was occupied with more immediate and elemental matters— the kiss of the following wind on the back of his neck; the glowing compass card in the binnacle, hovering around one-ten; the ghostly arc of the genoa; and the inky darkness ahead, which he scanned constantly for navigation lights.

The broad head of Ilyinsky appeared silhouetted at the top of the companion ladder. The Russian handed Paul a steaming mug of coffee. "How is it going?"

"No complaints. How are they doing below?"

"Toshka is very sick boy. Our other friends are both asleep. You need relief?"

"I'm fine. Just keep the caffeine coming."

Ilyinsky could steer a compass course, but the American dared not leave him alone in the cockpit for any length of time. With the *meltemi* likely to get fluky, having an inexperienced helmsman was inviting a whole catalogue of minor calamities, from an accidental jibe to dipping the boom and broaching to. Under the present conditions, he and *Alcyone* would go it alone. Surprisingly—at least to Paul—neither of the *Spetsnaz,* for all their training, had any basic seamanship.

"How fast we are going?" Ilyinsky asked.

"We're averaging around six and a half or seven knots."

"It seems not very fast to me."

"It won't, not with the wind behind us like this. Our speed through the water and the wind speed match, so you can't feel it or hear it. It seems like we're just drifting along." Paul pantomimed with his hands. "But we're moving."

"You cannot go faster?"

"Not really." They could do a bit better with a spinnaker, but it didn't seem worth the trouble. *Alcyone* would get them there in time. Feliks had originally wanted to hire a motor sailer, but even the smallest of these at Mandraki came with a minimum crew of two or three. Only sailing yachts were available on bareboat charter.

"We will be there when?"

"If this keeps up"—which, according to the English radio forecast out of Rhodes, it should—"sometime before dawn."

"Then you can sleep. We will do the rest."

"Maybe I'd like in on the fun."

"Believe me, you would not. Neither you, nor Toshka. Our new colleagues are not even sure about *my* abilities." Ilyinsky chuckled. "They prefer to do everything themselves."

"They do look fit." "They" were a couple of burly, hard-faced *Spetsnaz* noncoms in their mid-twenties, Viktor and Maksim. According to Feliks, both were *Afgantsy,* decorated veterans of Afghanistan, having served three years in a special forces brigade in Jelala-bad. As to their present status, Feliks would only say they were on loan from military intelligence.

And they'd come prepared. Paul had seen their equipment laid out on the bunks in the V-shaped forward cabin. AK-74 assault rifles, German HKMP5K compact submachine guns, nine-millimeter pistols with silencers, radios, several grenade launchers, even spring-loaded knives. The two seemed to feel that cleaning out a nest of Kurdish guerrillas would pose no particular problems. Their confidence was impressive.

Paul had felt awkward around them and, curiously, discovered he could converse with them only in French. But Anton Bessaraboff had been goggle-eyed, examining all their paraphernalia, asking rapid questions. The *Spetsnaz* were plainly amused by their grotesque-looking countryman.

While below checking stowage, Paul had witnessed a cruel practical joke. Viktor had been showing Anton his fighting knife, a wicked six-inch serrated blade of blackened steel, and apparently offered to demonstrate its use. When the young man nodded eagerly, the *Spets-naz* lunged with it at Bessaraboff's stomach in a blur of speed. Bessaraboff had grunted and doubled up, clutching himself as if to keep his guts from spilling all over the deck.

Maksim had doubled over, too, but in laughter, and Viktor with him. The two screwed up their eyes and giggled till tears squeezed out, miming Bessaraboff's terrified look again and again. By then, of course, the poor, ashen-faced wretch realized he had not been stabbed, only stomach-punched. The knife had been reversed in mid-air faster than the eye could see. Bessaraboff had tried to smile while the merry pranksters patted his thin shoulders.

Not very amusing, Paul had decided, heading topside. But what did he expect from professional killers? He'd already witnessed one torture-murder, committed by the stocky "diplomat" perched on the cockpit cushion to his left. But Paul had begged Ilyinsky to take him along. Was he going to wimp out now, over a nasty practical joke?

The answer was no. Paul wanted to be just where he was, among these cutthroats, riding to the rescue of Amanda Morgan with bugles and banners. Or, rather, with jib and mainsail, gliding over the waves toward the eastern horizon.

He smiled tensely to himself and drained his coffee. It sure as hell wasn't going to be boring.

21

By midnight, six hours out of Mandraki harbor, by Paul's dead reckoning the *Alcyone* was abreast of the Seven Capes, or Yedi Burunlar, on the Turkish Lycian Coast. The *meltemi* had slackened a little, but was still gusting from the northwest at around ten knots. Paul now calculated their arrival off Kastellorizo well before dawn.

Thirty thousand feet above them their position was also being plotted, on the radar of a Turkish RF-4E reconnaissance Phantom. The pilot, half-Kurdish himself, immediately relayed the information and headed home to the NATO air base at Adana, near the Syrian border.

Two minutes later, back in Istanbul, Colonel Ozsahin was handed a note and he marked *Alcyone*'s position on an overlay map of the southern coast. His office was one of the few still showing lights in the modern city hall, and only Majors Akalin and Yoruk, Captain Erol, and two young aides were present, the latter to handle communications traffic and brew coffee. All were vastly relieved to obtain the boat's location; the homing signal from the RDF device attached by Turkish agents on Rhodes to the *Alcyone*'s mast had petered out a half-hour earlier.

"Meis," the colonel said, pointing at the tiny Greek island opposite the Turkish town of Kas. With no Americans or British present, there was no need to go on using the Italo-Hellenic name, Kastellorizo. "I am sure of this."

"What about Ro or Strongili?" Akalin asked. These were two even tinier islets clustering around Kastellorizo, a fact that was responsible for the island's other Greek name of Megisti, meaning "the largest." "Aren't they inhabited?"

"If you count goats and lighthouse-keepers. Not places to hide kidnapped celebrities. On Meis there is plenty of room." Ozsahin crushed out a cigarette. "It is time, I think, for another call to Athens."

$$=$$

Acting upon Ozsahin's earlier warnings, the Greeks had sent two CH-47C Chinook transport helicopters island-hopping through the Cyclades and Dodecanese to Rhodes, where they disgorged three squadrons of Army para-commandos. These troops had just been joined by an elite unit from the Athens City Police Special Mission Platoon, which had recently undergone hostage rescue training with the British SAS and the West German GSG-9. Both groups were standing by at Rhodes Paradissi Airport.

Now, in response to Ozsahin's latest call and the

information relayed from the Turkish Phantom jet, further aerial photoreconnaissance of the Megisti island group was ordered. Within an hour of a high-level teleconference between Athens and Washington, a U-2/TR-1 spy plane, under authority of the U.S. Strategic Air Command, took off from Frankfurt's Rhein-Main Air Base, climbed to fifty thousand feet, and headed southeast through the night toward the Eastern Med.

There was also a call from Athens to the island itself.

≡

In the harbor town of Kastellorizo, Alekos Katapodis, a sixty-three-year-old veteran of World War II and his country's civil war, sat hunched on his bed, phone to his ear, nodding his head groggily in response to the crisp questions and directives from the other end of the line.

"No, I can do what you ask," he protested. "You do not need to send anyone. I will leave immediately."

Alekos put down the phone, ran a weathered hand over his wrinkled face, shook his bald head. *Terrorists on Megisti, with the film star they'd been showing on television! It could not be.*

The old policeman, who was also the island's postman, swung regretfully out of his bed, slowly dressed himself. In the back of a closet, wrapped in an oily blanket, he located his ancient Mannlicher bolt-action rifle, and beneath his underwear in the bureau, a half-full box of 6.5-millimeter cartridges. He trudged next into the kitchen and put a kettle on for tea. While it was coming to a boil he upended his old field pack over the pine table, spilling out his fishing gear and making room for the ammunition, a hunk of goat cheese, bread, a clove of garlic to combat fatigue, a bottle of *grappa,* binoculars, and a Japanese two-meter hand-held radio.

Fifteen minutes later Alekos Katapodis stepped out of his narrow harborside house into fog-shrouded darkness and shivered. It was 3:45 in the morning. Even the fishermen of Megisti weren't up yet!

He had come to the island in '48, sailing into a tiered amphitheater of abandoned, blackened houses, bombed by the Axis, then burned by the Allied occupation forces to hide the pillaging they had done after evacuating the islanders. The rebuilding had been slow, discouraging; many had emigrated to Australia and the town had never regained its prewar population. There were less than three hundred Kastellorizians now.

Alekos had been chief policeman since '69. The island was so isolated from the rest of the Dodecanese that in all that time he had never had to deal with anything more threatening than drunken tourists, hash-smoking hippies, some Italian kayakers trapped by the rising tide in the Fokiali sea cave, and occasional nude sunbathers of the more flagrant variety. Never anything like this.

He shivered again, watching the flashing beacon at the harbor mouth diffuse into the jeweled, swirling fog. The familiar twinkling lights along the bay of Kas on the Turkish mainland less than three kilometers away were nowhere to be seen. Alekos turned, heading past the shuttered quayside *tavernas* toward the flagged path behind the town that climbed in long switchbacks to the top of Mount Viglo and the ruins of a Dorian acropolis. Once he reached that, he promised himself, he'd rest for a while, have a drink of *grappa,* and watch the sun come up, before trekking south over the island's central plateau.

He could do this. Better one man already on the spot, with knowledge of the terrain, than a small planeload of commandos from Rhodes with all their high-tech gear and topographical maps. Alekos had barely managed to talk Athens out of that idea. If terrorists *were* hiding out there somewhere, they'd be instantly alerted by any unscheduled landing on the island's tiny airstrip. The weekly flight from Rhodes wasn't due for several days.

But where could they be? Beyond the monastery of Aghios Ioannis, there was little but barren rock. Only a hermit who lived in a cliffside cave—a harmless fellow who evidently found monastery life not solitary enough, and a bearded Englishman camped out at an abandoned dig on the island's southern tip.

Occasionally this huge fellow came lurching into town for provisions. He'd pass the day on the quayside, staggering from one *taverna* to the next, singing songs and buying drinks for everyone in sight. Then he'd sleep it off at a *pension* and leave the next morning. A noisy but harmless eccentric.

Still, Alekos would have to cover every square meter of the island with his binoculars. He reckoned he could finish his survey by noon, then radio the results on the frequency Athens had given him. With any luck he'd be back in his own bed by nightfall. And if he found something . . . well, he'd be damn careful. It was good to feel like a young soldier again, to be answering his country's call. But there was no point in getting shot at.

By the time he reached the top of Mount Viglo, the fog was beginning to shred. Bathed in sweat, his heart laboring, he made a three-hundred-and-sixty degree survey. To the east the coming day showed as a vermilion gash in the purple stratus banked over Asia. In the harbor far below lights were beginning to flicker on the fishing boats. Everything seemed normal.

As he searched for a favorite flat rock he recalled as an ideal resting spot, he heard a clatter of loose stones. A ghostly figure was coming down the misty path toward him! Alekos unslung his rifle, stepped behind an olive tree.

"Hallo there! Art thou not Constable Katapodis?"

A flashlight beam swept the path where Alekos had been standing. The policeman moved back into view. He recognized the voice, the stilted dialect. A moment later a young man appeared behind the weaving flashlight— a tall, blond Swede with soft, pleasant features, who'd arrived two days before on the *Panormitis* from Rhodes. The youth smiled, blinking pale limpid eyes, and adjusted his rucksack on his shoulders.

"Good morning," Alekos said.

"And to thee, Constable." The young man spoke an amusing Homeric Greek, obviously learned out of books. He had told Alekos he was an admirer of all things Hellenic and had come to tramp around the island and photograph some of the numerous archeological sites. "Thou seemst to have difficulty with thy breath, Constable. What has roused thee from thy bed so early?"

"Eh? What indeed? Looking for you, young man, in all this fog. I was worried when you didn't come back to the *pension.*"

"Thou needst not worry. I am accustomed to privation."

"Your name was Wulf, wasn't it?"

"Truly, it still is."

"Well, Wulf, tell me how you like our island. Find that lost city of Strabo you were looking for?"

"Cysthine? Yes, perhaps. Near Kampos there are some venerable fragments." ·

"Of course they're 'venerable.' They're ruins. But if you want to find our lost city, lad, it's right down there—harborside. The way I figure it, Cysthine is just another ancient name for our island. Now if it was me, I'd be searching for that chest of gold pieces buried by pirates somewhere around here."

The Swede nodded happily, but made no comment. Alekos framed the question he'd been leading up to: "Say, did you happen to meet anybody out there, beyond the monastery? Maybe that crazy Englishman I told you about, way down on the southern end?"

"Alas, I encountered no one, and proceeded so slowly I did not attain Pouliou Folia. Now I am without provisions."

"Well, if you hurry, you'll be just in time for breakfast at the *pension.*"

"Art thou coming as well?"

"No, now that I'm up, I may as well stretch my legs. I hardly ever get up here anymore. You should see this place in early spring. Blooming with narcissi and anemones."

"Perhaps I shall. Adieu, Constable Katapodis."

"And adieu to thee, Wulf."

Alekos continued up the rocky track, deciding to push on awhile. Show the lad his stride, try not to labor like an old mule. Nice enough young man, but what sort of a dawdler couldn't make the end of the island and back in two days?

≡

When the old man was out of sight, the young Swede sat down on the very spot Alekos had picked out for himself. Lovely view. Fished into his rucksack. Took out his dog-eared Homer. Quite appropriate, with dawn flexing its rosy fingers just over there. Uncapped his mineral water, took a swig. Unwrapped a honey pastry and swallowed it.

Lastly Wulf took out his portable VHF-UHF transceiver and extended the flex antenna. The spot was ideal for line-of-sight transmission—if his "friends" were where they were supposed to be. He punched a preset frequency button and verified it on the illuminated LED readout. Then he waited, checking his watch. Exactly on the hour he began transmitting.

≡

The *Alcyone* was hove to just north of the islet of Ro. Alone in the cockpit, Paul took a bearing on the blinking ruby-and-white eye of the lighthouse on Kastellorizo's northern headland, Aghios Stefanos, sweeping through the mist. Thanks to the *meltemi,* he had done his part nicely—in just under eleven hours from Rhodes. Now it was up to Ilyinsky to find out where on that ghostly hunk of rock the Kurds had gone to ground. The actual rescue operation, Ilyinsky indicated, would be carried out by himself and the *Spetsnaz.* But when the moment came, Paul intended to push for a piece of the action.

Ilyinsky was below, on the VHF radiotelephone in the little nav station forward of the main cabin. "Excellent," he was saying into the microphone as he hurried a felt-tip pen across a rough map of the island. "I have it. That's where we'll do our fishing. Good work, Wulf. You've earned a few more months of holiday."

≡

The Swede smiled, put away his radio, leaned against his rucksack, and stared out over the gradually lightening, fog-strewn channel. Both he and the Russian had played a little game, pretending they didn't know what was going on at the other end of the island in the little camp Wulf had spied upon. But the Russian had demanded to know every detail, while obviously trying to conceal his own excitement.

The big bearded man was certainly the English eccentric Alekos had mentioned. But the man and woman with rifles were certainly not archeologists. Then there was the lovely dark-haired creature, whose face, when Wulf's binoculars pulled her into close-up, was so terribly familiar and so very much in the news. What could this strange quartet be doing on the deserted end of a remote island, except hiding from the whole world?

It was dangerously exciting to be in possession of such a secret. Yet Wulf was more than discreet in such matters. It paid not to ask questions sometimes, and paid very well indeed. For the young Swede it was the perfect part-time job, running occasional errands for a Russian he'd never seen. Thanks to the regular infusion of *drachmas,* Wulf had managed another whole summer in the islands, with mostly nothing to do but pursue his favorite Philhellenic pastimes—reading Homer in the original, bronzing his lean body, and cruising the beaches and discos for other like-minded young Adonises.

Thinking of which, Apollo would be up and about

soon in his chariot. Time to hike on down for breakfast and a nap at the *pension.* Life was a very fine thing when you were young and free, blond and irresistible.

≡

Ilyinsky had just been handed another radio message by Bessaraboff. This one came through in code, on one of the higher FM frequencies not used for commercial broadcast. Translated, the message was simple. The Greeks had been tracking him, and now, apparently based on his position and course, were readying their own counter-terrorist forces at Rhodes airport.

In order not to jeopardize relations with Athens, the message concluded, the GRU (which had loaned the two *Spetsnaz* soldiers) and the KGB had jointly decided to cancel Ilyinsky's operation. On no account was he to proceed.

Bessaraboff read the translation through. Ilyinsky only shook his head. "So, the Greeks know we are here. But how did *they* become interested in me?"

"I think it is our friend, Colonel Ozsahin."

"I think so, too. Have you acknowledged?"

"Of course. Do you have a further reply?"

"Yes. 'Unable to decode. Message garbled. Please repeat.' Then turn off the radio. Don't laugh, Toshka. I'm serious. Reply exactly as I say."

The younger man waved the message. "This is an operational order, Feliks, not a suggestion. We are talking about careers and lives here—yours and mine, for instance."

"Toshka, I was promoted to major for disobeying explicit orders. Gelding that Lebanese Shia boy was a 'clear and flagrant breach of authority,' remember? And after the return of our hostages, my superiors were all drafting post-dated memoranda granting full authorization."

"Circumstances are different."

"How so?"

"We are not alone in the field anymore." Bessaraboff again flourished the message. "The Greeks are ready to jump on top of us the minute we reach Kastellorizo. It's their island, Feliks. We've no business there."

"God help them. They can't even secure their own airport."

"They've improved since 1985."

"Who knows? If they come roaring in over that tiny island, dropping commandos out of helicopters, they'll never take the Little Fox by surprise. In fact, they'll probably land in the wrong place. And even if, by strange accident, they do find Ismet, they'll either get Amanda killed or start another hostage standoff. No, my young friend, we are in position to do this thing. And only we. But we must move quickly.

He smiled at his protegé.

"Well, Toshka, are you just going to stand there blinking at me? Where is the intrepid soul who killed a charging sheepdog with only four bullets? Perhaps you want to snitch to our *Spetsnaz* friends up there, tell them Major Ilyinsky has lost his mind and is about to betray the Fatherland? Have them arrest me as a traitor? Let me know what you decide, will you?"

Bessaraboff gulped. He knew his mentor was embracing irrationality, just as he often did in launching poorly conceived chess offensives. Yet the narrowed look in Feliks's eyes warned Bessaraboff he was in a very dangerous position. In a showdown, he could not see Maksim and Viktor backing him against Feliks.

There was another thing. Ever since Feliks had agreed to take him along on a real operation, the young man had experienced a burgeoning excitement, akin to that of closing with an opponent over the chessboard. Only this was real. Had not Bessaraboff already fired a weapon and killed an adversary, albeit an animal? And in this arena of blood and bullets—wet operations—Ilyinsky, for all his lapses of logic, was a proven master. Who was Bessaraboff to say the KGB major couldn't pull it off, right under the eyes of the Greeks?

"All right, Feliks. I'll say nothing. On one condition."

"Which is?"

"That I be allowed to participate."

"With a gun, you mean? But of course, Toshka. I'm sure we can find something for you to kill."

22

AT LONGOS, ON THE WEST SIDE OF THE BAY OF KAS, AND less than four kilometers east of *Alcyone,* a *caique* motored out through the fog toward Kastellorizo. Hamzah had the tiller, and Ismet sat in the bow, watching the intermittent white-sector flashes from the Aghios Stefanos light on the island's northern cape. Both men were exhausted from a day and night of the exuberant Aussies, Susannah and Britt.

The images blurred: the innumerable glasses of beer; the bumpy ride in Susannah's battered Toyota van with everyone laughing; a secluded beach the girls had heard about, where there was more beer, and *cannabis* passed around by some North African guys at a camp fire; then swimming naked and partying in the back of the van, where Ismet had started out with Britt and woke up with Susannah.

The Little Fox shook off the reverie. In the stern-sheets Hamzah had on his usual grin.

"You are happy now, Cousin?" Ismet asked.

"As the Prophet has written: 'Those that have faith and do good works shall dwell in the gardens of delight forever.' " Hamzah began to giggle.

"I have had enough of this garden for now," Ismet said. "Besides, we are late, and there is work to do."

"Yes, but when we have done our work, and collected our ransom, we will be able to enjoy such delights whenever we wish."

"Be careful, Cousin. You begin to sound like the Big Angleesh." Ismet held a folded square of paper up to the breeze and let it flutter away.

"What was that?"

"The address of my 'Sheila,' in Melbourne."

"She liked you very much."

"Perhaps so. But she will forget me, and I her."

Another woman was waiting for him now, and a decision must be made. Trade her for millions, that's what they all wanted. Perhaps when they got away with all that money, Ismet would retire from the *pesh merga,* go somewhere he was not known, assume a new identity. The *Murshid*'s prophecy had been wrong, after all. The Little Fox was not born to save Kurdistan. The battle was too long, and he had grown weary of it.

He turned back to his cousin. "Hamzah, what we talked about last night, perhaps you are right."

"You will really do it?"

"When this is over, yes. We will go away, the two of us."

"Perhaps to Melbourne?"

Ismet shrugged. "Yes, perhaps. I don't care."

≡

Amanda awoke just after dawn. For long, dizzying moments she could not place herself. Above her head faint light showed through blue tent fabric. She must be on location—but where, on what film, for what company, playing what part? She stared at the blue light, alarmed by the memory void and a sudden sense that something truly awful had happened to her.

Then she glanced down. A young woman was curled on the ground beside her in a sleeping bag, a rifle by her side; a few feet away, at the tent opening, was another sleeping body. Fahri, Guldasa, John Courage— it all came back in a horrifying rush.

She could not recall the details of her last-second deliverance, only that it had happened, and that these two sleeping bodies at her feet had somehow saved her.

She looked at them with mild astonishment. They were the same two who had tied her to a kitchen chair in the hovel in Usküdar. They were still terrorists, after all, and she their prisoner—as she obviously had been since Fahri snapped a handcuff on her back in the Harbor Police building, only she'd been too arrogant to realize it.

What should she do? She felt dead, drained of energy and will. Did anything matter anymore, after what she'd been through?

Yes, answered a stubborn voice within, and made her push herself wearily off the cot and swing her lifeless legs from under the covers. Survival mattered. *Her* survival. She damn well wasn't going to lie around like dead meat waiting for Courage's next attack.

She set her feet on the ground, looked down curiously. Guldasa must have dressed her last night, after saving her life. Amanda had no memory of it. She was wearing cotton half-socks with fluffy pink tassels and an indigo batik tank-top that was probably fine for the slim Kurdish girl but which stretched taut across Amanda's fuller breasts, tracing her nipples. A pair of khaki Bermudas were also snug, baring her legs to mid-thigh, raising goose bumps in the morning chill. Amanda felt another surge of tenderness for the woman sleeping at her feet. But it wouldn't stop her from escaping.

She spotted the black Reeboks in a corner and lifted herself gingerly off the bed, fighting dizziness, stepping carefully over Guldasa. It seemed to take forever, moving in slow motion, to lace the shoes on over the silly socks.

Her eyes went next to Guldasa's assault rifle. Amanda wouldn't hesitate shooting the giant, but the Kurdish woman's hand was on the folding stock. Fahri's rifle was partly hidden beneath his sleeping bag. *Just get out!*

She tiptoed to the entrance.

"Amanda, where you going?"

Shit! Amanda forced herself to turn slowly. Guldasa's sleepy face protruded from her mummy bag.

"Um, just to the latrine, actually." Amanda whispered, hoping not to wake Fahri as well.

"My husband will go with you. Wake him."

"He needn't. I'll only be a moment. Really, I'll be all right." She hesitated. "Guldasa, I don't remember if I ever thanked you . . . for saving my life."

"You did, many times. I wanted to shoot him. Perhaps Ismet will do it when he gets back and learns what happened. But tell me how you are."

"I'm—I'm all right."

"Amanda, I think it better that Fahri go with you."

"No, really, he's sound asleep, and my kidneys are about to burst. I shan't be a moment." To forestall further debate, the actress turned and exited through the tent flap.

Outside, she blinked into pearlescent morning fog. The camp was silent. Amanda did exactly what she'd planned to do last night in the dark of the moon—before running into Courage. She headed swiftly and silently up the ramp.

At the top, thick, chilling vapors had effaced the world, leaving only a few shadowy olive branches. The ocean that lay beyond the trees had vanished as well, though Amanda could smell the cold salt breeze. *Good!* she thought. The lack of visibility would slow her flight, but hide her from pursuit.

She retraced in her mind the three paths diverging from the top of the excavation. One led off through bushes toward the malodorous trench that served as their latrine. A second wound down the steep cliff face to the shore, the path she had climbed blindfolded days before. The third ascended a steep shoulder of rock overlooking the camp, then headed inland—precisely where, Amanda didn't know. She began climbing in that direction.

At the top of the steep pitch, she paused for breath, then hurried along. She was desperate to put distance between herself and the camp before Guldasa began searching or sounded an alarm. The actress moved as fast as she dared, able only to see a few steps ahead—

the red earth at her feet and the ghostly tracery of branches looming out of the mist and glistening with dew.

Then, from somewhere ahead, there boomed a deep, drunken male voice:

"I can't get no . . . satisfaction!"

Amanda halted, her heart thudding. John Courage was out there, very near! The fog made it impossible to pinpoint the sound direction.

"But I try . . . and I try . . . and I try . . ."

She mustn't panic. If she made no sound, she might slip past him in the fog. Yet the gauzy curtain was starting to shred here and there, vignetting the rocky path ahead, and revealing for the first time, just above the eastern horizon, a pale, quicksilver sun through the mist. Amanda whirled. All around her the fog was coming apart. Then, nearer still, came the ghastly chorus:

"But I can't get no . . . satisfaction! No, no, no!"

She must hide! She crouched, peering through the eddying vapors, seeking cover, a rock to dive behind or crawl under.

"Amanda! Where are you?"

Bloody Christ! Guldasa was calling her, the stupid bitch—betraying her presence to Courage! Courage's voice followed, almost in her ear: "Mandy? You there, luv? Let me see you."

Amanda bolted, as heedless of direction as a flushed rabbit, praying she wouldn't run into the giant or plunge straight off a cliff. Instead she blundered into vines, feeling their wet, clinging slap against her face, tore free, tripped and tumbled and slid down a loose, gravelly slope, scrambled up and kept on running. Both voices continued to call after her.

More landscape opened up as the mist burned off. Bare brown hills took shape before her, a narrow path between. She ran for her life, glancing back as the bearded mercenary appeared out of the mist, stumbling after her like Frankenstein's monster. Where was Guldasa now, with her rifle?

It was right out of her childhood nightmares—fleeing over hill and dale, pursued by a fearsome, devouring giant, an ogre who was gaining on her, slowly and inexorably, as her legs maddeningly refused to go faster.

And Courage *was* gaining. Every time she looked back he seemed closer. Amanda Morgan had reached her limit. Her lungs felt on fire, her legs leaden, and with every stride a stitch knifed at her side. Soon she was gasping for each breath. The beating, the desperate struggle the night before, had taken too heavy a toll. It was almost over.

She looked back, expecting to see him almost on top of her. Instead he had slowed to a walk. Why?

All at once the remaining fog lifted and vanished, revealing her to be halfway down a path on a narrow headland. On each side of her lay sheer cliffs. Beyond sprawled the Mediterranean, a vast sheet of polished silver.

The bearded mercenary had just reached the neck of the headland. His face was split by a huge grin. He must have known for several minutes she was fleeing into a trap. There was no way out from the rocky point, except past him.

Courage opened his arms wide: "Come to poppa, that's the girl."

Amanda turned toward the bluff in a horror of despair. She staggered on a short way, till she stood on the very brow of the cliff. She looked down past her feet at a sheer drop into gray seas, seething at the base of the cliff. Fifty feet, or a hundred fifty? She couldn't tell, and it probably didn't matter. It was enough to fire off every alarm in her nervous system, and wring the last drop from her exhausted adrenals.

No stuntman or woman was handy to step in for her. The Turkish mainland was farther off here at the island's southern end. Much farther than she could ever hope to swim in her present condition. Maybe she could hide down there somewhere . . . if she survived the fall.

She turned a final time. Courage shuffled forward, one foot at a time, obviously worried by her behavior.

"Easy, girl," he coaxed. "Don't you be doing anything stupid. You're spooked—I see it—but I won't hurt you. Not anymore. I'm sorry about what happened. You gave me a real scare with that knife. But it's over now. You just stay right where you are, and I'll come get you."

Amanda turned away. *Whatever happens,* she vowed, *never again will he touch me.* She backed off from the edge several steps, said the briefest prayer. Then, banishing all thought, launched herself forward— and into the void.

23

WHEN ISMET AND HAMZAH TIED UP THE WEATHERBEATEN *caique* at the old wooden landing and started the slow trek up the switchbacks, *Alcyone* was still twenty minutes to the north, beating into a slackened *meltemi* that had backed to the south.

By the time the two weary *pesh merga,* each laden with sixty pounds of supplies, finally vanished over the clifftop, Ilyinsky, tracking ahead from the sloop's pulpit with his binoculars, had spotted the *caique* and ordered Paul to come about and anchor as near as possible. The dilapidated pier matched Wulf's description. The Soviets were closing in on their quarry.

Two hundred yards offshore, yet out of sight of the pier, Paul Cyrus lowered *Alcyone*'s anchor off the bow into forty feet of water, payed out two hundred feet of rode as the sloop drifted astern and snubbed it tight around a cleat. They were stopped; Paul couldn't promise much more. This side of the rocky island offered no real shelter, as he had explained to Ilyinsky. According to the Admiralty chart, the only safe anchorage was Megisti harbor on the north side.

The Russian was indifferent. "Just get us ashore here," he had said, jabbing the crude island map scribbled with notes from his chat with the Swede. They had only a couple hours for the rescue op, Ilyinsky emphasized. If they came back with Amanda Morgan and still wearing their heads, then they could worry about trivial matters like dragging anchors and lee shores.

Paul granted the point. With a little luck, he thought, the *meltemi* wouldn't kick up again, the current and swell would continue northerly, hugging the coast, and *Alcyone*'s plow anchor would hold.

Ilyinsky scanned the escarpments with his binoculars while cursing the increasing visibility that allowed him to do so. The Russian major wished desperately that the fog had not lifted, wished they could have landed on the island under cover of darkness.

Maksim and Viktor joined him in the cockpit. Both *Spetsnaz* fighters, like Ilyinsky, now wore tan camouflage uniforms over armored Kevlar vests, plus outer flak jackets bristling with weaponry. The silenced submachine guns were slung behind; front pouches and loops contained side arms, spare ammo, commando knives, stun grenades, and radio. Suspended from the *Spetsnaz*'s web belts were coils of nylon climbing rope, carabiners, and pitons. Feliks went over contingencies in rapid Russian, while all three applied light-colored stick camouflage to their faces and all metal or reflective surfaces.

Finally Ilyinsky turned to Paul, handed him a Kalashnikov and a rappelling harness. "One is for shooting, the other you wear. Think you can tell the difference?"

Paul began buckling on the harness. "I've done some rock climbing, and I've fired a few rounds. Mostly semi-automatic."

"And that is exactly how you will keep it. The clip is full, thirty rounds. That should be more than enough. On semi-auto it will take you almost a minute to empty it. But please don't do this. Just watch our backs and stay the hell out of our way. Okay, Yankee?" Feliks tossed him a camouflage stick.

Paul began daubing his face. Lacking the Russians' body armor, he had no great desire to take the point in a firefight. Basically, he was still dressed as a yachtsman out of the boutiques on Rhodes, after throwing out Jiraz Shikak's crappy wardrobe. He felt, in consequence, like the little brother tagging along to the ball field with the older guys. But what mattered was that he would be on the island with a weapon, not watching the action on TV or analyzing it the morning after in some think tank. In his own eyes, he was exorcising the demon of physical cowardice placed upon him, fairly or unfairly, by Amanda Morgan. Perhaps, in the next few hours, the actress would see him in this new guise—as a warrior, skin darkened and camouflaged, rifle in hand, part of the intrepid team that had rescued her.

What he needed to do most was slow down the pulse that pounded high in his throat and ears, and to stop injecting himself with his own adrenaline. He studied Maksim and Viktor. Both men were chewing gum with bovine placidity as they climbed down into the dinghy tethered aft. They moved with surprising stealth, Paul thought, considering their bulk and all the hardware they were packing. He followed, settling in the sternsheets, watching as they muffled the oarlocks with thick wrappings of gauze from a first-aid pack. *Alcyone* had swung slightly with the current, but the anchor was holding.

Feliks was last in, and Bessaraboff handed the final few items down to him. The gangly young Russian's resentment at being left behind was obvious; Feliks tried again to reassure him: "I know you are unhappy, Toshka, but here on the boat you are an essential part of the plan. If they try to escape, you must warn us. But be very sure they are Kurds, not Greek fishermen, and then just call me on the radio. Do not shoot unless you are actually attacked, you understand this?"

"You told me already five times, Feliks."

"So now it is six. All right, Toshka, wish us luck."

Bessaraboff managed to draw himself up in soldier-like fashion as he waved them off. As they pulled away with Viktor bent at the muffled oars, Paul saw the two *Spetsnaz* exchange contemptuous glances.

≡

The moment they were out of sight around the rocky point Bessaraboff yanked open one of the cockpit seat lockers where he'd seen a small inflatable life raft stowed. It took him several minutes to wrestle the blasted thing out of its canvas duffel bag and lay it out on the cabin top under the boom. Barely three meters long and designed to carry four, it must have weighed nearly forty kilos.

Bessaraboff began frantically working the foot pump. Fifteen fatiguing minutes later he decided the two

PVC side tubes and tubular floor were pumped enough to float him ashore—all he cared about. He hitched the painter to a cleat, heaved the inflatable over the lifeline and into the water, and began tossing in odds and ends—the assault rifle with a spare magazine, his radio, an Olympic Airways bag containing three Pepsis and a generous selection of chocolate bars. And—nearly forgotten!—the oars. Finally, he lowered himself onto the rubberized thwart.

Ever since Feliks had told him he wasn't going, Bessaraboff had been in a state of suppressed rage, dangerously close to tears. He would show everybody, he vowed, including those cocky *Spetsnaz* who had missed no opportunity to torment him. He cast off the painter and pushed away from the sloop, dipping the oars into the current and matching the course taken by the dinghy.

=

Amanda did not scream, her life did not pass before her. Instead she thought, *I'm going to survive this.* In the soul-searing seconds of free-fall there was a great rush of air, a far-off serenity, a smearing of light, a clenching of her solar plexus, an instinctive effort to stay feet-first and vertical. Then the water slammed up and hit her like a freight train.

After instantaneous blackout she came to, galvanized with shock, arms and legs thrashing on their own, struggling upward like a birthing fetus for air and life. She swam blindly, knowing that as long as she was moving she had a chance to live.

Then she burst into light and gulped air and seawater before sliding back under, choking, gagging, and rejoicing in the knowledge she *had* survived. She felt a sense of intoxicating triumph. She had escaped!

She came up again, flailing her arms and flinging a lank weight of wet hair off her face. The churning surface was in deep shadow, moss-green water and gray hissing foam sucking to and fro against dark varnished granite. The tide surged and rebounded against the rock wall, tossing her about dangerously. Triumph was replaced by alarm.

Rocks were all around her. How had she missed them in her mad plunge? She flung her arms forward, kicking out, trying to make headway and distance from the cliffs, yet fearing to swim too far out. What she needed, and quickly, was a ledge to grab onto, a place to hide and rest and think what to do next. Yet she must stay out of sight from above. The giant would be up there now, squinting over the edge, searching for her floating corpse.

Please God, let him think I've drowned. Make him go away.

She thrashed on, treading and swallowing water, fighting to keep her head above the waves, searching for a handhold. There was nothing.

The current swept her around a knife edge of rock, opening another stretch of coastline. She scanned ahead hopefully—and felt her heart sink. The island wall bulged out beyond vertical, with nothing along the wave-battered base to cling to. Amanda turned frantically to swim back the way she'd come. But the current bullied her on.

Dear God, what could she do now? Instinct battled to keep her head up, but her arms and legs seemed to sink deeper with each futile stroke and kick, and her will to fight was ebbing. A backwash slapped her hard, pulled her under. She swallowed brine, choked, panic vying with exhaustion.

She threw back her head for a last look at the world. Sunlight scattered sapphires and diamonds out beyond the island shadow. A seabird balanced high on a white wing tip, then was eclipsed by her own childish hand arching through the sky, grasping at air. She slipped deeper into the water, felt herself letting go of all the Gordian-knotted, unfinished business of her life. All sums zeroed, debts canceled, dreams abandoned. *Goodbye,* she thought. *I loved it all so much. And now it's over.*

Then something struck her on the head, and curiosity pulled her back to the surface. A reed basket bobbed in the waves just in front of her like a bath toy—or a drowner's delusion. From its handle a thick rope stretched upwards. Amanda grabbed for the basket, fell short, and sank. She scissor-kicked her exhausted legs, lunging out of the water and wrapping both arms around the basket. It was really there, and it held her up!

As she gorged on oxygen, she felt a strain on the rope. Then her head rose fractionally out of the water. After several gasping lungfuls, she lifted her eyes.

From a protruding ledge high up the overhanging cliff a round bearded face stared down. Beside the face was a pulley attached to the rope basket. The man was waving and shouting something. Amanda could not understand. It didn't matter. There was nothing she could do but cling here. The rest was up to him.

She felt the tug again, realized she was rising slightly out of the water. Was he really going to try and pull her up? She wrapped her hands more tightly around the rope, wedged her elbows inside the fiber basket. The task seemed impossible, but she would hang on as long as she could.

She rose in a series of small jerks, feeling quite like a corpse being fished out of the sea. Then her shoes broke the surface and she was completely out, twisting in the air against the massive cliffside.

She glanced upward again. Still a long way to go. Her fingers were being cut by the rope, her wrists ached, her shoulders and back muscles burned. She clenched her teeth, but it was no use. Her back muscles gave way first, causing her elbows to slip out of the basket. Amanda lurched downward, her throbbing hands barely clinging to the wet hemp.

She cried out, but held fast. Her arms felt like they were being uprooted from their sockets, but she refused to let go. As the strain flayed the muscles on her back, she continued to rise, inch by agonizing inch, hearing the rope screech through the block above. Far below the green water still seethed, as if eager to claim her again. She *must* hang on. She could never survive another fall.

Then her hips struck solid rock. The pain was searing, but followed by the glorious sensation of a strong arm around her waist, pulling her upward. She felt no pain as her bare knees scraped the rocky ledge. She let go in an exquisite swoon, tumbling onto blessed, solid rock.

≡

His name, said her bearded rescuer, was Brother Theodore. He was a monk of the Eastern Orthodox Church. He spoke a halting English, studied long ago as an Athenian schoolboy. He announced proudly that he had a brother who owned a restaurant—"in Chicago, America, South Side."

Amanda slumped against the stone wall of his cliff dwelling, a woolen blanket wrapped round her, saltwater staining the stones beneath her. Off to her left morning sunlight was winking around the island's shoulder. She realized it was probably only about seven. Her long nightmare had begun around midnight with the attack of John Courage. Pray God it was now over.

She was too exhausted to say much more than her name. The hermit repeated this several times—"A-man-da"—and said it was "beauty-ful," pronouncing the latter word like the ferret-faced Turkish cop who'd arrested her in front of the Pera Palas.

"You know what means 'A-man-da'?" Theodore asked.

She couldn't recall. "Is it Greek?"

"Is Latin. Means, I think to say, 'Worth to love,' yes?"

Worthy of love, yes, that was it. She managed a smile in response to his own.

He had an utterly benign face, surprisingly young, she thought, to have renounced the world. His head was quite round, bald and olive-shiny on top, black and curly-bearded on the bottom, with questioning blue eyes that were the most sympathetic she'd ever seen. When she had protested she was too weak to move, he had scurried inside his cave and fetched her a glass of tea, a dish of almonds, and a bowl of fresh water—the last for her to sip, then for him to dip a cloth into and bathe the cuts on her legs and arms. Never had Amanda felt so royally treated—and by someone without the slightest knowledge of "who" she was.

Brother Theodore went on in halting monologue, sensing perhaps that it comforted her. He had lived here five years, he said, having moved from a monastery in the middle of the island to more fully devote himself to what she gathered was the incessant practice of prayer and mental quietude.

In the back of her mind, Amanda felt a fuzzy qualm for his serenity. After all, in those first few moments before he'd brought her the blanket, Brother Theodore had been subjected to a rather copious display of female flesh. Guldasa's flimsy tank-top was technically intact, but the waterlogged fabric had given way at the already scooped neckline and armholes, sagging into maximal cleavage and barely clinging to her nipples. She couldn't help observing the monk's agitation as he had draped the blanket around her shoulders. *I must be more careful,* she thought.

After a few minutes she was able, with his help, to go inside. His home was a single room which, she realized, had been hewn out of solid rock. He guided her to a little straw pallet in the corner. She lay down and tucked the blanket carefully around herself. Turning her head, she could still see the ledge in morning shadow, azure sky beyond. His smiling countenance hove into view, bidding her sleep.

Something was triggered in her mind. She tried to sit up. "I must tell you . . ."

"No. Later tell me everything. Why you in *pelagos,* ocean."

"No, *now,* Theodore. There is great danger."

His puzzled look returned.

She told him about the giant. Brother Theodore did not know this man. His only contact with the world, he said, was with the fishermen of Megisti harbor who came every day to check his basket. They left him fish and bread and other supplies in exchange for rosaries that he made, which they could sell. Quite forgetting her urgent intentions, he went to a little shelf and brought her several of these rosaries—tiny things, some woven out of wool, others fashioned out of seashells. His blue eyes were bright, eager for her reaction.

As Amanda looked at the rosaries in his hand and read the tenderness in his face, she began to weep. She hid her face, watching her teardrops spill onto the stone floor. Theodore tilted her chin up again, smiling and pressing a black woolen rosary into her palm. "For A-man-da. I make hundred knots for hundred Prayers of Jesus. Later I teach you this prayer."

This made her cry harder, of course, her shudders suddenly painful as they stretched diaphragm muscles injured the night before by the giant's crushing weight. *Oh God, I'm endangering this saintly man,* she thought. *I must leave here at once.* She tried again to tell him of the peril.

He shook his head and pointed to the ledge. "No one find you here, A-man-da. To climb up—no. To come down from high up—very, very difficult."

"Then how did you get here, and all this?"

"Oh, there is a way, a rope. But you must know where to look. This bad man not find you. Here you are safe." Theodore smiled. "Also, it is too difficult for you now to climb this rope. You must rest here. When fishermen come—I think tomorrow—you go down to them." He pantomimed lowering the rope basket into the sea. "Now you sleep. And I watch you, A-man-da, beauty-ful lady from ocean."

Theodore saw her acquiesce. Watched her small hand close around the rosary, her eyelids lower and tremble. Within seconds her fingers had relaxed slightly, yielding to sleep. He decided she was the loveliest creature he had ever beheld, and he thanked God for being able to deliver her from the sea and having her in his home, if only for the briefest while. What she had suffered Theodore could not imagine.

He would like to sit here, he thought, just beside her, and stare at her all day while she slept, storing up the vision like warmth from a fire. But he knew this would be a most perilous thing to do.

Instead he forced himself to move away, to the opposite corner where he took up his *Philokalia,* a collection of mystical writings by the Orthodox Church Fathers. But he quickly found he could not concentrate on even his favorite texts; his eyes were invariably drawn to the quiet radiance across the room. Finally he lay down the holy book and composed himself to look at her.

She awoke to find Theodore seated across the cave, smiling beatifically. Beyond him sunshine streamed through, gilding the doorway. Memory came back gently this time, and, as she felt the woolen rosary in her palm, she gave thanks for being alive.

"Welcome," Theodore said. "May you live!"

"Is it still morning? How long have I slept?"

"One hour, perhaps. Sun is here." Theodore framed an acute angle with his hands, indicating it was still early in the forenoon. "You are wish to eat? I have good bread."

One hour! Could it be that she was truly safe, that Courage had given her up as drowned? But why wouldn't he? Only God had saved her—and only He knew why—through this lovely man.

She sat up and smiled—then made a grab for the blanket which had fallen open, revealing her bosom again. "I'm sorry," she said, actually blushing.

Theodore tipped his head this way and that, just as her little brother, Small Tom, used to do when caught stealing sweets. "No, no, I am forget to close eyes. I am sorry. If you wish it, A-man-da, I can make you robe."

"You can?"

"Oh, yes, I make everything here. Robe, shoes, candles. I make basket for you to come up here."

The sun peeking through the doorway formed a shining nimbus behind his head, like a Byzantine icon. *Maybe I'll just stay here,* Amanda thought. *Marry him and have children. No, that's not right! Become an Orthodox sister, then, make little rosaries, too.* She smiled to herself, glanced up again and screamed.

Behind Theodore, silhouetted in the sunlit doorway, two huge legs dangled in midair. The next instant, John Courage's huge torso and shaggy head appeared. The giant looked around almost casually, then dropped heavily onto the ledge outside.

He grinned at her. "Whatcha, Manda? Had a nice swim?"

24

AMANDA SCUTTLED BACKWARD AGAINST THE CAVE WALL, her eyes casting about wildly and vainly for a weapon.

"Ain't you gonna invite me in, luv?" Courage asked, and followed it with a deep belly laugh that exploded into the tiny room like the braying of a mule.

"No!" she screamed—not at Courage, but at Brother Theodore, who was walking straight at the Englishman. "Theodore, stay away from him! He'll kill you!"

Amanda leaped to her feet—too late to prevent what happened next. Ignoring her warning, Theodore tried to block the huge man's progress. "A-man-da not like you," he began, his voice quivering. "You must leave my home now."

Courage kept coming, brushing the monk aside like an annoying insect. Amanda saw the outrage in Theodore's eyes, saw him hurl himself at the intruder. Without bothering to turn, Courage swung his right arm in a backhand blow that flung the dark-robbed figure against the cave wall with a sickening impact.

"No!" Amanda screamed as the hermit slumped to the floor, and dark blood oozed thickly around his bald head. "You've killed him!"

"He shoulda taken your advice and kept out of it," Courage said, coming nearer.

Powerless to help the monk, Amanda decided her only hope was somehow to dodge past Courage and fling herself over the parapet and back into the sea. If she drowned, at least it would not be at his hands.

Courage saw her intention to get by him, and laughed. "Want to play, do you? Come on, then, luv. What a tasty little tart you are with your titties hanging out!"

The blanket had slid down around her feet, revealing her soaked and skimpy costume. Yet Amanda made no attempt to cover herself. Instead she cupped her palms under her breast and jiggled them forward, tauntingly. Then she spat at him. *"You* come on! You couldn't fuck me if your life depended on it. You proved that last night, didn't you, Ollie?"

"What—what did you call me?"

"Ollie. Oliver Fitzgibbon. Isn't that your adorable little name? D'you like boys better, Ollie, is that it? Is that what you dream of, sucking your bubble pipe, trying to whack off in your tent? Stripping the knickers off of schoolboys?"

Amanda kept the stream of abuse flowing, flaunting her body and watching carefully the simian twitch and flicker in his eyes. Paranoid rage was what she wanted, and she got it. She feinted to her right and, as he launched himself at her with a roar of animal fury, she slipped past to the left and rushed toward the doorway.

She was gauging the leap ahead when her foot slid in a pool of blood and sent her careening into a corner. She rolled over and scrambled up—just in time to see Courage's fist hurtling toward her.

Amanda sank to the floor, a sheaf of her hair flung to one side, where it touched the dark viscous flow from the monk who now lay close beside her.

≡

Ismet and Hamzah returned to find no sentry posted at the perimeter of the dig and the camp itself deserted. There were no signs of violence, but dire images flooded Ismet's brain, mostly involving Amanda Morgan.

Moments later Fahri and Guldasa appeared, rifles dangling, clothes sweat-stained, faces haggard. The two began to speak at once, one in excited Turkish, the other in Kurdish. From the bilingual crossfire, Ismet was able to piece together a rough sequence of events.

Finally he shouted them into silence. "All right, enough! In which direction did you not look?"

"We checked *every* direction," Guldasa pleaded. "They've disappeared."

"Perhaps *I* can help!" boomed John Courage from the brow of rock overlooking the camp. Over one shoulder was draped the body of a dark-haired woman, legs and arms dangling. "Our girl's right here, only a bit worse for wear. I had to fish her out of the water, after she jumped off a friggin' cliff."

The big man pounded down the steep path to them

and, heaving a massive sigh, deposited the unconscious woman at their feet.

"Saytan!" Ismet was the first to kneel, yanking the blood-stained tank-top down to cover the naked breasts, while Guldasa bent to check Amanda's pulse. More blood was matted in her hair and smeared with the dirt on her face. Beside her left eye was a livid bruise, and below the filthy khaki shorts her bare legs were scratched and bleeding.

Ismet turned to Guldasa, who was now unscrewing Hamzah's water bottle. "How is she?"

"I can't tell. I think she's in shock. Her pulse is fast."

"Oh, don't worry about her, Izzy," Courage said, pinwheeling one arm to work the cramp out of his shoulder. "Just tie her up good, watch her like a hawk, and ransom the bitch bloody quick."

Ismet got slowly to his feet beside the Englishman. "John, what did you do to her?"

"Hey now, take it easy, Izzy."

"He tried to rape her," Guldasa said, bathing Amanda's face. "He ripped off her clothes and beat her with his fists."

"Quiet, Guldasa!" Ismet said. "First I hear Angleesh and only him. Then I ask you."

"She's lying."

"You are calling my sister a 'liar'?" Hamzah fingered his machine pistol.

"Hamzah!" Ismet restrained his cousin. "I will handle this."

"I'm saying I didn't hardly touch her. Here's exactly what happened, and nobody saw it but me and Mandy. I'm standin' outside Mandy's tent last night when she comes rushing out with Guldasa's knife and starts slicing away. I got a big gash on my arse, if you want bloody proof. Christ, what was I supposed to do? Say, 'Beg pardon, m'lady, I'd prefer it ever so much if you didn't cut off my fuckin' balls'? All I did was push her away. I gave her a tap, I admit it, but that's all."

"You are the liar," Guldasa said. "You had your trousers off. I saw it."

"I sleep bare-arse, Mrs. Bayram, always have, which you can come and check out any time you like."

At the insult to his wife, Fahri leaped upon the Englishman, wrapping himself around the huge shoulders like an organ grinder's monkey.

"Excuse me, Fahri"—Ismet peeled the ex-policeman off Courage—"but I have not finished my questions. Now, John, how did Amanda escape?"

"Who knows? I was out walking, smoking some shit to ease the pain in my arse where the bitch stuck me, like I said. Fahri was on guard duty, and Guldasa was right in the tent with her. And sometime this morning Amanda just bloody walks out of camp."

"This is true, Guldasa?"

"Please, it is not Guldasa's fault."

"I did not ask you, Fahri. Guldasa?"

She glanced up from her patient. "Yes, it is true. Mandy said she was going to the latrine. She was very weak. This was after Angleesh had attacked her. I never dreamed she would try and get away."

"But she did?"

"Yes."

"And you never saw her again?"

"No, Ismet. I did not."

"But I did," Courage said. "Almost caught her in the fog, ran down to the end of the bleedin' island after her, watched her jump off the cliff—after I tried to talk her out of it. If I coulda swum, I'd have jumped right in after her. I mean, think of it—millions sinking to the bottom of the sea, not to mention her other fine qualities. Then I look down and see her swimming pretty good— right out of sight under where the cliff kind of sticks way out."

Courage rambled on, telling how he remembered hearing from fishermen in Megisti harbor about a Greek hermit who lived in a cave somewhere on the end of the island. Courage figured if he could find his way down to this cave, he could search the cliff bottom, see if she'd washed up. After an hour of scrambling around the cliffs and nearly falling a couple of times, he'd located a thick rope. He'd descended by this means, discovered Amanda hiding in the hermit's cave, and promptly fetched her home. "You can all thank me any time you feel like it," he concluded with a grin. "Or, if you don't like what I done, give me your shares of the fucking ransom."

"John, you say she was 'hiding.' Then she was awake, not like this?"

Courage shrugged. "Well, more or less awake. She musta clipped her head against the rocks when we climbed out. But she'll be all right. She's a fighter."

"Yes, she is." Ismet knelt again beside the supine figure. Her large dark eyes were open now, but unfocused. He prayed for her to come back to herself, so he could ask her to forgive him. But if the crazy Angleesh had beaten her into idiocy, he would surely die for it. Ismet felt anger not only at Courage, but at Guldasa and Fahri, for not watching her, and at Hamzah, for talking him into going along to deliver the videotape, and then into staying on with the two Sheilas.

Most of all Ismet was angry at himself, for betraying the promises he had made to Amanda, and being in a drunken orgy hundreds of kilometers away while she was being attacked—and forced to flee for her life. Ismet was responsible for these things. It was he who had sworn to protect her, not Hamzah. Had he kept his word to her, none of this would have happened.

"You have heard his filthy lies," Guldasa said. "Now do you want the truth?"

"No. Now I will speak, and in English, so everyone can understand. John, you listen good. I do not wish to know more. I know enough. I say that this brave lady will not suffer any more. She came to help us. Amanda is a great lady, I think. I promise her feedom. I promise her she will be safe—most of all from Angleesh, when he is shit-faced. Now you see what he has done to her, what *we* have done to her. This will be no more.

"Guldasa will stay with Amanda. Tonight Hamzah and I go to Kas, speak to Ugur. As soon as he can arrange a fishing boat to take us to Nicosia, we will all go, and leave Amanda with him to take to the Turkish police. Everyone understand?"

"Ain't you forgettin' something?" Courage asked.

"What is this, John?"

"The bleedin' ransom."

"There will be no ransom!" Ismet's voice boomed off the rock wall behind them. *"All this is finish!"*

John Courage took a step backward, shaking his head in disbelief. "Well, that's a fine, noble sentiment, Izzy, and you're welcome to it. But some of us can't afford to be so bloody noble. Five million francs, dollars, or whatever, lads? Forget about Kurdistan. Think what it could do for you, each of you. Because the truth is, your bleedin' 'omeland's a lost cause, and you all know it. You're losers, the lot of you Kurds—like red Indians or the humpbacked fuckin' whale. How many of your villages did the Iraqis wipe off the map last year—couple thousand, wasn't it?"

Ismet stood as if turned to stone by the Englishman's words.

"It's true, Izzy, face it. Hell, I've known it for years, just tagged along with you *pesh merga* for the fun of it. Same as I threw in with the Provos. They was doomed, too. The Brits aren't leaving Northern Ireland, like they did fucking India. It's never going to 'appen. And you lot are even more hopeless. Christ Almighty, you're like the fucking Polacks, building their country between Russia and Germany. Only you picked Turkey, Iran, Iraq, *and* Russia. Face it, you're all blokes without a country, like me. Be proud of it, I say.

"What you should do, see, is make your cause work for you. Get some money, ransom this little bitch, dead or alive. The bird in the bloody bush, or whatever the hell it is. Because if you don't, John Courage is the lad who will. Now, who's with me?"

The sun beat down in the small clearing. A cicada began drilling in the brush nearby. All eyes had shifted gradually to Ismet. Hamzah had dropped his smile. Guldasa had left her patient and picked up her rifle.

Finally Ismet's resonant voice sliced through the tension: "You must leave us now," he said to Courage. "In the *caique* there is a smaller boat. You take this and the money that is yours, and you leave Kastellorizo. Go now."

Courage backed off a step, shook his head. "I don't think you got the whole picture yet, Izzy. We *all* better get off this rock pile, like you said, only sooner. I forgot to mention one detail in my story about rescuing Amanda. I just killed me an infidel."

"Who is this?"

"The Greek hermit. I sorta forgot to ask his name. It was a pretty nasty head wound, Izzy, you know the kind what don't stop bleeding? So who's gonna miss a hermit? Except those fishermen told me they check this little basket he lowers every bloody day. So if they don't see it today, or maybe tomorrow, they'll know something is wrong and tell that old fart of a policeman down at the harbor, and what with one thing and another there's gonna be a big commotion down this end of the island real quick."

"You have killed a holy man, John?"

"An infidel," Courage corrected. "Didn't I say it?"

Ismet shook his head in disbelief. "Muhammad Himself did honor to Jesus and all Hebrew prophets. You have done a thing beyond forgiveness."

"Well, you may be right about that, Izzy. I'm not exactly up on theology. Guess we better go our separate ways, eh?" Courage was still grinning. "Here's my evac plan, Izzy. You four take the *caique*—that's a pun, but never mind—and me and Mandy'll take the dinghy. I think we can both squeeze in."

"Please God, no." Everyone turned to the figure on the ground, now trying to sit up. Amanda's voice was feeble, but full of urgency. And her eyes focused—directly up at the Little Fox. "Ismet, please, don't let him . . ."

"Allah be praised!" Ismet exclaimed. "Amanda, do not worry. He will never touch you again."

"Now, wait a minute, Izzy. You owe me, mate, you owe me a big one. Let's not be forgetting I saved your carcass more than once, Hamzah's too. I've never collected, but I aim to right now." Courage beckoned to the actress. "Come on, me darlin' girl, you and me got a boat to catch."

"John!" Ismet's growl was thick with menace, and his knuckles shone white around the Kalashnikov trigger. "Do what I tell you and go."

"Don't think so, Izzy. Not alone. And I'd appreciate your not pointing that thing at me, all right? We're still blood brothers, remember? That little ceremony you and me had in Basra, just before about a million Iranian Guards came screaming through the marshes? Kurdish blood oath is what you called it and it lasts a lifetime, as I recall." With a wink Courage reached and seized Amanda's wrist.

As he jerked her onto her feet, gunfire erupted in their midst. Brass shell casings sprayed from the breech of Guldasa's AK-47. Amanda screamed, but it was John Courage who stared down in bewilderment at a huge darkening stain on his shirt front. He let Amanda go and staggered backward against a boulder.

"*I* am not your blood brother, Angleesh," Guldasa's voice shrilled in the stunned aftermath. "*I* swore no oath."

Courage pushed forward off the boulder, looked down again at the spreading ruin of blood, opened his mouth to speak but spat a bloody froth of bubbles instead. He lurched forward two steps and then stood, swaying.

Guldasa held her ground, ready to fire another burst.

Ismet reached out and nudged the barrel aside. "Not necessary," he said softly. "Angleesh is already dead."

Courage heard the remark, seemed genuinely puzzled by it. Then, as if in grudging agreement, he nodded, and toppled forward into the dust—and into that final oblivion he had sought in so many ways for so many years.

25

GULDASA OFFERED HER RIFLE TO ISMET.

The Little Fox shook his head, looking down at the corpse whose blood was darkening the surrounding red earth. "You will need it. You heard what he said. We must leave here quickly."

There was no grief in him for this monstrous ruin sprawled at his feet. The huge man had died slowly and by his own hand over the years, ravaged from within by hashish and endless drink. Now there could only be relief that the shell, too, was destroyed and the blood bond finally broken. Relief—and a sense of shame, for Ismet had let a woman do his killing.

Amanda, on her knees where Courage had dropped her, watched the giant's death throes in terrible fascination. She saw the tree-trunk legs kick and thrash, the bloated, scaly hands clench and relax, heard and smelt a vile flatulence. Can it really be over, she thought? Shouldn't somebody drive a stake through its heart, or cut off its head? Of compassion or pity she felt not a trace. She lifted her hand toward the slim Kurdish girl.

"Guldasa, I'll never forget what you did."

Guldasa clasped her hand. "Can you walk?"

"Yes." Amanda rose with Guldasa's help. "But I can't leave the island. Not yet." She turned to Ismet. "The Greek hermit—we can't leave him to die."

"I thought he *was* dead."

"He may be—but he may be alive. Someone must go and see."

"There is no time."

"Please! He is a holy man, and you just said Islam honors all such men. It's not far, really. I can guide you there, but I can't get down to the cave. If he's alive, and we can save him, you can leave me behind to take care of him." She grabbed at Ismet's sleeve. "Something must be done and I can't do it alone. Help me, Ismet."

The Little Fox looked at the others, avoiding Amanda's gaze.

"Okay, I will go with you. We will take food, water, bandages. If this man is alive, you stay with him. Send a message to fishermen for help. Hamzah, Guldasa, Fahri and I will leave this island today, no matter. If this holy man is dead, you must wait here in this camp until the second day, and then you go to the harbor. You swear to do this?"

"I swear it. You know I'll keep my word."

"Yes, I know it." He turned to his comrades, spoke in Turkish for Fahri's benefit: "We must bury Angleesh at once. There below the cliff where the ground is less rocky. In the camp, by the big trench, there are two old shovels, also a mattock."

"Why not let him rot?" Guldasa said.

"Silence! Guldasa, this man once saved our lives. So you will make a cross to bury with him and say some words of Jesus—no matter what you think of Angleesh. Now, be quick with everything." He glanced at the plastic sportwatch. "It is almost ten o'clock. I will be back no later than noon, with or without Amanda. Then we will load the *caique* and leave this island."

He turned and offered Amanda his arm.

Alekos Katapodis shuffled along the narrow track on the island's southern ridge. He judged he was still a tough kilometer from the abandoned dig. The southernmost spit of land was a few hundred meters beyond that, at which point his survey, thank God, would be finished. For so would he be. His euphoria had evaporated, along with the fog and most of his energy reserves, several hours before. He was mule-weary, sweat-soaked, and every step in the stiff old infantry boots hurt his feet. He regretted not letting the young bravos from Athens carry out their own reconnaissance, no matter how ineptly.

He halted, swept his binoculars across the barren plateau for the hundredth time, watched the light glinting off the bony brown hills. The place was deserted, except for a few shrubs, lichen, and insects. The only other living things down at this end of the island were the seals in the grotto, the lunatic Englishman—if he hadn't succeeded in drinking himself to death—and Brother Theodore. The Englishman was worth a visit, but Alekos had no intention of risking his neck paying a call on the cavedweller.

He lifted his cap, mopped his bald head and brow with his kerchief. If he pushed on he could still be done by noon. Then maybe a nap in the Englishman's camp. Start home by three.

Suddenly, caroming over the hills, came the unmistakable stutter of gunfire. Alekos dropped to the ground, bruising his hip and knocking himself in the jaw with the binoculars.

"Skatá!" he cursed, spitting dust from his teeth and rubbing his jaw. His heart, already overworked, was beating even faster now. He unslung the field pack, began pulling its contents out. The radio was buried underneath everything—bread, cheese, garlic, *grappa.* He extracted the antenna, punched the frequency he'd been given.

It took him five maddening minutes to raise the emergency command post on Rhodes, and a couple more to convey the urgency of his message: There *were* terrorists on his island, and—by Christos!—they were shooting.

"Bring paratroopers!" he barked into the radio. "Drop 'em on the southern end of the island."

"How many terrorists are there?" asked the calm voice.

"Ask your fucking Virgin Mother!" Alekos shouted back. "How should I know?"

When they assured him help was on the way, he switched off. His job was over. The smartest thing to do now was stay here and wait for help, not go stumbling around attracting stray bullets. He chewed off a hunk of bread, reached for the bottle of *grappa,* and took a long pull. Fighting was a tough business.

Ilyinsky avoided the cove where the *caique* was tied up, assuming the steep track would be watched. Instead they nosed the dinghy against a sheer cliff around the corner, made the boat fast to a sharp edge of rock.

Paul first looked up at the towering slab, then at Ilyinsky, and shook his head dubiously. The Russian major grinned and tipped his head toward the two *Spetsnaz,* who were already breaking out their climbing gear. "Our friends here have scaled vertical cliffs in Afghanistan to ambush the *Mujahedeen.* For them this is a slice of cake."

Viktor set off first, scrambling upward from foothold to handhold, stopping at intervals to nail pitons and secure the rope through carabiners for those below to follow. On a ledge halfway up he stopped and waved. Feliks snapped his climbing harness to the rope and began crabbing upward, using a sliding ascender. Paul followed, finding the technique surprisingly easy, even exhilarating. In a few minutes he stood, smiling and bathed in sweat, beside the other two. Maksim joined them moments after, hardly out of breath as he coiled the twisted-nylon line he had retrieved. They were able to manage the next pitch without ropes, ending in a scramble over boulders.

At the top Ilyinsky checked his bearings with the map. Then they headed south along the cliffs, keeping low and taking care not to dislodge rocks. The thick-bodied middle-aged KGB officer moved surprisingly well, Paul thought, but neither he nor Ilyinsky could match the tireless pace of the two *Spetsnaz.* When Paul made an effort to go faster, Ilyinsky stopped him.

"Hey, you trying to catch a bullet?" the Russian

joked. "Stay back, and stay alive. This Little Fox and his men are experienced mountain fighters."

"What about you?"

"Me, I'm crazy."

"How far back you want me?"

"Just keep us in sight, okay?"

Paul nodded, letting Ilyinsky go ahead—and not very reluctantly. Like Bessaraboff, he wanted to be in the starting lineup. But the thought of charging into machine-gun fire had been churning away at his guts all morning, actually for several days. All he wanted to do was face danger—and survive. And help rescue Amanda in any way he could. If that meant standing on the side-lines, he could live with that. The Russians knew what they were doing; Paul did not.

Then somewhere ahead the humming silence was shattered by the explosive coughing of an automatic weapon—followed by a throttled cry.

Paul rushed forward, scrambling recklessly along the cliff edge and over an outcropping of rock—and ran into the three Russians, who had halted on the brink of another ledge, all scanning ahead with binoculars.

"What happened?" Paul asked.

Ilyinsky shook his head.

"I heard a cry," Paul continued.

"So did we."

Paul whipped out his little Japanese sport binoculars, focused straight down the sheer run of rock to a bright blue wedge of sea slapping against dark rocks and the dilapidated wooden dock at the foot of a zigzag path. Two boats were now tethered to the rotting timbers—the weatherbeaten *caique* they had seen earlier, and another boat that had *not* been there before, a four-man inflatable, rocking in the swell.

"That's the Avon from *Alcyone!*" Paul said.

"And there's Toshka!" Ilyinsky said, unleashing a torrent of Slavic invective.

Paul tracked upward along the switchbacks and saw, near the top, Anton Bessaraboff lunging along in his T-shirt, jeans, and deck shoes, rifle in hand. What the hell was *he* doing off the boat? Had he fired the burst they'd heard—or was he running toward the sound, as they were?

Ilyinsky was frantic. He was sure Toshka would blunder into the terrorist camp, get himself killed—and maybe Amanda and the rest of them in the process.

He tossed his silenced AK-47 to a surprised Maksim. The *Spetsnaz,* a qualified sniper with dozens of confirmed kills, shook his head violently.

"I'm not asking you to *waste* him," Feliks hissed. "Just get his attention, so he'll look up here. Aim in front of him."

Maksim nodded, flipped the fire selector to semiauto, shouldered the rifle, squinted through the eight-power scope, held his breath, squeezed off a round.

Ilyinsky focused the binoculars on Bessaraboff, saw him stop suddenly, wheel in panic and then, to Ilyinsky's amazement, bolt even faster up the trail, disappearing up a sharp switchback.

Ilyinsky swore and leapt to his feet, beckoning the others.

Assuming the invitation now included himself, Paul hurried after the three Russians, heart pounding, light-headed, trying to outrace his own fear.

≡

Bessaraboff had seen the puff of rock dust just above his head, followed by a two-tone ricochet. No matter who was shooting at him, Bessaraboff had to get the hell off the trail fast.

He'd never run so hard in his life, propelled by all-out terror, visualizing himself locked in the cross hairs of a sniper scope, ready at every instant for the fatal bullet to strike. His eyes leapt ahead, desperately seeking cover, but finding only the rising trail and beside his feet a dizzying drop to the cove below. Why hadn't he stayed on the damned boat, like Feliks told him to?

He crested the hill, amazed to be alive, and saw another slight rise. But there were odd sounds ahead, clinking and scraping. Bessaraboff stumbled on, his heart crashing against his frail chest, his breath rasping. But he didn't dare stop. Instead he felt to make sure the rifle was on full-auto, summoned his last dregs of energy, and charged over the hill.

The scene ahead seared starkly into his consciousness. Three people stood in a clearing in front of a big rock. A body lay at their feet. Two men bent over shovels, a woman rested on a pickax. Their rifles lay several meters away on the ground, well out of reach. A burial party. *The terrorists!* Bessaraboff realized with a kind of incredulous glee. *And they were absolutely at his mercy.*
Checkmate!

He planted his feet and swung the Kalashnikov to his hip, just as he had when that crazed sheepdog had come charging out of the twilight in Usküdar. The rest was child's play. Point, pull, and pivot—spray them with death and keep holding the trigger down till the magazine was empty.

≡

Despite her determination, the Western woman was on her last legs, Ismet could see. When they reached the rocky bluff overlooking the camp, he paused to rest.

"No," Amanda said. "If I stop now, I'll never go on."

Ismet nodded, took a last look down at the three grave diggers and the huge corpse. Something about the scene bothered Ismet, but he could not think what.

As he turned away, he heard Guldasa scream from below, then a rush of footfalls and erupting gunfire. Ismet checked his first impulse to fight and hurled himself on Amanda, throwing her to the ground as the lethal, irresistible sound went on and on, silencing the horrified screams from several throats. Ismet rolled off Amanda and gazed over the ledge.

A single figure stood in the clearing. Hamzah, Guldasa, and Fahri lay bloody and motionless, heaped in the postures of death alongside the man they'd been burying. Their hands were still on shovels, their rifles out of reach.

Ismet raised his rifle—then dropped once more behind the rocks. He had seen four more men sprinting over the hill from the ocean, carrying rifles and dressed in camouflage. Greek commandos, most likely.

Amanda's face was close beside him, her eyes huge and glazed with terror. "What's happened?" she whispered.

"Say nothing, not move." he dared not whisper more. Not since he had discovered Adila and all her family slaughtered in their beds, long years ago, had he beheld so terrible a sight. Not even the carrion fields of the Faw Peninsula. The last remnant of his *pesh merga,* his only remaining family, cut to bloody bits in a few seconds. All because of idiot carelessness.

Hadn't Courage warned him the Turks would torture Taufiq and learn they were here, that someone would surely come after them? And why hadn't Hamzah, wiliest of fighters, even posted a guard? Too late Ismet realized that it was this that had bothered him when he saw all three laboring on the grave.

But what should he do next? There were too many for him to take out by himself. He could only wait, and watch his own fears reflected in Amanda's face.

$$\equiv$$

Feliks Ilyinsky was in full pursuit when he heard the long mindless chatter of the automatic rifle over the rise ahead, then the agonized cries of the victims—one of which he assumed to be Toshka. But in the aftermath, as Maksim and Viktor sprinted ahead, came Bessaraboff's voice, screaming in Russian: "Feliks! Feliks! I've killed them all!"

Ilyinsky ran harder, with the American several strides back. Seconds later the Russian burst into a clearing and saw Bessaraboff. The young man's eyes were wild, his face contorted. He was dancing about in a circle of carnage, a rifle over his head and four bleeding bodies at his feet.

Ilyinsky struggled to comprehend the grisly sight. Bessaraboff must have surprised four terrorists—or three terrorists digging a grave for a fourth, he saw as he took a step nearer. Incredibly, it was Toshka who was responsible for this massacre. But where was Amanda?

Then Feliks saw something that chilled his heart and twisted in his guts like a knife. One of the bloody victims had a long spill of glossy black hair.

Bessaraboff went on shouting, apparently unaware that he'd killed Amanda Morgan. Maksim and Viktor, meanwhile, fanned out, one racing down the ramp into an excavation, the other working his way up a steep slope which skirted the overhanging rock.

Paul Cyrus walked slowly into the clearing and sank to his knees, his gaze also riveted on the shiny black hair of the lifeless female figure. "Oh Jesus Christ, no," the American said, and began vomiting into the dust.

"Oh, yes," Feliks said, and walked up to Bessaraboff, whose eyes still blazed in demented triumph. Feliks wrenched the rifle from the bony hands, then slapped Toshka hard.

"*Durok!*" he spat in Russian. "Don't you see what you have done?"

"But I've killed them, Feliks! I've killed the terrorists."

"*She* is not a terrorist! Look!" Feliks stepped over to Amanda's sprawled corpse, face down in the dust, wedged his boot under the waist, and heaved her over. A lifeless Kurdish woman stared blindly up at him.

"*Slava Bogu!* Paul, look!"

But the American was already at his shoulder, staring down, the incremental grief at this unknown woman's cruel fate lost in an overwhelming surge of relief. Amanda was alive! But where was she?

"You thought it was her?" Bessaraboff cackled hysterically. "It's just some Kurdish bitch! And I shot them all, Feliks. I did it. Not Viktor, not Maksim, but me!"

Feliks slapped him again harder, knocking him down. "Shut up, imbecile. How do you know you shot them all? There may be more." Indeed, there had better be. Ilyinsky had recognized two of the corpses—the carnival giant from the Emirgan quayside and his assistant. But the Little Fox remained unaccounted for.

Maksim came racing up from the excavation, shaking his head negatively.

"You're sure? You're fucking sure?"

"Yes, Feliks, I'm fucking sure. There's nothing down there."

Ilyinsky scanned the rocks above, in the grip of an impotent fury, as Maksim began to work his way up the sloping path.

Suddenly a figure appeared silhouetted atop the cliff. Maksim saw it, too, and raised his rifle.

26

As the gunpowder stench drifted up, Amanda felt herself sucked deeper into the day's vortex of horrors, heard pounding feet below, Russian voices. They were all dead, then—Hamzah, Fahri, Guldasa. The hideous fact was confirmed by Ismet's eyes, which were dilated and unfocused with horror. She could not conceive what had happened. What were Russians doing on a Greek island? Then she heard her own name, distinct in the torrent of Slavic syllables. Had they come to save her? If so, perhaps she could save Ismet.

She pressed her lips to his ears: "Russians. They won't hurt me. I'm going to stand up. You escape."

He seized her wrist.

"Let go," she whispered fiercely. Their eyes dueled

before he released her. "Get out of here, Ismet. Hide. Quick, while I distract them."

Because she was trying to help him, she found the strength to climb off the ground and expose herself to view. She stared down into surreal horror, a scene so ghastly it could only be a tableau of film gore, contrived by clever prop and makeup men with bladders of chicken blood, plastics, and liquid latex. Only it was real. Amanda gagged, looked away.

Her knees trembled, the blood drained from her head. Yet she did not faint. She had to keep the horror at bay if Ismet was to have a chance to get away. The Russians saw her now, their rifles lifting. She braced for bullets that didn't come, stared back at strange faces—an older man, blocky and balding, in commando camouflage with two rifles; a gangly, grotesque figure, weaponless and sobbing; a dark-skinned young man who seemed oddly familiar and called her by name.

A fourth soldier rushed up from the camp, flakjacketed, crew-cut, cradling a small machine gun. The older man barked, and all weapons were lowered. Then this man, whom she took to be the leader, asked her in English to come down, said they'd come to rescue her. While he spoke, a fourth man in commando gear drifted toward the path that led up to where she stood. Out of the corner of her eye Amanda saw a second commando already on that path. Ismet, for some idiotic reason, was still at her feet! Why didn't he run?

Then her eye was drawn back to Guldasa's dark hair, shining in the sunlight, her boyish body, her stylish safari outfit splattered now like a slaughterhouse apron. The horror struck her full force, caused her to vomit. And when she had wiped her mouth, the revulsion spewed forth in a torrent of words directed down at the Russians:

"You fucking bastards! Look what you did! They had no weapons!" She went on shrieking denunciation—while kicking at Ismet, desperate for him to flee before it was too late. The Russian leader, meanwhile, spread his palms in a gesture of innocence, claimed it was an accident, said they'd come only to rescue her.

"How can you rescue me? I'm not a prisoner—I never was! Those were my friends you murdered! They were sending me home today. I don't know who you are, or who sent you, but I'm going to tell the whole fucking world what you've done, every bloody detail!"

There was sudden alarm in the leader's eyes. "Miss Morgan," he called back, "you've been through an ordeal. You're hysterical. But it is over now—"

"Of course I'm bloody hysterical. And I'll *stay* hysterical. I'm bloody good at it! And the world will listen to every bloody hysterical word I say."

Before she could say any more, Ismet spun her around and began dragging her in a crouched run away from the camp.

She tried to tell him it was useless, that, unless he took off on his own, the Soviet commandos would run them down effortlessly. But she couldn't, because she was soon gasping for breath, while the Little Fox never slackened, yanking her in his wake. It took all of her strength just to keep from falling.

Twice she did fall and was jerked to her feet. Ismet not only herded her along, but kept yelling at her and shoving her head down. Why did it matter any more? Yet they ran on till she was nearly sick again from fatigue. When he did finally stop and dragged her back against a large rock, she was barely able to keep her head up. He shouted at her, seized her shoulders, stuck his fierce face close to hers.

"Listen to me, Amanda!" he shouted.

She nodded.

"Now you go alone!"

"I can't," she whined. "No more. You . . . go without me."

"Amanda, they *kill* you now—for what you said!"

"Let them."

"No! You must live! Tell the world, like you said!"

"Sorry."

He slapped her hard, venting a rage she was too exhausted to respond to. Couldn't he see that? Why wouldn't he leave her alone? But when he felt her limpness he slapped her again, then prodded her so cruelly with his rifle she cried out in pain and leaped to her feet.

"Now you get out of here, Amanda! Don't stop. Go to harbor town. Six kilometers only. I not let them catch you. For me you do this, Amanda. For Guldasa, and Hamzah, and Fahri. Go!"

Seeing the strange expression on his face, both fierce and tender, commanding and beseeching, she could not resist further. "Good-bye, Ismet."

"Go!"

She stumbled down the path away from him, feeling his will pushing her on, his viselike grip on her wrist. At a turning she glanced back and saw him sitting cross-legged against a rock, reloading his rifle. He didn't look up.

She turned and hurried down a gravelly slope and out of sight. She understood what he was trying to do.

Save her life with his own. He wished desperately for her to survive. Now it was up to her to grant his last wish.

≡

Paul Cyrus had been stunned to see Amanda Morgan appear suddenly above him. Moments before he had seen her corpse—or thought he had—and here she was utterly alive, though looking like a wild woman. She was smeared with blood and dirt, her black hair tangled, her crimsoned torso nearly bared, her dark eyes crazed. Yet she held her head high, as if careless of their weapons, and shrieked curses at them like some barbarian queen.

He called out her name, but she was in a kind of Medean madness, beyond hearing. Then she vanished, so abruptly Paul suspected someone—probably the Little Fox—had pulled her away. Maksim and Viktor hurried up the steep rocky path, with Ilyinsky only a beat behind.

Paul was left alone, hearing the receding flurry of bootsteps and the pitiful shudders of Bessaraboff, now curled fetally on the ground amid the carnage he'd wrought. The thought occurred suddenly: *Christ! They're going to kill her! And then they'll kill me too.*

He panicked and ran back the way he'd come. As his fear-maddened body plunged down the path, something in his mind held back, hovering and observing his headlong flight yet powerless to stop it.

He took a switchback too fast, lost his footing, and crashed against a rock, sprawling on stones and skinning his palms. He lay there a moment, feeling his heart pounding, his stomach knotted, his ragged breathing almost like the sobbing Bessaraboff. Another foot and he would have plunged to his death over the cliff. Christ, where was he going? Back to *Alcyone* to sail away? To radio a call for help—while Amanda was being executed? What kind of display of manhood was that?

But what could he do? Even if Ismet were with her, they were no match for the Russians. The *Spetsnaz* supermen would run them down playfully. Besides, Paul didn't even have a rifle anymore. He'd either dropped the Kalashnikov back at the clearing or Feliks had taken it away; Paul couldn't remember which. A fine soldier that made him. Maybe the only useful thing he *could* do was get back to the boat and radio for help.

Then he thought of the tortured old Kurd, a victim of Ilyinsky's KGB-trained ruthlessness. That was what Paul was leaving the actress to, while he scurried for safety. No, if Paul was going to do anything for Amanda Morgan, it had better be in the next few minutes.

But what?

He shoved himself off the ground, worked quickly back up the path—with no more plan in mind than putting one foot in front of the other. Fear still swarmed in his guts, but he'd at least located his backbone and a gear that moved forward instead of in reverse. When he reached the rise before the clearing, he veered off. Rather than being last dog in the hunt, he decided to scale a rocky escarpment to his left, angling north to intersect with Amanda and Ismet's flight from the Russians—assuming they'd also headed north toward the harbor. What he'd do if he met up with either or both of them he still had no idea. He'd think of something.

Halfway up the rock face he heard a single shot, over the crest and off to the right. So the *Spetsnaz* had caught up. Paul altered course in that direction, again contrary to his survival instincts. Weaponless or not, he couldn't run away without trying to save her—and live with himself later.

As he gained the top and hurried forward over the broad granite crown, the whole southern end of the island spread before him. A barren, boulder strewn waste, the fallout of some long-ago volcanic belch. Down the middle of this plateau was a long spill of larger rocks, sparkling in the morning sun. Beyond, a blue enamel sea reflected an enamel sky.

Again came the deadly chatter of automatic weaponry—not far off. He reached in the day pack, pulled out the small binoculars, swept the southern horizon. Sunlight struck a metallic spark. Paul held his breath, steadied his hands, focused slowly.

The Little Fox was barely visible, wedged between large rocks, the sharp silhouette well remembered from the hostage negotiation. The little guy's a real *mensch,* Paul thought, surprised by the admiration he felt. But why? For risking his life here, for being weaned on grenades and Kalashnikovs like other terrorist waifs, for being unable to value human life so he could gun down an innocent Turkish boy on a hostage ship?

No, it was something else. Ismet had achieved something Paul hadn't. Not just bravado or a willingness to face danger, but an inner decision that made such deeds possible. The Little Fox had taken all his dreams, his clay, and fired them in the kilns of crisis till they were adamantine. That was why he could put his life on the line. This was something Paul had not done. He had not found anything worth dying for.

Paul scanned the surrounding rocks. Amanda was nowhere in sight. He whipped the lens back to Ismet just as rock dust spurted over the Kurd's head, followed by a flat rifle crack and ricochet whine.

The Little Fox was pinned down, but holding them off. The Russians would be fanning out through the boulders, trying to get an angle on their quarry. Ismet sprang up, fired a short burst, and dove for cover, out of Paul's vision. As good as the *Spetsnaz* were, Paul thought, Ismet would lead them a merry chase in this deadly game of fox and hounds. The trouble was, if Paul had been able to get Ismet in his sights, so would the Russians.

The thought impelled him to scramble back and scan the slope he'd just climbed. Fifty meters below he saw Viktor leaping like an ibex from rock to rock. Once he gained the high ground, he'd be able to pick off Ismet—though, with only a submachine gun, he'd probably need to get closer. Paul wished desperately for a weapon, even a goddamned club to stop the *Spetsnaz*.

But where was Amanda? He swept the binoculars north, tracking across a narrow ridge through tumbled red rock. He caught a flash of khaki, bare arms, and black hair flying. Then she was gone, heading north.

So, Ismet had sent her on and hunkered down like Horatius at the Bridge to hold the Russkies off. Tough little sonuvabitch.

Keeping low, Paul moved diagonally down the slope. He was going after Amanda.

≡

These guys are good, Ismet thought. He ejected a spent magazine and inserted a new one. There was only one more thirty-shot clip in his pouch. He'd been traveling light, expecting to have to climb down to the monk's cave with Amanda.

Instead, he was in a fight for his life.

Judging the sound of the shots and the ricochet angles, there were at least three of them out there. But he had escaped worse predicaments—for instance a burning ship surrounded by the entire Turkish counter-terrorist apparatus.

Except his objective here was not to escape. That would have been easier. It was to keep the Russians pinned down so Amanda could get as far away as possible.

But it was Ismet who was pinned down. Every time he showed so much as a millimeter above the rocks, bullets would come zinging in, driving him to cover and allowing them to draw nearer. To make a better game of it he needed Hamzah beside him, flashing his old grin that said, *Don't worry, Cousin—this is fun!* This is how Hamzah would have preferred to die—Kalashnikov in one hand, Skorpion in the other, not cut down by some lunatic while holding a damn shovel. Yet, at least Hamzah and all Ismet's comrades had died as fighters.

Now they were all gone, vanished like lovely Adila, and Ismet was alone again. And if he spent another second feeling sorry for himself, he'd be gone, too. It was time to get moving.

He ducked behind a run of boulders, slid on his stomach over a sloping patch of open ground till he reached cover again. He raised his head slightly, scanning the rocks. The instant he caught a movement, he fired a short burst, then dropped. A split second later the rock above him splintered, steel slugs pinging off stone.

Saytan! but they were fast.

He wormed his way back up the slope away from

his pursuers, diving, crawling, slithering. He was running out of rocks here, he thought. He looked around, trying to plot a course that would leave him an exit, and also shield him from the escarpment off to his left. One of the Russians was sure to be up there, looking for an easy shot.

Ismet replaced the clip. He couldn't remember firing thirty rounds, but it was empty. This was the last one. Better make them count. He found a small notch between two boulders and surfaced his head like a periscope, checking the high ground.

Something moved and he sprang up, shouldered his rifle, fired a burst—and screamed, hopping laterally along the rocks for a second shot. The bastard was up there on the hill with a machine gun. Both men fired together. Ismet saw the Russian fold and fall before he was punched to the ground, tumbling and bashing his head.

The Little Fox came to, realized he was still exposed, and rolled into the lee of a nearby rock. There was a spreading numbness in his left shoulder, blood in his eyes, and a throbbing in his head from his fall. He jerked his chin sideways, checking his shoulder. It was a mess. Still, it wasn't his shooting shoulder. And one Russian was down. If Ismet could trade three such wounds for three deaths, he'd have won the game.

And he still had half a clip.

≡

Ilyinsky scrambled up the rocky slope to Viktor. The *Spetsnaz* was face down. Feliks turned him over. He'd been shot in the mouth. Feliks had suggested ballistic helmets for the assault, but both *Spetsnaz* had disdained them. Viktor had figured the *pesh merga* to be easy prey. Three years in Afghanistan, fighting *Mujahedeen* with hardly a scratch. On this Mediterranean holiday, he hadn't counted on meeting an even more experienced guerrilla fighter.

Ilyinsky reached down to the fallen *Spetsnaz,* unbuckled the scabbard of the big commando knife, and attached it to his own web belt. Now it was up to him and Maksim.

Ismet had to make a move. Amanda needed more time. But he couldn't seem to get to his feet. The shoulder wound had been worse than he'd thought. He'd ripped part of his sleeve off and tied a tourniquet, but it wasn't very tight. He could no longer feel his left hand, and the whole arm throbbed like it was being used as a target for bayonet practice.

With great effort he scooted back against a rock and levered himself to a sitting position. He rested a second, then slid farther up. Finally, he was more or less on his feet. He wrapped his right hand around the rifle trigger, looking for a target. Saw nothing, swung right, his lip bit open to keep from screaming as he moved the injured shoulder. He inched sideways, turned back and looked straight into a submachine gun in the hands of a Russian soldier on a nearby rock.

Ismet dived, felt bullets punching his legs as he tumbled down a stony slope, totally exposed. He was hit again as he rolled, solid blows, but managed to come up with the rifle still in his hand and squeezed off the rest of the clip, shooting blind, seeing only a red mist.

More bullets came then—a hailstorm of steel, ripping into his flesh and bone. The Little Fox had finally been tracked to his lair.

Light faded. He could not remember what he'd

been doing, only that these were his hills, and he had stayed out too late, tending the goats. He looked up and saw a woman bending over him. He was afraid she'd be angry with him for staying out so long. But her dark eyes were infinitely tender as she reached for him.

Ismet thought for a moment it was Adila, but that was wrong, because Adila was only a silly girl, an occasional playmate. No, it was his mother who bore him up now lightly, as though he were a babe, and carried him safely over the hills to home.

"The little bastard got Viktor," Maksim said, looking down at the crumpled, bullet-chewed body of the slain *pesh merga* chieftain.

"But I told you not to kill him," Ilyinsky said.

Maksim slung his submachine gun. "Yeah, well, it didn't work out that way. The whole thing makes me fucking sick."

"What about Amanda?"

Maksim grunted, tilted his head to the north. "Last time I saw her she was down there somewhere."

"You saw her?"

"Yeah, in the binoculars, running like hell. She must have got away from him."

"We've got to catch her. She's our last chance."

"Not me, Major. I'm through. You and your ugly little friend fucked it up."

"What do you mean by that?"

"Shut up a moment." The *Spetsnaz* pointed skyward. Then Feliks heard it, the far-off droning of a helicopter. "Somebody's coming this way. Probably Greeks. Whoever it is, they can pick up the bloody pieces."

Maksim shrugged and turned away. Feliks, confronting the broad, bullet-proofed back, plunged Viktor's commando knife into the side of the thick neck, putting all his weight behind it. Bright arterial blood geysered into the sunlight as Feliks drove the huge man down, ignoring the arms that clawed frantically, the glottal screams.

As Maksim sank lifeless on top of the Kurdish fighter, Ilyinsky stumbled back several steps. He, too, was drenched in blood now and dizzy from violence. Better calm down.

The droning sound was louder and had doubled, indicating two choppers, thrashing closer, though still not visible.

These would be Greeks, as Maksim had thought. His plan was in shambles. Too many people dead, and Amanda hysterical. But she was still the key.

He swept his field glasses north where Maksim had seen her. Saw nothing but naked rock. But she had to be out there, running for her life. She'd still have a few hard kilometers to the harbor. And she had to be exhausted, while Feliks was fit and relatively fresh. He could track her down.

And then?

Hope his luck changed.

He yanked the huge blade out of Maksim's neck, wiped it on his pants, scabbarded it. Then he set off on a steady jog north.

27

As GUNFIRE CONTINUED TO ERUPT BEHIND HER, AMANDA kept running and stumbling forward, sending a prayer over her shoulder for the gallant Little Fox, back there trading shots with the Russian commandos.

The island's leeward coast, chiseled against a cobalt sky, appeared a bleak and menacing landscape, veiled by her own exhaustion and despair. For her it was the last mile in a ghastly marathon that had begun in her suite at the Pera Palas with Leo's phone call, only a few days ago.

Maybe she should have stayed in her room, as the little tyrant had ordered her.

Another short salvo echoed off the rocks behind her. She sought a place to collapse, a hole to crawl into. But the path had widened into a sloping trough, whose sides were completely exposed. She had no choice but to keep on, though she was doubled over with a side stitch that brought a grimace at every step.

Suddenly she began picking up speed—the path was dropping away precipitously. Too late she found she could not control her played-out muscles on the steep slope. Her knees buckled and gave way, and she tumbled sideways off the path and down a hill, crashing through dry brush—till she hit something large and yielding, rolled twice over, and came to a jarring stop.

A voice cried out, but she could not react. She was staring at sky, gasping for air, unable to move. She panicked, believing she'd broken her neck and paralyzed herself for life. But after a few seconds she was able to swivel her head. She'd landed on her rear in a wide ditch, or was it a narrow ravine? Against the opposite side an old man was similarly sprawled, staring back at her. He had a droopy face, grizzled, tobacco-stained mustache, and sad black eyes under gray-thatched brows. On the ground beside him lay a rifle, along with his cap and the scattered contents of what looked like his lunch.

Amanda found her voice before her wits and began inanely, "Look, I'm so sorry. I was running—from guns—and I'm—"

"You are Amanda Morgan, of course. I see you on television. You are the reason why I, Alekos Katapodis, am here." He knocked the dust off his cap and replaced it on his bald head. Then he grabbed up his rifle, got heavily to his feet, and peeked over the top of the ditch. "They are coming after you, terrorists?"

"No, not them. Russians."

"Holy Virgin Mother! Russians? Where are Greeks?"

"What Greeks?"

"The ones I call on the radio. Commandos from Rhodos."

Amanda shook her head. "I don't know anything about that. Who are you?"

"You call me Alek. I am constable for Megisti, also postman. Athens tells me make investigation. So I come. Then I am hearing shots." He sighted quickly over the top of the ditch, then ducked down again.

"What did you see?" she asked.

"Nothing."

"But you think help is coming?"

"Oh, very soon, I hope it."

"Should we wait here then? Is it far to the harbor?"

"Very far now. Yes, let us wait for commandos. You are very tired lady, I think."

"Oh Christ, am I ever a tired lady."

Alekos scratched his head through his cap. "But you think Russians maybe come this way, eh?"

"I don't know, Alek. I'm afraid so."

"Skatá!" He worked the bolt action of his rifle, making sure a round was chambered. His hands were shaky on the mechanism. Somehow, despite all his precautions, he had landed right in the middle of big trouble, just like in the war. But he did not want such a most famous lady to see how frightened he was, and how even his legs were now trembling. He must pretend to be brave. He shouldered his rifle, then paused thoughtfully.

"Listen," he said. "Do you hear?"

"What?"

"The shooting, it has stopped."

Amanda listened. It *had* been quiet a long time. Which could only mean one thing—Ismet was dead. She felt a sudden and surprising sense of loss. The Little Fox was no more. She kept listening, hoping again to hear weapons fire, but there was only the thrum of insects, the old man's labored breathing, the sea breeze sighing over dry hills.

No, there *was* another sound, a distant, cyclical throb. Alekos heard it, too, and broke into a grin that curled his mustache and squinted his sad eyes. "Autogiros! Commandos are coming! We be safe now, lady."

God, could it actually mean the end of this carnival ride of horrors? Surely now the Russians would have to abandon their mad pursuit? She let her shoulders sag back against the ditch. Yes, perhaps it was all over, and she could just sit here, awaiting rescue and enjoying the comforting normalcy of this old man with his old rifle and funny cap and suspenders and the remains of his lunch all over his shirt.

The helicopter drone grew louder. Hang on, girl, she counseled herself.

The next instant one of the Russians leaped into the ditch with them—the bronzed, black-haired one. Amanda screamed, and Alekos swung his rifle. But the young Russian kicked out, knocking the weapon from the old man's hands just as it went off in a deafening detonation.

The Russian whirled next toward Amanda, and she backed away in fear, trying one of her few Russian words: "Please—*pozhalsta!*"

The young man grinned. "Amanda, are you all right?"

"You speak English?"

"American, anyway." He spun back toward Alekos, who had been reaching for a throwing-size rock. "Hey!

Take it easy, okay? I'm on your side. You're lucky I kicked that rifle out of your hand before it killed you." The ancient Mannlicher lay shattered on the ground, its breech having exploded in firing.

Paul turned back to Amanda. "You probably don't remember, but Bertie Giddings introduced us—in Istanbul. I'm Paul Cyrus."

"Yes! What are you doing here? And what happened to your hair and skin?"

"It's kind of complicated. Right now we've got to get out of here. Ilyinsky just—well, I won't tell you what I just saw him do to one of his own men. But he's gone totally psycho."

"What about Ismet?"

"I'll tell you everything later. Come on."

"Tell me now, dammit! Is he dead?"

"Yes. He was trying to save you, I think. I'd like to finish the job for him and get you the hell out of here."

"Wait!" Alekos said. "Greeks are coming!"

"I know, I hear the choppers. But we can't wait that long. Ilyinsky is a helluva lot closer than they are, and he knows which way you came." Paul extended his hand to Amanda.

"I've not much left, I'm afraid." She managed a laugh as he pulled her to her feet. "Christ, I've been telling people that all day, but nobody believes me."

Paul turned to Alekos. "Where can we hide near here?"

The old man thought a moment, then pointed seaward. "Fokiali."

"What's that, an island?"

"No, Fokiali is cave, here on Megisti."

"Okay, yeah, I read about it. A grotto. Seals live in it, right?"

"Yes. It is very close."

"Sounds good. After you, Alekos."

They set off, the old policeman leading them down the little ravine, which turned into a twisting path toward a sparkling wedge of sea. Paul stayed close beside Amanda, lending her encouragement and a helping hand over rough spots. She shook off any further support. Otherwise, God knew, he would have happily carried her in his arms. But with Ilyinsky on the loose, it was better Paul keep alert and not be distracted by her proximity.

The path degenerated abruptly into a steep rockfall, requiring them to back down single file, step by cautious step. Paul guided Amanda above him, placing her feet securely, now and again steadying her hips. Continued close-up contemplation of the actress's derrière, of course, constituted a major distraction; despite his resolve and the perilous circumstances, Paul found himself quickly and noticeably aroused. But, at least for the moment, she couldn't see him.

The last bit was a sit-down slide over loose scree to a tiny shingle beach, on which were two inverted wooden rowboats. One had a large hole in its bottom. Alekos helped Paul right the other and drop the oars they found underneath into the oarlocks. The distant chopper sound had ceased now, though perhaps it had only been drowned out by the incessant sea.

"Excuse me," Amanda said as the two men dragged the dinghy into the water. "But why don't we just hide down here till the commandos come?"

Paul surveyed the cliff line above and shook hi

head. "We'd be easy targets from anywhere up there." Along the coast to the north, however, as long as they kept the boat hugging the shore, it looked like they'd be shielded from above. "Alekos, exactly how far is this cave?"

"Not far."

"In meters? A hundred, a thousand?"

"Maybe one hundred, maybe two." Alekos pointed north.

"How far is the harbor?" Amanda asked.

"Too far. Cave is more close. You take boat inside, keep heads down, okay? I tell Greeks how find you."

"What do you mean? You're coming too, Alekos."

"No." The old man sat down heavily on the shingle beside Amanda. "Too much for Alekos one day. Bad for here." He tapped his chest. "Also, I am too big for such little boat. Crazy Russian, he not kill old man down here. You go."

"What'll we do?" Amanda asked Paul.

"What he says, I guess. Get in the boat and stay down."

She crawled into the bow. Paul stepped past her to the thwart and bent to the oars, as Alekos stood and shoved them off, swinging them north into the current.

After a few strokes Paul glanced over his shoulder. Amanda, after a last wave to the old man, lay back in the bow, her head just below the gunnel, her bare legs splayed out. She looked qualified for admission to an emergency room—cut and bruised, plastered with blood and dirt, obviously too far gone to worry about such minor matters as modesty.

"What are you grinning about?" she demanded.

"You. All you need is a parasol and a book of sonnets."

"Just turn around, shut up, and keep rowing, okay?"

Paul obeyed, swinging his gaze back astern and giving her privacy. But he couldn't help smiling as he recalled the set of her jaw and the flash of her dark eyes.

"Can you see Alekos?" she asked after a moment.

"He's okay. He sat back down."

"God, pray he doesn't have a heart attack. He'd be the second islander I've done in today."

"How's that?"

Amanda shook her head. She'd been thinking hopeless thoughts about Brother Theodore. "Never mind. I suppose there's nothing I can do to help you?"

"You're doing great. Just stay cheerful."

Paul's back and shoulders were feeling it already, as he labored to keep them close inshore while turning constantly to scan the wave-worn wall ahead for the cave opening.

"Paul, you came with the Russians. I don't understand?"

"It's a bizarre story, Amanda. They really did mean to rescue you, till that gangly Russian ran amok with a rifle and you started threatening to tell the world Ilyinsky was a murderer."

"That was pretty dumb, right?"

"Well, let's say it didn't set well with him. Anyway, they're the only ones who figured out where the hell you were, and Ilyinsky asked me to come along. Actually I asked *him.*"

"Why? I thought you were a consultant, or something?"

"I was. I am. I guess you got to me."

"I did?"

Paul chuckled, glancing back at her and at the fretted cliffs beyond. "You said I didn't have the balls for my job."

"I don't remember. I know I said a lot of things."

"Yeah, and I remembered all of 'em."

"I do have a way with words sometimes." She paused. "Paul?"

"Yes?"

"Whatever your reasons, thanks."

"Anytime." Sweat was pouring off him now, a noon sun beating down. They'd covered at least two hundred meters, he figured, and Alekos was out of sight. The cave opening had to show up pretty soon. Even if they somehow missed it, if they could just stay out here long enough and not get themselves shot, maybe the Greek commandos would force Ilyinsky to call off the hunt.

"Guess what?" Paul said. "I think we're going to make it."

An instant later there was a sizable *ker-plunk* astern. They both glanced up and saw a stocky figure in battle dress standing on the bluff high above, waving an assault rifle in mock greeting.

Paul cursed himself. He had let them drift too far out!

He spun the bow hard, pulling for the shelter of the cliffs with everything he had, in combined panic and fury. He didn't dare look up again, just put all his might into rowing till they glided into blessed shadow and bumped against the rocks. He wrapped a weary arm around an edge of rock to keep the boat from drifting out, then slumped over the oars.

"Why didn't he shoot us?" Amanda asked.

"I don't know. But let's not give him another chance."

The cliff shadow narrowed dangerously ahead, barely the width of the dinghy. He dared not row out, yet neither could they stay here indefinitely. For one thing, the current was tugging hard on the boat, and Paul was getting tired holding them back.

Amanda voiced the question: "What are we going to do?"

Paul decided. "I'm going to try and find the island's main tourist attraction, real fast." He shifted around on the thwart, pulled an oar out of its lock, and used it as a paddle to scull slowly ahead, scraping along the rocks out of Ilyinsky's view. Now, if only the grotto was where Alekos had said it was.

Paul heard it before he saw it, a sound like a locomotive letting off steam. A few seconds later they rounded a rock and heard it full force, a great slobbering of water rushing into the grotto mouth. The small opening was perhaps fifty feet ahead and barely three feet high—when it wasn't completely swamped by waves. Paul snagged another rock to halt their progress.

"You think we can get in there?" Amanda asked.

"I think so, but I'm not sure I want to do it Alekos's way. If we row out in front, we'll be in plain view. Even if Ilyinsky doesn't shoot us, I'd rather he didn't know where we're going."

"What other way is there?"

"How about a swim? I think it's our only chance."

She shook her head violently.

"You *can* swim, Amanda?"

"I've *been* in the ocean once already today, and—oh, bloody hell! Of course, you're right, Paul."

"Think of it this way. It's only about the length of a pool, and the current's with us." He began peeling off boots, shirt, pants, while having her steady the boat against the rocks. "Better take off whatever you can and drop it over the side." He wadded his clothes and demonstrated. "Ilyinsky'll see the empty boat and maybe think we're hiding down here somewhere."

When it came her turn Amanda unlaced the Reeboks and reluctantly tossed them overboard. Her feet had acquired several blood blisters. She glanced down at her ruined and drastically shrunken tank top and shorts and shook her head. "This is as far as I go," she said. "In case you hadn't noticed, I'm basically naked already."

"I'd noticed. Okay, when we're in the water, stay as close to the rocks as you can. Stay right behind me. Better yet, keep a hand on my shoulder—or, if you need to, around my neck. I'll hold you up. Now, over you go."

Paul followed her into the water, clinging to the dinghy beside her. While he expanded his lungs and measured the swim ahead, Amanda calmed herself by studying his face, close in the shadows—the strong profile, the oddly jaundiced-looking skin which highlighted the blue-gray eyes, his hair now jet black and slicked back. "You had freckles," she said.

"Still do, I think, under this gunk. Okay, here we go. Lights, camera, action."

They slipped free of the boat together, feeling the urgent embrace of the current. Amanda held tight to Paul's left shoulder, as directed. The American seemed strong, and she gratefully let him do the work. He dog paddled, working hard to stay along the base of the rocks. Farther on they swam into sunlight, yet were still shielded slightly from the clifftop. Amanda kept glancing up, almost expecting to see the giant John Courage up there. But this was one of those nightmares where the bogeyman kept changing faces. He had now become a Slav.

Halfway to the cave mouth they were caught in sudden turbulence, where the swell was surging both in and out. Amanda felt her own surge of fear at the prospect of being sucked into that dark vortex. She grabbed Paul so fiercely she forced him under.

"Sorry!" she shouted above the appalling noise as he rose quickly and cleared his vision.

"It's all right!" he yelled back. "The tide's rising, we gotta go for it. Hold on to me with both hands now. Just be ready to hold your breath if we go under. Here we go."

Paul moved laterally, battling the eddies, maneuvering directly in front of the cave. Twice they were nearly sucked inside, then washed back. Amanda gripped his shoulders, scissoring her legs, trying not to be a dead weight. Then she felt a strong swell pick them up and push them toward the dark maw. The next instant she went under, swallowing water and, far worse, losing hold of Paul. She grabbed blindly for him, missed, then felt his hand seize her wrist and pull her close.

They surfaced together, locked in embrace. "We're in!" Paul shouted, his voice echoing. Before Amanda could push the hair out of her eyes they sank together again, released each other reluctantly under water and came back up—into a vast, luminous blue cave, with the water suddenly as calm as a lake.

Overcome with relief and fatigue, she started to sink. Paul buoyed her up, pressed close against her. "Roll over on your back and float."

She obeyed, staring up at a rocky dome that seemed to arch a hundred feet above her, vaulted with stalactites, flooded with undulant light, echoing end to end like a cathedral with the murmurous motion of waves against rock. Suddenly the grotto reverberated with a cacophony of frantic barking.

"Seals!" she said in delight.

"Yeah," Paul spoke into her ear. "I did read about this place. 'Fokiali' means something like 'playground of seals.' This is their indoor swimming pool. Guess we woke 'em up."

"It's fantastic. But I don't think I can go on much longer, Paul. Help me."

His hand came quickly under her back. "Just relax, breathe, look at the pretty sights. I'll tow you along. There's supposed to be an island in here somewhere, if I recall my guidebook. If not, remind me to send a nasty note to the publisher when we get home."

Together they glided through echoing, dreamlike immensity, deeper into the cave.

28

FELIKS ILYINSKY PEERED OVER THE CLIFF, WAITING FOR THE dinghy to reappear. Time was running out. Now that the Greek para-commandos were on the island, they'd work their way up here, following the trail of bodies. Ilyinsky hadn't perfected his cover story yet, but if Bessaraboff could keep his mouth shut, Feliks could deal with the Greeks. First, however, he had to deal with Amanda. And Paul.

Then the empty dinghy slid out from beneath the overhang. Was he supposed to think them drowned? He shook his head at their naïveté. They were clinging to a ledge down there, of course, praying he'd go away. No such luck, children. Ilyinsky had already scouted the cliff below and judged it climbable. He slung his rifle and, using tricks the *Spetsnaz* had shown him, began working his way down.

As he descended, he glanced over his shoulder at the empty boat rotating in the current and gliding slowly in his direction. Then he reached a narrow ledge and found, to his chagrin, further descent impossible without rope and pitons. Nothing to do but climb back up. He cursed silently.

An alternative, however, presented itself immediately. It was suggested by a crescendoing sound from below—the tidal wash into and out of that grotto Toshka had mentioned being on this side of the island. So *that* was where they were hiding! They must have swum in. A smile creased Ilyinsky's face. How clever of them, and how fortuitous for him! An ideal place to play the final hand, without fear of interruption. They had even left him the oars. But Ilyinsky had to act quickly, before the boat drifted past.

He yanked off his boots, unslung rifle, pack, and flak jacket, then pulled off his shirt and ballistic inner vest, and unbuckled his web belt. He left on only his undershirt and trousers, rolled the rest of his clothes into his pack and wedged it firmly behind some rocks. Then he stood, strapping Viktor's commando knife to his trouser belt.

Gauging the drift of the rowboat, he tossed the rifle away from the cliff in a lazy arc. It turned end over end in the air and knifed cleanly into the Mediterranean a half-meter off the bow. So much for that brilliant idea. He had one more chance.

He hefted the Makarov pistol, braced his legs, and stared straight down—at least ten meters—into water that *seemed* free of submerged rocks. Mumbling a prayer, he stepped into midair, pinwheeling his arms. Halfway down he underhanded the Makarov toward the rowboat, an instant before splashing feet first into the sea.

He came up thrashing and gasping. The major was a poor swimmer, but he hadn't far to go. He clawed through the waves toward the rowboat, expending too much energy. He almost capsized the dinghy before crawling waterlogged over the side and coughing onto the floorboards. Then he opened an eye and saw the blue-steeled pistol winking an arm's length away. God was good! He'd have at least a full clip of eight shots.

He heaved himself onto a thwart, placed the Makarov beside him and looked around. As he'd suspected, the grotto was close, piercing the rock wall a bare thirty meters to his right. Down here the sound was much more impressive, like a blowing whale. Ilyinsky stroked toward the opening, but was spun around by strong eddies and had to fight his way out, flailing the oars.

When he did escape, he rowed directly offshore, came about, and pointed the bow a little south of the cave to allow for the northerly current. It would be a tight squeeze. He'd have to flatten himself to pass through.

As he launched the dinghy forward, he glimpsed off to the north the sleek sparkle of a motor yacht. It was probably just a pleasure craft. And even if it were the Greek Navy, they'd never spot him now.

He concentrated on rowing. A dozen meters from the opening, the tidal race seized the tiny boat and shoved it north, on a collision course with solid rock. Frantically Ilyinsky dug in the left oar, and again, throwing the bow south, then dipped both oars to straighten out. A panicky glance over his shoulder showed he'd compensated neatly, but an instant later the matter was taken out of his hands as a wave muscled the dinghy broadside and flung it toward the cliffs.

Ilyinsky had only an instant to boat the oars and hit the floorboards before the transom crunched against solid rock. He felt the boat lurch forward, bump again, then spin off into darkness. He shut his eyes, face down, shielding his head. He remained thus till he realized the crashing surf had abated, and the boat was now drifting . . . through suddenly cool air . . . on a gentle swell . . . in an enveloping hush. He lifted his head and eyes to eerie, flickering light which bathed a cave beyond measurement. He'd made it!

Ilyinsky checked the floorboard for leaks, but the dinghy seemed intact. Wild doves darted above him. Aqua-blue light streamed from the cave entrance across the vast grotto ceiling and through the water itself. It rippled like an interior *aurora borealis,* caused apparently by the sun refracting through the narrow opening. It would be spectacular at sunrise, Ilyinsky thought. Better than Capri's Blue Grotto, and minus the tourist flotillas.

What else had Toshka told him about the grotto? Something about a little island formed by a partial collapse of the cave roof. He got the dinghy turned around, let it glide forward. Then he checked the Makarov, working the slide to feed a round into the breech and flipping the safety on.

They were in here with him somewhere, with no way out.

≡

Paul felt Amanda's hand tighten on his arm. She was pointing at the barely visible cave entrance. "There," she whispered. "The silhouette of a boat, just for an instant."

Paul squinted into the fading light, saw nothing. "Your eyes must be better than mine."

"But you heard it?"

"Uh-huh." A sharp echoing crack, like something striking the rocks. More than anything, he *sensed* the presence of someone else in the cave with them. Someone keeping damn quiet, for the only sound was the ambient lullaby of lapping waves.

"Ilyinsky?" she whispered.

"Who else?" The Greek commandos would make themselves known. Keeping silent themselves, they scooted farther back on their tiny island. In the diminishing light with Amanda close beside him, Paul's hearing and sense of smell had expanded, so that he detected now the effluvium of fear compounding her female scent. He found it, in some atavistic way, powerfully erotic.

Amanda's hand clenched his; he felt her shiver with fear.

"What shall we do?"

He'd been trying to think creatively along those lines and had drawn a complete blank. He had nothing, no weapon, no ideas. The tiny island was just smooth, bare rock, except for a few fallen stalactite fragments. He was down to his shorts, Amanda little more. Bare feet, bare hands. And Ilyinsky might have an arsenal aboard, though Paul couldn't figure how the KGB officer had tracked them and gotten hold of their dinghy so quickly.

"Paul?" Her lips grazed his ear.

"I don't know, Mandy." He, too, pressed close,

afraid of the vast echo chamber. "He knows we're in here, and he'll keep coming till he finds us. One thing we could do is get back in the water, keep swimming away from him." He sensed her reaction in silence. "No, I guess we're beyond that, aren't we?"

"I just can't, Paul. I'm sorry. If we survive this, some-one's going to have to bring a boat for me."

"I know. Listen, you stay put, but I'm going to slip into the water—"

"Paul, please don't leave me."

"I'll be right here. But if he gets close and sees the island, or sees you, I'll have a chance to attack him. And I'll kill him, Mandy. I swear it. I'll drown the bastard."

He felt her cold hand clench his fiercely. After a long moment, her lips brushed his ear, her muted voice urgent and deeply thrilling. "All right, Paul. Do it! Kill the bastard! Do it, *caraed!*"

He felt the warm exhalation of her breath as her fingers moved slowly across his face, tracing his lips once, before pushing him reluctantly away.

He crawled away in a daze, feeling himself totally linked to this woman. He slid silently back into the water, holding onto an outcropping of rock, then found a sub-merged ledge on which to stand. Waiting now to kill a man.

He might not measure up as Lancelot, but Amanda Morgan made one hell of a Guinevere. *"Do it, caraed!"* For a cynical instant he wondered what Welsh soap opera she had pulled that out of. But it didn't matter. She'd said it. And though he felt the icy tentacles of fear as he thought about what was to come, the fire she had ignited in him was stronger. Whatever happened, he would give it his best.

He waited, staring off into flickering obscurity, seeing and hearing nothing. The seals had quieted; the rising tide eclipsed the last feeble sun rays from the distant cave opening. He was just able to discern the faint, viscid gleam of Amanda's eyes. Could Ilyinsky be close enough to see it, too?

Then, from very near, came the Russian's insinuating voice, echoing in the darkness:

"Amanda? Paul? I see one of you, on an island just ahead there. Which one? Where is the other?" Paul heard the kiss of wavelets against the dinghy's side. The Russian had to be very close.

"It's all over, you're both safe. There's no reason to hide in here." Now Paul even heard the Russian breathing. "Amanda? You must know it was the Little Fox we were chasing, not you. And Paul—I could have shot you, my friend, a moment ago from that cliff, instead of throwing a stone.

"All right. You decide. Stay in here all day, all night, if you wish. But you will hear the truth from me. And the truth is, Amanda, that your Kurdish 'friends' intended to ransom you for five million Swiss francs. *Five million*—for your *life*. Paul knows this is true. Indeed, the whole world knows it."

Silence, all around.

"You may not wish to believe me, Amanda, and I'm sorry the rescue was so . . . ugly. But the truth is, you *were* a hostage, and you *have* been saved from a very bad situation.

"There is something else you must know. Somewhere on this island these Kurds have hidden a dozen steel cylinders that look like ordinary SCUBA tanks. They are yellow. Only they do not contain air to breathe, but the most deadly nerve gas. It will kill you in seconds. The Kurds have stolen these cylinders, to what evil purpose I do not know. And I do not wish to find out.

"I *must* recover these canisters, Amanda. And you must help me. The terrorists are gone from the island, but they have comrades elsewhere, who would very much like these weapons. You have been with these criminals, all the way from Istanbul. You will have seen these tanks, or heard them speak of them. A dozen metal cylinders. Bright yellow. Think very hard, Amanda . . ."

So that was it, Paul thought. It was stolen nerve gas all along, not Amanda Morgan, that had brought Feliks riding to the rescue with such a vengeance. Somehow Paul had never believed the KGB would fret about damsels in distress, even glamorous ones of the correct political stripe. And if the Soviets had developed a new and particularly lethal chemical agent, they would certainly not want it recovered, along with the actress, by Turkish or Greek commandos—and thus fall into NATO hands.

And yet all this changed nothing. Paul thought. He still did not trust Ilyinsky; he'd seen the man's viciousness, through binoculars and at close quarters. He sensed that Feliks was only lulling them, trying to locate Paul in the gloom. And Paul had no intention of betraying his position by so much as a blink. He held perfectly still and prayed Amanda would do likewise. Long seconds passed with only the muffled spank of water along the hull.

The Russian went on: "Amanda, please help me. Say something . . ."

≡

Ilyinsky was almost certain the person on the tiny island was Amanda, from the shadowy silhouette he had glimpsed in the dying light. But there was no response from the darkness, no movement. Why were they being so irrational? He was getting panicky. If he could get the cylinders back before the Greeks stumbled on them, all else would be forgiven—disobeying orders to pull back from the island, even the loss of two more *Spetsnaz.*

Amanda had to know something. All that was standing in his way from interrogating her—and taking her by force, if he chose, as he had first taken Noorsheen—was the American. Feliks had nearly shot the blundering fool that night in Usküdar, and again, minutes ago. Now, sitting in the gently rocking dinghy with the Makarov in his fist, Feliks was ready to fire that long-delayed bullet.

The boat nosed softly against the island, with Ilyinsky crouched in the bow. As he lunged forward, a hand grabbed his ankle and pulled him off balance.

He cried out as the boat slid beneath him. The gun went off, the explosion repeated endlessly across the vaulted darkness. The Russian crashed sideways into water and was pulled immediately under. He thrashed violently, eager to come to grips with the American who had somehow surprised him. Feliks had no doubt of his superior strength, once he got his hands on the bastard. But the American came from behind, pinned his arms and plunged them both deeper into black water.

Feliks felt the clutch of real panic. He needed oxygen, now! His hands began to flail, then struck something hard against his thigh—Viktor's commando knife strapped to his belt! His fingers slid the steel blade from its scabbard.

≡

Paul wrestled with Ilyinsky, trying to hold him under till he blacked out. During the Russian's speech, Paul had been silently hyperventilating, expanding his lungs, hoping to use oxygen as his only weapon against the Russian.

But Ilyinsky was more powerful than Paul had anticipated. He broke an arm free from Paul's bear hug. Paul grabbed at him, slapped the empty scabbard on Feliks's leg and knew, with sickening terror, the fate that would be his. At the moment, he was saved from it only by the Russian's desperate need to breathe.

Feliks burst to the surface, gulping air and whirling to find Paul. But the Russian was confused by the reverberating bedlam throughout the cavern, as the little colony of Mediterranean monk seals, terrified by the gunshot, joined together in a paroxysm of barking. When Ilyinsky hesitated, Paul, still behind him, was able to lock his hands on the wrist that held the knife.

He held on like a man wrestling an alligator. Finally Ilyinsky tore free, but, as he did, Paul's blind punch crashed against his broad skull, driving the Russian back. Paul followed the advantage, and they grappled once more beneath the water.

Again they churned to the surface, again the Russian wrestled free. Something slashed the air beside Paul's cheek. He lunged forward, his hands finding and closing on the Russian's throat, compressing the windpipe with both thumbs. He strained, pouring every ounce of strength into it, as Ilyinsky's arms writhed, trying to stab him in the back.

Better kill me with the first one, you bastard! Paul thought. Because short of death—and maybe not even then—Paul was not going to let go. He'd keep on strangling till Ilyinsky was a corpse . . . so Amanda could live.

It was then the entire cave collapsed on Paul's head and knocked him senseless.

≡

He came to, coughing his guts out, a heavy weight crushing his ribs. As he fought to make his lungs work, something warm and rubbery clamped on his mouth. Before he could struggle free, a blast of warm air was blown into him. He kicked his legs and flailed his arms, as a second breath was forced deep into his lungs.

He jerked his head away, opened his eyes, saw darkness.

"Paul, thank God you're alive!" Amanda Morgan's husky voice was near. He pictured her heart-shaped face hovering somewhere above him. "I was sure I'd killed you."

Paul raised up, yelped in pain, and fell back. "Feliks, is he—?"

"He's dead. You're safe. We're both safe." Her hands cradled him, shifting his head now into her lap. Paul felt a surge of exquisite relief, though his lungs and sinuses were burning from salt water, and there was a horrible throbbing in his head. Then he tasted blood.

"Oh shit! Did he stab me?"

"Stab you? Did he have a knife?"

"You didn't know?"

"I couldn't see anything! Oh, my God!" Her voice came closer in the dark, more urgent.

"What in hell happened? What's this blood?"

"It's yours. From your scalp. I had to bash you with an oar."

"You *what?*"

"Paul, I couldn't see anything, but the sounds you were both making were horrifying! And I . . . I didn't think you'd win the fight. I was afraid you wouldn't. I couldn't take that chance, don't you see? So when the dinghy drifted back to me, I grabbed an oar and decided to bash away and knock you both out if I had to, then save the one I wanted. Which happened to be you."

Paul shook his head—a dumb thing to do, since it started the whole percussion section in his skull pounding and throbbing. "You were right," he groaned. "I was going to lose."

"See? I don't have to apologize, then, for almost killing you, do I?" He felt her tears splash down, tasted their saltiness mingling with the blood on his lips.

"Paul, it was so awful! Oh God, I was sure I'd killed you!" She gave way then to wrenching sobs, while he mumbled meaningless words, too weak to offer real comfort. After an impressively noisy few moments she subsided, snuffling and caressing the side of his face, but a little absently, as she might a house pet.

"Mandy, sorry, but that hurts. Especially around my eye."

"Paul, I'm sorry! I forgot."

"Mandy?"

"Yes?"

"You're sure? Ilyinsky drowned?"

"Yes."

"How do you know?"

"Well, he—he was drifting face down when I last saw him."

"Are you sure? I mean—"

"Yes, I'm sure! After I made sure it was you I'd saved, I went back and . . . and kept hitting him with the oar, over and over in the darkness. It was horrible, but I wanted him dead. I even went and checked after . . . it was right here, where it's shallow . . . and his head was a bloody mess. Then I thought of sharks and screamed and pushed him away. Is that good enough?"

"Christ!" Paul exhaled. "I was supposed to rescue *you,* not the other way around."

"I guess things don't always work out the way you plan."

≡

Suddenly the cave re-echoed with mad barking. Paul woke up as a powerful beam of light stabbed through the cave, sweeping back and forth. Amanda started awake beside him. He felt her tense convulsively.

"Paul, what is it?"

"I don't know."

A second light lanced forth, then a third, arcing, crossing, foreshortening, finally finding and blinding them.

"Do not move!" a man's voice reverberated. "We are Greek Navy here. We are coming now!" The lights winked out, and the frantic barking continued, reaching a mad crescendo with the oncoming thrash of the swimmers. Then Paul heard the sounds of men all around him, emerging from the water onto the island. The flashlights flicked back on, held by big, dripping, wet-suited figures in full SCUBA gear, peeling off their masks and swim fins. SEALs, UDTs, whatever the Greeks called them.

"Kalispera," Paul said.

"Yes, sir! *Kalispera*—Good afternoon to you!" replied a cheerful voice. "You peoples are okay, eh?"

"Yes, thank God." He and Amanda turned at the

same moment, seeing each other for the first time in hours. "Well, Mandy, looks like the cavalry's here. And just when we were getting to know each other."

Amanda's relief was profound. "Paul, think of it! A real bed to sleep in!"

Epilogue

EVENTS MOVED SWIFTLY AFTER THAT. AMANDA AND PAUL, lying side by side in a Zodiac, were towed out of the grotto by the SEAL team, while the little seals barked farewell. Because of the tide, the raft's vinyl tubes had to be slightly deflated to scrape through the scant opening. Outside, while the SEALs mounted a small outboard onto the Zodiac's transom, the two exhausted passengers were blinded by sunlight—incredibly, it was only late afternoon. Neither looked back at the cave, and both were spared a last look at Ilyinsky's corpse, which was picked up separately.

They were ferried out to a big gaudy motor yacht lying just offshore—half again as large as *Pegasus,* Paul estimated. And none other than Leopold Bouchard stood at the polished teak rail to welcome them aboard—or, more particularly, to welcome Amanda. He gave Paul only a perfunctory handshake before enfolding the actress in an oversized white terry robe and whisking her away. Paul had a final wave as she was escorted aft, flanked by miscellaneous security types.

Paul was then helped to the ornate saloon where a young Greek medical corpsman examined his head wound. He would remember those brief moments on deck later—for all the things he never got to say to Amanda.

The French film producer, Paul was amazed to find out, had actually assembled his own amateur strike force, chartering an amphibious plane to Kas and hiring the motor yacht out of the marina there. On board were a couple of ex-French Foreign Legionnaires and a scary-looking giant of a fisherman from Marseille, who turned out to be the brother of the slain security cop from the *George Washington*.

Unfortunately, with no hard information to go on, Bouchard and his men had been simply steaming around the island most of the day, scanning the bluffs, checking their equipment, and putting down quantities of *ouzo*—until the Greek SEAL team had commandeered the yacht.

Now, of course, the Frenchman was back in command, captain's cap perched on his mostly bald head and his erstwhile leading lady exactly where he wanted her, confined to her stateroom.

Within the hour the big yacht was moored in Kastellorizo's picturesque horseshoe harbor and Paul was sitting at a quayside table, head sutured and bandaged, eating freshly grilled swordfish. At the next table Alekos Katapodis was holding court among several young para-commandos. It was Alekos, Paul had learned, who had directed the Greeks to the seal grotto.

Leo Bouchard was still on the yacht, and on the phone, trying to reconnect the myriad links of his financial empire. As a consequence, Paul had to go to the harborside OTE office to take a call from Istanbul, where Mike Mitchell was waiting to talk to him. The U.S. vice consul had both chided and congratulated Paul for playing James Bond and told him for Christ's sake to go home now and take his holiday.

Paul should not expect to see his name featured in any of the impending media avalanche, Mike explained. Athens was being given official credit—not only for the rescue of the actress, but for the taking out of the entire Kurdish terrorist cell—and the recovery of the nerve gas. Ironically, the Greek SEAL team had found the canisters submerged in the grotto, not far from Ilyinsky's floating corpse. There was to be no mention of American involvement, nor of *KGB, GRU,* or *Spetsnaz.* All parties— including the Soviet Union and Amanda herself—had agreed to this arrangement.

Paul saw no reason to rock the boat. It made a neater story. As for Amanda, she was already gone, helicoptered by the Greek para-commandos from the airstrip above the harbor to the southern end of the island, where she'd directed them to the cave of Brother Theodore. The monk had been alive—though just barely. The actress had been last seen at his side en route by the same helicopter to a hospital in Rhodes, where both would be treated.

Already, then, she had found a new cause. Paul was happy for her. She had seemed more affected by what happened to Theodore than by her own ordeal. She'd probably arrange adjoining rooms. From now on Paul could follow her career from afar, with a mixture of awe and affection.

He turned down a couple of rides home. There were still several days left on *Alcyone*'s charter, and he wanted to sail her back to Rhodes himself, in the daytime, enjoying the craggy Lycian coast he'd missed at night. Beating back through the *meltemi* might also heal some of the physical and emotional aches of the past few days and allow him to savor some of the sweeter memories.

He sailed the following dawn. Paul's bandaged head was still aching as he cleared the headland and hoisted the main, but he'd survive. All in all, he felt like he'd gone the distance with Mike Tyson—beat up but proud of it. Except his opponent had been a hundred-pound woman wielding an oar.

He took the haul in two stages, stopping over at Fethiye. He reached Mandraki Harbor on the second afternoon and made inquiries about Amanda. Her image was everywhere—tabloids, newspapers, magazines, television. But her actual whereabouts remained a mystery. Paul got conflicting reports—from the press, from the British consulate, from yachtsmen at Mandraki.

According to one version, she'd been whisked away to London by British security and Kronos Limited, and was already barricaded in her Hampstead house to avoid the press.

Another Garboesque scenario had her checking into a famous spa outside Bern specializing in celebrity traumas.

A last one, which Paul heard from his chartering agents in the harbor, claimed she was still hiding out in

Rhodes and about to embark on the yacht of a certain Saudi prince for a cruise to the Balearics. The "yacht" was certainly in evidence—*Aldebaran,* two hundred blinding white feet, flying the Liberian flag on Mandraki's luxury row.

Wherever she was in the lubricous world of the rich and famous, Paul thought, she deserved it after the hell she'd walked through. He only hoped she'd come out of all this as idealistic and intransigent as she'd gone in. Amanda, in other words, and nobody else.

After a final debriefing from some of Josh Nevins's men, Paul was at liberty. Planes were leaving every hour for all points of the globe. He was still on leave, had only spent a few days of it, actually. And he still didn't want to go home.

He decided to charter *Alcyone* again, rig some self-steering gear for single-handing and poke on up through the Dodecanese. Maybe, if he felt ambitious, the Southern Sporades.

The yacht agent said Paul could drop the sloop off in Kos. By that time, a couple weeks hence, the black hair dye would have grown out, the ugly skin stain replaced by a real tan, and just maybe Paul would have gotten over Amanda.

And have a plan for the rest of his life.

So, after dispatching some cables home, he found himself back on *Alcyone,* laying in provisions. When the stowage was completed he stripped off his shirt, opened a bottle of beer, set it on the top of the cambered deckhouse, and lounged back in the cockpit, arms draped on the lifeline like a punchy fighter.

Then, down the sun-blasted quayside, past the Saudi's *Aldebaran* and the other floating palaces, he saw an honest-to-God mirage—or some kind of déjà-vu mind trick. A blonde in dark sunglasses was walking down the jetty in Paul's general direction, and making a one-woman parade out of it.

Darryl Ann? But why not? *Pegasus* must be in port. Forrest had toyed with the idea of heading south into the Dodecanese. Damn! How did she know he was here? Or did she? Paul felt the knotting in his viscera, the old susceptibility. Yet found himself hoping it was someone else.

The blonde slowed, then came to a full stop abreast of *Alcyone.* A cute figure in white baggy slacks and black blouse knotted at the waist, exposing a slice of tanned tummy. Definitely not Darryl Ann—thank heaven! Darker-skinned and more compact.

The woman lifted the dark glasses—just for a second, then replaced them on her button nose. It was Amanda Morgan, smiling at him. Amanda Morgan in a flamboyant blond wig.

She took a step nearer. "Don't say anything. I'm in disguise. Like you." She flounced the blond wig like Mae West.

"I can see that." He bounded onto the quayside, checking, just in time, the impulse to embrace her, but delighted when she gave him her hand to hold in both of his.

"God, it's wonderful to see you," he began, his voice cracking like a high-school kid's. Well, that figured. His heart was pounding like a kid's, too. Seeing her again *was* wonderful. "I—I heard you were in Switzerland, or off to Majorca, or somewhere."

Her dark throaty laugh made him shiver. "No, not

yet anyway. Somebody told me you were getting ready to ship out."

"Yeah. Somehow, in all the confusion, I—I—uh never got a chance to say good-bye."

She nodded.

He stared down at the improbable yellow hair and his own tiny reflection in the dark glasses.

"Hey, how's Theodore?"

"Much, much better. What a dear man. He'll be going back to the island next week, to the monastery this time. I guess I've got a new pen pal. I think he has a crush on me."

"I bet. Just the thing to brighten up monastic life."

"Paul, really."

He felt a little uncomfortable standing there, so he invited her aboard, gave her a Coke, and explained his sailing plans, which she said sounded idyllic. They chatted about loose ends, avoiding anything of real significance.

Paul was shocked to learn that Leo Bouchard was actually planning to revive "Barbary!"—apparently based on his insurance settlement and substantial new financing. He even intended to include actual video footage of the frigate burning in Istanbul harbor. "It's being written into the script," she laughed. Media interest in the project had skyrocketed, for obvious reasons. And, of course, Leo wanted Amanda.

"You're not going to do it?" Paul asked.

She shrugged. "I've got a few months to decide. Not now. Not anything for a good while. But maybe yes, a few months down the road. I can use the money."

"What for?" Paul found himself both surprised and annoyed by her attitude.

"Political reasons. To finance my causes. Do something for the Kurdish refugees in Iran and Turkey. There are thousands of them now. Other things. Peace in our time, and all that."

Paul was embarrassed by his earlier reaction. "I'm glad. I was afraid what happened would . . . make you give it all up."

"Oh, no!" she said, mildly horrified. "I wouldn't know what to do with myself if I wasn't fighting for something."

He felt his heart stumble a bit, watching her strong chin and neck as she tipped up the Coke. Lust aside, he admired the hell out of her. Maybe he could get on her pen-pal list with Brother Theodore. If having a crush qualified you, Paul was in.

Then she turned and waved at someone.

Paul looked in the same direction. Down the jetty a topaz Rolls-Royce Corniche had pulled up adjacent to the *Aldebaran.* A tall, elegant man in white flannels was directing a muscular Greek boy in the transfer of steamer trunks out of the convertible's boot, over the gangway, and onto the yacht.

"Who's the dapper fellow?"

"That's Tony, my agent, and one of his new friends. And yes, that's my luggage."

"So, one rumor was true, after all."

"Don't make that face. It's damn useful. Tony's spread the word to the media that I'm cruising the Med with Prince Rashid. In total seclusion. Out of camera range. Which at least keeps the vultures circling high. Right now, for instance, I can spot a couple of *paparazzi* at that cafe down there, watching my bags go up the bloody ramp."

"But they'll be waiting for you at every port," Paul said.

"But they won't find me," she smiled, "because I won't be on the damn boat. It's just a ruse, don't you see?"

He nodded, though he was not exactly up on Jet Set tactics. Then he noticed the muscular Greek boy heading toward them with a single soft-sided bag. The boy moved casually, not looking at them. He set the bag down on the quayside beside the *Alcyone*'s little gangway, then walked on.

"What's that all about?" Paul asked. "Is that yours?"

"Mm-hmm. I travel light. Got room for one more?"

"What?"

"Prince Rashid is a dear, but he's seventy-five years old. I prefer sailing with younger men."

"You're not serious? You want to come sailing? Just you and me?"

She nodded.

"Look, I'm heading out for two weeks here . . . although I could, uh, I mean I'm willing to—"

"Two weeks sounds fine. On one condition."

"Name it, for pete's sake."

"When we go ashore I have to wear this god-awful wig. At such times you can call me . . . oh, shall we say, Rita?"

"Listen, I'll call you any damn thing you want."

"Now, if you'd have the steward see to my luggage."

"Just don't move, okay?" Paul stood up, walked across the gangway, hefted the little seabag—it wasn't weightless, she'd have at least a hair dryer in there—and turned about. As he sauntered back aboard, the last of her steamer trunks was being manhandled into the *Aldebaran.*

Paul sat across from her in the cockpit, feeling a perfect euphoric idiot. She seemed to be enjoying all this as well, he thought. But, while his blood kept pounding its anthem of full speed ahead, there was one matter troubling him:

"Listen . . . Rita. There's a couple dumb things I feel called upon to say here. Maybe you can tell I'm real agreeable to this whole thing, okay? And we've got separate cabins here on *Alcyone,* so you'll have complete privacy. Whatever you want. And I won't even ask if you can cook." He swallowed.

"Paul, what is it?"

"It's just that . . . after everything that's happened . . . I don't know, dammit. *Isn't it risky?* For you, I mean."

Amanda nodded. It was, she thought, and in more ways than one. But she had chosen her companion carefully. She wanted two weeks with this eager, gentle young man, alone on the Aegean. To grow close, bake in the sun, heal deep wounds, regain her physical and emotional courage. And when everything was exactly right, she wanted him to make love to her.

"Yes," she said. "It is risky."